STRANGE WEATHER

Also by Joe Hill from Gollancz:

JOE HILL

FOUR SHORT NOVELS

STRANGE WEATHER

GOLLANCZ

LONDON

First published in Great Britain in 2017 by Gollancz
an imprint of the Orion Publishing Group Ltd
Carmelite House, 50 Victoria Embankment
London EC4Y 0DZ

An Hachette UK Company

1 3 5 7 9 10 8 6 4 2

Art credits:
Gabriel Rodriguez—Snapshot
Zach Howard—Loaded
Charles Paul Wilson III—Aloft
Renae De Liz—Rain

Running head art courtesy of Shutterstock

"Snapshot" first appeared in a different form as "Snapshot, 1988" in
Cemetery Dance: The Magazine of Horror and Suspense, Issue #74/75,
copyright © 2016 by Cemetery Dance Publications.

A CIP catalogue record for this book is
available from the British Library.

ISBN (Cased) 978 1 473 22117 8
ISBN (Export Trade Paperback) 978 1 473 22118 5

Printed in Great Britain by CPI Group (UK) Ltd, Croydon CR0 4YY

www.joehillfiction.com
www.gollancz.co.uk

For Mr. Blue Sky:
Aidan Sawyer King. Love you, kid.

Contents

1

SHELLY BEUKES STOOD AT THE bottom of the driveway, squinting up at our pink-sandstone ranch as if she had never seen it before. She wore a trench coat fit for Humphrey Bogart and carried a big cloth handbag printed with pineapples and tropical flowers. She could've been on her way to the supermarket, if there were one in walking distance, which there wasn't. I had to look twice before I registered what was wrong with the picture: She had forgotten to put on her shoes, and her feet were filthy, almost black with grime.

I was in the garage, doing science—my father's term for what I was up to anytime I decided to ruin a perfectly good vacuum cleaner or TV remote. I wrecked more than I built, although I had successfully wired an Atari joystick into a radio, so I could jump from station to station by pressing the Fire button—a fundamentally stupid trick that nevertheless impressed the judges of the eighth-grade science fair, where it earned me the blue ribbon for creativity.

On the morning Shelly turned up at the base of the driveway, I was working on my party gun. It looked like a death ray from a pulp-era science-fiction novel, a big horn of dented brass with the butt and trigger of a Luger (I had in fact soldered together a trumpet and a toy gun to create the body). When you pulled the trigger, though, it sounded an air horn, popped flashbulbs, and blew a storm of confetti and paper ribbons. I had an idea that if I could get the gun right, my dad and I could bring it to toy manufacturers, maybe license the idea to Spencer Gifts. Like most budding engineers, I honed my craft on a series of basically juvenile pranks. There isn't a single dude at Google who didn't at least fantasize about designing X-ray goggles to see through girls' skirts.

I was aiming the barrel of the party gun into the street when I first spotted Shelly, right there in my sights. I put down my bozo blunderbuss and narrowed my eyes, looking her over. I could see her, but she couldn't see me. For her, looking into the garage would've been like staring into the impenetrable darkness of an open mine shaft.

I was going to call to her, but then I saw her feet and the air snagged in my throat. I didn't make a sound, just watched her for a bit. Her lips moved. She was whispering to herself.

She darted a look back the way she'd come, as if afraid someone might be sneaking up on her. But she was alone in the road, the world humid and still under the lid of an overcast sky. I remember that all the neighbors had put their garbage out and the trucks were late and the avenue stank.

Almost from the first, I felt it was important not to do anything to alarm her. There was no obvious reason for caution—but a lot of our best thinking takes place well below the level of conscious cogitation and has nothing to do with rationality. The monkey brain absorbs a great deal of information from subtle cues that we aren't even aware we've received.

So when I came down the slope of the driveway, I had my thumbs hooked in my pockets and wasn't even looking directly at her. I squinted into the horizon as if watching the flight of a far-off airplane. I approached her the way you'd close in on a limping stray dog, one that might lick your hand with hopeful affection or might lunge, upper lip drawn back to show a mouthful of teeth. I didn't speak until I was almost within arm's reach of her.

"Oh, hi, Mrs. Beukes," I said, pretending to notice her for the first time. "You okay?"

Her head swung toward me, and her plump face instantly settled into a look of pleasant benignity. "Well, I've got myself all turned around! I walked all the way down here, but I don't know why! This isn't my day to clean!"

I hadn't seen that one coming.

Once upon a time, Shelly had mopped and vacuumed and tidied the house, four hours every Tuesday and Friday afternoon. She was already old by then, although she had the brisk, muscular vigor of an Olympic curler. On Fridays she left us with a plate of cake-soft, date-filled cookies protected by a film of Saran Wrap. Man, those were some cookies. You can't get anything like them anywhere anymore, and no crème brûlée at the Four Seasons ever tasted so good with a cup of tea.

But by August 1988 I was just weeks away from beginning high school, and it had been almost half my life since Shelly had cleaned for us on a regular basis. She'd stopped working for us after her triple bypass in 1982, when the doctor told her she ought to take some time to rest herself. She'd been resting ever since. I'd never given it much thought, but if I had, I might've wondered why she ever took the job in the first place. It wasn't like she needed the money.

"Mrs. Beukes? Did my dad maybe ask you to come in and help out with Marie?"

Marie was the woman who'd replaced her, a sturdy, not terribly bright girl in her early twenties, with a big laugh and a heart-shaped can, who provided imagery for my nightly sausage-pounding ceremonies. I couldn't imagine why my father might think Marie would need a hand. We weren't, as far as I knew, anticipating company. I'm not sure we ever even *had* company.

Her smile faltered briefly. She shot one of those anxious looks back over her shoulder, down the road. When she returned her gaze to me, there was only the faintest trace of good humor on her face, and her eyes were frightened.

"I dunno, bucko—you tell me! Was I supposed to clean out the tub? I know I didn't get to it last week, and it's pretty dingy." Shelly Beukes pawed through her cloth tote, muttering to herself. When she looked up, her lips were squeezed together in an expression of frustration. "Piss on it. I walked out of the house and forgot the fucking Ajax."

I twitched, could not have been more startled if she'd pulled open that trench coat and revealed she was naked. Shelly Beukes wasn't anyone's idea of an uptight old lady—I had a memory of her cleaning our house in a John Belushi T-shirt—but I had never heard her use the word "fuck." Even "piss on it" was quite a bit saltier than her usual conversational fare.

Shelly didn't notice my surprise, just went on to say, "Tell your dad I'll take care of the tub tomorrow. I don't need more than ten minutes to make it shine like no one ever put their ass in it."

Her cloth shoulder bag drooped open. I looked into it and saw a battered, grimy lawn gnome, several empty soda cans, and a single raggedy old sneaker.

"I'd better go home," she said suddenly, almost robotically. "The Afrikaner will be wondering where I got to."

The Afrikaner was her husband, Lawrence Beukes, who had emigrated from Cape Town before I was born. At seventy, Larry Beukes was one of the most powerfully built men I knew, a former weight lifter with the sculpted arms and vein-threaded neck of a circus strongman. Being huge was his primary professional responsibility. He had made his money on a series of gyms he'd opened in the seventies, just as the oiled, mind-boggling mass of Arnold Schwarzenegger was muscling its way into the public consciousness. Larry and Arnie had once both appeared in the same calendar. Larry was February and flexed in the snow, wearing nothing but a tight black hammock for his nuts. Arnie was June and stood glistening on the beach, a girl in a bikini perched on each gargantuan arm.

Shelly darted a last look over her shoulder and then began to shuffle off, moving in a direction that would take her even farther from her house. The moment she looked away from me, she forgot me. I could see it in the way all expression dropped from her face. Her lips began to move as she whispered quiet questions to herself.

"Shelly! Hey, I was going to ask Mr. Beukes if . . . about . . ." I struggled to think of something Larry Beukes and I might have to discuss. "If he ever thought of hiring anyone to mow the lawn! He's got better things to do, right? Mind if I walk to your house with you?" I reached for her elbow and caught her before she could drift out of reach.

She jerked at the sight of me—as if I had craftily snuck up on her—then gave me that brave, challenging smile. "I've told that old man we need to hire someone to cut the . . . the . . ." Her eyes dimmed. She couldn't remember what needed cutting. At last she gave her head a lit-tle shake and went on: ". . . the *thing* for I don't know how long. Come on back with me. And you know what?" She clapped a hand over mine. "I think I've got some of those cookies you like!"

She winked, and for an instant I was sure she knew me and, more than that, knew herself. Shelly Beukes flickered into crisp focus, then went fuzzy again. I could see awareness slip away from her, a light on a dimmer switch being turned down to a dull glow.

So I walked her home. I felt bad about her bare feet on the hot road. It was muggy, and the mosquitoes were out. After a while I noticed a red flush across her face and a dew of sweat in her old-lady whiskers, and I thought maybe she should take the trench coat off. Although I admit that by then the notion had crossed my mind that maybe she really *was* naked under there. Given her disorientation, I didn't think it could be ruled out. I fought down my unease and asked if I could carry her coat. She gave her head a quick shake.

"I don't want to be recognized."

This was such a wonderfully daffy thing to say that for a moment I forgot the situation and responded as if Shelly were still herself, a sensible person who loved *Jeopardy!* and cleaned ovens with an almost brutal determination.

"By *who*?" I asked.

She leaned toward me and in a voice that was practically a hiss said, "The Polaroid Man. That slick fucking weasel in his convertible. He's been taking pictures when the Afrikaner isn't around. I don't know how much he's taken away with his camera, but he can't have any more." She gripped my wrist. Her body was still stout and big-bosomed, but her hand was as bony and clawlike as a fairy-tale crone's. "Don't let him take a picture of you. Don't let him start taking things away."

"I'll keep an eye out. Hey, really, Mrs. Beukes, you look like you're melting in that coat. Let me have it and we'll watch out for him to-gether. You can jump into it again if you see him coming."

She leaned her head back and narrowed her eyes, inspecting me the way she might've studied the small print at the bottom of a dubi-ous contract. Finally she sniffed and shrugged out of the big coat and handed it to me. She was *not* naked underneath but wore a pair of black gym shorts and a T-shirt that was on inside out and backward, the tag flopping under her chin. Her legs were knotty and shockingly white, her calves crawling with varicose veins. I folded her coat, sweaty and wrinkled, over one arm, took her hand, and went on.

The roads in Golden Orchards, our little housing development north of Cupertino, were laid out like overlapping coils of rope, not a straight line in the whole thing. At first glance the houses appeared to be a scattershot mix of styles—a Spanish stucco here, a brick Colonial there. Spend enough time knocking around the neighborhood, though, and you came to recognize they were all the same house, more or less—same interior layout, same number of bathrooms, same-style windows—dressed up in different costumes.

The Beukes house was mock Victorian, but with some kind of beach theme going on: seashells embedded in the concrete path leading to the steps, a bleached starfish hung from the front door. Maybe Mr. Beukes's gyms were called Neptune Fitness? Atlantis Athletics? Was it maybe a goof on the Nautilus machines that were used in the facilities? I don't remember anymore. A lot of that day—August 15, 1988—is still sharp in my memory, but I'm not sure I was too clear on that particular detail even then.

I led her to the door and knocked, then rang the bell. I could've just let her in—it was her house, after all—but I didn't think that suited the situation. I thought I ought to tell Larry Beukes where she had wandered and find some hopefully not-too-embarrassing way to let him know how confused she'd been.

Shelly gave no sign she recognized her own house. She stood at the bottom of the steps looking placidly around, waiting patiently. A few moments earlier, she'd seemed sly and even slightly threatening. Now she looked like a bored granny going door-to-door with her Boy Scout grandson, keeping him company while he sold magazine subscriptions.

Bumblebees burrowed into nodding white flowers. For the first time, it struck me that maybe Larry Beukes really *did* need to hire someone to cut his grass. The yard was unkempt and weedy, dandelions spotting the lawn. The house itself needed a power wash, had spots of mold high under the eaves. It had been a while since I'd walked by the place, and who knew when I had last really *looked* at it, not just let my gaze slide over it.

Larry Beukes had always maintained his property with the diligence and energy of a Prussian field marshal. He was out there twice a week in a muscle shirt, pushing a powerless hand mower, his delts tanned and rippling, his cleft chin lifted dramatically (he had great fuckin' posture). Other lawns were green and tidy. His was *meticulous.*

Of course, I was only thirteen when all this happened, and I understand now what I didn't at the time: It was all getting away from Lawrence Beukes. His ability to manage, to keep up with even the mild demands of suburban living, was being overwhelmed, a little at a time, as he wore down under the strain of looking after a woman who could no longer look after herself. I suppose it was only his inherent sense of optimism and conditioning—his sense of personal fitness, if you will—that allowed him to go on, kidding himself that he could handle it all.

I was beginning to think I might have to walk Shelly back to my house and wait with her there when Mr. Beukes's ten-year-old burgundy Town Car swerved into the driveway. He was driving it like an outlaw on the run from Starsky and Hutch and bumped one tire up over the curb as he swung in. He got out in a sweat and almost stumbled and fell coming into the yard.

"Oh, Jesus, dere you are! I hoff been looging all over to hell and gone! You almost giff me a heart attack." Larry's accent just naturally made you think of apartheid, torture, and dictators sitting on gilt thrones in marble palaces with salamanders scampering along the walls. Which was too bad. He had made his money hauling around iron, not blood diamonds. He had his flaws—he'd voted for Reagan, he believed that Carl Weathers was a *great* thespian, and he grew emotional listening to ABBA—but he revered and adored his wife, and balanced against that, his personal blemishes were no matter at all. He went on, "What did you do? I go next door to ask Mr. Bannerman if he hoff detergent, I come bagg, you are gone like a girl in a David Cobberfelt trick!"

He grabbed her in his arms, seemed like he might be about to give her a hard shake, then hugged her instead. He looked over her shoulder at me, his eyes glittering with tears.

"It's okay, Mr. Beukes," I said. "She's fine. She was just kind of . . . lost."

"I wasn't lost," she said, and she showed him a small, knowing smile. "I was hiding from the Polaroid Man."

He shook his head. "*Hush*. Hush yourself, woman. Let's ged you out of the sun and— Oh, Lord, your feet. I should make you take your feet off before you go inside. You will track your filth everywhere."

All this sounds kind of savage and cruel, but his eyes were wet and he spoke with a gruff, wounded affection, talking to her the way you might speak to a beloved old cat that had gotten itself into a fight and come home missing an ear.

He marched her past me, up the brick steps, and into the house. I was about to go, thought I had already been forgotten, when he turned back to jab a trembling finger at my nose.

"I hoff something for you," he said. "Do not float off, Michael Figlione."

And he banged the door shut.

2

FROM A CERTAIN POINT OF view, his choice of words was almost funny. There was really no danger I was going to float off on him. We have not yet touched upon the elephant in the room, which is that at the age of thirteen I was the elephant in any room I stepped into. I was fat. Not "big-boned." Not "sturdy." Certainly not merely "husky." When I walked across the kitchen, glasses rattled in the cupboard. When I stood among the other kids of my eighth-grade class, I looked like a buffalo wandering among the prairie dogs.

In this modern age of social media and sensitivity to bullying, if you call someone a fat-ass, you'll likely find yourself on the receiving end of some abuse yourself, for body shaming. But in 1988 "twitter" was a verb used only to describe what sparrows and gossiping biddies did. I was fat, and I was lonely; in those days if you were the former, the latter was a given. I had plenty of time for walking old ladies home. I wasn't neglecting my buddies. I didn't have any. None who were my age anyway. My father sometimes drove me to the Bay to attend monthly meetings of a club called S.F. GRUE (the San Francisco Gathering of Robotics Users and Enthusiasts), but most of the others at those get-togethers were much older than I. Older and already stereotypes. I don't even need to describe them, because you can already see them in your mind's eye: the bad complexions, the thick-lensed glasses, the unzipped flies. When I dropped in on this crew, I wasn't just learning about circuit boards. I believed I was looking at my future: depressing late-night arguments about *Star Trek* and a life of celibacy.

It didn't help, of course, that my last name was Figlione, which, when translated into 1980s elementary-school English, became Fats-Baloney or Fag-Alone or just plain old Fags, monikers that stuck to me like gum on my sneaker until I was in my twenties. Even my beloved fifth-grade science teacher, Mr. Kent, once accidentally called me Fag-Alone, to uproarious laughter. He at least had the decency to blush and look sick and apologize.

My existence could've been much worse. I was clean, and I was neat, and by never studying French I was able to avoid honor roll: that list of smug know-it-alls and teacher's pets who were just begging for a wedgie. I never faced anything worse than the occasional low-grade humiliation, and when I was teased, I always smiled indulgently, as if I were getting ragged by a dear friend. Shelly Beukes couldn't remember what had happened yesterday. As a rule, I never wanted to.

The door was flung open again, and Larry Beukes was back. I turned to see him wiping one enormous callused hand across his wet cheek. I was embarrassed and looked away, out toward the street. I had no experience with weeping adults. My father was not a particularly emotional man, and I doubt that my mother was much for tears, although I couldn't say for sure. I only ever saw her two or three months out of every year. Larry Beukes had come from Africa, whereas my mother had gone there for an anthropological study and, in a sense, never *really* came back. Even when she was home, a part of her remained six thousand miles away, beyond reach. At the time I was not angry about this. For children, anger usually requires proximity. That changes.

"I droff all around dis neighborhood looging for her, the goddem simple old thing. Dis is the third time. I thought dis time, *dis* time she will walg into traffig! The silly goddem—thang you for bringing her bagg to me. Bless you, Michael Figlione. Gott bless your heart." He pulled a pocket inside out, and money sprayed everywhere, crumpled bills and loose silver scattering across the walk and the grass. I realized, with something like alarm, that he meant to tip me.

"Oh, jeez, Mr. Beukes. It's okay. You don't have to. I'm glad to help. I don't want . . . I'd feel stupid taking . . ."

He narrowed one eye and glared at me with the other. "Dis is more than a reward. Dis is a down payment." He bent and scooped up a ten-dollar bill and held it out to me. "Go on. Take dis." When I didn't, he stuck it in the breast pocket of my Hawaiian shirt. "Michael. If I hoff to go somewhere . . . can I call on you to loog after her? I am home all day, all I do is loog after dis crazy woman, but sometimes I hoff to buy groceries or run to one of the gyms to put out a fire. Dere is always a fire to put out. Every musclehead who works for me can lift four hundred pounds, but not one of dem could count past ten. Dat is where they run out of fingers." He patted the money in my shirt and took his wife's coat away from me. It had still been hanging over my forearm, like a waiter's towel, forgotten. "So? We hoff a deal?"

"Sure, Mr. Beukes. She used to babysit me. I guess I can . . . can . . ."

"Yes, babysit *her*. She has entered her second childhood, Gott help her and me, too. She needs someone to make sure she doesn't go wandering. Looging for *him*."

"The Polaroid Man."

"She told you about him?"

I nodded.

He shook his head, smoothed a hand back over his thinning, Brylcreemed hair. "I worry someday she will see someone walging by and decide it is him and stig a kitchen knife into him. Oh, Gott, what will I do then?"

This wasn't such a smart thing to say to the kid you were trying to hire to look after your old, mentally disintegrating wife. It was impossible not to consider the possibility that she might decide *I* was the Polaroid Man and stick a carving knife into *me*. But he was distracted and distressed and running his mouth without thought. It didn't matter. I wasn't scared of Shelly Beukes. I felt she could forget everything about me, and everything about herself, and it still wouldn't change her fundamental nature, which was affectionate, efficient, and incapable of any real malice.

Larry Beukes met my gaze with bloodshot, miserable eyes. "Michael, you will be a rich man someday. You will probably make a fortune, inventing the future. Will you do something for me? For your old friend, Larry Beukes, who spent his last years desperate with worry for his fool of a wife, with her oadmeal brains? The woman who gaff him more happiness than he ever deserved?"

He was crying again. I wanted to hide. Instead I nodded.

"Sure, Mr. Beukes. Sure."

"Invent a way not to ged old," he said. "It is a terrible goddem trick to play on someone. Gedding old is no way to stop being young."

3

I WALKED WITHOUT A PLAN, hardly aware I was moving, let alone where I was going. I was hot, I was dazed, and I had ten dollars crushed into my shirt pocket, money I didn't want. My grimy Run DMC Adidas carried me to the nearest place I could get rid of it.

There was a big Mobil station across the highway from the entrance to the Golden Orchards: a dozen pumps and a deliciously refrigerated convenience store where you could buy beef jerky, Funyuns, and, if you were old enough, skin magazines. That summer I was drinking my own frozen slush concoction: a thirty-two-ounce cup of ice drenched in vanilla Coca-Cola and topped with a squirt of something called Arctic Blu. Arctic Blu was the color of windshield-wiper fluid and tasted a little of cherry and a little of watermelon. I was mad for the stuff, but if I came across it nowadays, I probably wouldn't try it. I think to my forty-year-old palate it would taste of adolescent sadness.

I had my heart set on an Arctic Blu–Coca-Cola Slush Special and just didn't know it until I saw the Mobil's revolving red Pegasus atop its forty-foot pole. The parking lot had recently been repaved with fresh tar, black and thick as cake. Heat wobbled off it, causing the whole place to quiver faintly, a hallucinated oasis glimpsed by a man dying of thirst. I didn't notice the white Caddy at Pump Ten, and I didn't see the guy standing next to it until he spoke to me.

"Hey," he said, and when I didn't react—I was in a sunstruck daydream—he said it again, less nice. "Hey, Pillsbury."

I heard him that time. My radar was attuned to any blip that might represent the threat of a bully, and it pinged at "Pillsbury" and the man's tone of good-humored contempt.

He didn't have a lot of room to go ragging on people about their looks. He was dressed well enough, even if his clothes looked out of place: In duds like his, he belonged at the door to a nightclub in San Francisco, not at a Mobil pump in a nowhere California suburb. He wore a silky black short-sleeved shirt with glassy red buttons, long black pants with a blade-sharp crease, black cowboy boots embroidered with red and white thread.

But he was feverishly ugly, his chin sunk most of the way back into his long neck, his cheeks corroded with old acne scars. His deeply tanned forearms were covered in black tattoos, what appeared to be lines of cursive script running around them in long, snakelike swirls down to his wrists. He wore a string tie—those were popular in the eighties—secured with a Lucite clasp. A yellowing scorpion was curled within.

"Yes, sir?" I asked.

"You goin' in? Get yourself a Twinkie or somethin'?" He thunked the pump's nozzle into the gas tank of his big white boat.

"Yes, sir," I said, thinking, *Suck my Twinkie, asshole.*

He reached into his front pocket and wiggled out a wad of yellowing, dirty bills. He peeled off a twenty. "Tell you what. You take this inside, tell 'em to switch on Pump Ten and— Hey, Land O'Lakes, I'm talkin' at you. Listen up."

My attention had drifted away for a moment, my gaze caught by the object sitting on the trunk of his Caddy: a Polaroid Instant Camera.

You probably know what a Polaroid looks like, even if you're too young to ever have used one or seen one used. The original Polaroid Instant is so recognizable, and represents such an enormous technological leap forward, that it became an icon of its era. It *belongs* to the eighties, like Pac-Man and Reagan.

These days everyone has a camera in his pocket. The idea of snapping a picture and being able to examine it immediately strikes absolutely no one as spectacular. But in the summer of 1988, the Polaroid was one of just a few devices that would allow you to shoot a picture and have it develop more or less instantly. The camera popped out a thick white square with a gray rectangle of film in the center, and after a couple minutes—faster if you shook the square back and forth to activate the developing agent within its chemical envelope—an image would swim up out of the murk and solidify into a photograph. That was cutting-edge back then.

When I saw the camera, I knew it was him, the guy—the Polaroid Man that Mrs. Beukes was hiding from. The slick-looking weasel in his white Cadillac convertible, with its red top and red seats. He color-coded like a motherfucker.

I knew that whatever Mrs. Beukes believed about this guy had no basis in fact, of course, that it was a misfire from an engine already choked up and giving out. Yet something she'd said stuck with me: *Don't let him take a picture of you.* When I put it all together—when I realized the Polaroid Man was not a senile fantasy but a real dude, standing right in front of me—my back and arms prickled with chill.

"Uh . . . go ahead, mister. I'm listening."

"Here," he said. "Take this twenty in and get 'em to light up this pump. My Caddy is thirsty, but I'll tell you what, kiddo. If there's any change, it's all yours. Buy yourself a diet book."

I didn't even blush. It was a nasty swipe, but in my distracted state it barely grazed my consciousness.

On second glance I saw that it *wasn't* a Polaroid. Not exactly. I knew the devices pretty well—I had taken one apart once—and recognized that this was subtly different. It was, for starters, black with a red face, so it matched the car and the clothes. But also it was just . . . different. Sleeker. It sat on the trunk, within hand's reach of Mr. Slick, and it was turned slightly away from me, so I couldn't see the brand name. A Konica? I wondered. What struck me most, right away, was that a Polaroid had a hinged drawer you opened at the front, to slide in a package of instant film. I couldn't see how this one loaded. The device seemed to be made of one smooth piece.

He saw me eyeing the camera and did a curious thing: He put a protective hand on it, an old lady gripping her purse a little tighter as she walks past some street toughs. He extended the dingy-looking twenty with his other hand.

I came around the rear bumper and reached for the money. My gaze shifted to the writing scrolled up his forearm. I didn't recognize the alphabet, but it looked similar to Hebrew.

"Cool ink," I said. "What language is that?"

"Phoenician."

"What's it say?"

"It says 'Don't fuck with me.' More or less."

I tucked the money into my shirt pocket and began to shuffle away from him, moving in reverse. I was too scared of him to turn my back on him.

I wasn't looking where I was going and veered off course, bumped into the rear fender, and almost fell down. I put a hand on the trunk to steady myself and glanced around, and that was how I saw the photo albums.

There were maybe a dozen of them stacked along the backseat. One of them was open, and I could see Polaroids slid into clear plastic sleeves, four on each sheet. The photos themselves were nothing special. An overlit shot of an old man blowing out the candles on a birthday cake. A rain-bedraggled corgi staring into the camera with tragic, hungry eyes. A muscle-bound dude in a hilariously orange tank top, sitting on the hood of a Trans Am straight out of *Knight Rider*.

That last one caught my gaze. I felt I vaguely knew the young man in the tank top. I wondered if I'd seen him on TV, if he was a wrestler, had climbed into the ring with the Hulkster to go a few rounds.

"You got a lot of pictures," I said.

"It's what I do. I'm a scout."

"Scout?"

"For the movies. I see an interesting place, I shoot a picture of it. I see an interesting face, I shoot a picture of that." He lifted one corner of his mouth to show a snaggly tooth. "Why? You wanna be in movies, kid? You want me to take your picture? Hey, you never can tell. Maybe some casting agent will like your face. Next thing you know—*Hollywood*, baby." He was fingering the camera in a way I didn't like, with a kind of twitchy eagerness.

Even in the theoretically more innocent time of the late 1980s, I wasn't keen to pose for photographs taken by a guy who looked like he bought his clothes at Pedophiles "R" Us. And then there was what Shelly had said to me: *Don't let him take a picture of you.* That warning was a poisonous spider with hairy legs, crawling down my spine.

"I don't think so," I said. "It might be too hard to fit all of me in one shot." I gestured with both hands at my paunch, straining against my shirt.

His eyes bulged in his corroded face for an instant, and then he laughed, a raw, horsey sound that was part disbelief, part real hilarity. He pointed a finger at me, thumb cocked like the hammer of a gun. "You're okay, kid. I like you. Just don't get lost on the way to the cash register."

I walked away from him on unsteady legs, and not just because I was escaping a creep with an ugly mouth and an uglier face. I was a rational child. I read Isaac Asimov, hero-worshipped Carl Sagan, and felt a certain spiritual affinity with Andy Griffith's Matlock. I knew that Shelly Beukes's ideas about the Polaroid Man (only I was already thinking of him as the Phoenician) were the addled fantasies of a mind sliding apart. Her warnings shouldn't have rated a second thought—but they did. They had, in the last few moments, assumed an almost oracular power and worried me as much as it would've worried me to learn I had Seat 13 on Flight 1313 on Friday the 13th (and never mind that 13 is a pretty cool number, not just a prime or a Fibonacci but also an emirp, which means it stays prime if you reverse the digits and make it 31).

I got inside the mini-mart, dug the money out of my shirt pocket, and dropped it on the counter.

"Put it on Pump Ten for the nice guy in the Caddy," I said to Mrs. Matsuzaka, who stood behind the register alongside her kid, Yoshi.

Only no one ever called him Yoshi except her; he went by Mat, one *t*. Mat had a shaved head and long, ropy arms, and he affected a laconic surfer-dude ease. He was five years older than me and heading off to Berkeley at the end of the summer. He was looking to put his parents out of business by inventing a car that didn't need gas.

"Hey, Fags," he said, and tossed me a nod, which cheered me up some. Yeah, all right, he called me Fags—but I didn't take it personally. To most kids that was just my name. That may sound savagely homophobic now—and it was!—but in 1988, the era of AIDS and Eddie Murphy, calling someone a fag or a queer was considered high wit. By the standards of the day, Mat was a model of sensitivity. He read *Popular Mechanics* faithfully, cover to cover, and sometimes when I wandered into the Mobil mini-mart, he'd give me one of his back issues, because he'd seen something in there he thought I'd dig: a prototype jet pack or a personal one-man submarine. I don't want to misrepresent him. We weren't friends. He was seventeen and cool. I was thirteen and desperately *un*cool. A friendship between us was about as likely as my scoring a date with Tawny Kitaen. But I believe he felt a certain pitying affection for me and had a nebulous urge to look after me, maybe because we were both circuitheads at heart. I was grateful for any kindness from other kids in those days.

I went to grab an extra-large cup of my frozen Arctic Blu–Coca-Cola Slush Special. I needed it more than ever. My stomach was restless and gurgling, and I wanted something with a little fizz to settle it.

I had hardly finished adding the last neon-bright splash of Blu when the Phoenician pushed in the door with his forearm, giving it a hard shove like he had something personal against it. The open door blocked his view of the soda dispenser, which is the only reason he didn't see me as he cast his glare around the room. He didn't miss a step but stalked up to Mrs. Matsuzaka.

"What's a man got to do to get a tank of fucking gas around this joint? Why'd you shut off the pump?"

Mrs. Matsuzaka was barely five feet tall and delicately built, and she had mastered the blank, uncomprehending expression common to first-generation immigrants who understand the language just fine but occasionally find it easier to feign bafflement. She lifted her shoulders in a weak shrug and let Mat do the talking for her.

"You pay ten dollars, brah, ten dollars of gas is what you get," Mat said from his position on a stool behind the counter, under the racks of cigarettes.

"Either of you two know how to count in English?" said the Phoenician. "I sent the kid in with a fucking twenty."

It was like I drank my entire Arctic Blu–Coca-Cola Slush Special in one swallow. My blood surged with cold shock. I clapped a hand to my shirt pocket with a thrill of horror. Right away I knew what I'd done. I had reached into my pocket, felt money there, and tossed it on the counter without looking at it. But I'd handed over the ten that Larry Beukes had forced on me earlier, not the twenty the Phoenician had given me in the parking lot.

The only thing I could think to do was abase myself, as quickly and fully as possible. I was ready to cry, and the Phoenician hadn't even screamed at me yet. I reeled into the front of the store, hip-checking a wire shelf of potato chips. Bags of Lays scattered everywhere. I clawed the twenty out of my shirt pocket.

"Oh man oh man I'm sorry oh man. Oh, I screwed that up. I'm sorry, I'm so sorry. I didn't even look at the money when I threw it on the counter, mister, and I must've put down my ten instead of your twenty. I swear, I *swear*, I didn't—"

"When I said you could keep the change to buy yourself some weight-loss pills, I didn't mean you could fuck me out of a sawbuck." He lifted one hand as if he had a mind to catch me upside the head.

He'd come in with his camera—it was clutched in his other hand—and even as rattled as I was, I thought it was odd he wouldn't have just left it in the car.

"No, really, I'd never, I swear to God—" I was babbling, my eyes tingling dangerously, threatening to spill tears. In my haste I set my enormous thirty-two-ounce Blu slurry on the edge of the counter, and the moment I let go of it, a bad situation turned so, *so* much worse. The cup toppled and dropped, hit the floor, and exploded in a vibrant gout of blue ice. Glowing blue chips sprayed the Phoenician's perfectly pressed black pants, splashed his crotch, and threw sapphire droplets on his camera.

"*The fuck!*" he screamed, dancing back on the toes of his cowboy boots. "Are you fucking *retarded*, you enormous pile of turd?"

"'Ey!" shouted Mat's mom, pointing at the Phoenician. "'Ey, 'ey, 'ey, no fight in store, I call cop!"

The Phoenician looked down at his Blu-spattered clothes and back up at me. His face darkened. He put the Polaroid-that-wasn't on the counter and took a step toward me. I don't know what he meant to do, but he was shaken up, and his left foot skidded in the spreading pile of Arctic Blu–Coke slush. Those boots had high Cuban heels, and they looked good but must've been as tricky as walking around in six-inch stilettos. He came very close to slamming down on one knee.

"I'll clean it up!" I cried out. "Oh, man, I'm so sorry, I'll clean it all up, and, oh, Jesus, believe me, I've never tried to cheat anyone out of anything, I'm *really* honest, if I fart, I always cop right to it, even when I'm on the school bus, swear to God, swear—"

"Yeah, brah, chill," Mat said, rising from his stool. He was sinewy and tall, and with his dark eyes and shaved head he didn't need to make a threat to look like one. "Take it easy. Fags is okay. I guarantee he wasn't trying to screw you."

"And you can stay the fuck out of it," the Phoenician said to him. "Or try paying attention before you choose sides. Kid rips me for ten bucks, throws his drink on me, and then I just about break my ass in this puddle of shit—"

"Don't put the boots on if you can't walk in 'em, pard," Mat said, without looking at him. "You might get hurt one of these days."

Mat handed a big roll of paper towels across the counter, and as I took them, he gave me a wink so quick, so subtle, I almost missed it. I felt almost shaky with gratitude, that was how relieved I was to have Mat on my side.

I tore off a fistful of paper towels and immediately dropped to my knees in the slush to begin swiping at the Phoenician's trousers. You could be forgiven if you thought I was getting ready to give him a blow job by way of apology.

"Aw, man, I've always been clumsy, always, I can't even roller-skate—"

He danced away (almost slipping again), then leaned in and snatched the clod of sodden paper towels away from me. "Hey! Hey, no touch! You get down there on your knees like someone who's had *way* too much practice. Keep your hands off my dick, thank you. I got it."

He gave me a look that said I had crossed the line from someone who needed an ass-stomping to someone he didn't want anywhere near him. He swiped at his pants and shirt, whispering bitterly to himself.

I still had the paper-towel roll, though, and I splashed through slush and grabbed his camera to clean it off.

By then I was so nervous and wretched I was moving in spastic bursts, and when I picked up the camera, my hand pressed the big red button to take a shot. The lens was pointing across the counter, into Mat's face, when the Polaroid went off with a snap of white light and a high-pitched mechanical whine.

The photo didn't just pop out. The camera *launched* it from the slot, firing the square of plastic across the counter and over the far side. Mat snapped his head back, blinking rapidly, blinded by the flash perhaps.

I was a little blind myself. Weird, coppery glowworms crawled before my eyes. I shook my head, stared stupidly down at the camera in my right hand. The brand was "Solarid," a company I'd never heard of and as far as I know never existed, not in this country or any other.

"Put that down," the Phoenician said, in a new tone of voice.

I thought I'd heard him at his scariest when he was yelling at me, but this was different and much worse. This was the sound of the cylinder turning in a revolver, the click of the hammer cocking back.

"I was just trying to—" I began, my tongue thick in my mouth.

"You're trying to get yourself hurt. And you're about to succeed."

He held out a hand, and I put the Solarid in it. If I dropped the camera—if it slipped out of my sweaty, shaking hand—I believe he would've killed me. Put his hand on my throat and squeezed. I believed that then, and I believe it now. His gray eyes regarded me with a cold, curdled fury, and his pocked face was as inexpressive as a rubber mask.

He tugged the camera away from me, and the moment passed. He swung his gaze to the young man and elderly woman behind the counter.

"The picture. Give me the picture," he said.

Mat still seemed dazed from the camera's flash. He looked at me. He looked at his mother. He seemed to have lost the thread of the entire conversation.

The Phoenician ignored him and focused his attention upon Mrs. Matsuzaka. He held out a hand. "That's my photo, and I want it. My camera, my film, my photo."

Her gaze swept the floor around her, and then she looked up and shrugged again.

"It popped out and fell on your side of the counter," the Phoenician said, speaking loudly and slowly, the way people do when they're hideously angry with a foreigner. As if translation were aided by volume. "We all saw it. *Look* for it. Look around your feet."

Mat rubbed the balls of his palms into his eyes, dropped them, and yawned. "What's up?" As if he had just shoved back the sheets and walked out of his bedroom into the middle of an argument.

His mother said something to him in Japanese, her voice rapid and distressed. He stared at her in a kind of foggy daze, then lifted his chin and looked at the Phoenician.

"What's the problem, brah?"

"The picture. The photograph the fat kid took of you. I want it."

"What's the big deal? If I find it, you want me to autograph it for you?"

The Phoenician was done talking. He stalked around to the waist-high door that would let him in behind the counter and the cash register. Mat's mom had returned to scanning the floor in a forlorn sort of way, but now her head twitched up, and she put her hand on the inside of the swinging door before he could come through. Her expression became *severely* disapproving.

"No! Customer stay other side! No, no!"

"I want that fucking photograph," the Phoenician said.

"Yo, brah!" If Mat had been in a daze, he shook it off then. He stepped between his mother and the Phoenician, and suddenly Mat seemed very large. "You heard her. Back off. Company policy, no one on this side of the counter who don't work here. You don't like it? Buy a postcard and send your complaint to Mobil. They're dying to hear from you."

"Can we move this along? I have a baby in the car," said the woman who was standing behind me with an armful of cat-food cans.

What? Did you think it was just the four of us in the Mobil Mart all this time? While I threw my Arctic Blu special at the Phoenician and he cursed and sulked and threatened, people were coming in, grabbing drinks and chips and plastic-wrapped hoagies and forming into a line behind me. By now the queue stretched halfway to the back of the store.

Mat moved behind the register. "Next customer."

The mom with the armful of cans stepped carefully around that sci-fi-colored puddle of vividly glittering blue, and Mat began to ring up her purchases.

The Phoenician stared in disbelief. Mat's curt dismissal was an outrage on a par with my flinging frosty Blu down his pants.

"You know what? *Fuck* this. Fuck this store and fuck this fat waste and fuck *you*, slant. I got enough gas to get out of this shithole, and that's more than enough. I wouldn't want to blow one penny more than absolutely necessary in this toilet."

"That's one eighty-nine," Mat said to the woman with the cat food. "No extra charge for the afternoon's entertainment."

The Phoenician reached the door but paused, half in, half out, to glare back at me. "I won't forget you, kid. Look both ways before you cross the street, know what I mean?"

I was too choked up with fright to squeak any kind of reply. He banged out the door. A moment later his Caddy blasted away from the pumps and onto the two-lane highway with a shrill whine of tires.

I used the rest of the paper towels to mop the slush off the floor. It was a relief to get down on my knees, below eye level, where I could have a semiprivate cry. I was *thirteen*, man. Customers stepped around me, paid for things, and left, considerately pretending they couldn't hear my sniffling and choked gasps.

When I had the mess swabbed up (the floor was tacky but dry), I carried a great mass of sopping paper rags over to the counter. Mrs. Matsuzaka stood to one side of her son, her eyes far away and her mouth crimped in a frown—but when she saw me with my load of wet towels, she came out of her thoughts and reached for the big industrial wastebasket behind the counter. She wheeled it over toward me, and that's when I saw it: The snapshot was face-down on the floor, in the corner, had slid under the bin and out of sight.

Mrs. Matsuzaka saw it, too, and went back for it, while I dumped my soggy paper towels into the trash can. She stared down at the photo with incomprehension. She looked over at me—then held it out so I could have a look.

It should've been a close-up of Mat. The lens had been right in his face.

Instead it was a photograph of *me*.

Only it wasn't a shot of me from a few minutes ago. It was from a few weeks earlier. In the picture I sat in a molded plastic chair by the soda machine, reading *Popular Mechanics* and sipping on a giant plastic cup full of soda. In the Polaroid (Solarid?) I was wearing a white Huey Lewis T-shirt and a pair of knee-length denim shorts. Today I had on khakis and a Hawaiian shirt with pockets. The photographer had to have been standing behind the counter.

It didn't make any sense, and I stared at it in complete bafflement, trying to figure out where it had come from. It couldn't be the picture I'd just accidentally shot, but I also didn't see how it could be a snap from a few weeks back. I had no memory of Mat or his mom taking my picture while I read one of Mat's magazines. I couldn't imagine *why* they'd want to do such a thing, and I had never seen either one of them with a Polaroid camera.

I swallowed and said, "Can I have that?"

Mrs. Matsuzaka took one last bewildered look at the photograph, then pursed her lips and put it on the counter. She slid it across to me, and when she took her hand back, she rubbed the tips of her fingers together, as if it had left a disagreeable coating on her skin.

I studied it for a moment longer, with a clenched, ill feeling behind my breastbone, a cramped sensation of anxiety that wasn't entirely a product of the Phoenician's rage and threats. I tucked the picture into my shirt pocket and eased over to the cash register. I put the twenty on the counter, thinking, with a shudder, *That's his money, and what's he going to do when he realizes you never gave it back? Better look both ways when you cross the street. Better look both fucking ways, Fags.* See, I even insulted myself.

"Sorry about the mess," I said. "That's for the thirty-two-ounce soda."

"Whatever, brah. I ain't gonna charge you for that. Just a little spilled sugar water." Mat pushed my money back toward me.

"Okay. Well. I owe you one for not letting him kick my ass. You saved my life there, Mat. Sincerely."

"Sure, sure," he said, although he had narrowed his eyes and was giving me a puzzled smile, as if he weren't quite sure what I was talking about. He considered me for a moment longer, then gave his head a little shake. "Hey, ask you something?"

"Sure, what, Mat?"

"You talk like we know each other. Have we met before?"

4

I WALKED OUT OF THERE with my nerves jangling and a sick buzz in my head. By the time I left, I was reasonably certain that Mat didn't have any goddamn clue who I was, and had no memory of ever seeing me before, never mind that I walked into that Mobil every day and had been reading his used copies of *Popular Mechanics* for more than a year. He simply didn't know me anymore—an idea that rattled me badly.

I told myself I didn't understand, that it was crazy, that it didn't make sense, but this wasn't entirely the truth. I already had a notion about Mat's sudden forgetfulness nibbling at the edge of my consciousness. I was aware of it in the way you might be aware of a rat scuttling inside the walls. You can hear the furtive scrabble of its claws, the thump of its torso against the drywall. You know it's there, you just haven't set your eyes on it. My notion about Mat and the Solarid was so horror-movie terrible—so Steven Spielberg impossible—that I couldn't bear to consider it straight on. Not yet.

I returned home in a state of persistent, low-grade panic. It took me ten minutes to cross the distance between the Mobil and my house on Plum Street. In my mind I died seven times on the way.

Twice I heard the Phoenician's tires squealing on the blacktop and turned to see the shiny chrome grille in the half second before the Caddy slammed into me.

Once the Phoenician slid to a stop behind me, got out with a tire iron, chased me into the woods, and beat me to death in the brush.

He ran me down as I tried to scamper across the Thatcher family's front yard, and he drowned me in their purple inflatable wading pool. The last thing I saw was a headless G.I. Joe sunk to the bottom.

The Phoenician drove past nice and slow and hung his left arm out the window with a gun in it, put two bullets in me, one in my neck, one in my cheek.

He drove past nice and slow and lopped my head off with a rusty machete. *WHACK.*

He drove past nice and slow and said, *Hey, kid, how's it going?* and my weak heart stopped in my fat chest and I fell dead of a massive cardiac arrest at age thirteen, so young, so full of promise.

The snapshot was in my shirt pocket. I felt it there as if it were a square of warm, radioactive material, something that could give me cancer. It could not have made me more uneasy if it were kiddie porn. Possessing it felt criminal. It felt like *evidence* . . . although of what crime, I could not have told you.

I cut across the grass and let myself into the house. I heard a mechanical whirring and followed the sound into the kitchen. My father was out of bed and using the electric beater on a bowl of orange-tinted whipped cream. Something was baking in the oven, and the air was redolent of the warm scent of gravy, an odor quite like a freshly opened can of Alpo.

"I smell dinner. What's in the oven?"

"Battle of Stalingrad," he said.

"What's the orange stuff you're whipping up?"

"Topping for the Panama Thrill."

I opened the fridge looking for Kool-Aid and found the Panama Thrill, a mountainous sculpture of Jell-O, cherries suspended within its quaking mass. My father only knew how to make a few things: Jell-O, pasta dishes with ground beef in them, chicken topped with sauces made out of Campbell's canned soups. His real gift in the kitchen was for naming the meals. It was Battle of Stalingrad one night, Chainsaw Massacre the next (that was a weird mess of white beans and meat in a bloody red sauce), Fidel's Cigar for lunch (a brown tortilla stuffed with shredded pork and pieces of pineapple), and Farmer Pizza for breakfast (an open-faced omelet piled with cheese and random chopped leftovers). He wasn't a fatso like me, but thanks to our diet he wasn't anyone's idea of trim. If we passed each other in the hall, we both had to turn sideways.

I poured the Kool-Aid, drank off the entire glass in four swallows. Not good enough. I poured another.

"It's almost ready," he said.

I made a humming sound of acceptance. Battle of Stalingrad was mashed potatoes topped with shaved steak and a bottled gravy-and-mushroom sauce. Eating it was roughly like consuming a bucket of liquid cement. I felt boiled after my hike to the Mobil and back, and the dog-food smell of dinner was making me ill.

"You're not enthusiastic?" he asked.

"No. I'm eager."

"Sorry it's not Mom's apple pie. But I got to tell you, even if she was here, I don't think she makes pie."

"Do I look like a kid who needs pie?"

He glanced at me sidelong and said, "You look like a kid who maybe needs a shot of Pepto-Bismol. You okay?"

"I'm just going to sit in the dark and cool off," I said. "I haven't been this hot since I was fighting off the Cong outside Khe Sanh."

"Let's not talk about that. If I start thinking about the boys we left behind, I'll begin crying in the whipped cream."

I went out whistling "Goodnight Saigon." My dad and I had an ongoing riff about the time we'd spent fighting the North Vietnamese together, the arms we'd run to the Contras, the helicopter crash we'd barely survived on a mission to save the hostages in Iran. The truth was, neither of us had ever been out of California, except for one trip to Hawaii, when we were still a family in the traditional sense. My mother was the one who had adventures in faraway places.

My parents were technically still married, but my mother lived with the tribal peoples of the southwest African coast and was only home for a month here and a month there. When she was stateside, she made me uneasy. We did not have conversations—talking with my mother was more like taking a series of oral quizzes on subjects ranging from feminism to socialism to my feelings about my own sexual identity. She would sometimes ask me to sit on the couch with her so she could read me an article about genital mutilation from *National Geographic*. She would announce that the practice of women shaving their armpits was a form of patriarchal control and then look at me with a certain hostile fascination, as if she expected me to disapprove of the wiry gray thatch beneath her arms. Once I asked my father why they didn't live together, and he said because she was brilliant.

She was, too, I think. I've read her books, and they aren't what you'd call page-turners. But I admire the way she could fold together a series of small observations and then suddenly spread them out before you—open them like a fan—to reveal a single great insight. Her curiosities gripped her entirely, held her transfixed. I don't think there was room in her head to wonder about her husband and son.

I stretched out on the couch, underneath the picture window, in the dimness of the living room. I was running my thumb along the edge of the photo in my shirt pocket for maybe half a minute before I realized what I was doing. A part of me didn't want to look at it now or ever, which was a peculiar way to feel. It was, after all, just a photo of me sitting next to the soda machine, reading a magazine. There was nothing wrong with it, as long as you didn't know that it had been taken today but showed something that had happened days, or maybe weeks, ago.

A part of me didn't want to look at it—and a part of me couldn't help myself.

I picked it out of my pocket and tilted it to examine it in the afternoon's weird stormlight. If ghosts have a color, then they are the color of an August thunderstorm getting ready to break. The sky was the exact filthy gray of a Polaroid just beginning to develop.

In the photograph I hunched over that crumpled copy of *Popular Mechanics*, looking fat and unlovely. The fluorescent lighting above gave me the bluish tinge of the undead in a George Romero picture.

Don't let him take a picture of you, Shelly Beukes had told me. *Don't let him start taking things away.*

But he *hadn't* taken a picture of me. I was in the picture, but he hadn't pointed his camera at me and pressed the button. In fact, he hadn't taken a picture at all. *I* had—and I'd been pointing the Solarid at Mat.

I dropped the photo with a kind of revulsion, as if I had suddenly realized I was holding a squirming maggot.

For a while I sprawled in the shadowy cool, trying not to think, because everything in my head was rotten and strange. Ever try not to think? It's like trying not to breathe—no one can do it for long.

Maturity is not something that happens all at once. It is not a border between two countries where once you cross the invisible line, you are on the new soil of adulthood, speaking the foreign tongue of grown-ups. It is more like a distant broadcast, and you are driving toward it, and sometimes you can barely make it out through the hiss of static while other times the reception momentarily clears and you can pick up the signal with perfect clarity.

I think I was listening for Radio Adulthood then, remaining perfectly still in the hopes that I could catch a transmission carrying useful news and emergency instructions. I can't say anything came to me— but in that moment of enforced stillness my gaze happened to settle on the small collection of family photo albums that my dad had arranged on the top shelf of the bookcase in the corner. My dad liked to keep things in order. He wore a tool belt to work, and everything was always in just the right place—the pliers in a holster, the wire stripper snug in a loop that was meant for it.

I picked an album at random, dumped myself back onto the couch, and began to turn through the pages. The oldest photos were glossy rectangular squares and—hold on to your hats, kids, I'm not making this up—were in black and white. The earliest showed my parents to-gether in the days before they married. They were both too old and too square to be hippies, and I'm not sure I can honestly describe them as an appealing couple. My father's only concessions to the time period were bushy sideburns and tinted sunglasses. My mother, the great Afri-can anthropologist, wore khaki shorts pulled up above her belly button and heavy hiking boots, even to family reunions. She smiled like it pained her. There wasn't one shot of them hugging or kissing or even looking at each other.

There were at least a few shots of them taking turns holding *me*. Here was my mother on the floor, dangling enormous rubber keys above a chubby infant on his back, who grasped at them with fat fingers. Here was a picture of my father up to his waist in someone's aboveground swimming pool, clutching his naked toddler in his arms. I was already a butterball.

My most frequent companion, though, was not my father or my mother but . . . Shelly Beukes. It was kind of a shock, really. When she retired five years earlier, I'd felt nothing in particular, was as indifferent as I would've been if my father had told me we were replacing an end table. Are you shocked to hear that a privileged seven-year-old from the Valley took the help for granted? My dad didn't talk to me then about her open-heart surgery. He just said that she was a little older and older people needed more rest. She was in the neighborhood, and I could go see her anytime.

And did I? Oh, I dropped in on rare occasions, for tea and date cookies, and we sat in front of *Murder, She Wrote*, and she asked me how I was doing. I'm sure I was polite and ate my cookies quickly so I could go. When you're a kid, spending an afternoon in an overheated living room with an old lady in front of daytime television is like winning a ticket to Guantánamo Bay. Love doesn't figure into it. Whatever I owed her, or whatever I might've meant to her, never entered into my thoughts.

But here she was, in photo after photo.

We clutched the bars of a jail cell in Alcatraz, both of us putting on mock-horrified faces.

I sat on her shoulders to pluck a peach from the branches of a peach tree—my free hand crushing the brim of her straw hat down into her face.

I blew out candles while she stood behind me, hands raised, ready to clap. And yes . . . by this stage, the pictures were all Polaroids. Of course we had one. Everyone had one. Just like everyone had a VCR, a microwave, and a WHERE'S THE BEEF? T-shirt.

The woman in these photos was old but had bright, almost girlish eyes and a mischievous smile to match. In one Polaroid her hair was the red of a neon beer sign in a bar. In another it was a comical shade of carrot, and her nails were painted to match. In the snapshots she was always grabbing me, tousling my hair, sitting with me in her lap while I ate one of her date-filled cookies—a chubby little kid in Spider-Man Underoos with grape-juice stains on his chin.

About two-thirds of the way through the book, I came across a photo of a long-forgotten backyard barbecue. Shelly's hair was Arctic Blu–colored this time. She had Larry with her, the Afrikaner wearing too-tight sand-colored trousers and a white button-down shirt with the sleeves rolled back to display his Popeye forearms. Each of them had one of my hands—I was a blur swinging between them in the dusk. Shelly was frozen in the act of whooping. Bemused grown-ups stood around watching, holding plastic cups of white wine.

The idea that these days had been taken from her struck me as vile. It was a swallow of curdled milk. It was indecent.

There was no justification for the loss of her memories and understanding, no defense the universe could offer for the corruption of her mind. She had loved me, even if I'd been too witless to know it or value it. Anyone who looked at these pictures could see she loved me, that I delighted her somehow, in spite of my fat cheeks, vacant stare, and tendency to eat in a way that smeared food all down my bad T-shirts. In spite of how I thoughtlessly accepted her attention and affection as my due. And now it was all melting away, every birthday party, every BBQ, every plucked ripe peach. She was being erased a little at a time by a cancer that fed not on her flesh but on her inner life, on her private store of happiness. The thought made me want to fling the photo album at a wall. It made me feel like crying.

Instead I swiped at the water in my eyes and flipped to the next page—and made a sound of surprise at what I found there.

When I had glanced into the back of the Phoenician's car, I'd seen a photo of a bodybuilder, a darkly tanned youth in an orange tank top, perched on the hood of a Trans Am. Some part of me had recognized him—had known I'd seen him before—even though I couldn't place him or guess where we'd crossed paths. And here he was again, in my own photo album.

He held two straight-backed chairs over his head, one in each hand, gripping each by a wooden leg. I sat in one, hollering in what looked like joyous terror. I was in a damp swimsuit, jewels of water glittering on my fat-boy boobs. Shelly Beukes sat in the other, gripping the seat with both hands, laughing with her head tipped back slightly. In this photograph the big guy was dressed not in a tank top but in navy whites. He grinned wolfishly beneath his Tom Selleck mustache. And—*look*—even the Trans Am was there. I could just see the rear end of it, sitting in the driveway, visible around one corner of Shelly's house.

"Who the hell are *you?*" I whispered.

I was talking to myself and didn't expect an answer, but my father said, "Who?"

He stood in the doorway to the kitchen, wearing a single oven mitt. I wasn't sure how long he'd been standing there, watching me.

"Guy with the muscles," I said, gesturing at a picture he couldn't see from halfway across the room.

He wandered over, craned his neck for a look, "Oh. *That* jackass. Shelly's boy. Sinbad? Achilles? Something like that. That's the day before he shipped out to the Red Sea. Shelly had a going-away barbecue at her house. She made a cake looked like a battleship and was almost as big. We brought home the leftovers, and you and I ate battleship for breakfast all week."

I remembered that cake: a three-dimensional aircraft carrier (not a battleship), churning up waves of blue-white frosting. I also remembered, faintly, that Shelly had told me that the party was a graduation party—for me! I had just finished the third grade. What a Shelly Beukes thing to do: tell a lonely little kid that a party was all about him, when it had nothing to do with him at all.

"He doesn't look so bad," I said. It bothered me, my dad calling him a jackass. It seemed like an offhand criticism of Shelly herself, and I wasn't in the mood.

"Oh, you *loved* him. He was Larry's boy through and through. Competed in bodybuilding contests, liked to show off with his muscle-boy tricks. Pick up one end of a car with his dick or whatever. You used to think he was the Incredible Hulk. I remember that stunt. Picking both of you up at the same time and walking around with you while you balanced on those chairs. I was afraid he'd drop Shelly on her head and I'd have to find a new babysitter. Or he'd drop you and I'd have to find a new kid to eat my Panama Thrill. Come on. Food's done. Let's tuck in."

We sat catty-corner to each other at the dinner table with the Battle of Stalingrad on our plates. I wasn't hungry and was surprised when I found myself using a roll to mop up the last of the gravy. I moved my bread around and around, smearing juice and thinking of all those photo albums in the back of the Phoenician's car. Thinking of the picture in my shirt pocket that showed something it couldn't possibly show. An idea was developing, not unlike a Polaroid, swimming slowly, inevitably, into clarity.

In a distant, artificially calm voice, I said, "I saw Mrs. Beukes today."

"Oh, yeah?" My father gave me a thoughtful glance, and then asked, in a mild tone that was as artificial as mine, "How'd she look?"

"She was lost. I walked her home."

"I'm glad. I wouldn't have expected you to do anything different."

I told him about finding Shelly in the street and how she thought she was supposed to work today and how she wouldn't say my name because she didn't know it. I told him about Larry Beukes swerving into the driveway in a panic, how he'd been scared to death she might go wandering into traffic or wind up lost for good.

"He gave me money for bringing her home. I didn't want to take it, but he made me."

I didn't think my dad would like that, and a part of me expected—was maybe even hoping—to be shamed. But instead he got up for the Panama Thrill and said, over his shoulder, "Good."

"It is?"

He set down the Jell-O, wobbling under four inches of sherbet-colored whipped cream, and began to scoop globs of it into bowls.

"Sure. Paying you is the way a man like Lawrence Beukes makes himself feel that he's back in control. He's not a man who lost his senile wife because he's too old to see to her needs himself. He's a man who knows how to pay someone to solve a problem."

"He asked if I'd help out sometimes. If I'd . . . you know, come by and sit with her when he has to go out. For groceries or whatever."

My dad paused with a spoonful of Panama Thrill at his lips. "I'm glad. You're good to help out. I know you loved that old lady."

Funny, huh? My father had known I loved Shelly Beukes, something I hadn't known myself until only a few minutes before.

"Anything else happen this morning?" he asked.

My thumb crept to my shirt pocket, ran along the edge of the Polaroid (Solarid?) there. I'd been touching it off and on in a nervous, restless, helpless way ever since getting home. I considered saying something about the Phoenician and the clash at the Mobil mini-mart, but I didn't know how to bring such a thing up without sounding like a rattled little kid.

And then there was that idea creeping around the edge of my awareness, a thought I was studiously trying to ignore. I didn't want to go anywhere near that idea, and if I started talking about the Phoenician, I wouldn't be able to avoid it.

So I didn't say anything about the run-in at the gas station. Instead I said, "I'm almost done working on the party gun."

"Outstanding. It'll be easy to celebrate when you're finished. All you have to do is pull the trigger." He got up and carried our plates to the sink. "Mike?"

"Yeah?"

"Don't get too down if Shelly doesn't know you or says things that don't make sense."

"I won't."

"It's like . . . a house after someone moves out. The house is still there, but all their stuff is gone. Someone took away the furniture and rolled up the rugs. The movers crated all the parts of Shelly Beukes up and shipped her away. There's just not much left of her anymore except the empty house." He scraped the ruins of Stalingrad into the disposal. "That and what's in old photographs."

5

"YOU'LL BE ALL RIGHT HERE?" my father asked me on his way out the door. He had one foot on the front step and the other on our pea-green shag carpet. Lightning lit the low, boiling clouds behind him in a soundless flicker.

"Been a while since I needed Shelly Beukes to tuck me in," I said.

"Yeah, it has. I don't know that's how it should be, but that's how it is, huh?"

That was such an uncharacteristic thing for my dad to say—to acknowledge, even a little, that our life was somehow not quite ideal— that I opened my mouth to answer him and found I had no reply at all.

He glanced out into the turbulent, thundercloudy dusk. "I hate working nights. When Al gets back in the rotation, I'll put in for days."

My father had been pulling night shifts with the utility company all summer. They had a staffing gap. His best pal, Al Murdoch, wasn't working while he received treatment for lymphoma. One of the line engineers, John Hawthorne, had recently been arrested for assaulting his ex-wife. Piper Wilson had left to have a baby. Suddenly my father was the senior lineman and working sixty hours a week, most of them after I went to bed.

At first I liked it. I liked staying up after I was supposed to be asleep, catching soft-core porn on what we called Skinemax in those days. But by mid-July all the fun had gone out of being alone in the house at night. I had a vivid imagination and in late July had made the mistake of reading *Zodiac*. After that the emptiness of the house began to seriously creep me the fuck out. I'd lie in bed dry-mouthed at two in the morning, listening to the silence, breathlessly expecting to hear a splintering crunch as good old Zodiac forced open a window with a crowbar. He'd use one of the kitchen knives to cut astrological signs into my fat gut—not after I was dead but while I was still alive, so he could hear me shriek.

I never talked about any of this with my father, because the only thing worse than my nighttime anxiety attacks was the idea that he might decide to hire someone to babysit me. All the Zodiac Killer could do was torture and kill me. If my dad hired some teenage Valley girl to put me to bed at nine-thirty and then spend the rest of the night on our phone jawing with her friends, I'd *wish* I were dead. The indignity would stomp up and down on my brittle, thirteen-year-old boy's ego.

After my run-in with the Phoenician, I especially dreaded being alone *that* evening. Plus, there were those thunderheads and a sense of electrical charge in the air, a prickling energy I could feel in the fine hairs on my forearms. The thunder had been rolling all afternoon, and you could just tell it was going to cut loose soon—cut loose and *roar*.

"Think you'll work on the party gun some more?" he asked.

"Probably. I—"

What followed was not melodramatic horror-movie thunder but more like a world-splitting sci-fi missile launch, a single obliterating cannon blast. It was noise at such a volume that it drove the air out of me.

My father would spend his evening offered up to that sky on an iron crane, repairing power lines, a thought that made my insides bunch up with worry when I allowed myself to think about it. He only looked disgruntled and a little weary, as if the thunder were a tiresome irritation, like the sound of kids fighting in the backseat. He cupped one hand behind his right ear to indicate he hadn't heard me.

"I almost had it working this afternoon when Shelly showed up. If I finish, I'll show you tomorrow."

"That's good. You have to hurry up and make your first million bucks so I can retire and focus on what I really love—doing original things with Jell-O." My father took a few steps down to his panel van, then turned back, frowning. "I want you to call if—"

There was another cannonade of thunder. My father went right on talking, but I didn't hear a word. That was very like him. He had an unmatched gift for tuning out background details that didn't concern him. The Dallas Cowboys cheerleaders could've romped by naked, shaking their pom-poms, and if he was up in his crane repairing a transformer, I doubt he would've so much as glanced down.

I nodded as if I'd heard him. I supposed he was dishing out a standard-issue caution for me to call the office and have them radio him if anything came up. He waved and turned away. A blue light snapped on, high in the clouds, a flash on the world's biggest camera. I flinched (*Don't let him take your picture*) and half shut the front door.

The headlights of the panel van blinked on and the afternoon blinked off in the same moment. It was only six-fifteen in mid-August, and the sun wouldn't be down for another three hours, but the day was lost in a smothering darkness. The van backed away. I closed the door.

6

I DON'T KNOW HOW LONG I stood in the foyer, listening to the tick of my pulse in my ears. The taut, expectant hush of the afternoon held me in place. At some point I realized I had my hand over my heart, as if I were a child about to pledge allegiance.

No—not over my heart. Over the Polaroid.

I had a powerful impulse to get rid of it, to throw it away. It felt awful to have it there in my pocket—awful and dangerous, like walking around with a vial of infected blood. I even went into the kitchen and opened the cupboard under the sink, meaning to cram it down into the garbage.

But when I slipped it out of my pocket, I just stood there looking at it: looking at the fat, red-faced boy in a Huey Lewis T-shirt, bent over *Popular Mechanics*.

Have we met before? Mat asked, smiling apologetically.

A flash snapped outside, and I lurched back, dropped the photo. When I looked up, for an instant I *saw* him, the Phoenician, right on the other side of the kitchen window, and don't let him take your picture, oh God, don't let him—

But it wasn't the Phoenician with his Solarid. The flash was only another blue crackle of lightning. The face I saw in the window was my own, a faint reflection suspended in the glass.

When the next crash of thunder came, I was in the garage. I carefully set the snapshot down, aligning it with the edge of my worktable. I switched on my Luxo lamp and twisted its hinged arm to nail the picture down in a hot circle of white light. Finally, and with a kind of nasty pleasure, I stuck a pushpin through the top, to hold it in place. I felt better then. It was in my operational theater now, fastened to my autopsy table. This was where I pried things apart and made them tell me everything, all their powers and vulnerabilities.

To add to my feeling of confidence and control, I unbuttoned my pants and let them fall around my ankles and stepped out of them. I had discovered some time ago that nothing frees the mind like dropping the pants. Try it if you doubt me. American productivity would, I believe, nearly double if everyone were free to work pantsless.

Just to show the photo who was boss, I ignored it and worked on the party gun. I squeezed the trigger to hear the fan whir inside the casing. I unbolted the side and lifted out the circuit board, picked and prodded at it. At first I was distracted. I kept looking at the picture that had no right to exist, and then, when I turned back to my new toy, I couldn't remember what I'd been doing. After a while, though, I settled into my own capsule of focus, and the Phoenician, Shelly Beukes, the Solarid, all of it went gray—like a Polaroid developing in reverse, returning to unmixed blank chemicals.

I soldered and wired. It was warm in the garage and fragrant with that smell I still love: melted rubber and hot copper and oil. I had oil on one of my hands, a little WD-40, and I wiped it with a rag, to expose pink skin. I studied the rag, watched the way the ink stain spread, leeching into the fabric. Sponged away. Absorbed.

I had snapped a picture of Mobil Station Mat, Yoshi Matsuzaka, but what the Solarid captured was something in his *head*, a picture he held in his mind—of *me*. It soaked it up, like the rag in my fist, absorbing oil.

Blue light flashbulbed outside the windows.

I was not alarmed. The idea, when it came to me, was no shock. I suppose, down below the level of my conscious mind, I already knew. I believe that our subconscious often finishes ideas hours, days, weeks, even years before it decides to present them to the higher reaches of the brain. And after all, Shelly had already explained everything to me.

Don't let him take a picture of you. Don't let him start taking things away.

It's odd that when I knew—when I *understood*—I wasn't more afraid. That I didn't go clammy and shivery and try to tell myself I was being crazy. Instead I was almost serene. I remember I calmly turned a shoulder to the photo and bent back to the party gun, screwing it together again and then shaking a packet of glitter down into the barrel, loading it like a musket. I behaved as if I had solved a math problem of no particular import.

The last part of the gun was the flash, which could be snapped into the top, where a sharpshooter might put his scope. I had in fact swiped the disposable flash from our own Polaroid for this purpose. I held the flash in my hand, as if I were weighing it, and thought of the camera going off in Mat's face, that hot, white snap of light, and how he had staggered away, blinking rapidly.

I thought of Shelly Beukes, casting her baffled stare around the neighborhood she'd lived in for at least two decades, looking as dazed as if a flash had just gone off in *her* face. I thought about the black photo albums in the back of the Phoenician's Caddy. I thought about the photo I'd seen in one of them, a photo that was almost certainly of Shelly's own son.

There was a long rolling peal of thunder that seemed to cause the whole garage to shudder, and afterward the air rang strangely. Then I decided I was the one shuddering, and abruptly I stood up, feeling dizzy. I switched off the Luxo and stood in the dark, taking deep breaths of the coppery-smelling air. I wondered if I was going to be sick.

The ringing sound in my ears went on and on, and all at once it came to me that I wasn't hearing an aftershock from the thunder. Someone was leaning on the doorbell.

I was afraid to answer it. By some thirteen-year-old logic, I felt sure it had to be the Phoenician, who somehow knew I had solved the riddle of his Solarid and was here to shut me up forever. I looked around for something I could use as a weapon, considered the screwdriver, then took the party gun instead. I had the wild idea that in the shadows of the foyer it might look like a *real* gun.

As I approached the front door, the storm clouds launched a fresh salvo of house-shaking thunder, and I heard a whispered curse in a heavy South African brogue. My anxiety drained away, leaving my legs loosey-goosey and my head light.

I cracked the door and said, "Hi, Mr. Beukes."

His Rock Hudson features were haggard, deeply lined, and his lips were discolored, as if he'd been walking for a long time in the cold. He might've aged ten years since I'd last seen him.

For all the crashing and flaring lights, it still wasn't raining. The wind, though, lashed at his trench coat, so it flapped frantically around his massive torso and narrow hips. It was the same coat Shelly had been wearing that morning. It looked better on him. The gale flung his silver hair across his seamed, bold forehead.

"Michael," he said, "I did not eggspect I would have need of you so soon or on a night like this. I am so sorry. I am just— Oh, Gott. What a day. I am sure you must be busy. Doing something with your friends. I hate—on such short notice—"

Under other circumstances this would've sounded like the setup for a punch line. I was less a social butterfly than a social death's-head moth. But in the rushing darkness of that storm that refused to break, I hardly registered his line about how I must be doing something with my friends.

The storm, the feeling of electric charge in the air, Mr. Beukes's strained, raspy breath, and all the strangeness of the day had me keyed up, almost quivering with tension. Yet for all that, I wasn't surprised to see him on the front step. Some part of me had been expecting him all afternoon . . . had been waiting for the third act of today's performance to begin, the conclusion to an absurdist drama in which I was both the lead and the audience.

"What's up, Mr. Beukes? Is Shelly all right?"

"Is she . . . ? Yes. No." He laughed bitterly. "You know how she is. At the moment she is asleep. I hoff to go out. Something has happened. Today I am a man in a sinking boot, trying to bail out the water with a spoon." It took me a moment to realize that "sinking boot" was Larry Beukesese for "sinking boat."

"What happened?"

"Do you remember what I tolt you about my gyms, how there is always a fire to put out?" He laughed again, bleakly. "I shoot watch my metaphors. My gym, the one next to the Microcenter? There has been a fire—an actual fire. No one is hurt, thank Gott for his blessings. It was closed. The fire department eggstinguished the blaze, but I must go inspegg the damage."

"What kind of fire?"

He wasn't expecting that question, and it took him a beat to process it. I don't blame him for being surprised. I was surprised, too. I didn't know I was going to ask him that until I heard the question come out of my mouth.

"I . . . I thingg it must be the lightning. They didn't say. I *hope* it is the lightning and not old wiring. The insurance company will heave me by my shriveled olt ball sack."

I barked with laughter at this passing mention of his shriveled olt ball sack. I had never heard an adult—let alone an elderly man like Lawrence Beukes—speak to me this way: with a profane, desperate honesty, with such a mix of black humor and undisguised vulnerability. It was a jolting experience. At the same time, I had a thought, two simple, dreadful words—*It's him*—and felt a light touch of vertigo.

Thoughts flashed by, like cards glimpsed as the dealer shuffles the deck.

Tell him not to go, I thought. But there'd been a fire, and he had to go, and I had no argument to make him stay, none that made sense. If I told him there was a man with a camera that stole thoughts circling his wife, he would never let me near Shelly again. In that case he might stay home—to protect her from *me*.

I thought, *He will go, and I will call the police and warn them his wife is in danger*. Again I asked myself, In danger from what? From *who*? A man with a Polaroid camera? I was thirteen, not thirty, and my dread, my anxieties, would count for nothing with the police. I would sound like a hysterical child.

Also, a quadrant of my brain held out hope that I was only scaring myself with a lunatic ghost story, the result of a childhood spent reading too many comic books and watching too many episodes of *The Tomorrow People*. The rational counterargument presented itself to me in a series of forceful, unequivocal points: Shelly Beukes did not suffer from a curse inflicted by a knockoff Polaroid. She was the victim of Alzheimer's disease, no magical explanation required. As for the snapshot that showed me reading *Popular Mechanics*—so what? Someone must've taken my picture weeks ago, and at the time I hadn't noticed. Simple explanations have the disappointing tendency to be the best explanations.

Only the rational counterargument was a pile of shit, and I knew it. I *knew* it. I just didn't *want* to know it.

All this flickered through my mind in a moment. The wind blew a can rattling down the road, and Mr. Beukes turned to watch it go, then cast a distraught and distracted look at his idling Town Car.

"I will drive you. This weather. If not for this morning, I might've risked leafing her by herself tonight. She has had the pill for her arthritis, and she sleeps so heavy, sometimes ten hours. But tonight there is the thunder. What if she wake up and is afraid? You must imagine me very wicked to have left her even for a minute."

At not quite thirteen, I wasn't emotionally equipped to respond to a distressed and elderly man, viciously finding fault with himself. I mumbled some eloquent words of comfort, like, "Uh, no, not at all."

"I tried to dial you, but when there was no answer, I thingg he is in his garage and cannot hear the phone ringing. I kissed her goot-bye, very softly, so not to wake her, and came straight over." He showed me a smile that was close to a grimace. "When she is asleep, she look like her olt self. Sometimes I thingg in her dreams she gets it all back. The path to her old self is overgrown, lost in the briars. But her sleeping mind . . . you thingg, Michael, the sleeping mind has paths of its own? Trails the waking self has never walked?"

"I don't know, Mr. Beukes."

He dismissed his own question with a weary nod. "Come. I will drive you now. You should get a book maybe and I dunno what else." He lowered his eyes, took in the fact that I was wearing boxers and socks. He lifted one white, stupendously shaggy eyebrow. "Trousers perhaps."

"I don't need you to drive me around the corner. Go see if your gym is okay. And don't worry about Shelly. I'll be over there in five minutes."

Thunder growled at his back. He cast another aggrieved look up at the sky, then leaned through the door and took my hand in both of his.

"You are a goot damn kid," he announced. "Shelly always tolt me this, you know. Every time she came home. 'That is a goot damn kid, Larry. All the funny things he talks about building. Beware, Afrikaner. I will ask him to build me a new husband, one who doesn't shave in the shower so it looks like a ferret exploded in there.'" He smiled at the memory, while the rest of his face crumpled, and for a horrible moment I thought he was going to cry again. Instead he lifted his hand and rested it on the back of my neck. "Goot damn kid, she said. She always knew when someone had greatness in them. She didn't waste her time with second-rate people, not never. Only the best. Always."

"Always?" I asked.

He shrugged. "She married me, didn't she?" And winked.

7

ON THE WAY TO COLLECT my pants, I took a detour into the kitchen and dialed NorWes Utility. I knew the direct number to the switchboard by heart and thought maybe they could patch me straight through to my dad's radio. I wanted to let him know where I was going to be—I thought there was a very reasonable chance I'd wind up sacking out on the Beukeses' couch that evening. Only no one picked up on the other end because it never rang. There was just a long, dead hiss. I hung up and was about to try again when I realized there wasn't any dial tone.

It came to me, suddenly, that it was very dim in the kitchen. Experimentally, I flipped the light switch. The room didn't get any brighter.

I went to the picture window in the living room and looked out at the dead street; not a light on in a single window, in spite of the darkness of the day. The Ambersons, across the road, always had their TV on by midafternoon, but tonight there was no spectral blue glow pulsing in the windows of the den. At some point while Mr. Beukes and I had been talking, a line had gone down somewhere, cutting the juice to the whole neighborhood.

I thought, *No. It's* him.

My stomach flopped. Suddenly I wanted to sit down. The aftertaste of Panama Thrill was in my mouth, a flavor like sweet bile.

The house buckled in the wind, creaking and popping. Probably a lot of lines were going down tonight. As far as that went, it was entirely credible to imagine that the fire at the gym had something to do with the storm—a fire that had conveniently left Shelly all alone, with no way to raise an alarm if there was trouble, because even if she could remember how to call the police, her phone would be as dead as mine.

I considered running across the road and beating a fist on Mr. Amberson's door and yelling for help and—

And then what? What was I going to tell him? That I was afraid a cruel man with tattoos had engineered a fire and a power outage so he could take Polaroids of a senile old woman? Let me tell you how *that* would look: like a fat kid with a headful of horror movies getting hysterical because of a little thunder and lightning.

I wondered if I could just stay home. I don't like admitting that, but it crossed my mind that Mr. Beukes would never *really* know if I'd walked over to watch his wife. Yeah, sure, in a couple of hours he would get back from his gym and I wouldn't be there. But I could always bullshit him, say I'd only gone home for a minute to get my pillow and was coming right back.

The idea briefly filled me with a shameful throb of relief. I could stay home, and if the Phoenician came and did something to Shelly— something awful—I wouldn't be in the way and wouldn't have to know. I was only thirteen, and no one could expect me to try to protect a mentally crippled old woman from a sadistic freak with a mile of ink on his body.

I was afraid to go—but in the end I was even more afraid to stay. I envisioned Mr. Beukes coming home and finding Shelly toppled out of bed, her neck snapped, head turned halfway around to look back between her shoulder blades. When I closed my eyes, I could see it: her lips wrinkled in a grimace of terror and anguish, her stiffening corpse surrounded by hundreds of Polaroid snapshots. If the Phoenician visited her while I cowered at home, I might be able to lie my way out of it with Mr. Beukes. But I could not lie my way out of it with myself. The guilt would be too much. It would rot my insides and spoil every good thing in my life. Worst of all, I felt that my dad would somehow intuit my cowardice and I'd never be able to look him in the eye again. He would know I hadn't really gone to watch Mrs. Beukes. I'd never been any good at lying to him, not about anything that mattered.

One idea got me into my pants and out the door. I thought maybe I could just creep up to the house and peek in the windows. If Mrs. Beukes was alone and asleep in her bed—if all was clear—I could park myself in the kitchen with a knife in one hand and my party gun in the other, next to the back door, ready to run and scream like hell if anyone tried to force his way into the house. I still thought, in the late-day gloom, that the party gun might make someone hesitate for a moment. And if it didn't fool anyone, I could always throw it.

Before I left, I sat down at the kitchen table to write a note for my father. I wanted to put into it all the things I might never have a chance to say to him if the Phoenician turned up. I wanted to let him know how much I loved him and that I'd had a pretty good time on earth right up until I was butchered like a steer.

At the same time, I didn't want to make myself cry writing the thing. I also didn't want to scrawl anything terminally embarrassing if I wound up spending the night doing crosswords at Mrs. Beukes's kitchen table and nothing happened. In the end I wrote:

I'M OKAY. MR. BEUKES ASKED ME TO SIT WITH SHELLY. THEY HAD A FIRE AT HIS GYM. WOW, HAS HIS DAY BIT THE BAG. LOVE YOU. THE PANAMA THRILL WAS GREAT.

8

WHEN I OPENED THE DOOR, the wind hit me with a shove, a guest banging past me and reeling drunkenly into the house. I had to back my way out, hunching my shoulders against the gale.

But when I got around the corner and was on my way up to the Beukes house, I had the wind at my back. The gusts ran at me, turning my light Windbreaker into a sail and carrying me along at a trot. A house on the corner was on the market, and as I went by, the real-estate agent's metal sign, which was pitching back and forth, snapped free and soared twenty feet before doing a meat cleaver—*whap!*—into the soft dirt of someone's front yard. I did not feel I was walking to Shelly's house so much as I was being blown there.

A fat, warm drop of water splatted the side of my face, just like a mouthful of spit. The wind surged, and a burst of rain, barely a dozen drops, struck the blacktop ahead of me, producing the smell that is one of the finest odors in the world, the fragrance of hot asphalt in a summer shower.

A sound began to build behind me, a thunderous rattle that I could feel in my teeth. It was the sound of torrential downpour driving into trees and against tar-paper roofs and parked cars: a mindless, continuous roar.

I picked up my pace, but what was coming couldn't be outrun, and in three more steps it caught me. It came down so hard that the rain bounced when it hit the road, creating a shivering, knee-high billow of spray. Water began to pour into storm drains in a brown, foaming flood. It was amazing how quickly it happened. It seemed like I ran fewer than ten steps before I was splashing ankle-deep. A plastic pink flamingo rushed past, carried by the tide.

Lightning popped, and the world became an X-ray photograph of itself.

I forgot my plan. Did I even have a plan? You couldn't think in a storm like that.

I fled through pelting water, cut across the yard of the house next to Shelly's. Only the lawn was melting. It came apart under my heels, long runners of grass peeling up to reveal the waterlogged earth beneath. I fell, went down on one knee, caught myself with my hands, and came up filthy *and* wet.

I staggered on, across the Beukeses' driveway, which was a wide and shallow canal by then, and around to the back of the house. I scrabbled at the screen door and leapt inside as if I were on the run from wild dogs. The door banged behind me, only slightly less loud than a crack of thunder, which was when I remembered I'd been aiming for stealth.

Water dripped off me, off the party gun. My clothes were sopping.

The kitchen was still and shadowed. I had sat there plenty of times in the past, munching Shelly Beukes's date cookies and sipping tea, and it had always been a place of pleasant smells and reassuring order. Now, though, there were dirty plates in the sink. The garbage can overflowed, flies crawling on heaped paper towels and plastic bottles.

I listened but couldn't hear anything except the rain rumbling on the roof. It sounded like a train going by.

The screen door opened behind me and slammed again, and I choked on a scream. I spun, ready to drop to my knees and begin begging, but there was no one there. Just wind. I pulled the screen door tight—and almost immediately a fresh gust overpowered the old latch and sucked the screen open once more, then thumped it shut. I didn't bother to secure it again.

My insides squirmed at the thought of going any farther into the house. I felt strongly that the Phoenician was already there, had heard me coming in and was patiently waiting for me somewhere in the gloom, down the hall and around the corner. I opened my mouth to call hello, then thought better of it.

What finally got me moving wasn't courage but manners. A puddle was forming under my feet. I snatched a dish towel and wiped up. It gave me a way to stall going any farther into the house. I liked it close by the screen door, where I could get outside in two steps.

Finally the floor was dry. I was still wet, though, and needed a towel myself. I edged over to the doorway and stuck my head around the corner. A dim and lonely hall awaited.

I crept down the corridor. I used the barrel of the party gun to nudge open each door as I came to it, and the Phoenician was in every room. He was in the tiny home office, standing motionless in one corner. I spotted him in my peripheral vision, and my pulse did a hectic jig, and I looked again and saw it was only a coatrack. He was in the guest bedroom, too. Oh, at first glance, the place *seemed* empty. It could've been a room in a Motel 6, with its neatly made queen-size bed, striped wallpaper, and modest TV. The door to the closet, though, was slightly ajar, and as I stared at it, it seemed to wobble slightly, as if it had only just been pulled closed. I could *feel* him in there, holding his breath. It took all the will I possessed to walk the three steps to the closet. When I threw open the door, I was prepared to die. The little cabinet within contained a collection of curious costumes—a pink jumpsuit with a fur collar, white silks of the sort Elvis Presley liked to wear in the seventies—but no psychopaths.

Finally only the door to the master bedroom remained. I gently turned the knob and carefully pushed it inward. The screen door in the kitchen chose that exact moment to bang once again, going off like a pistol shot.

I looked behind me and waited. It came to me then that I was trapped here at the end of the corridor. The only way to get out of the house (without leaping through a window) was to retrace my steps. I swayed, ready for the Phoenician to step into the hall, planting himself between me and escape. One moment turned into another.

No one came. Nothing moved. Rain hammered on the roof.

I stuck my head into the bedroom. Shelly was asleep on her side beneath a puffy white comforter, nothing of her showing except her dandelion puff of white hair. Her snore was a soft, rasping buzz, barely audible over the steady rumble of the downpour.

I inched into the room in mincing little steps, feeling jumpy and weak—but quite a bit less jumpy and weak than I'd been when I first entered the house. I used the party gun to push aside curtains. There was no one behind them. No one in the closet either.

My nerves were still jangly, but I wasn't scared of the house anymore. I didn't see why a guy like the Phoenician would hide in a closet anyway. What kind of predator hid from a fat thirteen-year-old with a big plastic gun that looked about as threatening as a bullhorn?

The signal from Radio Adulthood was sharpening by then, making its way through the usual static of adolescence. The newscaster was reading tonight's report in a dry, droll tone. He reminded me of Carl Sagan's maxim that extraordinary claims require extraordinary evidence. He pointed out that I had in the past believed that the Zodiac Killer might break into my house and murder me, simply because I'd once read a book about him. He reminded his listeners that Michael Figlione had, when he was twelve, saved his allowance for six months to buy a metal detector because he thought there was a strong chance of finding Spanish doubloons buried in his backyard. Radio Adulthood wanted its audience to know that my current theory—that the Phoenician possessed a camera capable of stealing thoughts—was based on the sturdy evidence of an old lady's demented ramblings and a random scuffed snapshot discovered beneath a trash can.

But, but, but—what about the fire at the gym? Yes, Radio Adulthood admitted, there'd been a shocking blaze at Mr. Beukes's gym. Considering the lightning storm that had just rolled in, the Cupertino fire department would probably be responding to a lot of fires that evening. Did I think perhaps that the storm was *also* the work of the Phoenician? Was that another of his "superpowers"? He had a camera that destroyed minds. Did he also have an umbrella that squirted thunderstorms into the sky? I should count myself lucky he hadn't used his sorcery to make it rain nails.

That was about all the jeering from Radio Adulthood I wanted to hear at the moment. I was wet, and I was cold, and I was safe, and that was good enough. But later—yes, later—maybe I would be tuning back in to hear the rest of the program. Maybe a part of me was looking forward to tearing myself down, taking a good rip at my own overworked *Twilight Zone* imagination.

I was sick of my soggy clothes and poked my head into the master bathroom. There was a big white robe trimmed in gold thread hanging off a hook by the shower, the kind of robe you'd expect to find in a five-star hotel. It looked like the next best thing to curling up in a bed somewhere.

I patted the party gun dry, set it down next to the sink, and schlopped off my wet shirt. I left the door open between the bathroom and the bedroom, but I stood behind it so if Shelly Beukes woke, she wouldn't be startled by the sight of my exposed pink blubber.

The rain was slackening by then, had softened to a deep, lulling crackle on the roof. As I toweled off my boy boobs and back, I felt myself softening with it. I had planned to sit in the kitchen, next to the screen door, ready to run at the first sign of a psycho, but now I was beginning to indulge fantasies of hot cocoa and Girl Scout cookies.

The rain was tapering off, but the lightning was still going full throttle. It flashed, close enough to fill the bathroom with a throb of almost blinding silver light. I wrestled off my pants, which were soaked through. I peeled off my waterlogged socks, too. The lightning blinked again, the brightest flash yet. I wiggled into the robe. It was even softer and fluffier than I'd imagined. It was like wearing an Ewok.

I toweled off my wet hair, my neck, and the lightning snapped for a third time, and Shelly responded to it with a low moan of unhappiness. Then I understood and I wanted to moan myself. All those flashes of lightning and not one crack of thunder.

Fear inflated within me like a balloon, a thing expanding in my midsection, pushing organs out of the way. The white glare flashed again, not outside but from within the bedroom.

There was a single window in the bathroom, but I wasn't getting out that way: it was made of glass bricks, set inside the shower, and couldn't be opened. The only way out was past *him*. I reached for my party gun with a shaking hand. I thought that maybe I could throw it at him—at his face—and run.

I peeked around the edge of the door. My pulse thrummed. The flash flashed.

The Phoenician stood by the bed, bent over Shelly with his camera, peering through the viewfinder. He had pulled the covers completely off her. Shelly was curled on her side, a hand protecting her face, but as I watched, the Phoenician grabbed her wrist and forced her arm down.

"None of that," he said. "Let's see *you*."

The flash went off again, and the camera whirred. The Solarid spit a photo onto the floor.

Shelly made a low, wounded sound of refusal, a noise that was almost but not quite *No*.

A heap of snapshots surrounded his fancy boots with the high Cuban heels. The flash pulsed again, and another picture fell into the pile.

I took a small step into the bedroom. Even that required too much coordination for a shambling slob like myself, and the party gun clicked against the doorframe. The sound of it made me want to cry, but the Phoenician didn't look my way, so intent was he on his work.

The camera whined and snapped. Shelly tried to raise her hand to shield her face again.

"No, bitch," he said, and grabbed her wrist, and shoved her hand down. "What did I tell you? No covering up."

"Stop it," I said.

It was out of my mouth before I knew I was going to speak. It was the way he kept shoving her hand down. It offended me. Does that make sense? I wanted more than anything to run, but I couldn't, because I couldn't bear the thought of him touching her like that. It was indecent.

He glanced over his shoulder without any real surprise. Flicked his gaze down at the party gun and snorted softly in contempt. It wasn't fooling anyone.

"Oh, look," he said. "It's the fat boy. I thought the old bastard might send someone around to sit with her. Of all the people in the world, if it could've been just one person, I would've picked you, fat boy. I'm going to remember the next few minutes with great pleasure, all the rest of my life. I am—but you aren't."

He turned toward me with the camera. I jerked up the gun. I'm sure I meant to throw it, but instead my finger found the trigger.

The air horn shrieked. Confetti exploded in a shower of glitter. The flashbulbs kapowed. The Phoenician went backward as if someone had struck him in the chest. His high right heel came down on that little pile of photographs—those slick plasticky squares—and squirted out from under him. The backs of his legs thumped an end table. A lamp toppled, hit the floor, and the bulb exploded with a sharp pop. He jumped forward a step, and Shelly reached out and grabbed his pant leg and *yanked*. He stumbled, with his eyes shut—right toward me.

He made a sound between a snarl and a roar. Glitter spackled his cheeks, flecked his eyelashes. He even had some in his mouth, bright gold flakes on his tongue. He cradled his camera to his chest like a mother with her infant and reached for me with his free hand. In that moment I found a decisive grace I'd never known before and would never know again.

I stepped *into* him, knowing he couldn't see me, had been blinded by the flash. When we thudded together, the Solarid slipped. My knee found his groin, not a good hard thump but a weak jostle that made him instinctively clamp his knees together. He bobbled the camera, and I lifted it right out of his hand. He choked on a scream and grabbed for the Solarid. I handed him the party gun instead. He caught it by the trigger, and it went off with another loud squawk. I kept going, was past him in two steps, and then I was behind him, next to the bed.

He stumbled almost as far as the bedroom door before he realized what had happened. He put out his free hand and steadied himself against the doorframe. He blinked rapidly down at the party gun with complete bafflement. He didn't drop it. He *threw* it onto the floor with a crack and kicked it away.

A hand stroked the outside of my leg, gently patted my knee. Shelly. She had relaxed and gazed up at me with a dreaming affection.

The pale, colorless worms of the Phoenician's lips flexed in a look of rage masquerading as humor.

"You can't imagine what I'm going to do to you. I'm not going to kill you. I'm not even going to hurt you. Either would be showing you a respect you don't deserve. I'm going to fucking *erase* you." His dark eyes shifted to the camera in my hands, then went back to my face. "Put that down, you fat piece of shit. Do you have any idea what that does?"

"Yes," I said in a shaking voice, and lifted the viewfinder to my eye. "Yes I do. Say cheese."

9

THERE ARE A LOT OF things I don't understand about that night.

I took photo after photo of him. The Solarid pictures fell, one after another, into a pile at my feet. A standard Polaroid cartridge contained twelve pictures. The extra-large cartridges allowed you to take eighteen photographs. But the Solarid never needed to be reloaded, and it never ran out.

He didn't come get me. The first picture dazed him, just as it had dazed Mat. It seemed to put him back on his high Cuban heels, his eyes blank, staring far away at some distant view he would never see again. He stood there fixed in place, a computer trying to boot up. But he could never get unstuck, because I kept firing the camera at him.

After the first dozen photos, he did finally move. But not to charge me. Instead he carefully, almost daintily, crossed his ankles and then slid to the floor to sit like a disciple meditating in an ashram. After another twenty snapshots, he began to tilt over to one side. Ten pictures later he was curled in the fetal position on the floor. In all this time, a sly, subtle, knowing smile remained on his face, but at a certain point one corner of his mouth began to glisten with drool.

Shelly stirred from the narcotic fog created by the Solarid and was able to sit up, blinking sleepily. Her hair floated in bluish tangles around her shriveled-dumpling face.

"Who's that?" she asked, looking at the Phoenician.

"I don't know," I said, and took another picture.

"Is it Alamagüselum? My father says Alamagüselum lives in the walls and drinks tears."

"No," I said. "But maybe they're related." I don't think the Phoenician drank tears, but I believe he enjoyed seeing them quite a bit.

Maybe fifty photos in, the Phoenician's eyelids sank halfway shut and his eyes rolled back to show the whites, and he began to shiver. His breath shot out of him in short, harsh bursts. I lowered the camera, scared he was going to have a seizure. I regarded him carefully, and after a minute the tremors began to subside. He was rag-doll limp, and his face had assumed an expression of forlorn imbecility.

It was perhaps like electroshock therapy. You could fry the brain for only so long before you risked overloading the system and stopping the heart. I decided to give him a chance to get his breath back. I bent and grabbed a fistful of the pictures on the floor. I knew it would be a mistake to look at them, but I looked anyway. I saw:

- A crying man, mid-fifties, on his knees in a gravel driveway, fleshy and naked and holding out a pair of car keys in a desperate offering. He was cut all over, lots of fine red slashes trickling blood. The big white Caddy—the one the Phoenician went around in—could be seen in the background, parked under a willow, so shiny and clean it might've just rolled out of a 1950s-era magazine ad.
- A snapshot of a reflection in the Caddy's driver's-side mirror: dust roiling over a dirt drive, partially obscuring a naked man, facedown in the road with what looked like a garden trowel in the small of his back. I could not tell you why this picture was so joyous, so carefree. Some quality of the late-spring light. Some sense of escape, of effortless motion.
- A child—a girl—in a winter cap with earflaps, clutching a lollipop of enormous size. She smiled uncertainly for the photographer. A Paddington Bear peeked out from under one arm, where she held it clutched against her side.
- The same child in a coffin, her plump hands folded on the velvet bodice of her gown, her face smooth and untroubled by dreams. A

scarf the color of darkest wine had been arranged artfully around her throat. Paddington Bear was under the same arm, peering out in much the same way. A gaunt hand reached into the frame, as if perhaps to push a curl of yellow hair back from the girl's brow.

- A basement. The background was a wall of old whitewashed brick, with a narrow cobwebbed window set six feet above the floor. Someone had crudely drawn black marks in what I am sure was Phoenician script just below the window. Three rings of ash, slightly overlapping one another, had been sketched on the cement. In the one farthest to the left was a circle of smashed mirror. In the one farthest to the right was a Paddington Bear. In the central circle was a Polaroid camera.

- Old people and more old people. There had to be at least a dozen. A scrawny old man with an oxygen tube in his nose. A baggy old hobbit of a fellow with a peeling, sunburned nose. A dazed-looking fat woman, one corner of her mouth twisted in the snarl of someone who has suffered a severe stroke.

- And, finally . . . me. Michael Figlione, standing beside Shelly's bed, an expression of sick terror on my moon-shaped face, the Solarid in my hands, the flash igniting. It was the last thing he'd seen before I started shooting.

I collected the slippery squares into a stack and put them in the deep pockets of the fluffy white robe.

The Phoenician had rolled back onto his side. Some clarity had returned to his eyes, and he watched me with a foolish look of fascination. He had wet himself, a dark stain soaking his crotch and down his thighs. I don't think he knew.

"Can you get up?" I asked.

"Why?"

"Because it's time to leave."

"Oh."

He didn't move, though, until I bent and took his shoulder and told him to stand. Then he did, docile and bewildered.

"I think I'm lost," he said. "Do . . . we . . . know each other?" He spoke in little bursts that suggested he was having trouble finding the right words.

"No," I said firmly. "Come on."

I steered him down the hall and to the front door.

I thought I had absorbed all the shocks the night had to offer, but there was one more waiting. We got as far as the front step, and then I caught in place.

The yard and the street were littered with dead birds. Sparrows, I think. There had to be almost a thousand of them, stiff little black rags of feathers and claws and BB-pellet eyes. And the grass was full of fine, glassy pebbles. They crunched underfoot as I walked down the steps. Hail. I sank to one knee—my legs were weak—and looked at one of the dead birds. I poked it with a nervous finger and discovered that it was flash-frozen, as stiff and cold and hard as if it had just been pulled out of an icebox. I rose again and looked down the street. The feathered dead went on and on, for as far as the eye could see.

The Phoenician rocked on his heels, brainlessly surveying the carnage. Shelly stood behind him, just inside the open front door, a far more serene expression on her face.

"Where'd you park your car?" I asked him.

"Park?" he said. His hand had dropped to the front of his trousers. "I'm wet." He didn't say it like it bothered him.

The thunderheads had blown off to the east, coming apart into mountainous islands. The sky to the west was a bright burning gold, darkening to a deep red along the horizon—a hideous shade, the color of the human heart. It was a hideous hour.

I left him in the yard and went looking for his car. Are you surprised by that? That I left the Phoenician alone in the yard with Shelly Beukes, just walked away from the both of them? It never crossed my mind to worry. By then I understood the stunning effect of exposure to the Solarid multiplied, each time the camera went off. After zapping him more than fifty times, I had just about lobotomized him—temporarily anyway. Even now a part of me thinks I did enough damage inside his head to leave him permanently impaired.

Certainly Shelly never recovered. You knew that, didn't you? If you were hoping somehow that that kind, brave old woman was going to get it all back in the end, then this story is going to disappoint you. Not one of those birds got up and flew away, and not a bit of what she lost was ever returned to her.

Almost as soon as I was walking up the street, I began to cry. Not out-and-out racking sobs—just a weak, miserable trickle of tears and a hitching of breath. At first I tried not to step on any of the dead birds, but after a couple hundred feet I gave up. There were too many of them. They made muffled snapping sounds underfoot.

The temperature had dropped while I was inside, but it had started climbing again, and when I found the Phoenician's Caddy, steam was rising from the wet blacktop surrounding it. He hadn't parked far away, just along the curb around the corner, where the development hadn't really developed yet. There were ranch houses along one side of the road, pretty spread out, but a dense wall of forest and scrub brush on the other. A good place to leave a car for a while if you didn't want anyone to notice.

When I returned to the Beukeses' house, the Phoenician had sat down on the curb. He was holding a dead bird by one scaly leg and inspecting it closely. Shelly had found a broom and was futilely sweeping the lawn, trying to collect up the little corpses.

"Come on," I said to him. "Let's go."

The Phoenician put the dead bird in his shirt pocket and obediently stood.

I walked him down the path, up the street, and around the corner. I didn't notice Shelly following us with her broom until we were almost to the Phoenician's big Caddy.

I opened the car door, and after a moment of staring blankly into the front seat the Phoenician slid behind the wheel. He looked at me hopefully, waiting for me to tell him what to do next.

Did he still remember how to drive? I wondered. I leaned in to pat his pant pockets for his keys, and that's when I caught an eye-watering reek of gasoline. I glanced into the back and saw a red fuel can sitting on the rear seats, next to the stack of photo albums. I knew then what it would ultimately take arson investigators another three weeks to determine: that the fire at Mr. Beukes's Cupertino gym had been caused not by a stroke of lightning but by a stroke of malice.

The power outage in the neighborhood, on the other hand, was really just a by-product of the storm. I'm less sure that the storm itself was a purely natural event. An hour earlier, I had considered the possibility that the Phoenician might have some occult influence over the weather and rejected the idea with a certain amused disgust. But the notion seemed less absurd as I looked out upon those acres of slaughtered birds. Did he have a hand in the storm after all? Perhaps—perhaps not. I said there was a lot about that evening I don't understand.

I imagined reaching into the back of the Caddy and sprinkling what little was left in the can on the Phoenician, then dropping the car lighter in his lap. But of course I wasn't going to do that. I felt sick about stepping on a dead sparrow. I was hardly going to murder a living man. I left the gas can where it was, but on impulse I grabbed the topmost photo album and stuck it under my arm. I discovered the keys in the dashboard ashtray and started the Caddy for him.

The Phoenician gazed at me devoutly.

"You can go now," I said.

"Go where?"

"I don't care. As long as it's nowhere near here."

He nodded slowly, and then a sweet, dreamy smile appeared on his leprous face. "That Spanish gin will fuck you up, huh? I should've stopped at one! I got a feeling I'm not going to remember any of this tomorrow morning."

"Maybe I ought to take your picture," Shelly said from behind me. "So you don't forget."

"Hey," he said. "That's a good idea."

"Smile real big, bucko," Shelly said, and he did, and she thudded him in the teeth with the handle of her broom.

It made a bony *thwack* and snapped his head to the side. She cackled. When he looked up, his hand was clapped over his mouth, but there was blood dribbling between his fingers. His eyes were childlike and frightened.

"You want to keep that crazy bitch away from me!" he cried. "Hey, bitch! You better watch out. I know some real bad men."

"Not anymore," I said, and slammed the car door in his face.

He banged down the lock and stared at us with a mute terror. His hand fell away from his mouth to show blood in his teeth and a swiftly fattening upper lip twisted in a painful sneer.

I didn't wait to see him take off. I gripped Shelly by the shoulder and turned her around and started back. We were almost to the yard when he drove by. He hadn't forgotten how to steer his big Caddy after all, and looking back from my more informed adult perspective, I'm not surprised. Motor memory is compartmentalized, set aside from other thought processes. Many people, lost entirely in the blinding white fog of senility, can still flawlessly perform certain piano pieces they learned as children. What the mind forgets, the hands remember.

The Phoenician didn't so much as glance at us. Instead he was bent forward over the steering wheel, looking this way and that, his eyes shiny with anxiety. I had seen the exact same look on Shelly's face earlier in the day, when she was desperately scanning the neighborhood for something—*anything*—that might seem familiar.

At the end of the street, he struck his blinker, turned right for the highway, and drove out of my life.

10

WHEN I PULLED THE SHEETS over her, Shelly gave me a sleepy smile and reached out to grasp my hand.

"Do you know how many times I tucked *you* in, Michael? Lives have bookends, but you have to keep your eyes peeled if you wanna see 'em, bucko."

I bent and kissed her temple, which had the soft, powdery texture of ancient vellum. She never said my name again, although there were days when I'm sure she remembered me. There were more days when she didn't, but now and then her eyes would flash with recognition.

And I'm certain she knew me at the end. Not a doubt in my mind.

11

MR. BEUKES DIDN'T GET HOME until 2:00 A.M. Time enough for me to straighten up and put my clothes through the dryer. Time enough to rake up the dead birds in the yard. Time to pour a glass of strawberry Quik—Mr. Beukes liked to use it as an ingredient in his protein shakes, and I liked to use it as an ingredient in my fat ass—and take stock.

Time to leaf through the stolen photo album. The one marked S. BEUKES in black Sharpie on the inside cover.

It could've been anyone's collection of memories, although the oldest Polaroids in the book showed scenes that had occurred well before color photography was available to the masses. And so many snapshots were of things no one would've photographed.

Here was a wooden horse on wooden wheels, with a rope strung through a hole in its head, being pulled along a concrete sidewalk.

Here was a sunlit blue sky with a single cloud in it, a cloud shaped like a cat, tail curled in a question-mark shape. The chubby hands of a toddler reached up toward it from the bottom edge of the photograph.

Here was a brawny woman with big, crooked teeth, peeling a potato at a sink, a radio in a walnut case glowing on the kitchen counter in the background. Based on the resemblance, I guessed it was Shelly's mother and that the year might be somewhere around 1940.

Here was a twenty-year-old knockout with the body of an Olympic swimmer, wearing white underwear, her arms crossed over her bare chest, a fedora perched on her head. She inspected herself in a full-length mirror. A big mule of a man, completely naked, could be seen in the reflection as well, sitting on the edge of a mattress. He grinned wolfishly and studied her with frank admiration. I had to look at this image for half a minute before it sank in that the girl was Shelly herself and the man behind her was her future husband.

Midway through the book, I came across a series of four Polaroids that gave me a very nasty shock—four snapshots I cannot explain. It was the girl again—the girl with the Paddington Bear. The dead girl I'd seen in the Phoenician's mind photographs ("thoughtographs"?). They had both known her.

In these images it was the late sixties, early seventies. In one the girl sat on a kitchen counter, her cheeks wet with tears, a scrape on one knee. She bravely clutched her bear to her chest, as Shelly's big, freckled hands reached into frame with a Band-Aid. In another Polaroid, Shelly's strong, confident fingers worked a sewing needle, stitching Paddington Bear's hat back on his head, while the girl looked on with dark, grave eyes. In the third picture, the child slept in a rich girl's bed, surrounded by stuffed bears. But it was Paddington she clutched tight to her chest in sleep.

In the last photograph, the little girl was dead at the bottom of the world's steepest stone staircase, facedown in a spreading puddle of blood, one arm flung out as if reaching back for Paddington, who had wound up only about halfway down the steps.

I don't know who she was. Not Shelly's daughter. Someone she'd looked after when she was younger, a first nannying job? That steep stone staircase didn't look like Cupertino; San Francisco maybe.

I can't be sure how the girl with the bear connected Shelly and the Phoenician—I've said there's a lot I don't understand—but I have my ideas. I think the Phoenician was trying to erase *himself.* That he was visiting people who knew him, or *might* have known him, before he *was* the Phoenician. I think every photo album in his car belonged to someone who might've remembered the man or boy he'd been before his body became a profane manuscript in a tongue that has been perhaps rightfully forgotten. As to *why* he needed to scrub that former version of himself from living memory, I will not hazard a guess.

The last pages of Shelly's memory album were the hardest to look at. You know what was in them.

There I was, sitting on a concrete step, placidly allowing Shelly to tie my shoes with worn, age-freckled hands that were so much older than the hands that appeared in the Paddington Bear photos. I sat in her lap while she read me *Alexander and the Terrible, Horrible, No Good, Very Bad Day*. A plump seven-year-old version of me, with hopeful eyes underneath tousled bangs, held up a green-and-golden frog no bigger than a quarter, for her inspection and approval.

It should've been my mother's arms around me and my father reading to me, but it wasn't. It was Shelly. Again and again it was Shelly Beukes, loving—cherishing—a lonely fat boy who desperately needed someone to notice him. My mother didn't want the job, and my father didn't really know how to do it, so it fell to Shelly. And she adored me with all the enthusiasm of a woman who's just won a new car on *The Price Is Right*. Like *she* was the lucky one—to have *me*, to have the good fortune to bake me cookies, and fold my underwear, and endure my grade-school tantrums, and kiss my boo-boos. When really I was the lucky one and never knew it.

12

IN THE YEAR AND A half that followed, Shelly had two kinds of days: bad and worse. Mr. Beukes and I tried to look after her. She forgot how to use a knife, and we had to cut her food for her. She forgot how to use the toilet, and we changed her diapers. She forgot who Larry was and was sometimes frightened of him when he walked into the room. She was never frightened of me, but she often didn't know who I was. Although maybe there was a little tickle of a memory back there somewhere, because often when I walked into the house, she would shout, "Daddy! The repairman is here to fix the TV!"

Sometimes when Larry wasn't around, I sat with her and looked at the Phoenician's album of stolen memories, trying to get her interested in those thoughtographs with their muddy colors and bad lighting. But usually she would sulk and turn her head away so she didn't have to see them and say something like, "Why are you showing me this? Go fix the TV. *Mickey Mouse Club* is on next. I don't want to miss anything good."

Only once did I see her respond to an image in the photo album. One afternoon she looked at the picture of the dead girl at the bottom of the steps with sudden, childlike fascination.

She pressed her thumb to the photograph and said, *"Pushed."*

"Yes, Shelly? Was she? Did you see who did it?"

"Disappeared," she said, and sprayed her fingers out in a theatrical *poof* gesture. "Like a ghost. Are you going to fix the TV?"

"You bet," I promised. *"Mickey Mouse Club,* coming up."

In the fall of my sophomore year in high school, Larry Beukes dozed off in front of the TV and Shelly wandered out of the house. She was not found until four o'clock the next morning. Two cops discovered her three miles away, looking for something to eat in a dumpster behind the Dairy Queen. Her feet were black with filth, ragged and bloody, and her fingernails were broken, her fingers raw, as if she'd fallen into a gully and had to claw her way out. Someone had helped himself to her wedding and engagement rings. She didn't know Larry when he came to get her. She didn't respond to her own name. She couldn't say where she'd been and didn't care where she was going as long as there was TV.

I came by to see her the next afternoon, and Larry answered the door in a baggy MEXICO! T-shirt and his boxers, his silver hair standing up on one side of his head. When I asked if I could help with Shelly, his face shriveled and his chin began to quake.

"Hector took her away! He took her while I was asleep!"

"Dad!" shouted a voice from somewhere behind him. "Dad, who are you talking to?"

Larry ignored him and came down the step, into the light. "What must you thingg of me? I let Hector take her away. I signed all the papers. I did as I was tolt because I was tired and she was too much trouble. Do you believe she would've ever given *me* up?" And he took me in his arms and began to sob.

"Dad!" Hector shouted again, coming to the door.

There he was: the bodybuilder and navy boy, proud owner of a mint '82 Trans Am straight out of *Knight Rider*, the son I only sometimes remembered that Shelly and Larry had. The kid who made a party trick of picking up a chair one-handed while his mother sat in it.

He had put on a spare tire of fat, and the ink on his Sailor Jerry tattoo had begun to blur and fade. His fashion sense hadn't matured in the years he'd been away and might best be described as Richard Simmons chic. He wore a bright red sweatband to hold his frizzy hair out of his eyes and a tank top with a pirate on it. He looked embarrassed.

"Jesus, Dad. Come on. You're gonna make the kid feel awful. It isn't like you sent her to the pound. You can see her every day. We both can! It was best for her. You're putting yourself inna early grave chasing after her. You think that's what she'd want? Come on. C'mon now." He put an enormous arm over his dad's shoulder and gently peeled Larry off me. As he turned his father back into the house, he flashed a chagrined smile and said, "Come on in, bucko. I just made date cookies." When he called me "bucko," I shivered.

Shelly had been admitted to a place called Belliver House. Hector had driven her there that morning, while his father was napping. It wasn't the Four Seasons, but she'd get her pills on time and wouldn't be digging in a Dairy Queen dumpster for edibles. Hector said his father had been crying ever since. He told me this after Larry Beukes had shuffled back to bed, where he'd spent almost the entire day. By then Hector and I were sitting in front of *The People's Court* with tea and warm date cookies, their insides sweet and gluey, bits of walnut in them to give a little crunch.

Hector leaned forward over his plate to speak to me in a confidential tone that was entirely unnecessary, since we were all alone. "I used to be kinda jealous of you, you know. The way my mom talked about you. The way you did everything right. Good grades. Never talking back. I'd call Ma from Tokyo to tell her I just ate sushi with a relative of the emperor, and she'd say, 'Oh, great. By the way, bucko just invented a working nuclear reactor out of spare Legos and rubber bands.'" He shook his head, grinning beneath his Tom Selleck mustache. "She was right about you, though. You were every bit the stand-up kid she said you were. If not for you, I don't know how my dad would've managed the last year and a half. And Ma . . . back before it all slipped away from her, you gave her a reason to get up every morning. You made her laugh. You made her a lot happier'n I ever did, I guess."

I was mortified. I didn't know what to say. I fixed my gaze on the TV, and with my mouth half full I said, "Great cookies. Just like your mom used to make 'em."

He nodded wearily. "Yeah. I found the recipe in one of her notebooks. You know what she called 'em?"

"Date cookies?"

"Mike's Favorite," he said.

13

I WENT TO SEE HER now and then over the next couple years. Sometimes I went with Larry, sometimes with Hector, who'd moved to San Francisco to be closer to his parents. Later I drove myself.

The first year or so, she was always glad to see me, even if she thought I was the TV repairman. But by the time I was a senior in high school, she no longer acknowledged me when I visited—or anyone else. She sat in front of the TV in the overcrowded common room, a sunlit space that smelled of urine and old people and dust, a place with dirty tile floors and fraying secondhand furniture. Her head lolled forward on her neck, the folds of her chin sunk into her chest. Sometimes she would whisper to herself, "Next channel, next, next, *next*." She got very excited whenever someone changed the channel, would bob up and down in her seat for a couple moments before settling back into her melted slouch.

Maybe a month before I left for MIT, I drove into San Francisco for a meeting with the home-brew computer hobbyists, and on the way back I got off the interstate two exits early and swung by Belliver to look in on Shelly. She wasn't in her room, and the nurse at the desk couldn't tell me where to find her if she wasn't in front of the TV. I discovered her sitting in a wheelchair by some vending machines in a side hallway, down the corridor from her bedroom, unattended and forgotten.

It had been a while since Shelly even seemed to notice me, let alone recognize me. But when I knelt next to her, something, some dim awareness, brightened in those green eyes of hers that had gone as soft and faded as sea glass.

"Bucko," she whispered. Her gaze shifted away and came back again. "Hate this. Wish. I could forget. How to breathe." And then that faint, almost amused light flickered in her eyes. "Hey. What'd you do with that camera? Wouldn't you like to take my picture? Something to remember your best girl by?"

My whole back went as goose-bumpy and cold as if someone had dumped a bucket of ice water on me. I leapt away from her, then went around behind her and grabbed the handles of her chair and rolled her out into the hall, rumbled her briskly on to the lobby. I didn't want to know what she meant. I didn't want to think about it.

I cornered the nurse behind the desk and made ugly noises at her. I said I wanted to know who had left my mother by a fucking vending machine and how long she'd been there and how much longer she would have been there if I hadn't randomly stopped by. When I spoke of her as my mother, I had no sense that this was in any way a lie. And it felt good to be angry. It was a sorry second to being loved, but it was better than nothing.

I yelled until the nurse was flushed and looked stricken and shamed. It satisfied me to see her dab at her eyes with a tissue, to see the way her hands shook when she picked up the phone to call her supervisor. And while I vented, Shelly sat in her wheelchair, head lolling on her chest, as forgotten and invisible as she'd been by the vending machines.

How easily we forget.

14

THAT NIGHT A HOT WIND—it was like air blowing from an open furnace—tore through Cupertino, and thunder banged, but no rain fell. When I went out to my car in the morning, I found a dead bird on the hood. The gale had flung a sparrow into the windshield hard enough to snap its neck.

15

MY DAD ASKED IF I planned to visit Shelly before I left for Massachusetts. I said I thought I would.

16

THE SOLARID WAS IN A box in my bedroom closet, along with the photo album of Shelly's thoughts and a manila envelope containing the Phoenician's memories. What—did you think I threw any of that away? That I *could've* thrown any of it away?

Once, a few weeks after I saw the last of the Phoenician, I got his not-a-camera down from the top shelf in my closet and brought it to the garage. Just touching it made me nervous. I remembered how when Frodo put on the Ring, he became visible to Sauron's infected red eye, and I was afraid that merely by coming in contact with the Solarid I might somehow summon the Phoenician back. *Hey, fatso. Remember me? Yeah? You do? Not for long.*

But in the end, after turning it over and over in my hands, I put it back in the closet. I never did anything with it. I didn't take it apart. I couldn't see how to. There were no seams, no places where the plastic parts joined together. It was, impossibly, all of one piece. Perhaps if I took a picture, I might've learned something more, but I didn't dare. No, I shoved it back in the closet and then hid it behind a box of wires and circuit boards. After a month or two, I was sometimes even able to go fifteen minutes without thinking about it.

The weekend before I was set to depart for Boston—my dad and I were flying there together—I opened the closet and went looking for it. A part of me didn't expect it to be there, had almost come to believe that the Phoenician was someone I'd dreamed up in a day of fever and emotional distress, years earlier. But the Solarid *was* there, just as I remembered it. Its blank blind glass eye stared down at me from the top shelf, a mechanical cyclops.

I set it gently in the backseat of my Honda Civic, so I wouldn't have to look at it while I drove to Belliver House. Just staring at it felt dangerous. Like it might suddenly, vengefully go off and wipe my mind, to punish me for letting it gather dust for four years.

Shelly was in her bedroom, a compartment just a little larger than a prison cell. I knew that Hector and Larry had been by to see her a few hours before—they always dropped in on Saturday morning. I had timed my own visit to fall shortly after theirs, so they would have had a last chance to be with her.

I found her in her wheelchair, turned to face the window. How I wish she'd had something beautiful to contemplate. A green park of oaks, a place with a fountain and benches and children. But her room looked out on a sun-baked parking lot and a pair of dumpsters.

She had her Walkman in her lap, a pair of headphones on her head. Hector always put her headphones on when he left, so she could listen to the soundtrack of *Stand by Me*—the songs she and Larry had danced to when he was new in the country and she was just out of high school.

The music was long over, though, and she was just sitting there, her head twitching on her neck and spit hanging off her chin, sitting in a diaper that needed changing. I could smell it. Oh, the dignity of the silver years.

I slipped off her headphones and eased the chair around to face the bed. I sat on the mattress across from her, so our knees were almost touching.

"Birthday," Shelly said. She looked at me briefly, looked away. "Birthday. Whose birthday?"

"Yours," I said. "It's your birthday, Shelly. Can I take your picture? Can I take some pictures of the birthday girl? And then—then we'll blow out the candles. We'll make a wish together and blow them all out."

Her gaze snapped back to me, and there was suddenly an almost avian interest in her eyes. "Picture? Oh. Okay. Bucko."

I took her picture. The flash flashed. And again.

And again. And again.

Pictures fell to the floor and developed: Shelly's bent grandmother drawing a pan of date cookies from the oven, a cigarette poked in one corner of her mouth; a black-and-white TV set, children wearing Mickey Mouse ears; the name Beukes written in blurred black ink on a raised pink palm above a phone number; a fat baby with his fists raised in the air and jam smeared on his chin, Hector's hair already a mess of fizzy curls.

I shot a little more than thirty pictures, but the last three didn't develop, which is how I knew I was done. They were gray, toxic blanks, the color of thunderheads.

By the time I rose, I was crying, silently and furiously, a coppery taste in my mouth. Shelly slumped forward, her eyes open but seeing nothing. Her breathing was congested, hitching. Her lips were pursed—as if she were about to blow out the candles on her birthday cake.

I kissed her forehead, breathing deep the fragrance of the room where she'd spent the last years of her life: dust, feces, rust, neglect. If I was wretched in that moment, it was not because I'd pointed the camera at her—but because I'd waited so long to do it.

17

HECTOR CALLED THE NEXT DAY to let me know she had passed away at two in the morning. I didn't care what the cause of death was and didn't ask, but he told me anyway.

"Her lungs just quit," he said. "Like her whole body suddenly forgot how to breathe."

18

AFTER I HUNG UP THE phone, I sat in the kitchen listening to the clock on the oven *tick-tick-tick*. It was a very still morning, very hot. My dad was out, had the A.M. shift then.

I went into my bedroom and got the Solarid. I wasn't scared to pick it up now. I carried it outside and put it down in the driveway, behind the front driver's-side tire of my Civic.

When I backed over it, I heard it shatter with a plasticky crunch. I put the Civic into park and got out to have a look.

When I saw it, though, in the driveway, my heart leapt like a bird caught in a gale, thrown helplessly into the hard wall of my ribs. The case had been smashed into big, glossy splinters. But there was no machinery within. No gears, no ribbons, no electronics of any kind. Instead it was filled with something that looked like tar, a thick gallon of black soup—a soup with an *eye* in it, a great yellow eye with a slit pupil at the center. A great blackberry-colored glob of Panama Thrill with an eyeball in it. As that tarry crap spread out in a puddle, I swear that single eye rolled to look at me. I wanted to scream. If I'd had enough air in my lungs, I would've.

As I watched, though, the black liquid began to harden, rapidly turning silvery and pale. It stiffened at the edges, crinkling up, fossilizing. The shiny hardness spread inward, reaching that yellow eye at last and freezing it solid.

When I picked it up, the whole black splash had become a blob of dull, lightweight steel, a little smaller than a manhole cover, and about as thin as a dinner plate. It smelled like lightning, like hail, like dead birds.

I held it for only a moment. That was all I could stand. No sooner had I picked it up than my head began to fill with hiss and static and lunatic whispering. My skull became an AM tuner dialing in a distant station: not Radio Adulthood but Radio Madness. A voice that was ancient when Cyrus the Great crushed the Phoenician people under his heel whispered, *Michael, O Michael, melt me down and* build. *Build one of your thinking machines. Build a com-*puh-*ter, Michael, and I will teach you everything you want to know. I will answer every question, Michael, I will solve every riddle I will make you rich I will make women want to fuck you I will—*

I flung it away with a kind of revulsion.

The next time I picked it up, I used tongs to slide it into a garbage bag.

Later that afternoon I drove to the ocean and threw the fucking thing in.

19

HA-HA. SURE I DID.

20

I *DID* USE TONGS TO handle it, and I did put it in a garbage bag. But I didn't throw it into the ocean—I threw it into the back of my closet, where I had kept the Solarid for so many years.

That fall my mother flew to America to meet my father and me in Cambridge and see me installed at MIT. I had not set eyes upon her for over a year and was surprised to discover that her mouse-colored hair had gone completely silver and that she had taken to wearing rimless bifocals. We had a meal together as a family at Mr. Bartley's Gourmet Burgers on Mass Avenue, one of only a few meals I can recall us sharing together. My mother ordered shoestring onion rings and just picked at them.

"What are you looking forward to the most?" my father asked me.

My mom answered for me. "I imagine he's glad not to have to hide it anymore."

"Hide what?" I asked.

She pushed her shoestring onions away. "What he can do. Once you're in a place that lets you be your fullest self . . . well, you never want to leave."

I have no memory of her ever saying she loved me, although she did give me a stiff hug around the neck at the airport and reminded me that contraception was my responsibility, not the responsibility of my future dates. She was killed in June of 1993 by members of the Lord's Resistance Army, on a mountain road along the northwestern border of the Congo. She died with her French lover, the man with whom she had lived, it turned out, for most of a decade. Her death made the *New York Times*.

My father absorbed the news in the same way he'd responded to the space shuttle *Challenger* disaster—gravely, but with no great sign of personal grief. I could not tell you if they ever loved each other or what led them to make a baby together. That is a mystery greater than anything concerning Shelly Beukes and the Phoenician. I will say that as far as I know, my father had no woman in his life in all the years when they were apart, first when they were separated by Africa and later when they were divided by her death.

And he read her books. Every one. He kept them on the shelf right below the photo albums.

My father lived to see me graduate from MIT and return to the West Coast to pursue my master's (and then my Ph.D.) at Caltech. He died the week before I turned twenty-two. A live subtransmission line let go on a wet and windy night and caught him across the back where he stood at the side of the repair van, collecting his toolbox. He was nailed with 138 kilovolts.

I went into the twenty-first century alone, an angry orphan who resented it whenever people my age bitched about their parents ("My mom is pissed because I don't want to study law," "My dad fell asleep at my graduation"—blah, blah, blah). But then I also resented people who *didn't* complain about their parents but spoke of them with affection ("My mom says she doesn't care what I do as long as I'm happy," "My dad still calls me Little Trooper"—blah, blah, blah).

There is no system of measurement that can adequately quantify how much resentment I carried in my heart when I was young and lonely. My sense of personal grievance ate me like cancer, hollowed me out, left me gaunt and wasted. When I set off for MIT at eighteen, I weighed 330 pounds. Six years later I was a buck-seventy. It wasn't exercise. It was fury. Resentment is a form of starvation. Resentment is the hunger strike of the soul.

I spent most of a musty, stultifying April vacation clearing out the house in Cupertino, boxing up clothes and chipped dinner plates to bring to Goodwill, delivering books to the library. That spring the pollen was heavy, coating the windows with a bright yellow haze. Anyone who had come into the house would've found me with tears dripping off the end of my nose and assumed it was grief when really it was allergies. Packing up the house where I'd lived out my entire childhood was a surprisingly dispassionate business. With our generic furniture sets and our inoffensive striped wallpaper, we had left almost no mark on the place at all.

I had genuinely forgotten about the weird plate of steel shoved to the rear of my closet until I reached back there and put my hand on it. It was still in its garbage bag, but I could feel the bulges and planes of the metal through the plastic. I lifted it out and held the wrapped bundle in both hands for a long time, in a heavy, suspenseful silence, the sort of silence that settles on the world in the moments before a hard summer thundershower breaks.

That whispering iron never spoke to me again—not in my waking thoughts anyway. Sometimes it spoke to me in dreams, though. Sometimes, in dreams, I saw it as it had been when it first spilled out of the crushed Solarid: a tarry liquid with an eyeball in it, a weird thinking protoplasm that didn't belong in our reality.

I had one dream in which I found myself sitting across the dinner table from my father. He was dressed for work, staring down into a bowl of purple Panama Thrill, the Jell-O quivering and jiggling uneasily in its dish.

Aren't you going to have some dessert? I asked.

He looked up, and his eyes were yellow, with cat's-eye pupils. In a strained, unhappy voice, he said, *I can't. I think I'm going to be sick.* And then he opened his mouth and began to vomit onto the table, gouts of that black goop coming out of him in a slow, sticky gush. Bringing with it a hiss of static and a babble of madness.

In my final years at Caltech, I began to develop the architecture for a new sort of memory system, crafting an integrated circuit board the size of a credit card. My prototype leaned heavily on components crafted out of that grotesque, impossible metal and it achieved computational effects that I'm sure have never been matched, not in any lab, anywhere, by anyone. That first board was my Africa, was to me what the Congo had been to my mother: a splendid alien country where all the colors were brighter and where every new day of study promised some fresh, thrilling revelation. I lived there for years. I never wanted to come back. I had nothing to come back to. Not in those days.

Then the work was done. Ultimately I found I could get impressive, if less remarkable results, by employing certain rare-earth metals: ytterbium mostly, and cerium. It wasn't anything like what I could do with the whispering iron, but it still represented a major leap forward in the field. I was noticed by a company named after a crisp and juicy fruit and signed a contract that made me a millionaire on the spot. If you have three thousand songs and a thousand photos on your phone, you're probably carrying some of my work in your pocket.

I'm the reason your computer remembers everything you don't.

No one has to forget anything anymore. I made sure of it.

21

SHELLY HAS BEEN GONE FOR more than a quarter of a century now. I lost her, my mother, and my father before I turned twenty-five. None of them saw me marry. None of them ever had a chance to meet my two boys. Every year I give away as much money as my father earned in his entire lifetime, and I am still far richer than any man has any right to be. I have had an indecent share of happiness, although I confess most of it only came after I was no longer mentally able to keep up with the latest breakthroughs in computer science. I am a professor emeritus at the company I signed with out of Caltech, which is a nice way of saying they only keep me around out of nostalgia. I haven't made a significant contribution in my field for over a decade. That weird, impossible alloy has long since been all used up. The same goes for me.

Belliver House was demolished in 2005. There's a soccer pitch where it used to stand. The land beyond has been pleasantly groomed and planted, professionally landscaped into meadowy park with winding trails of white stone, a man-made pond, and a vast playground. I paid for most of it. I wish Shelly had lived to see the place. I am as haunted by her dying view of a parking lot and dumpsters as I am by my memories of the Phoenician. I don't like to think about her last days in that dismal little room—but I wouldn't erase those recollections even if I could. As awful as they are, those memories are *me*, and I would be less without them.

We all went down to the park for the big opening: my wife and our two boys. It was August, and there was thunder in the morning—big, rolling cannonades of it—but come afternoon the skies were stripped clean and blue, and you couldn't have wished for a better day. The town put on a good show. A thirty-piece brass band played old-timey swing music in the bandstand. There was free face-painting, and one of those guys who makes animals out of balloons, and my old high school turned out the cheerleading troupe to do some jumping and tumbling and rah-rah-ing.

What my boys liked most was a roaming magician, a guy with slicked-back hair and waxed mustaches. He wore a purple tailcoat and a ruffled green blouse, and his great trick was making things disappear. He juggled burning torches, and somehow, as each one came down, it vanished as if it hadn't been. He held an egg in one hand and smashed his fist into it and it was gone—shell and all. When he opened his fist, a chickadee sat chirping in his palm. He sat on a straight-backed chair and then collapsed into the dirt, because the chair was gone. My boys, six and four, knelt in the grass with dozens of other children, watching raptly.

Me, I mostly watched the sparrows. There was a flock of them settled on the slope above the pond, picking contentedly. My wife took pictures—with her phone, not a Polaroid. Tubas and trombones blatted in the dreamy distance. When I closed my eyes, the past seemed very close, only the thinnest of membranes separating yesterday from today.

I was close to dozing off when one of my sons, Boone, the younger boy, tugged on my shorts. The magician had walked behind a tree and dematerialized. The show was over.

"He's all gone!" Boone cried in wonder. "You missed it."

"You can tell me about it. That will be just as good."

The older boy, Neville, laughed scornfully. "No it won't. You should've kept watching."

"That's Daddy's magic trick. I can close my eyes and make the whole world disappear," I said. "Anyone want to see if we can make some ice cream vanish? I think there's a place selling soft-serve on the other side of the pond."

I got up and took Neville's hand. My wife took Boone's. We started away, crossing the greensward and startling the sparrows, which took off in one great rustling swoop.

"Dad," Boone said, "do you think we can always remember today? I don't want to forget the magic."

"Me neither," I said—and I haven't yet.

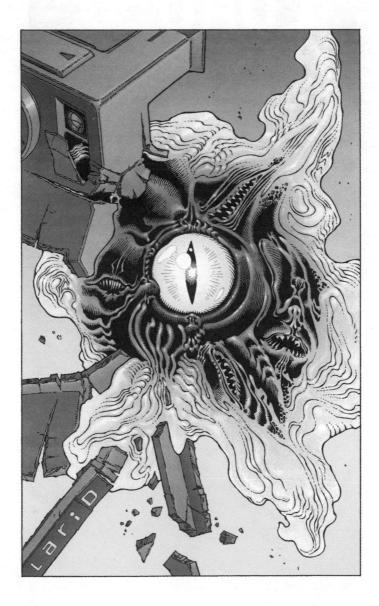

October 14, 1993

AISHA THOUGHT OF HIM AS her brother, even though they weren't blood.

His name was Colson, but his friends called him Romeo, because he had played that role in the park last summer, getting fresh with a white Juliet who had teeth so bright she should've been in a chewing-gum ad.

Aisha had watched him perform on a hot July evening, when dusk seemed to last for hours, a line of glowering red light on the horizon, the clouds shavings of gold against the dark sky behind. Aisha was ten and didn't understand half of what Colson said, up there on the stage, dressed in purple velvet like he was Prince. She couldn't follow the words, but she didn't have any problem making sense of the way Juliet looked at him. Aisha didn't have any problem figuring out why Juliet's cousin hated Romeo either. Tybalt didn't want some smooth-talking black kid crowding in on any white girl, let alone someone in his family.

Now it was fall, and Aisha was getting ready for a performance of her own, the Holiday Vogue, which meant modern-dance classes twice a week after school. Practice didn't end on Thursday nights until six-thirty, and her mother wasn't there to collect her when it was done. Instead Colson showed up, twenty minutes late, after all the other girls had left and Aisha was waiting alone on the stone steps. He looked good in a black denim jacket and camouflage pants, coming up the path, out of the dark, in long strides.

"Hey, Twinkletoes," he said. "Let's dance."

"I already did."

He bumped his fist on the top of her head, grabbed her school backpack by one strap. She had the other and didn't let go, so he towed her along after him, into the darkness, which smelled of grass and sun-warmed asphalt and—distantly—the sea.

"Where's Mom?" Aisha asked.

"At work."

"Why's she at work? She's supposed to get off at four."

"Dunno. 'Cause Dick Clark hates black people, I guess," he said. Her mother worked the grill at a Dick Clark's Bandstand Restaurant, an hour-long bus ride south in Daytona Beach. On the weekends she vacuumed at the Hilton Bayfront in St. Augustine, an hour's bus ride north.

"How come Dad didn't pick me up?"

"He's cleaning up after the drunks tonight." Her father was an orderly at a blue-collar rehab facility for alcoholics, work that combined the pleasures of janitorial labor—there was always puke to mop up—with the invigorating effort of wrestling hysterical junkies in the throes of withdrawal. He often came home with bite marks on his arms.

Colson lived with Aisha's father and Aisha's stepmother, Paula. Colson's mother was Paula's sister, but Paula's sister couldn't look after herself, let alone anyone else. *Why* she couldn't look after herself had never been adequately explained to Aisha, and in truth she didn't much care. If Colson Withers had a Coca-Cola and she wanted a sip, he'd let her have one, no hesitation. If they were out where there was a video game and he had a quarter in his pocket, it was hers. And if he didn't listen to her when she told a long, rambling story about the stupid things Sheryl Portis said in dance class, he also never told her to shut up.

They trotted along Copper Street to Mission Avenue. The east-west streets in that part of town were all colors: copper, gold, rose. There was no Blue Street, and there was no Black Street (although there *was* a Negroponte Avenue, which Aisha suspected might be racist), but the whole area had always been called the Black & Blue. Much as it had never occurred to her to find out why Colson didn't live with his own mother, she'd never thought to ask anyone why she lived in a part of town that sounded like a beating instead of a neighborhood.

Mission Avenue was four lanes wide where it intersected with Copper. A big strip mall, the Coastal Mercantile, ran for a few blocks along the far side of the road. The lot was desolate, only a handful of cars parked there.

The night was warm—almost hot—perfumed with exhaust from the passing traffic. A police cruiser flew past, blowing through a yellow light just as it turned red, the darkness stuttering with blinding blue flashes.

"... and I said over in England 'pants' means 'underwear,' and Sheryl said English people ought to use the right words for things, and I said if they use the wrong words, how come we go to school to study English instead of American?" Aisha was especially proud of this riposte, which she felt had properly put Sheryl Portis in her place, at the end of a long, wearying argument about whether or not British accents were *real* or just faked for movies.

"Mm-hm," Colson said, waiting for the WALK light. At some point he had wrestled her backpack away from her and slung it over his own shoulder.

"Oh! Oh! That reminds me. Cole?"

"Mm-hm."

"How long are you going to live in England?"

Aisha had England on the brain, had been thinking about the place all week, ever since she heard that Colson had sent an application to the London Academy of Music and Dramatic Art. He hadn't heard back yet—wouldn't hear back until spring—but he hadn't bothered applying anywhere else, acted like he'd already been accepted, or at least wasn't worried about being turned down.

"I don't know. However long it takes to meet Jane Seymour."

"Who's Jane Seymour?"

"She Dr. Quinn, Medicine Woman. She also going to be my first wife. First of many."

"Doesn't she live out west? That's where the show is set."

"Naw. She from London."

"What will you do if she doesn't want to marry you?"

"Pour my sadness into my art. It'd be tough if she didn't want me, but I'd just take all that heartache and use it to be the best Hamlet ever stalked the boards."

"Is Hamlet black?"

"He is if I'm playing him. Come on. We going to run for it. I think the walk light is busted."

They waited for an opening and beat feet across Mission, holding hands. As they slowed and stepped up onto the curb on the far side, they heard the ugly squall of a police siren, and another cruiser slammed past. Aisha started singing the reggae song that began every episode of *Cops*, hardly aware she was doing it. It was not at all uncommon for the police to kick up a racket this time of the night, booming along the streets with their disco lights pulsing and their sirens scaring the bejesus out of people. You never knew why or even wondered. It was like the hum of crickets, just another night sound.

As it happened, the police were crisscrossing the Black & Blue looking for a stolen Miata. Forty minutes before, out on the north edge of St. Possenti—where there were mansions with stucco walls and roofs of red Spanish tile—a couple had been followed into their house by a man in fatigues, wearing a woman's stocking over his face. William Berry had been stabbed twice in the abdomen. His wife had been stabbed nineteen times in the back as she tried to run away. The assailant then calmly helped himself to her purple Hermès purse, the jewelry in the bedroom, their DVD player, and some admittedly pornographic DVDs. The man with the knife whistled while he took what he wanted and occasionally chatted to Bill Berry while the forty-two-year-old investment banker lay on the floor groaning. He complimented them on their interior decoration and particularly admired their drapes; he promised he would pray for both of them to recover. Cathy Berry did not, but Bill Berry was expected to survive, although he was in intensive care with a perforated large intestine. Bill had been coherent enough to report that the killer "sounded black" and smelled of alcohol. The Miata had been spotted by a crossing guard, entering the Black & Blue not twenty minutes before.

The lot spread out around Coastal Mercantile was pitched and cracked, the fissures badly sealed with scribbles of tar. The strip mall housed a check-cashing joint (open), a liquor store (open), a tobacconist's (open), a dentist's office (closed), a Baptist church called the Holy

Renewal Experience (closed), a jobs office called Work Now Staffing (permanently closed), and a coin-op Laundromat that was open now, would be open at 3:00 A.M., and would probably continue to offer the use of its overpriced, underpowered washers and dryers right through the Rapture.

Colson slowed alongside an Econoline van with a desert scene painted on it and tugged on the handle of the driver's-side door. Locked.

"What are you doing?" Aisha asked.

"This looks like the kind of van kidnappers drive," Colson said. "I want to make sure there isn't a girl tied up in the back."

Aisha cupped her hands around her face and pressed her nose to the tinted bubble window. She didn't see anyone tied up.

Satisfied that the van was locked and empty, they walked on. Soon they would pass around the corner of the building, down along one side of the Mercantile, over a fence, and into the Tangles: four acres of buttonwood, cabbage palms, anthills, and beer bottles.

Colson slowed again as they passed a blue Miata, too nice for Coastal Mercantile—black leather interior, glossy cherry dash. He tugged on the latch.

"Why'd you do that?"

"Had to make sure the lady locked her doors. Anyone who'd park a car like this in the Black & Blue don't have the sense to look after their stuff."

Aisha wished Colson would stop yanking on door handles. He didn't worry about getting in trouble, so she had to worry for him.

"How do you know it's a lady's car?"

"'Cause a Miata look more like a lipstick than a car. They won't even sell you a car like this if you're a man, less you turn your balls in first." They walked on.

"So after you marry Jane Seymour, when you going to come back to Florida so I can meet her?"

"You'll come to me. Come to London. You can study dance same place I'm going to study being famous."

"You're studying acting."

"Same thing."

"Are you going to get a British accent while you're there?"

"You bet. Pick one up in the gift shop at Buckingham Palace, first day I'm there," he said, but in a distant, disinterested voice.

They were passing a battered Alfa Romeo, the driver's-side door painted an ashy matte black, the rest of the car the too-bright yellow of Gatorade. CDs were scattered across the dashboard, a collection of reflective silver Frisbees. When Colson tested the driver's-side door, it sprang open, one Romeo welcoming another.

"Oh, lookit," he said. "Someone has not been putting safety first."

Aisha kept walking, willing Colson to come with her. When she'd gone five steps, she dared to look around. Colson remained back by the Alfa Romeo, ducked down and leaning inside, a sight that gave her an ill feeling.

"Colson?" she asked. She meant to shout it, to say it like a scold— Aisha had a fine voice for scolding—but it came out in an unhappy waver.

He straightened up, looked back at her with blank eyes. He had her purple backpack balanced on his knee, half unzipped, and was rooting around inside.

"Colson, come *on*," she said.

"Just a minute." He dug a spiral-bound notebook out of the backpack, felt inside for a pencil. He tore a sheet out, spread it on the roof, and began to write. "We got to do an important public service here."

Aisha cast a glance at the strip mall. They were parallel with the coin-op, the brightest storefront in the whole row. The door was propped open with a cinder block, and they were close enough that she could hear the sound of tumbling dryers. She was sure at any moment someone would appear in the doorway and yell.

She crept toward him. She wanted to grab his hand and pull him along, but when she got close enough to take his sleeve, he yanked his arm free and kept writing.

As he scribbled away, he began to read. "'Dear Sir. It has come to our attention that you neglected to lock the doors of your mint-condition Alfa Romeo this evening. We have taken the liberty of locking the doors for you. Please be aware that this neighborhood is full of smelly, ungroomed hoboes who might have used your vehicle for a toilet. If you are not currently sitting in a puddle of stanky wino piss, you can thank the Promoters Of Normal Urination team. Support your local P-ON-U squad today!'"

In spite of herself, Aisha laughed. Colson drifted from one moment that belonged in a play to another, with a serene, spacey calm that approached indifference.

He folded the letter and placed it on the dash. When he drew his arm back, the sleeve of his denim jacket caught a CD and knocked it to the floor. He picked it up, considered it, then set it on the roof of the car. He grabbed up his note and began to write again.

"'Pee Ess,'" he said. "'We have taken the further step of absconding with your copy of *Pocket Full of Kryptonite* to protect you from the Spin Doctors—'"

"Colson!" Aisha cried out, heartsick to go.

"'—who can be harmful to your hearing. Please replace with Public Enemy and treat yourself with daily doses until you are less of a lame-ass.'"

"Colson!" she shouted again, almost screamed. It wasn't funny anymore. It had never been *really* funny, even if he'd tricked a giggle out of her.

He slammed the door and wandered on, her backpack hitched over his shoulder. He had a finger through the hole in the center of the CD. Rainbows shimmied across the surface. He went three yards, then paused to look back with a certain impatience.

"We going or not? Don't yell at me to hurry up, then stand there like you can't remember how to move your feet."

When she began to run after him, he turned and walked on.

Aisha chased him down, grabbed his wrist, set her heels, and pulled. "Put it back."

He stopped, looked at the CD on his finger, then over at Aisha's hands on his right wrist. "Naw."

He walked on, mostly dragging her.

"Put it back!"

"Can't. This is my good deed for the day. I just rescued someone's ears."

"Put! It! Back!"

"*Can't.* I locked the door so no one steals something actually worth stealing, like the gold St. Christopher medal hanging from the rearview mirror. Come on, now. Quit it. You're ruining my buzz."

She knew why he took it: not because he was a thief but because it was funny, or *would* be funny when he told his friends. When he told them about P-ON-U, the CD was his proof it wasn't just a story. Colson needed stories to tell like a gun needed bullets, and for the same reason—to slay.

But Aisha also knew about fingerprints and felt it was only a matter of time before the police dropped in to arrest him for grand theft Spin Doctors. And he wouldn't get to go to London and be Hamlet, and his life would be ruined, and hers, too.

He grasped her hand, and on they went, around the corner, along a buckled side road in even worse condition than the main parking lot. He led her to the back corner of the lot and into the weeds, to a sagging chain-link fence, half smothered by the high grass and undergrowth. By then she was weeping steadily and silently, drawing deep, shaking breaths.

Colson bent to help her up onto the fence—and seemed genuinely shocked to see the tears dripping off her chin.

"Hey! What's going on, Twinkletoes?"

"You! Should put! It! BACK!" she shouted in his face, hardly aware of how loud she was being.

He bent backward, like a bush in a gale, and opened his eyes wide. "Whoa! Whoa, Godzilla! I can't! Told you. I locked the dude's car."

She opened her mouth to shout something else and sobbed instead. He caught her shoulder and held her while she shook and made big, racking sounds of misery. He used his tee to wipe her face. When her vision came unblurred, she could see him smiling with a kind of bewilderment. All you had to do was see him smile to understand why Juliet would die for him.

"No one cares about a Spin Doctors CD," he said, but she already knew she had won and was able to catch her breath, hold her next sob in. "Damn, girl. You're going to ruin a perfectly good joke, you know that? You're like the joke police. Going to write me a ticket for being flagrantly amusing? How about I go back and put the CD on the roof of the car? Will that make it better?"

She nodded, didn't trust her voice. She told him she was glad by hugging him instead, throwing her wiry nine-year-old arms around his neck. For years afterward she could close her eyes and bring it back, exactly what that hug had felt like, the way he laughed, one hand between her shoulder blades. The way he hugged her good-bye.

He rose, turned her toward the fence. Her fingers found the chain-links. He scooped one hand under her butt to help her over the top, and she dropped down onto the other side, into the thick brush.

"Wait for me," he said, and slapped the fence.

He went, still unconsciously carrying her Little Mermaid backpack over one shoulder, the CD hanging off the index finger of his right hand. The disc flashed silver in the darkness, as bright as Romeo's bodkin. In a moment he had disappeared around the corner.

Aisha waited in the velvety darkness, a night orchestra of insects playing their sleepy lullaby in the undergrowth.

When Colson came back, it was at a trot that accelerated to a sprint when someone yelled. He'd been gone only a few seconds, half a minute at most. He darted along the shattered side road, head down, backpack slapping against his shoulder.

A man came running after him, a man in a heavy belt with things rattling and jangling on it. The night lit up in a flurry of silver and blue lights, flashing like a simulated thunderstorm in a theater. The man in the belt was slow, panting for breath.

"Put it the fuck down!" screamed the man in the jangling belt—a police officer, a white kid, Aisha saw now, not much older than Colson himself. "Drop it! Drop it!"

Colson hit the fence with a steely crash, hit it so hard that Aisha unconsciously staggered even farther back into the gloom of the thicket. Colson went halfway up and then snagged in place.

The Little Mermaid backpack—later Officer Reb Mooney would state that he had believed it was the Hermès purse stolen from the scene of the stabbing earlier that evening—had dropped off Colson's shoulder as he ran, and by the time he slammed into the fence, he was holding it by just one strap. A bent hook of old steel at the bottom of the fence snared the fabric, and as Colson climbed, the backpack was yanked out of his hand.

Colson glared down at it and grimaced, considered it for an instant, then dropped back down. He sank to one knee to collect Aisha's backpack out of the dirt.

The police officer came to a stumbling stop eight feet away. That was the first Aisha saw the gun in his right hand. Mooney, a big freckled boy who planned to marry his high-school sweetheart in just two weeks, gasped for breath, red in the face. A cruiser rolled into view, coming around the corner of the Mercantile, lights flashing.

"Down on the ground!" Mooney screamed, coming closer, lifting the gun. "Hands in the air!"

Colson looked up and began to raise his hands. He still had the CD ridiculously stuck to the end of one finger. The kid cop put his boot on Colson's shoulder and shoved. Colson hit the fence, grunted, and rebounded. He bounced off the fence so hard he almost seemed to lunge at the officer. The CD flashed in his hand.

The gun went off. The first bullet pounded Colson Withers into the fence once more. Mooney fired six times in all. The last three rounds went into Colson's back, after he had sprawled onto his face. Later both Mooney and his partner, Paul Haddenfield, told the grand jury they'd believed the CD was a knife.

In the aftermath, the night ringing with the echoes of those shots, neither officer heard Aisha Lanternglass fleeing into the Tangles.

The following summer the St. Possenti Players would dedicate that year's performance of Shakespeare in the Park to Colson's memory. It was *Hamlet*.

A white guy starred.

September 2012–December 2012

BECKI AND ROG ALWAYS MET at the gun range. First they'd unload a few hundred rounds, then he'd unload into her in his cherry Lambo.

The very first time they went shooting together, they took turns with his Glock, emptying the thirty-three-round magazine into a human silhouette.

"Goddamn," Becki said. "Is a clip that big even legal in this state?"

"Honey," Rog told her, "this is Florida. I don't know if *you're* legal, but the mag is fine." Like she was still in high school and not taking college courses in business management.

He stood behind her, his crotch pressing against her backside and his arms reaching around her. He smelled good, like lemons and sandalwood and the sea, and when he held her, she thought of yachts and gem-bright waters. She wanted to dive for treasure with him and soap the Atlantic off him afterward in a hot shower.

"One hand cups the other," he told her. "Press your thumbs together. Keep your feet apart. Just like that. No, not that wide."

"I'm already wet," she whispered to him.

She pumped thirty-three bullets into the target, pretending it was his wife's big fake tits. Afterward her whole body hummed in a nice postorgasmic kind of way. It was always foreplay for them.

She had met Roger Lewis for the first time when she was sixteen. Her father had brought her to the mall, to Devotion Diamonds, so she could pick out a gold padlock on a gold chain, a gift for her to wear to her chastity pledge at church that Sunday. Rog helped her try a couple things on, and she turned this way and that in front of a little mirror on the glass counter, admiring the sparkle around her neck.

"You look good," Rog said. "Unblemished."

"Unblemished," she repeated. It was a curiously entrancing word.

"We're hiring salesgirls this summer. If you sold a friend a padlock like the one you're wearing now, you'd get ten percent of the price, on top of your paycheck."

Becki looked at the price tag on the gold chain and let the heavy weight of the lock fall back against her breastbone. Ten percent of what she was wearing was more than she made in a whole week of packing bags at Walmart.

She wore her padlock out of the store and had an application folded into her clutch. That Sunday she swore to her parents, her grandparents, her little sisters, and her entire church that there wasn't going to be any man in her life until marriage, except her father and Jesus.

Becki was still wearing her padlock the first time Rog rubbed her off through her panties, in the office in the back of the shop. By then she was out of high school and making almost five hundred dollars a month in commissions alone.

The first few times they went to the range together, they stuck with the Glock. She pulled her hair back in a do-rag to keep it out of her face and to feel more street. Rog was okay with that, but the first time she tried to shoot like a gangster—the gun turned sideways, arm stretched out and wrist bent downward slightly, like she'd seen the bangers do in movies—he let her squeeze off only a single round before he reached in and took her forearm. He forced her to point the barrel at the floor.

"What's that shit? You've emptied a few mags at the range, so now you think you're Ice Cube? You couldn't be more white if you were shoved down and drowned in a vat of cream cheese. Don't do that again. I don't want anyone here seeing you shoot that way—it'll make me look bad."

So she shot the way he told her, feet slightly apart, one a bit forward, the other a bit back, arms outstretched but not fully extended. Becki aimed for the center mass, because Rog told her if you hit the chest, you were going to get something juicy. Pretty soon she was bunching her shots together from thirty feet, grouping them in the area of the heart.

After that he switched things up, met her at the range with his

SCAR 7.62mm, loaded with 149-grain full-metal-jacket rounds. She pumped them out in bursts, *bap-bap-bap, bap-bap-bap*. Becki liked the smell of the propellant even better than Rog's cologne, liked to smell gun smoke in his clothes, in his thinning blond hair.

"It looks like a machine gun," she said.

"It is," he said, and took it out of her hands and swiveled a selector switch. He fitted the extended stock into his left shoulder and narrowed his eyes and pulled the trigger, and it went off in a furious, thudding clatter that made Becki think of someone hammering fiercely at an old manual typewriter. He cut the silhouette in half. She was so eager to shoot it herself that she almost snatched it out of his hands. Becki didn't know why anyone had to have cocaine when you could just get a gun.

"Don't you need a special license to blaze away with an automatic weapon?" she asked him.

"All you *need* is ammunition and a reason," he said. "You might *want* a license, I don't know. I've never looked into it."

He was vain about his hair, was always patting it to make sure the thin yellow swirl covered his bald spot. He had deep creases at the corners of his eyes, but his body was as pink and clean as a boy's, fine golden hairs spun on his chest. She liked to play with that fine down, was pleased by the silky feel of it. Silk and gold always came to mind when he was stretched out naked beside her. Silk and gold and lead.

Ten days before Christmas, she climbed into the Lambo after work, believing he was going to drive her to the range. Instead he drove her to the Coconut Milk Bar and Inn, twenty miles south of St. Possenti. They had a suite on the first floor under the names Clyde Barrow and Bonnie Parker, which she sensed was one of Rog's jokes. She was well practiced at smiling blandly and indulgently to keep him from realizing she didn't get the reference. His conversation was sprinkled with lines from movies and music she knew nothing about: *Dirty Harry* and Nirvana and MTV's *The Real World*—old stuff like that, not even worth googling.

He carried a black Teflon bag with him, the handles padlocked together. She'd seen him move jewelry in that kind of bag but didn't ask questions.

The old woman behind the counter looked from Becki to Rog and back and made a face like she had a bad taste in her mouth. Becki met her bitchy stare with calm indifference.

"Isn't it a school night?" the clerk asked when she pushed their key across the counter.

Becki took Rog's arm. "I think it's so great that places like this hire old folks to give them something to do besides play bingo in a senior center somewhere."

Rog laughed his hoarse smoker's laugh and swatted Becki on the rear. To the old woman with the tinted orange hair, he said, "You're lucky she didn't bite. She ain't had her shots. You don't know what you might catch."

Becki chomped her teeth together at the offended old bitch behind the register. Rog took her by the elbow and steered her down a corridor with thick white carpet that looked like it had never been walked on. He led her past brick arches that opened onto an outdoor patio, built around three swimming pools, each on a different terrace, waterfalls splashing between them. Couples sat on wicker chairs flanked by tall patio heaters, columns of caged fire. The palm trees had been done up for the holiday, the fronds hung with emerald Christmas lights, so they looked like fireworks frozen forever in spectacular mid-explosion. Becki shut her eyes to better hear the sound of ice clinking in glasses. You didn't need to drink to get drunk. That sound alone made her feel intoxicated. She didn't look around until he stopped at the door to their suite.

The sheets were slippery silk, or something like silk, the color of vanilla frosting. The bathtub in the enormous bathroom had been hewn out of a hunk of lava rock. He put the chain on the door while she sat on the edge of the king mattress.

He carried his bag to the bed. "This is just for tonight. Everything goes back tomorrow morning."

He popped the lock, unclasped the wire jaws of the bag, and poured out a heap of treasure. Gold hoops and freshwater pearls on silver ropes, bracelets crusted with diamonds, and necklaces hung with brilliant stones. It was as if he had dumped a bag full of light onto the opalescent sheets. There was white powder, too, in a crystal bottle like one you might fill with perfume. It might almost have been crushed diamonds. Rog had taught her to like a little coke before sex. It made her feel good and dirty, made her feel like a degenerate aiming to do something criminal.

She was almost breathless at the sight of all those gems, all those shining threads.

"How much . . . ?" she asked.

"About half a million dollars. Go on. Wear it. Put on all of it. I want to see you chained in it. Like a sultan's concubine. Like I bought you with all this." Rog used words better than anyone Becki knew. Sometimes he sounded like a lover in an old movie, tossing off poetic dialogue in a clipped, indifferent way, as if it were the most ordinary thing to talk like that.

Amid the pile of treasure was a bra-and-panty set, gold straps speckled with rhinestones. There was also a long box wrapped in metallic gold paper, bound in a silver ribbon.

"The loot has to go back to the shop tomorrow morning," he said, and pushed the gift box toward her. "But this is yours to keep."

She grasped the wide, slippery package. Becki loved presents. She wished Christmas came every month. "What's this?"

"A girl doesn't wear that much bling," Rog told her, "unless she knows she can keep it."

She tore away the paper and ribbon and tugged open the box. It was a .357 Smith & Wesson with a satin-white grip that looked like pearl, the stainless-steel finish of the barrel engraved with fleurs-de-lis and curlicues of ivy.

He tossed something at her, a web of black leather straps and buckles, and for an instant she wondered if they were moving in a bondage direction that evening.

"That goes on your leg," he said. "If you wear the gun on the inside of your thigh, you could walk around in a pencil skirt and no one would know you're armed. I'm going to shower off. You?"

"Maybe later," she said, standing up and rising onto her toes to kiss him. She bit his lower lip, and he took the front of her tight black slacks and pulled her against him. He was playing it cool, but he was already hard, poking her through his khakis.

The shower was blasting for fifteen minutes. Time enough to drop her clothes and drape herself in a small fortune. The gun went on last. She liked the way the leather straps cinched around the high part of her thigh, liked the silver buckles and the black lines against her skin. She knelt on the bed in chains, diamonds sparkling between her breasts, a silver choker around her throat, and practiced aiming at herself in the mirror.

She was waiting when he came out in a towel, his chest glittering with beads of water. She lifted the gun in both hands.

"Drop that towel," she said. "And do exactly what I say if you want to live."

"Point it somewhere else," he said.

She pouted. "It isn't loaded."

"That's what everyone thinks, right up to the moment someone's cock gets blown off."

She opened the cylinder and spun it clickety-click, so he could see for himself it was empty. Then she slapped the cylinder back into the gun and pointed at him again.

"Get naked," she said.

He still didn't like her aiming the S&W at him—she could tell—but the sight of her breasts decorated with blazing diamonds was getting to him. He dropped the towel, his skinny cock bobbing in front of him (a sight both hilarious and thrilling) and crawled across the bed toward her. He kissed her, his tongue tasting her upper lip, and she was conscious of her composure and personhood sliding away in a familiar rush of want.

He pulled her down on the bed, using the gold chain and a fistful of her own hair, forcefully but not too rough. She managed to get the gun into the holster, just before he pushed open her legs with one knee. She must've strapped the S&W on too loosely. His thigh forced the butt of the gun back against her crotch.

Truth was, she never came harder than in those first few minutes, when he was kissing her, and her clit was grinding against the soft-hard rubber of the .357's pearly grip. She went off like a pistol. The actual sex was just the recoil.

April 12, 2013

AT THE END OF HIS shift, Randall Kellaway let himself into the security office and found a sheriff's deputy waiting for him, a grinning Latina in one of those ugly Hillary Clinton pantsuits, a Glock on her massive hip. You never saw white cops anymore; it was all about increasing diversity now. After Iraq, Kellaway had applied to the state police, the local police, the sheriff's office, and the FBI and never so much as got an interview. State cops said he was too old; sheriff's office wouldn't hire him because he'd been AdSep'd; the feds told him there were suitability issues after he took their psych test; the local cops didn't have any openings and reminded him he had nine hundred dollars in unpaid speeding tickets. What it came down to, a black guy who talked in ebonics could get hired if he had just managed to graduate high school without murdering someone in a drive-by. A white guy had to have matriculated at Yale and volunteered to work with orphans who had AIDS to even get a foot in the door.

When Kellaway entered the security office, he was on the customer side of the desk, with Officer Chiquita Banana. The receptionist, Joanie, was on the other side of the Plexiglas window, sitting in her rickety rolling office chair. There was one other security guard there, too, Eddie Dowling, taking off his belt and hanging it up in his locker. It was just like Ed to decide to call it a night ten minutes before quitting time.

"Here he is, Officer Acosta. I told you, he doesn't clock out until the minute his shift ends. Mr. Kellaway is very punctual. Randy, this is Officer Acosta from the sheriff's department—"

"I know where she's from, Joan. I recognized the uniform."

Folks from the police department and the sheriff's office dropped in all the time. In January it had been to show him the mug shot of a wanted felon who was engaged to a girl who worked in the food court. In March it had been to warn him there was a known pedophile just down the road and to keep an eye out for him.

He was thinking it might be something about the black kid who had just started working at Boost Yer Game. A week ago Kellaway had found him carrying boxes out the Boost Yer Game service door and loading them into a rusty, rinky-dink Ford Fiesta. Kellaway had told him to get against the car and put his hands on the roof, had thought the kid was boosting *his* game by boosting some shoes. It was an hour before opening, and the boy wasn't in uniform, and Kellaway had never seen his face, didn't know he was a new hire, didn't know the kid had been instructed to drive some fancy Nikes to the Boost Yer Game outlet in Daytona Beach. Naturally, now it looked like Kellaway was a racist and not a guy who'd made an honest mistake.

If it really *had* been a mistake. Kid had a bumper sticker said LE-GALIZE GAY MARIJUANA, which was pretty much a raised middle finger to a world where rules mattered. Kellaway could hope that Acosta had come to tell him the kid was a known banger and she wanted to search his Fiesta for crack and guns. (And why, he wondered, did the most American of American car companies name one of their vehicles a *Fiesta*, which sounded more like a bargain meal at Taco Bell? Although probably the plant making those cars was in Tijuana, so the name actually suited.)

Just before Acosta spoke, though, Kellaway noticed the wan look on Ed Dowling's face. He saw, too, that Joanie was willfully not looking at him, pretending to be interested in something on the screen of her antique Dell—Joanie, who inserted herself in the middle of every conversation and couldn't bear to let any visitors to the office escape without forcing them to answer a dozen mindless questions about what they did, where they were from, and if they had seen last week's *Dr. Phil*. Kellaway felt the briefest of misgivings, a kind of grim flicker, the psychological equivalent of dull, distant heat lightning.

"Let's have it," he said.

"You got it, darling," said Acosta, and she slapped some folded papers into his hands.

His gaze skipped across blocks of text: TEMPORARY INJUNCTION FOR PROTECTION AGAINST DOMESTIC VIOLENCE and NOTICE OF HEARING and SCHEDULED TO APPEAR AND TESTIFY.

"You are instructed by the State of Florida not to physically approach Holly Kellaway, either at her current place of residence at 1419 Tortola Way or at her place of employment with the Tropic Lights Cable Network at 5040 Kitts Avenue, or to approach her son—"

"Our son."

"—George Kellaway, at the Bushwick Montessori on Topaz Avenue. If you are found within five hundred feet of their place of residence, her place of employment, or your son's school, you will be subject to arrest for violating this restraining order, are we clear?"

"On what grounds?"

"You'll have to ask the judge at the hearing, the date of which—"

"I'm asking *you*. On what grounds can the State of Florida decide to keep me away from my own child?"

"Do you really want to do this in front of your co-workers, Mr. Kellaway?" she said.

"I never put a hand on the hysterical bitch. Or the boy either. If she says anything else, it's lies."

Acosta said, "Did you ever point a gun at her, Mr. Kellaway?"

He didn't reply.

Joanie exhaled a snorting breath, like a tired horse, and began typing furiously, her eyes fixed on the screen of her computer.

"You're going to want to call her," Acosta said. "Don't. You are forbidden to contact her directly. You want to say something to her? Get a lawyer. Have him say it. You're going to want a lawyer for the hearing anyway."

"So if I call to say good night to my six-year-old, someone's going to arrest me? Should I hire a lawyer to call on a nightly basis to read bedtime stories to him?"

Acosta went on as if he hadn't spoken. "You have been scheduled for a hearing. The date and time is in the injunction. If you do not appear at the hearing, you can expect the restraining order to be continued in force, indefinitely. You may attend the hearing with your legal counsel, or you may be a dumb-ass, it's up to you. Now, you've been eating frozen dinners ever since your wife moved out, and you may be getting tired of them. Let me tell you, they're better than what's on the menu in the county jail. Take my advice and don't put eyes on your ex until you see her at the hearing, got me?"

He felt sick. He felt like taking his chrome-handled flashlight to her fat, dykey face. She had a dyke haircut—could've been in the marines with a haircut like that.

"That it? We done?"

"Nope."

He didn't like the way she said it, didn't like how happy she sounded. "What else?"

"Do you have any guns here or in your car?"

"The fuck that matter?"

"You are instructed by order of the State of Florida to turn in your firearms to the sheriff's department until a judge concludes it is safe for you to possess them."

"I am a *security* guard," he said.

"Do mall cops pack? Your co-worker wasn't carrying when he walked in." When Kellaway didn't answer, Acosta looked through the window at Joanie and Ed. "Are you required to carry while you're on the job?"

A strained quiet settled upon the room. The vending machine kicked on, a soft *whump* and a hum.

"No, ma'am," Eddie Dowling said at last, grimacing and glancing apologetically at Kellaway.

"Are you even *allowed* to carry a gun?" she asked.

"Not in your first year, ma'am," said Ed. "But after that, if you wear it discreetly, it's not prohibited, ma'am."

"Right," she said, and looked back at Kellaway. "Are you packing now?"

Kellaway could feel a vein throbbing in the center of his forehead. She inspected him then, glanced at his belt—nothing attached to it except his walkie-talkie and his flashlight—then down along the length of his body and back up.

"What's that on your ankle?" she asked. "That the Colt Python or the SIG?"

"How do you—" he started, then clenched his teeth together. Holly. The silly, fragile bitch had given the sheriff's department a list of all his guns.

"Mr. Kellaway, would you please surrender your weapon? I'll be glad to give you a receipt for it."

For a long time, he just glared at her, and she smiled pleasantly back at him. Finally he put his foot up on the mustard-colored love seat against the wall, the one with the patched cushions, and yanked up his pant leg.

"Like anyone could carry a fucking Colt Python in an ankle holster. You ever seen a Colt Python?" he said, unbuckling the entire holster and wiggling it loose and pulling it off.

"It would be a pain in the ass with a full-size Python, but it's doable if it's the snub. Your ex wasn't sure which you owned."

He gave her the SIG. She briskly removed the mag, pumped the slide, and squinted into the chamber to make sure it was unloaded. When she was sure it was safe, she zipped it into a big clear plastic bag and put it aside on the Formica counter. She rummaged in her leather satchel, came up with a slip of paper, and squinted down at it.

"So is the Colt in your locker?"

"You got a warrant to find out?"

"I don't need one. Not for that. I have permission from Russ Dorr, the CEO of Sunbelt Marketplace, the firm that owns this mall. You can call him yourself and ask if you're wondering. Your locker isn't your locker. It's his."

"What are you going to do if it's not there? Follow me to my house? Better have a warrant for that."

"We don't need to go to your house, Mr. Kellaway. We've already been there. Your wife gave us a key and granted us permission to enter the premises, as is her right. She's co-listed on the mortgage. But we didn't find the Colt or the SIG"—she scanned the sheet of paper—"or the Uzi. Really? *An Uzi?* That's some real Rambo shit, Mr. Kellaway. For your sake, I hope that hasn't been converted."

"It's a legacy piece," he said. "From 1984, grandfathered in. If your boys looked in my file cabinet, they would've found all the paperwork on it. It's legal."

"That must've cost some money. I guess patrolling the mall pays good. That right? You get top dollar making sure no one snatches a Cinnabon and runs for the doors?"

He opened his locker and got the Colt and handed it to her butt-first, the cylinder open. She shook the bullets out into the cup of her palm, spun the cylinder, and snapped it back into the frame with an agile flick of her wrist. It went into the plastic bag with the SIG. Acosta wrote him a receipt in a notepad that resembled what a waitress would use to take an order. That was what Acosta *should've* been doing, copying down orders in a Waffle House somewhere.

"The Uzi in the car?" she asked.

He was going to ask if she had a warrant, but as he opened his mouth, her gaze swept up and met his, and she looked at him with a benign calm he could hardly stand. Of course she had one. She was waiting for him to ask so she could show him up, humiliate him again.

She followed him down the long corridor, out the metal door, and into the parking lot. The late-afternoon sunshine always surprised him after he'd spent a day in the mall: the sharp-edged clarity of the world and the taste of the ocean in the air. Sheaves of palm leaves moved with a dry rustle. The sun was deep in the west, and the sky was shot with a smoggy golden light.

Acosta followed him across the blacktop. When she saw the car, she laughed.

"Really?" she asked. "I didn't see that one coming."

He didn't look at her. His car was a bright red Prius. He'd bought it for the kid, because George was worried about the penguins. They went to see the penguins almost every weekend at the aquarium. George could watch them swim all day.

He opened the hatchback. The Uzi was in a black hard case. He entered the code, popped the locks, and stood back so she could have a look at it, placed neatly in its black foam cutouts. He loathed the Spanish woman and her butch haircut, and he was surprised to feel a certain pleasure anyway, letting her look it over, every piece of it oiled and black and so clean it might've been brand-new.

She wasn't impressed, though. When she spoke, her voice was flat, almost disbelieving. "You leave a fully automatic Uzi in your car?"

"The firing pin is in my locker. You want it? I'll have to go back and get it."

She slammed the plastic case shut, got out her waitress check pad, and began to write once more.

"Read that restraining order, Mr. Kellaway," she said, tearing off his receipt and handing it to him. "And if you don't understand any of it, have a lawyer explain it to you."

"I want to talk to my son."

"The judge will make a provision for that, I'm sure, in fifteen days."

"I want to call my boy and tell him I'm fine. I don't want him to be afraid."

"Neither do we. That's why you're holding a restraining order. Good afternoon, Mr. Kellaway."

She took one step away with the black plastic case, and he threw the restraining order at her back, couldn't help himself. It was that last bit, the thing about how she saw her job as protecting his son—from *him*. The papers struck her between the shoulder blades, like a dart. She stiffened, stood there with her back to him. Then she gently set the case with the Uzi in it down on the asphalt.

When she turned to face him, her smile was enormous. He wasn't sure what would happen if she took the handcuffs off her belt, what he would do. But instead she only bent and picked up the papers and stepped toward him. Up close—when she was only an inch away—he was surprised at her mass. She had the stocky density of a middle-weight. She gently tucked the papers into his shirt pocket, where they sat nestled against his multitool in its little leather case.

"Now, hon," she said, "you're gonna want to hold on to those to show your lawyer. If you want visitation rights to see your kid—any rights to see your son at all—you're going to want to know what you're up against. You are lost in the woods, and this is the closest thing you got to a compass. Do you understand me?"

"Right."

"And you're going to want to avoid assaulting or threatening or ha-rassing officers of the State of Florida who might lock your ass up and disgrace you in front of your colleagues and passersby and God and ev-eryone. You might want to avoid troubling men and women of the law who could drop in on your hearing to talk about you throwing things and showing poor control of your emotions. Do you follow me?"

"Yeah. I got it. Any other questions?"

"No," she said, and picked up the case with the Uzi in it and then paused to meet his gaze. "Yes. Actually. One. I asked you if you ever pointed a gun at your wife, and you didn't answer me."

"No, and I damn well won't."

"Okay. I was wondering something else, though."

"What?"

"You ever point a gun at your son? Tell her if she tried to take him away, you'd put his brains on the wall?"

His insides boiled with sick, with acid. He wanted to throw some-thing else, throw something in her face, bust her lip, see some blood. He wanted to go to jail—but if she locked him up, he'd lose his rights to George forever. He didn't move. He didn't reply.

It didn't seem possible that Acosta's smile could broaden any more, but it did. "Just curious, hon. Don't do anything that'll get you in trou-ble, y'hear? Because as much as I don't want to ever see you again, you don't want to ever see me again even more."

July 1, 2013

ON JIM HIRST'S BIRTHDAY, KELLAWAY drove out of St. Possenti and into the smoke, with a gift for his old pal in the passenger seat.

The smoke blew across the highway in a gray, eye-stinging haze, carrying the stink of a dump fire. It was kids that had done it, getting started on the July Fourth celebrations a few days early, tossing Black Cat firecrackers at one another in some scrubland out behind their trailer park. Now there were something like three thousand acres on fire. The Ocala National Forest was going up like a pile of straw.

Jim Hirst's farmhouse was a quarter of a mile from the highway, at the end of a gravel track, crowded on either side by black mangrove and swampy ground. It was all a single story, the roof sagging in places, overgrown with moss and mildew, the gutters choked with leaves. Plastic sheeting covered half of the house, where the siding had been pulled away and windows had been extracted like teeth, leaving gaping sockets behind. It had been that way for three years. Jim had scraped together some money to begin a remodeling project, but not enough to finish one. The lights were off, and the wheelchair van wasn't there, and if Kellaway hadn't heard someone shooting out back, he might've thought no one was home.

He walked around the unfinished half of the house. The big sheets of plastic flapped desultorily in the breeze. The gun went off with the steadiness of a metronome sounding 4/4 time. The shooting stopped just as he came around the corner into the backyard.

Jim Hirst was in his electric wheelchair with a six-pack on the ground beside him, two cans already empty and tossed in the grass. He had the gun in his lap, a small automatic with a fancy sight, the magazine out. An AR rifle leaned against the wheelchair. Jim had a lot of guns. A *lot* of guns. He had a fully automatic M249 light machine gun in the garage, hidden under some floorboards below the workbench. It was identical to the one mounted on the Humvee they'd shared for six months in the Gulf. Kellaway wasn't in it, though, when it went over a Russian land mine that nearly tore both the vehicle and Jim Hirst in two. By then Kellaway had been transferred to the MPs, and the only thing that blew up on him there was his future in the army.

"I didn't see the van. I thought you forgot I was coming by, maybe went out somewhere," Kellaway said. "Happy birthday to you."

Jim turned and held out his hand. Kellaway tossed him a bottle, a Bowmore Single Malt, aged twenty-nine years. The scotch was a brassy, mellow gold, as if someone had found a way to distill a sunrise. Jim held it up by the neck and admired it.

"Thank you, man," he said, "Mary bought a lemon cake at the supermarket. Get a slice and come play with my new toy."

Lifting the pistol out of his lap. It was a gray Webley & Scott with a laser sight like something out of a spy movie. He had a box of 95-grain Starfire rounds next to his hip, hollow points that would open like toadstools when they struck soft tissue.

"Mary get you that? That's love."

"No, man, *I* got me that. She massaged my prostate, that was what she did for me."

"Is that the finger up the ass?" Kellaway said, trying to mask his distaste.

"She has a vibe. That and a vacuum pump on my cock, it all works out. *That's* love. Especially since for her it's less like sex, more like clearing a clogged drain." He started out laughing, but it turned into a rough, rumbling cough. "Christ, this fuckin' smoke."

Kellaway scooped the bottle of scotch out of Jim's lap. "I'll bring us glasses."

He batted through the screen door and found Mary in the kitchen, sitting at the table. She was a thin, bony woman, with deep lines around her mouth and hair that had once been a rich, glossy chestnut but had long since faded to a shade of mouse. She was texting and didn't look up. The garbage pail was full to the brim, an adult diaper on the very top, and the room smelled of shit. Flies buzzed around both the trash and the lemon cake on the table.

"I'll trade you a glass of scotch for a slice of cake."

"Sold," she said.

He rooted in the cupboard, came up with a few coffee cups. He poured her an inch of whiskey and set it down next to her. When he leaned forward, he saw her texting a series of hearts to someone.

"Where's the van?" he asked.

"It got took."

"What do you mean it got took?"

"We were six months behind on the payments," she said.

"What about the check from the VA?"

"He spent it on other necessities."

"What other necessities?"

"He's out there squeezing the trigger of one right now." The gun began to go off again. They both listened until the firing stopped. Mary said, "He'd rather finger one of those than me."

"That's a lovely thought, Mary. I want to thank you for putting that image in my head."

"Well, maybe if he sold one or two off, we could have windows in the living room instead of holes in the walls. That might be nice. Live in a place with windows."

He cut two slices of cake. As he did, he leaned in for another look at her phone. She didn't glance up at him, but she did turn it over so the screen was facedown.

"Jim already had a slice this morning. He doesn't need another."

"No?"

"He's overweight and diabetic, and he didn't need the first slice." She looked tired, dark rings under her eyes.

"What are you doing to get around without the van?" he asked.

"I got friends from work who don't mind helping out with rides."

"Was that who you were texting with just now? Friend from work?"

"How's your kid adjusting to only seeing Dad on court-supervised visits? That must be strange for both of you. Like family visits in prison."

Kellaway put a slice of cake on a plate for Jim and another on a plate for himself and went out, mugs under one arm, scotch under the other.

He balanced one of the plates on Jim's left knee and took the gun away from him. Kellaway began to feed rounds into the magazine, while Jim ate cake with his fingers. Jim had been a big man even in the army, but in those days most of it had been in his chest and shoulders. Now he was carrying it around the waist, and his fat, round face had a corrugated quality, pocked with little dimples.

At the back of the yard was a splintery, tilting slat fence, with targets pinned up along it: a zombie version of Barack Obama, a zombie version of Osama bin Laden, and a blown-up photograph of Dick Cheney. Politically speaking, Jim Hirst was a man who liked to spread his contempt equally among all parties.

"You bought this gun for yourself?" Kellaway said, hefting it. "Feels like a squirt gun. What's up with this grip?"

"Why don't you shoot it before you bitch about it?"

The gun was so small it almost disappeared in his hand. Kellaway lifted it, looked down the sight, and saw a green dot floating across Barack Obama's forehead.

"When did you start to go for James Bond shit like this?" Kellaway asked.

"I've always dug the James Bond shit. Laser sights, incendiary bullets. I look forward to our smart-gun future if the NRA ever lets us have it. I'd like a gun that knows my name and how I take my coffee. Who doesn't want that?"

"Me," Kellaway said, and fired. He put one in Obama's left eye, one in his forehead, one in his throat, one in zombie bin Laden's mouth, two in Dick Cheney's pacemaker. "Give me Bruce Willis over Roger Moore any day. I don't want a gun with a laser beam and a British accent. I want a gun that speaks American and looks like it was built to make holes in school buses."

"Why would you need to shoot through a school bus?"

"If you knew what my neighbor's kids were like, you'd understand."

He traded the gun for a glass of scotch, had a swallow. It tasted sweetly of vanilla and went down like kerosene, ignited the lining of his throat, made him feel like an explosive just waiting for someone to pull the pin.

"Mary is in a mood," he said.

"Mary's always in a mood," Jim said, and waved at the haze in the air, blinking reddened eyes and coughing weakly. Kellaway wondered if it was just the smoke or if he was carrying a cold. "She was gone late Saturday night, and my piss bag got too full, popped a tube, and soaked my pants."

Kellaway didn't have any sympathy for that. "You can't change your own piss bag?"

"I forget to check it. Mary does that for me. But she was off getting shitfaced at TGI Fridays with the girlfriends. They like to go out on the weekend and talk trash about their men. I assume Mary has more trash to talk than most. Her friends can say they don't get laid enough, but none of their men need a hydraulic device to get a thirty-second stiffy." He reloaded methodically. "I'm sitting there in urine, she gets back and starts in on me about money, about how her credit card bounced. Like I haven't already been pissed on enough."

"Yeah. She was saying inside. She wants you to sell some of your guns."

"Like I could get anything for them. Everyone is selling guns online. They're cheaper than the steel they're made out of."

"You got anything you want to dump? I mean, the kind of thing you can own without shame as an American. Not one of these guns where you feel like you got to shoot it with one pinkie sticking out, like it's a teacup and you're sitting down to scones with the queen."

Jim lifted his mug of scotch, held it under his lips without drinking. "You want to feel like a gunslinger, I've got a .44 SuperMag that'll make holes the size of a cabbage in the unlucky target of your choice."

"Maybe something a little smaller."

Jim drank deeply, swallowed, coughed a rough, barking cough into his fist. "I got a few things. We could talk, I guess. It would get Mary off my back, you wanted to take one of the older guns for a few bucks."

Kellaway said, "Jim, I can't pass a background check. I've got that injunction hanging over me. That bitch lawyer of hers destroyed me in court."

"Hey, you didn't tell me, and I didn't ask. I don't got to do a background check. I'm not a gun dealer. I won't get in trouble. You might, but I won't." Jim touched the joystick on the right armrest of his wheelchair. The chair spun halfway around with a whine of servo motors. Then he stopped and angled a dark, almost belligerent look up into Kellaway's face.

"I sell you a gun, though, you gotta swear one thing."

"Yeah? What's that?"

"You ever decide to go on a killing spree," Jim Hirst said, "promise you'll start with me."

July 6, 2013

9:38 A.M.

ROG TEXTED HER TO SEE if she could pop into work a half hour before opening. Becki texted him back, I need it 2, SO BAD, but he didn't reply.

In the car she put on a pale lipstick that gave her mouth the appearance of being lightly frosted in jizz. She adjusted her cardigan so the upper lacy bits of her black-and-emerald bra were showing, and after consideration she reached under her skirt and wiggled out of her panties. She poked them into the glove compartment, next to the present that had been there ever since Christmas.

The Miracle Falls Mall was cool and quiet at that hour, hardly anyone there, most of the stores still closed, steel grates pulled down across their wide entrances. The gate was pulled up at Boost Yer Game, but the two dudes who had the morning shift were just horsing around, taking three-point shots on the basket located in the center of the store. Their happy shouts and the squeak of their sneakers echoed all the way down the corridor to the central atrium.

Becki didn't see anyone else the whole walk to Devotion Diamonds, except for Kellaway, the top cop in the mall—although of course he wasn't really a cop at all. Rog said the real cops didn't want him, that he'd done some skeevy Abu Ghraib shit in Iraq and had been discharged in disgrace. Rog said Kellaway would follow black kids around in the mall, fondling his foot-long flashlight, like he was just looking for a reason to crack some skulls. Becki and Kellaway were both heading in the same direction, but she fell back a few paces, let him march away from her up the central staircase. He had oddly colorless eyes that gave an unsettling impression of blindness. He had eyes the hue of very cold water over very pale stone.

Devotion Diamonds was at the top of the stairs, the Plexiglas doors halfway open. She turned sideways and slipped between them.

The display area always smelled like money to her, like the inside of a new car. The gems weren't out yet but still locked away in their drawers.

When it was closed, the door to the office blended in with the fake cherry paneling in the back of the shop, but at the moment it was partly ajar, looking into a cube of fluorescent light.

She pushed it the rest of the way in. Rog was behind the desk, wearing a yellow shirt and a wide brown knit tie. He was smoking, which surprised her. She had never seen him smoke in the morning. The big window at the back of the room was cranked open, probably to air out the smell of the cigarette, which was funny, actually. He was letting more smoke in than he was venting, the haze from the Ocala fire giving the air a filmy texture. He typed something on his big silver iMac, clicked a key, and pivoted in his leather chair to look at her. He flicked his cigarette out the open window without looking to see where it went. His gestures were jerky and abrupt and unlike him, and it made her nervous.

"Hey, Bean," he said.

"What's up?" she asked. The thing about calling her "Bean" unsettled her even more. That was what he had called her right up until they started fucking. He called some of the other girls who worked for him "Bean," too, a term of fatherly endearment.

He squeezed the bridge of his nose between his fingers. "So one of my wife's friends told her to look at your Instagram feed."

Her stomach cinched tight, but she kept her face expressionless. "Yeah? Who cares? There aren't any photos of us together."

"There's a photo of you on my boat."

"How would anyone know it's your boat?" She narrowed her eyes, trying to visualize what had been in that picture. A selfie, her grinning up into her phone, holding a green appletini in one hand, a drink that matched her lime-green bikini top. The caption read something like, Until we go to the south of France, the only place to sunbathe naked is on bae's yacht! LOL. "It could be anyone's boat."

"You think my wife doesn't know my boat when she sees it?"

"So . . . tell her I asked if I could use it. Tell her I was out with my boyfriend." She put her hands on the edge of the desk, using her arms to squeeze her breasts together, and leaned in to kiss him. "You won't even be lying," she breathed.

He wheeled back from her in his chair, putting himself out of reach. "I already told her a different story."

She straightened up and hugged herself. "What'd you tell her?"

"That you took the keys out of my desk without asking me. That you must've gone for a joyride. She asked if I was going to fire you. I said you'd be gone by the time we opened." He pushed a small cardboard box across the desk. Until he touched it, she hadn't noticed it there. "I had some of your stuff in my car. And you had a few personal items in your cubby. I think I got all of it."

"Well, shit. I guess we have to start being more careful. Sucks you have to fire me, though. I made plans around my next few checks. It also sucks that your first instinct was to lie to your wife in a way that made me sound like a skeeve."

"Bean," he said. "I don't regret one minute of it. Not one. But I will if there's one minute more."

So. There it was.

He gave the box another slight nudge. "There's something else in there for you. Token of my feelings."

She folded back a flap and picked out a small black velvet box on the top of the mess. It contained a silver bracelet, crafted to look like a stave on a piece of sheet music, with a fake diamond G clef set on it. Cheap junk they couldn't give away.

"You were the music in my days, kiddo." That sounded cheap, too. It would've been corny in a sympathy card.

She dropped the black velvet box on the desk. "I don't want that shit. What do you think you're doing?"

"You know what I'm doing. Don't make it any harder. It's hard enough already."

"How can you pick her over me?" Becki found it hard to breathe. The room had a bitter blue campfire smell, the stink of the Ocala blaze, and it was impossible to get enough air. "You *hate* her. You told me you can't stand hearing her voice. You spend all day trying to figure out how to avoid spending time with her. Besides. What do you have to lose? You told me you had a prenup." Thinking that sounded very adult, calling it a "prenup."

"I do have a prenuptial agreement. *Her* prenuptial agreement. Becki . . . these stores are all *hers*. I don't keep the shirt on my back if she walks. I thought you understood that." He looked at his watch. "She's going to call in ten minutes to see how it went. Plus, I have to open. We better go over the ground rules. Don't try to meet up with me. Don't come back to the store. I'll send you your last check. *Don't text.*"

Her throat tightened some more. It was the blunt, almost impersonal efficiency in his voice. He might've been discussing store policy with a new employee.

"This is bullshit," she said. "You think this is how you get to end things? You're out of your fucking mind if you think you can just throw me out like a used rubber."

"Hey, now."

"Something you blew a load in and don't want to look at anymore."

"Don't. Bean—"

"Stop calling me that."

"*Becki.*" He laced his fingers together and looked tiredly down into the bowl of his palms. "Things end. Cherish the good times."

"And get the fuck out. With my shitty half-price bracelet."

"Keep your voice down!" he barked. "Who knows who's walking around? Anne Malamud in Bath & Body Works is friends with my wife. Personally, I think Anne is the one who told her to look at your Instagram feed. She must've seen us together, making out in the Lamborghini or something. Who knows what Anne has said to my wife?"

"Who knows what *I* might say to her?"

"What's that mean?"

"It would teach you something, wouldn't it?" What she wanted to say was, if his wife knew about them, then there wouldn't be any reason to break up anymore. If it was a choice between his wife's forty-eight-year-old pussy and hers, she had a pretty good idea which one Rog would pick.

"Don't go there."

"Why?"

"Because I want this to be nice. I'm trying to end it nice. I'm trying to protect us both. You go to her with a story about us sleeping together, she'll think you're just a disgruntled clerk who got busted."

"I didn't *steal* your boat, douchebag. You think she'd believe that shit if she talked to me?"

"I think she'd believe you walked out of here with a pair of eight-hundred-dollar diamond earrings, since you used your pass card to log them out of the store in December and they never came back."

"The fuck are you talking about? I never stole any eight-hundred-dollar earrings."

"Christmas," he said. "The hotel."

"The hotel?" she asked. She didn't get it—and then she did, remembered the night he gave her the ivory-handled pistol, the night she draped herself in almost half a million dollars of gems for him.

"When I took all that jewelry for us to play with, I used *your* security card, not mine. I guess we missed the earrings when we cleaned up the room. Honest accident. We were both pretty trashed. The point is, they went missing after *you* checked them out."

That thought—and everything that came with it—took a moment to settle upon her.

"You knew you were going to break up with me all the way back in December," she said in a soft, disbelieving voice. Speaking to herself more than to him. "Half a year ago. You already knew you were going to blow me off, so you planned some bullshit to make me look like a thief. You were plotting this blackmail shit half a *year* ago." She didn't believe for one second those earrings had been carelessly left behind at the hotel. They weren't an accident; they were insurance.

He shook his head. "No, Bean. It's terrible you'd even think that."

"What'd you do with them? The earrings?"

"I dunno what happened to them. I honestly don't. All I know is they never came back. Come on. I hate that I even have to say any of this. My marriage is older than you are, and I'm not going to let some hysterical, vindictive kid tear up my life just because she wants something she can't have."

She felt cold, shivery, so cold she almost expected to see her own breath. "You can't do this to someone. It isn't right."

He cocked himself back in his chair, turning slightly, sticking out his legs and crossing his ankles. For the first time, she noticed he had a little beer belly, a soft roll of fat hanging over his belt.

"I want you to go home, kid. You're upset. You need some time to be alone, feel what you got to feel. Believe it or not, I'm in mourning, too. You're not the only one who lost out here."

"What did you lose out on? You haven't lost out. You have everything you ever had."

"I don't have you. I'm mourning that." He looked at her through lowered eyelashes. "Go on. Be good. Don't try to contact me, and for God's sake, *don't* try to contact my wife. Let's not be stupid. I just want what's best for both of us."

"You're in mourning? You're in fucking *mourning*?"

"Believe it or not, I am. It makes me sick we can't end things on a . . . a more positive note."

She quivered. She felt fevered one moment and frozen the next. She really thought she was going to be sick.

"I'm not mourning you," she said. "And no one else is going to either."

He looked a question at her, furrowing his brow, but she didn't say any more. She didn't know she was backing up until her hip struck the edge of the open door. The impact turned her partly away from him, and she let it, swung around, and went out into the shop. She did not run. She walked very stiffly, without bending her legs, in no hurry.

She was gone for only about thirty minutes.

10:03 A.M.

Becki didn't cry.

For a long time, she sat clutching the steering wheel, holding it so tightly her knuckles were white, even though she wasn't going anywhere. She was just sitting there in the parking lot, looking at a bank of black Plexiglas doors leading into the mall. There were moments when rage seemed to push down on her whole body, as if she were an astronaut experiencing the gravity of some larger, denser, more terrible world. She was *squeezed,* felt the air being crushed out of her.

When he left work, Rog usually came out on this side of the mall. If she saw him now, if he stepped through those shiny black doors, squinting into the morning sunlight, she'd start the car and stamp on the gas and launch her little VW right into him. The thought of hitting him with the car—the thud, the yelp, the crunch of the tires going over him—thrilled her and made it easier to stand up against that cruel alien gravity.

He had fucked her for months while he was figuring out how to get rid of her. He came in her face, in her hair, and she acted like she enjoyed it, batting her eyelashes at him and purring, and it struck her now that he thought she was pathetic and childish, and he was right. It made her want to scream until her throat hurt. Gravity doubled. Tripled. She could feel it squashing her organs.

It maddened her, how easy it had been for him to stomp on her, to squash her under his heel. He had boxed her in with such tidy efficiency. He was probably on the phone with the wife now, telling her some story about how he'd confronted her, how hard it had been to fire her while she begged and wept and made excuses. The wife was probably comforting him, as if *he* were the one who'd been through something awful this morning. It wasn't right.

"It. Isn't. Right," she said through her teeth, unconsciously pumping her foot on the gas pedal to punctuate each word. The car wasn't running, but she mashed the pedal anyway. "It. Isn't. *Right.*"

She needed something to steady her and yanked open the glove compartment, fumbled around, and found a bottle of Rog's Putumayo cocaine, razor-blade-sharp stuff he'd picked up himself on an emerald-buying trip to Colombia. The coke went off like a bullet in the brain.

Becki spotted her black lace panties crumpled in the open glove compartment. The sight of them was vaguely humiliating, and she grabbed for them to put them back on. They'd gotten tangled around the butt of her Christmas gun, and it came tumbling out with them. The .357 was shoved into the thigh holster with the straps and buckles, which was the way she kept it, although she'd never worn it anywhere.

The sight of it was like drawing a deep breath. She took it in her hands and held it and was very still.

As a child, in the days before Christmas, Becki would sometimes pick up a favorite snow globe, showing a little pond and people in nineteenth-century dress skating amid the glitter, and she would crank the key in the base and listen to the music—"Noel, Noel"—and tell herself stories about the people under the glass.

She found herself doing the same thing now, only with the gun instead of a snow globe. She stared down at its etched-silver barrel and pictured herself walking into Devotion Diamonds with it. In her imagination Rog was still in the office, on the phone with his wife, wasn't aware of her entering the store. She floated to the extension in the customer-fulfillment nook and picked up the line.

"Mrs. Lewis?" she said in a pleasantly social voice. "Hi. It's Becki. I just wanted you to know that whatever Roger told you about me isn't true. He just doesn't want you to know he was fucking me. He said if I ever tried to tell you the truth about us, he'd make it look like I stole things from the store and have me arrested. But I know I couldn't survive even one day in jail, not even overnight, and I feel sick to have committed the sin of adultery with him. I can't ever make it up to you, but I can apologize. And I am so sorry, Mrs. Lewis. You will never understand how much." And then she'd shoot herself, right in his store, right by the phone. That would stick it to him. Leave him with a corpse and blood all over the white shag carpet.

Or maybe she'd march into his office and jam the gun into her temple and pull the trigger in front of him. She wanted to hear him

scream before she did it. She'd been in the car screaming the word
"No!" over and over again in her head for almost half an hour. Now
it was his turn. She felt if she could hear him scream it just once—
NO!—it would almost be worth it to blow her brains out. She needed
to see some horror on his face, needed him to know he didn't have
control of everything.

But then if she wanted to see some horror in his face, it might be better to point the gun at *him*. Point it at his cock. See if he'd plead like she
had pleaded. Or make him text the truth to his wife. Make him eat ten
thousand dollars of diamonds. Make him write an e-mail to everyone
at Devotion Diamonds and apologize to them personally for fucking
a twenty-year-old employee, disgracing himself in the eyes of his wife
and the Lord. The possibilities swirled, like bright flecks of snow in a
snow globe, like bright flecks of diamond-bright Putumayo cocaine.

At some point she wriggled back into her underwear. She felt a little
less dirty then. The sun was well up over the trees, and it was getting
stuffy in the car, and suddenly she needed to get out into cooler air. She
brought the gun with her.

The hazy bright of late morning made her head ache. She reached
back into the car for her cheap pink sunglasses. Better. It would hide
her bloodshot eyes, too. She wasn't sure what she was going to do, but
she knew she wanted to look good doing it. She leaned back into the
car, collected the flower-print do-rag she wore to the gun range, and
wrapped her hair to keep it out of her face. Last she rucked up her skirt
and buckled the holster onto her thigh.

It was still early, and it wasn't busy inside the mall. A scattering of
people strolled among the shops. Her heels cracked on the marble like
gunshots. With each step she felt she was leaving all thought behind,
all anxiety.

Becki climbed the stairs in the atrium for the second time that
morning. She was halfway up when the holster began to slip down her
thigh. She was hardly aware of it happening until it abruptly dropped
to her knee. She tugged it awkwardly back up without slowing. She
wasn't looking where she was going, and her shoulder thudded into a
guy going down the stairs past her. It was the tall, skinny black kid who

worked in Boost Yer Game, carrying a pair of frosty coffee drinks. She didn't make eye contact with him and didn't look back as she wrestled the holster into place. She had a sense he'd stopped walking and was staring at her.

She didn't feel emotional at all. She felt as glassy and inanimate as one of the skaters in her old snow globe. So it surprised her when, at the very top of the stairs, she turned her ankle and stumbled. She hadn't known that her legs were trembling. A fat dude with curly hair came out of nowhere to grab her elbow and steady her. He had a breakfast Crunchwrap in his free hand. Scrambled eggs fell out of it and spattered across the floor.

"You okay?" he asked her. He was a pimply, moon-faced boy in a too-tight striped polo that clung to his man boobs. He smelled of hot salsa and virginity.

"Fuck off me," she said, and jerked her arm out of his soft hand. It was horrible to be touched.

He lurched aside, and she clacked unsteadily along, but the holster had slipped down to her knee again, the fucking thing. She hadn't cinched the straps tight enough. Becki cursed, pulled at the buckles, tore the holster off, and clutched the whole mess to her stomach. Anyone who looked might think it was a purse.

Devotion Diamonds was a labyrinth of glass display cases, bulletproof coffins for artfully arranged bracelets and earrings and crosses and medallions. Rog was at the fulfillment center in a back corner. He was completing a transaction with a pretty, dark-skinned lady in a dove-colored cloak or dress and one of those head scarves the Arabs wore. A hijab, that was the word. Becki was obscurely proud of herself for knowing it. She wasn't as ignorant as Rog thought.

Rog took the Muslim woman's order with an air of hushed calm, speaking in the fond, approving tone he always used when someone was about to give him money. He had left the panel into the back office open, and Becki aimed herself at it, keeping her hands low, the gun beneath the level of the display cases, where he couldn't see it. She caught his eye on the way past, nodded for him to follow.

His jaw tightened. The Muslim saw his change of expression and glanced around. Becki took in that the Muslim lady had an infant in a BabyBjörn, worn against her chest. The baby was facing inward, asleep beneath a striped blue cap. The mom had enormous eyelashes above her dark eyes and was really very pretty. Becki wondered if she had tried something on and Rog had told her she was unblemished.

She swept by them both and into the office, pushing the panel partway shut behind her. She shook with adrenaline. She hadn't thought about other people being around. The window overlooking the rear lot was still open wide, and Becki went behind the desk, thinking that another deep breath of the outside air might calm her.

Then Becki was in a position to see what was on the screen of Rog's iMac, and she went very still. She took off her sunglasses, put them down, blinked at the screen.

"One moment, ma'am," Rog was saying in his smooth, hushed voice, but Becki knew him well enough to recognize the barely suppressed urgency just beneath the surface. "I'll be right back."

"Is everything all right?"

"Yes, perfect, perfect. One more moment and we'll get you rung out. Thanks. Thanks so much."

Becki heard him murmuring away, but it hardly registered. It was only background noise, like the whoosh of the air-conditioning vents.

A messaging program was open on the big iMac. Rog had been trading texts with someone named Bo. The most recent was a picture of Becki on her knees in slick silver panties, mouth open, hair blown across her face, leaning forward for some cock. Beneath that was Rog's most recent text: At least I'll always have this to remember her by. Plus, she LOVED it up the ass. I didn't even have to ask. Second date.

And Bo's reply: Shit, dude, I hate you. How come good things never happen to me?

Rog slipped into the office, saw her staring at the computer, and deflated.

"Okay," he said. "I admit, that was inconsiderate. I shouldn't have shared that photo with anyone. I was depressed and trying to cheer myself up by being callous and nasty. So shoot me for having feelings."

Becki barked with laughter.

10:37 A.M.

When he heard the first shot, Kellaway slopped his coffee. He didn't react to the second shot at all, just stood midway down the food court, head cocked, listening. Independence Day was barely over, and the thought was in his mind that it might be kids fucking off with some firecrackers. He'd managed to scald the shit out of his hand, but he made no move, letting the sounds sink in. When the gun went off a third time, he threw his cup at the wastebasket. He missed—the paper cup hit the side of the can and erupted—but he wasn't around to see coffee going everywhere. By then he was running in a crouch toward the sound of pistol fire.

He ran past Spencer Gifts and Sunglass Hut and Lids, saw women and their kids crouched behind pillars and displays, and felt his heartbeat thudding in his eardrums. Everyone knew the drill, had seen it all on TV. Get down, be ready to run if the shooter comes in sight. Kellaway's walkie-talkie awoke in a blast of noise, frightened voices, and feedback.

"What is that, guys? Guys? Guys? *Anyone know—"*

"Oh, fuck! Shots fired! That's shots fired! Holy fuck!"

"I'm in Sears—should we lock it down? Can someone tell me if we're in a lockdown situation or am I sending people to the exits or—"

"Mr. Kellaway? Mr. Kellaway, it's Ed Dowling. What's your twenty? Repeat, what's your—"

Kellaway turned his walkie-talkie off.

A fat twenty-something—a kid who kind of looked like that actor Jonah Hill—was sprawled facedown on the glossy stone floor, just outside Devotion Diamonds. He heard Kellaway coming, looked back, and began waving one hand in a gesture that seemed to mean, *Get down, get down.* He had a wrapped sandwich or burrito in the other hand.

Kellaway dropped to one knee, thinking it had to be an armed robbery. He imagined men in balaclavas, using sledgehammers to smash the display cases, grabbing jewels by the fistful. His right hand went to the heavy iron on his left ankle.

Fat kid gasped for breath, was having trouble getting words out. He flailed one hand toward Devotion Diamonds.

"Tell me what you know," Kellaway whispered. "Who's in there?"

The fat kid said, "Muslim female shooter. And the owner, he's dead, I think."

Kellaway's own breath whistled thin and fast. A fucking al-Qaeda thing, then. He had thought he'd left the black veils and the suicide bombers in Iraq, but here they were. He jerked up his pant leg and unsnapped the Ruger Federal that Jim Hirst let him have for a hundred and twenty bucks. He tugged its lovely weight out of the ankle holster.

Kellaway scuttled to a mirrored column at the entrance to the shop, pressed himself against it so hard his breath clouded the glass. He darted a look around the corner. Display cases divided the floor into zigzagging corridors. The paneled door into the private office at the rear was open. A black-tinted globe on the ceiling hid the camera that monitored the store floor. That wasn't one of the mall's cameras, which watched only common areas. That would be Devotion Diamonds' private security. Kellaway couldn't see anyone in the store, not another soul.

He moved, dropped to his hands and knees, and crawled into the shop. The air smelled of gun smoke. Kellaway heard a rustle of movement to his right, in the corner, near the fulfillment nook. He didn't have a good angle on it, not where he was. He made it to the end of one Z-shaped display counter. The open office door was just a yard away. This was the moment. Maybe the last moment. He closed his eyes. He thought of his son, thought of George, saw him clearly, squeezing a stuffed penguin to his chest, then holding it up for Daddy to kiss.

He opened his eyes and came uncoiled, threw himself against the wall just to one side of the office door. He lifted the gun and swiveled to cover the fulfillment nook. The woman rose at the same time, a small, almost elfin Muslim in the hijab and gown, bomb vest strapped to her chest, bulging with explosives, and a silver trigger in one hand. He put a bullet through her center mass. The moment he did it, he realized he had shot right through the packed explosive, too. He waited for the spark and the flash, waited to be carried away in a clap of light.

But it didn't go off. She fell. The bullet had punched right through her and into the mirror behind her, the glass splintering in a red spiderweb.

Something clattered in the office, to his left. He saw movement at the edge of his vision, glanced, saw another woman. She wore a hijab, too, this one a pretty, flowered, gauzy cloth. She clutched a silver pistol with a lot of fancy filigree on it. This shooter was white, but that didn't surprise him. They were pretty good at turning white girls into soldiers for Allah online.

There was a corpse on the floor between them, at their feet: Roger Lewis, the guy who owned the place. He was on his stomach, the back of his shirt soaked with blood. It looked like he had collapsed onto his desk, maybe grabbed at his big iMac to stay on his feet, and then slid off and rolled onto his face. He had almost pulled the computer off the desk with him. The big silver monitor was precariously balanced on a back corner, looked like it might crash at any moment.

The convert was so close he could've reached out to grab her. Some of her blond hair had come loose from the wrap over her head. A long golden strand was stuck to one damp, flushed cheek. She gaped at him, then looked into the next room, but from here she couldn't see the body in the fulfillment nook.

"Your partner is gone," he said. "Put it down."

"You shouldn't of done that," she told him, perfectly calm.

Her gun went off with a crack and a pop and a flash of light. He fired back, instinctively, and flung most of her right lung up onto the desk.

His scalp tingled. The barrel of her .357 was still pointing at the floor. If he was shot, he couldn't feel it, not yet. She stared at him with bewildered, stunned eyes. When she tried to speak, she gurgled blood. Her right hand began to drift up with her weapon. He caught it and twisted it out of her grip, and that was when he saw that the iMac had tilted off the desk and hit the floor. He played the crack and pop and flash of light back in his head, then pushed the notion aside before it could even fully form. No. He had heard a shot. He was sure it had been a shot, and not the sound of a falling computer. He even had a half memory of the slug passing by so closely it had seemed to twitch the fabric of his shirt.

The convert sagged. He almost stepped in to catch her, but at the last moment he deflected her with his left arm to keep her from tumbling into him. She wasn't a person anymore. She was just evidence. She flopped across Roger Lewis and was still.

His ears rang strangely. The world expanded and brightened around him, and for a moment he had the ridiculous idea that he was close to fainting.

The air was blue from gunfire. He stepped out of the office, backing away from the pile of dead.

Kellaway saw the other radical on her back, staring at the ceiling, still clutching the trigger for the explosives. He took a step nearer to kick her hand free from the button. He wondered what kind of explosive she had packed into the vest, which looked a bit like a converted BabyBjörn.

He saw a pair of small dusky fists clutching the front of her gown, but the image didn't make sense to him, not at first. He looked at the trigger in her right hand and saw a silver letter opener with an opal in the handle instead of a black button. He frowned. He glanced at the bomb vest again. The cap covering the infant's head had come loose. He could see an inch of scalp, lightly dusted in tan fuzz.

"Holy shit, dude," came a voice from his right.

He looked and saw the fat kid who resembled Jonah Hill. He had walked right up to stand behind Kellaway, had wandered in, still clutching his breakfast burrito. He looked at the bodies heaped in the office, then at the dead woman and her dead baby.

"D'joo shoot her for?" the fat kid asked. "She was just hiding, man."

"I asked you who was in the store. You said Muslim female shooter."

"No I didn't!" the fat kid said. "You asked who was in here. I said a Muslim, female shooter, and the owner. Holy shit. I thought you'd go in and save her, not blow her the fuck away like a fucking madman!"

"I didn't blow her away," Kellaway said in a dull, leaden voice. "The crazy bitch in the office killed this one. Understand? It wasn't me. It was her. Tell me you understand."

The fat kid laughed, a little wildly. He didn't understand. He didn't get it at all. He waved a hand at the mirrored wall where the bullet had struck after passing through the Arab and her baby. A silvery pink web of shatter lines that spread across the glass marked the point of impact.

"Dude, I *saw* you shoot her. I *saw* you. Plus, they're gonna pick the bullet out of the wall. Forensics." He shook his head. "You were out of your fucking mind. I thought you were going to stop a rampage, not go on one yourself. You killed more people than she did! Christ, I'm just glad you didn't shoot me!"

"Huh," Kellaway said.

"What?"

"Now that you mention it," Kellaway told him, and raised the shooter's fancy filigreed gun.

10:59 A.M.

Harbaugh was first up the stairwell, lumbering to the top in sixty pounds of black Teflon armor. Halfway up he stepped on something fleshy and heard a cry. A skinny black kid was stretched out flat on the stairs, and Harbaugh had mashed his hand with one boot heel. Harbaugh kept going, didn't apologize. When you were in the middle of a mass shooting, manners were the first thing out the window.

At the top of the steps, he put his back against a round plaster pillar and snuck a look along the second-floor gallery. It was fucking apocalyptic: two acres of polished marble floor, brightly lit, and only a few people scattered around, all of them hiding behind potted plants or spread prostrate on the floor. Like that movie about the walking dead taking over the mall. Matchbox Twenty played on the sound system.

Harbaugh made his move, sprinting across the corridor, two other guys on the team right behind him, Slaughter and Velasquez. He was on his sights the whole way. The guys called it Xbox time, hunt and shoot.

He hit the wall to one side of the store entrance and dipped his helmeted head around the corner into the shop. After his very first glance, though, he lowered his weapon a few inches. A single security guard stood in one corner, facing a shattered mirror. The guy was tranced out, in a daze, poking one finger at a bullet hole in the center of the glass. He wasn't carrying, but there were a pair of pistols resting on one of the display cases beside him.

"Hey," Harbaugh said, in a soft voice. "Police."

The guy seemed to rouse himself, shook his head, stepped away from the smashed mirror.

"You can stand down. It's all done," the security guard told him.

The mall cop was in his forties, sculpted, big arms, big muscley neck, hair in a marine crew.

"How many down?" Harbaugh asked.

"Shooter is in the office, on top of one of the victims," the mall cop said. "They're both dead. I've got three more in here. One's a baby." He didn't choke on that last word, but he did need to clear his throat before saying it.

Harbaugh's insides went sick and loose at that. Harbaugh had a nine-month-old himself and didn't want to see an infant with its skull smashed open like a pink egg. He padded into the store all the same, boots almost silent on the thick carpet.

A fat kid, maybe twenty, had been thrown across one of the display cases, a bullet hole almost perfectly between his eyes. His mouth was open as if to object. Harbaugh glimpsed a dead girl in a do-rag, sprawled over a white male in the office.

"Are you hurt?" Harbaugh asked.

Mall cop shook his head. "No . . . just . . . I might have to sit down."

"Sir, you should exit the premises. My colleagues will walk you out."

"I want a moment here. With the woman. I want to sit with her for a bit to say I'm sorry."

The mall cop was looking at his feet. Harbaugh glanced past his ankles and saw a woman in a pigeon-gray robe, eyes open and staring blankly at the drop ceiling. The baby was tucked into an infant carrier, perfectly still, facedown against his mother's breast.

The mall cop put a hand on the display counter and gently lowered himself to the carpet and sat beside her. He took her hand, moved his fingers over her knuckles, lifted them to his mouth and kissed them.

"This woman and her baby shouldn't be dead," the mall cop said. "I hesitated, and that crazy cunt in the office killed her. Killed her and the baby both. One shot. How am I going to live with that?"

"The only one to blame for what happened to them is the person who pulled the trigger," Harbaugh said. "You remember that."

The mall cop considered this and then nodded slowly, his colorless eyes vacant and far away.

"I'll try," he said.

11:11 A.M.

The ESU officer named Harbaugh helped Kellaway stand up and kept an arm around him as they walked into the corridor. They left the guns and the dead behind.

Harbaugh walked Kellaway to a stainless-steel bench in the hall and eased him down onto it. A pair of EMTs wheeled a gurney past. Harbaugh told Kellaway to sit tight and stepped away.

It was getting crowded in the hall. Uniformed police had turned up. Kellaway saw a gang of Indian kids—India Indians, not American Indians—standing ten yards off, and two of them were filming everything with their cell phones. Someone yelled to push the onlookers back. A pair of cops stalked past carrying a sawhorse.

Ed Dowling, with mall security, appeared at one side of the bench. He was a ridiculous stork of a man with a prominent Adam's apple and an inability to make eye contact with anyone.

"You okay?" Dowling asked, looking at his own feet.

"No," Kellaway said.

"You want water?" Dowling said. "I could get you some water."

"I want to be alone for a minute."

"Oh. Okay. Yeah, I get that." He began to shuffle away, moving sideways, like a man creeping along a high, narrow ledge.

"Wait. Help me up, Edward. I think I'm going to be sick, and I don't want it all over YouTube." Nodding toward the pack of fifteen-year-old Hindus or whatever they were.

"Oh, yeah, okay, Mr. Kellaway," Dowling said. "Let's go into Lids.

They've got a can in the storage room out back." He took Kellaway by the forearm and winched him to his feet.

They crossed to Lids, next door to Devotion Diamonds, and made their way past racks of baseball caps. A dozen Kellaways walked with them, reflected in the mirrored walls—a big, tired-looking man with circles under his eyes and blood on the hip of his uniform. He wasn't sure how that had gotten there. Dowling used his key ring to open a mirrored panel that doubled as the door to storage. Just before they stepped through into the back, Kellaway heard someone shout.

"Hey!" called a uniformed officer with a plump, pink face. It amazed Kellaway that the force took such soft, out-of-shape, suburban-dad types and yet had turned him down. "Hey, wait. He needs to stay out here. He's a witness."

"He's sick is what he is," said Dowling, with a sharpness that took Kellaway by surprise. "He ain't gonna york up out there with a bunch of nimwits filming him. He just nearly got himself killed stopping a mass shooting. Now he ought to be allowed thirty seconds to compose himself. That's just being decent." He nudged Kellaway into the storage room and then turned and stood in the doorway, as if to physically block anyone from following him. "Go on, Mr. Kellaway. Take care of yourself."

"Thank you, Edward," Kellaway said.

Dusty steel shelving stood against the walls on either side, boxes on top of them. A grimy couch, patched with duct tape, had been shoved into a back corner next to a stained counter with a Mr. Coffee on it. A very narrow doorway opened into a dingy bathroom. A chain dangled from the fluorescent bar above the sink. Graffiti on the wall over the toilet—he didn't read it.

He shut the door and slid the bolt. He sank to a knee, fished around in one pocket, and came up with the deformed lead slug he'd picked out of the wall behind the shattered mirror. It had popped right out after a moment of working on it with his little multitool. He dropped it into the toilet.

He had his story straight in his mind. He would tell the police he'd heard shooting and approached Devotion Diamonds to assess the situation. He'd heard *three* shots, but in his statement he would say he'd heard *four*. It didn't matter what anyone else said. When people were panicked, details became mutable. Three shots or four—who could be certain how many they'd heard?

He had entered and discovered three dead: the Muslim woman, her baby, and Roger Lewis. He'd encountered the shooter, the blonde, and they'd exchanged words. She moved to shoot, but he fired first, discharging his gun twice. He hit her with his initial shot, missed her with the second. They'd think that when he missed, the bullet went out the open window. Finally the kid who looked like Jonah Hill had entered the shop, and the shooter, with her dying breath, had put a bullet in his fat, foolish face. In fact Kellaway had fired her gun twice. Once into the kid, once out the window. When forensics did the math, the empty shell casings would all add up right: three for Lewis, one for the Arab woman and her infant, and one for the fatso.

He hit the flush. It clanked uselessly. He frowned and hit it again. Nothing. The lead slug sat in the bottom of the basin like a little squashy lump of turd.

Someone knocked.

"Mr. Kellaway?" said a voice he didn't know. "Are you all right in there?"

He cleared his throat. "Just a minute."

His gaze drifted up to the wall, and for the first time he read what was scrawled in Sharpie: TOILET FUCKED UP—USE THE PUBLIC RESTROOM.

"Mr. Kellaway, there's an EMT out here who'd like to examine you."

"I don't need medical assistance."

"Yep. But he'd still like a look at you. You've been through what you'd call a traumatic experience."

"A minute," he said again.

Kellaway unbuttoned his left cuff and folded it back to the elbow, then plunged his hand into the water. He fished out the slug that had killed Yasmin Haswar and her child, Ibrahim, and set it on the floor.

"Mr. Kellaway, if I can do anything to help you—"

"No, thank you."

He lifted the heavy lid on the water tank behind the toilet and very gently set it on the seat. His left hand dripped. He picked up the slug and sank it in the water tank. Then he hefted the lid and carefully, quietly put it back in place. There would be time, in a day or two—a week at the outside—to return and collect the slug and ditch it more permanently.

"Mr. Kellaway," came the voice on the other side of the door, "you need to let someone look at you. *I'd* like to have a look at you."

He ran the sink, washed and soaped his hands, splashed water on his face. He grabbed for a hand towel, but there weren't any left in the dispenser, and wasn't that always the way? There wasn't any toilet paper either. When he opened the door, his face was still wet, drops glittering in his eyebrows, in his eyelashes.

The man on the other side of the door was a full foot shorter than him and wore a blue baseball cap that said st. possenti police. His head was an almost perfect cylinder, an effect exaggerated by the close cut of his pale yellow hair. His face was a burnished shade of red, the deep painless sunburn that all men of German descent acquired when they lived in the tropics for any length of time. His blue eyes glittered with humor and inspiration.

"Here I am," Kellaway said. "What'd you want to look at?"

The man in the cap pressed his lips together, opened his mouth, closed it, opened it again. He looked like he might cry. "Well, sir, my two grandchildren were in the mall this morning, with their mother—my daughter. And they're all still alive, and so are a whole bunch more people. So I guess I just wanted to know what a hero looks like."

And with that, St. Possenti police chief Jay Rickles took Kellaway in his arms and hugged him.

11:28 A.M.

Lanternglass saw the lights and heard the scream of sirens and was on her way to the mall before Tim Chen called to ask if she was busy.

"I'm about to be," she said. "I'm driving toward it now."

"The mall?"

"Uh-huh. What are they saying on the scanner?"

"Shots fired. All units. Multiple homicides."

"Oh, shit" was her thoughtful reply. "Mass shooter?"

"Looks like it's our turn. How was the fire?"

Lanternglass had spent the morning in a helicopter, buzzing up and down the edge of the fire blazing through the Ocala National Forest. The smoke was a filthy wall of brown cloud, climbing ten thousand feet high and throbbing with a feverish umber light. Her escort was an official from the National Park Service, who had to yell to be heard over the steady *whap* of the rotor blades. He shouted unnerving trivia about state cuts to emergency services, federal cuts to disaster relief, and the good luck they'd had so far with the wind.

"*Good luck?* What do you mean you've had *good luck* with the wind?" Lanternglass had asked him. "Didn't you say you're losing a thousand acres a day to this thing?"

"Yeah, but at least the wind is blowing north," said the Park Service man. "It's pushing the fire into uninhabited scrub. If it turns to the east, this thing could be on top of St. Possenti in three days."

Now Lanternglass told her editor, "The fire was a fire. Hot. Greedy. Impossible to satisfy."

"Hot. Greedy. Impossible to satisfy," Tim said, speaking very slowly, weighing each descriptive in turn. "How do you satisfy a fire?"

"*Timmy.* That was a setup. You were supposed to say, 'Sounds like my ex-wife.' You gotta work with me here. When I give you a perfect setup like that, you have to take it."

"I don't have an ex-wife. I'm happily married."

"Which is amazing, considering you are the least funny, most literal man in the ranks of American journalism. Why does she stay with you?"

"Well, I suppose the kids exert a certain pressure to remain together."

Aisha Lanternglass made a buzzing sound, as if he'd replied with the incorrect answer on a game show. "WRONG. Wrong. Try again, Timmy. You're the least funny man in American journalism, so why does your wife stay with you? Think carefully. This might be another prime setup."

"Because . . ." His voice trailed off uncertainly.

"You can do it. I know you can do it."

"Because of my thick, uncircumcised penis?" he asked.

Lanternglass whooped. "There you go! Much better. I knew you had it in you." By then she was turning in to the lot at the mall and could see yellow sawhorses, ambulances, half a dozen cop cars. Blue and silver strobes stammered weakly in the near-equatorial heat. It wasn't quite noon, and she already had doubts that she would get to Parks & Rec on time to pick her daughter up from tennis camp. "Gotta go, Tim. Gotta figure out who killed who."

She parked and got out, threaded through the crowd to a line of saw-horses outside the entrance to the mall's central atrium. TV vans were pulling in, the local guys, Channels 5 and 7. She figured there were only three or four dead, not enough to catch the attention of the national cable networks. On the other side of the sawhorses, it was the usual crime-scene chaos. Cops milled about. Walkie-talkies crackled and bleeped.

She didn't recognize any of the uniforms, and after a while she sat on the hood of her twelve-year-old Passat to wait. The lot broiled, heat wavering up from soft blacktop, and pretty soon she had to stand again, her buns getting too hot against the steel of the car. All kinds of folks had driven in to see what was happening, or maybe they'd shown up to shop and decided to stick around to see what all the excitement was about. A hot-dog truck was parked at a discreet distance, outside a party-supply store across the road encircling the mall.

Lanternglass's eight-year-old daughter, Dorothy, had gone vegetar-ian three weeks ago. She didn't want to eat anything that had felt feel-ings. Lanternglass had done her best to play along, eating pasta and fruit salad and bean burritos, but the smell of hot dogs was making *her* feel feelings, and not empathetic ones.

She was wandering over to buy herself a lunch to regret when she passed some black girls standing around a sporty little bubblegum-colored ride and heard one of them say, "Okello had a front-row seat. EMT is looking at his hand, 'cause one of the SWAT stepped on it. SWAT ran right by him, carrying machine guns and everything."

That was interesting, but Aisha Lanternglass kept going, couldn't eavesdrop without being noticed. The hot-dog truck specialized in Asian fusion, and she wound up with a jumbo draped in cabbage and plum sauce. She could tell Dorothy she had cabbage and fruit for lunch and it wouldn't even be a lie—it would just be leaving out details.

She meandered back toward the scrum but slowed and stopped to chug her dog while standing near the rear bumper of the bubblegum-mobile, license plate OOHYUM. Three girls, a little past high-school age, wearing jeans so tight that none of them could fit their cell phones into the back pockets, loitered around the front end. A car like that—it was an Audi—they weren't out of the Black & Blue. More likely they were from the Boulevards north of town, where every house had a driveway of crushed white shells and usually a fountain with a copper mermaid in it.

The girl who'd been talking about the SWAT typed something on her phone, then said to the other two, "Okello is waiting to see if they'll let him get his stuff and change back into his street clothes. He can't stand that Boost Yer Game uniform. Taking it off is the best part of his day."

"I thought it was the best part of *your* day," one of the other girls said, and they all had a good dirty cackle.

Lanternglass saw cameras collecting in front of one of the sawhorses, like pigeons charging a fresh scattering of bread crumbs, and had to go. She finished her dog in a hurry and squeezed in among the local TV newsfolk. She was the only print journo in the bunch, the only one who would be using her phone to record whatever was said. She was used to it. The *St. Possenti Digest* employed eight full-timers, and two of them were on Sports, down from a staff of thirty-two just ten years before. Some days as many as five articles ran under her byline.

Chief Rickles emerged from the mall, trailing a small gang of uniformed officers and someone from the D.A., a slim, good-looking Latino in a cowboy hat. Rickles was built like a fire hydrant and wasn't much taller. His blond hair was so fair that his eyebrows disappeared against his pale Germanic skin. He crossed the tarmac, closing in on the cameras, stopped before them, and doffed his baseball cap. Lanternglass had somehow wound up almost nose-to-nose with him, but he didn't appear to see her, just gazed at some point in the distance over her left shoulder.

"I'm Chief Jay Rickles with the St. Possenti police, and I'll be making a brief statement about the incident that occurred here today. At
approximately ten-thirty this morning, shortly after the mall opened,
shots were fired on the upper level of the galleria, and four were slain
in an apparent mass shooting. The perpetrator was taken out by a
security guard on the scene, before the shooter was able to reach the
crowded food court. I speak of a single perpetrator because at this
time we only know of the one. The shooter was pronounced dead at
the scene at eleven-sixteen. The heroic individual who eliminated the
threat as it unfolded is in good health but is not prepared to make
a statement at this time." He lowered his chin and scratched at his
pink scalp, and Lanternglass was surprised to see the chief struggling
against some surge of intense emotion. When he lifted his head, his
very blue eyes glittered with joyful tears. "On a personal note, two
of my grandchildren were at the mall today, with their mother—my
daughter—riding the carousel in the food court, less than three hundred feet from the shooting. They were just three of the many children, moms, and shoppers who may well owe their lives to the selfless
action of the man who stepped up to stop the shooting before it could
escalate. I was able to express my gratitude to him personally, only a
few minutes ago. I am sure I will be just the first of many. I can take
a few questions now."

Everyone shouted at once, including Lanternglass herself. The chief
was right in front of her, but he still didn't look at her. She wasn't entirely surprised. Rickles and Lanternglass had a complicated history.

"You said four casualties, plus the shooter. How many injured?" hollered the woman from Channel Five.

"Several people are receiving treatment for shock and minor injuries,
both here on the scene and at St. Possenti Medical."

More shouts. "No comment at this time." More hollering. "Still too
early to know." Lanternglass was jostled and shoved as microphones
were thrust past her. She felt that Rickles was willfully ignoring her,
but then she called out something that caused him to jerk his head
toward her and fix her with his bright, humorous, affectionate stare.

She had yelled, "Was the alleged shooter known to law enforcement before today? Did he have a criminal record?"

"I never said the shooter was male," he told her. There was no smile on Rickles's face, but his eyes glittered. He did like saying the unexpected thing in front of the cameras. And maybe he liked, too, that he'd been able to catch Lanternglass out on making assumptions about the perpetrator of a crime.

The crowd around her went bananas. The other reporters loved it. Rickles backed away, raising a hand, palm outward in a gesture of peace, and said that was all for now. As he retreated, someone shouted to ask the names of his grandkids, and he returned to say Merritt and Goldie. Someone asked if he could at least confirm the age and gender of the killer, and he frowned and said, "Let's keep the focus on the people who died today. They're the ones the media should be thinking about, instead of glorifying the demented acts of the perpetrator to collect easy ratings." Another roar—they loved that, too. Every reporter Lanternglass knew adored coming in for a bit of public flagellation.

Then he was going, turning away from them. Lanternglass half expected him to be lured back yet again. Chief Rickles was a man who loved to make a statement, enjoyed his role as a public wit, scold, moralist, and legal thinker. In that way he reminded her a bit of Donald Rumsfeld, who had so clearly delighted in toying with the press and dropping a quotable line. Lanternglass thought, uncharitably, that Rickles was probably glad his grandchildren had been on the scene, because it gave him the opportunity to play two roles at once: firm enforcer of the law and grateful, relieved family man.

But she didn't care if he came back and had some more to say. He wasn't going to share anything else worth knowing—if he answered more questions, it would be to suit his needs, not theirs. And besides . . . a flicker of pink had caught her attention, moving through her peripheral vision. When she stood on her toes and craned her neck, she saw the girls in the bubblegum-colored car zipping away, not onto the highway but around the corner of the mall and out of sight.

Lanternglass went after them.

2:11 P.M.

The northeastern face of the mall was a long stretch of windowless sand-stone brick, featureless doors painted dull brown, and loading docks. No one entered on this side except employees. The lot was narrow and faced a twelve-foot-high chain-link fence with overgrown weeds on the other side. Such places set Lanternglass on edge. They made her think of the day she'd watched a twenty-four-year-old cop named Reb put six bullets in Colson Withers.

A pair of police cruisers bracketed the lot, one at either end. Lantern-glass slowed down for a big, smooth-faced cop in mirrored sunglasses. He stood in her way until she eased to a stop, and then he walked around to the driver's-side window and made a lazy circular gesture with one hand to indicate she should roll down the glass.

"Family of the employees only, ma'am. You family?"

"Yes, sir," she lied. "My son, Okello, he works at Boost Yer Game? He was in the building when it happened. I'm with those girls you just let through." She pointed to OOHYUM, which was just sliding into a space a third of the way down the lot.

But he had stopped listening as soon as she said a name, just waved his hand, stepped aside.

When she pulled into a spot, the three girls had already spilled out of their strawberry-milkshake-colored Audi, and the driver was stand-ing on her tiptoes, hugging a gangly black kid. A thin crowd lingered among the cars, employees who'd been evacuated from the building and who were hanging around, high on excitement, telling and re-telling the stories of their own narrow escapes. Perhaps because she was remembering Colson, who'd been so at home on a stage, the busy, cheerful swarm of onlookers reminded her of being backstage after a successful performance: a good bloody tragedy perhaps.

She parked and got out, just as the boy and his girl broke their em-brace. She intercepted them as they walked back toward the pink car.

"You in there when it happened?" she asked the boy without any preamble, her phone already out to record. "I'd love to hear about it."

The kid slowed, a thought line appearing between his eyebrows. He wasn't just black but *black*-black, like a lava-sand beach. Light disappeared into him. Good-looking, of course, but then you had to be to get hired at Boost Yer Game. Youth, health, and blackness were a lot of what they sold—to a mostly white, suburban clientele. He was still wearing the store uniform; apparently the cops hadn't let him change.

"Yeah. I was in there. I was the closest person to the action who didn't get shot. Not counting Mr. Kellaway."

The three girls eyed Lanternglass with a mix of wariness and curiosity. The girlfriend, the prettiest of them—snub nose, slim neck, and bobbed, straightened hair—said, "Why you askin'?"

"I'm with the paper. *St. Possenti Digest.* I'd love to know what it was like—to be three steps away from a bullet. The inside story. How you made it out," she said, answering the girl but looking at the boy while she spoke.

"My picture in the paper?" he asked.

"You bet. People will be asking you for your autograph."

He grinned, but the girlfriend said, "It's a hundred dollars," and stepped in front of him, as if to physically block Lanternglass from getting any closer.

"If I had a hundred dollars in my purse, I could afford a babysitter. But I can't, which means I've only got about a half an hour before I have to pick my girl up from town summer camp."

"Shit," his girl said. "You want to know his story, you can watch all about it on *Dateline.* I bet they're good for a grand."

Lanternglass figured a girl with a brand-new pink Audi probably had a higher limit on her credit card than she did. She thought the girlfriend was bringing up money as a pose, a bit of spontaneous performance art. Maybe the boyfriend was from the Black & Blue and the girlfriend was from the Boulevards, and now she was trying to impress him by acting like she was street.

"I'm not sure *Dateline* will be calling," Lanternglass said. "But if they do, don't you want them to talk to *your* guy instead of one of a hundred other people who were in the mall today? The person who gets their story out first is usually the *only* person who gets their story out. Besides"—and now she fixed the girlfriend with a direct stare—"I'd really like to talk to *both* of you. I'd like to know how you felt when you heard about the shooting, knowing your boyfriend was in the building, not knowing if you'd ever see him again."

That softened her. She glanced at her boy, Okello, who had not said anything about money and who attended to Lanternglass with calm interest.

"I'll tell you what happened," he said. "You don't have to pay me."

"Can I record you?" Lanternglass asked, gesturing with her smart-phone.

He nodded.

"What's your name?" she asked, because it was a good place to start, even if she already knew the answer.

"Okello Fisher. Like Othello but with a *k*."

In Aisha Lanternglass's mind, Colson died again. He died three or four times every day, even now. Facedown in his own blood. If he had not bled to death, he might've drowned in it.

"What kind of name is Okello?" Lanternglass asked.

He rolled his shoulders in an easy shrug. "My mom's big into African history. She made me a cake with num-num berries for my tenth birthday, bought me a tribal drum. I'm like, damn, what's wrong with chocolate cake and PlayStation?"

She liked him already, knew he was going to give her good quotes. The girl's name was Sarah. To keep everyone happy, Aisha got the friends' names, too, Katie and Madison. Boulevard names, all three.

"When's the first you knew something was wrong?"

"Prolly when I saw the gun," he told her.

"You *saw* the shooter?"

"Mall only opened a few minutes before. I went up to the food court to grab Frappuccinos for Irving and myself. Irving and I have the morning at BYG. I don't know why he works there—his family is pretty well-off. I guess his mom wants him to experience what it's like to have a job." Doubt flickered in his big, sensitive eyes, and he said, "You better not print I said that. Irving's cool. They've had me over for dinner."

"I won't publish anything you don't want me to publish."

"Anyway, there's a hoop in the BYG, and we play HORSE. Loser has to pay for the winner's Frappuccino, but the winner has to go get them."

"When's the last time you paid for his drink?" the girlfriend, Sarah, asked him with a certain teasing pride.

"Irving's okay. I have to pay sometimes. He's not too good from the left side, though. So—yeah, usually he pays and I go get them."

"I won't publish you said that either," Lanternglass promised. "I don't want to give away your secret winning strategy."

He grinned again, and Lanternglass liked him even more. She thought again that he was from the Black & Blue, not because he sounded street but because he didn't. He spoke effortlessly, yet with a certain care in his phrasing. Lanternglass was familiar with the impulse to choose words with some precision. It flowed from the anxious certainty that a single verbal slip would make you sound like you slung drugs on the corner. Lanternglass had spent a year studying journalism in London, doing some of the things Colson never got to do, and while she was there, she'd read an essay about the English class system. Englishmen, she read, were branded on their tongue. You knew whether someone was posh or trash the moment he opened his mouth and spoke. It was even more true of being black in America. A person would make up his mind about you as soon as you said hello, just from the way you said it.

Okello continued, "I was walking back to Boost Yer Game when she went by. We passed each other on the big flight of stairs in the central atrium. I was going down, and she was going up. I had to look at her twice because she was fooling with something high up on her leg. Like, I thought she was messing with a stocking at first. Only it was a holster. A thigh holster. She pulled it off just as I went by. She'd been crying, too. Even though she had sunglasses on, I could tell from the mascara streaks under her eyes."

"How would you describe her?"

"Petite. Blond. Real pretty. I think her name was Becki. Or Betty? No. Kinda sure it was Becki."

"How do you know her name?"

"She worked at Devotion Diamonds, same place she shot up. The whole mall has an employee-appreciation event on the last Saturday morning of every month, before opening. Rog Lewis—he runs the store—gave her an award once. Employee of the Month or something. She killed him first. At least I think that's what happened. He shouted right before the first shot. I know he's dead. I saw them wheel him out."

"Go back. She passed you on the stairs. She had a gun. Then what?"

"I turned to watch her go. I might even have started to walk after her. To see if she was— Ow!"

His girlfriend had punched him in the shoulder. "You ass. She had a *gun*, O.K.!" She hit him a second time.

He rubbed his shoulder, and when he spoke again, it was as much to Sarah as to Lanternglass. "I didn't follow too close. She left me behind anyway. After a moment I began thinking I ought to find someone in security. I had just started back down the steps when I heard Mr. Lewis shout and then a gun popping off. I got down flat on the stairs and froze. Then I heard Mr. Kellaway yelling—he's the head of mall security—and more shots."

"Do you remember how many?"

Okello closed one eye, looked into the sky with the other. "Three at first. That was when she killed Roger Lewis. About a minute after that, another shot and a sound like something falling over, then a fifth shot. And about five minutes later, two more."

"You sure about that? Five whole minutes between the fifth shot and the last two? In a stressful incident, it's pretty easy to lose track of time."

He shook his head. "Uh-uh. Four, five minutes. I know because I was texting with Sarah, so I could see the time on my phone."

Lanternglass nodded but doubted him. Eyewitnesses reshaped memories into stories very rapidly, and stories were always at least partly make-believe, dramatic interpretations of half-recalled facts.

Okello shrugged again. "That was it. I stayed put, and a couple minutes later the police charged up the stairs in their armor, carrying machine guns, ready to fight off ISIS. Only impact they made was on my hand. One of them stepped on it running by." He paused, then shook his head. "You can leave that part out, too. They went in to save lives. For all they knew, they might've been about to face a hail of gunfire. I don't want to put them down. EMTs had a look at my hand while I made a statement. No bones broke."

"And you're out and you're O.K.," Sarah said, and stretched up on tiptoe to kiss his cheek. "And don't you *dare* say it or I'ma twist your nipple."

Okello grinned, and his lips found hers, and in spite of herself Lanternglass decided OOHYUM was all right.

"Don't say what?" Lanternglass asked.

"That he's *always* O.K.," Sarah said, and rolled her eyes. "Him and his stupid dad jokes."

"I'm even more O.K. than usual. I mean, I'm not okay a baby got killed—"

"A baby?" Lanternglass asked.

His eyelids lowered, and a sudden scared, unhappy look crossed his face. "Yes, ma'am. Shot with his mom. A woman in a hijab, her baby, a chubby dude, and Mr. Lewis. Those are the four casualties, everyone who died—not counting the shooter. But you think about some of what's happened in other places, like Aurora and Columbine, and I'm glad it wasn't worse. I'm sure the cops are glad they didn't have to shoot it out with anyone." He laughed then—a harsh, jarring sound that carried no real humor in it. "And I bet Mr. Kellaway is glad he finally got to shoot someone."

Lanternglass was thinking she ought to wrap it up, get a couple quotes from the girls she wasn't going to use and split. If she didn't get moving soon, she'd be late to pick her daughter up from camp. She still recalled, keenly, the sick and lonesome feeling of being the last to go home, staring out the rain-speckled windows of her modern-dance class, wondering if someone, anyone, would turn up to get her. But there was no walking away from that last line, which grabbed her attention and held it.

"What do you mean, he's probably glad he finally got to shoot someone?"

The almost hungry grin on Okello's face slipped away. "Ah, maybe you better leave that out, too."

She paused the recording. "I won't print anything that makes trouble for you here, Okello. I'm just curious. What's the story with Kellaway?"

Okello met her stare with a sudden chill in his own Mississippi-colored eyes. "Old Nazi bastard put a gun in my neck on my third day of work."

"He . . . *what*?"

"Mr. Boston, the floor manager at Boost Yer Game, he asked if I could use my car to run some merch down to Daytona Beach. I was doing a bunch of errands because I didn't have my uniform yet." Tugging at the silly gold basketball shirt that bore the words BOOST YER GAME and showed a black hand gripping an orange ball of flame. "I was out here sticking boxes in the back of my car when Kellaway sneaks up behind me and sticks the barrel of a gun against my neck. He says, 'Jail or the morgue—it's up to you. It's the same to me either way.'"

"Bullshit," Lanternglass said, although she believed him, and her tone said she believed him.

Sarah's jaw was set, her mouth a grim line, and she was squeezing her boyfriend's fingers tightly. She'd heard this story already, Lanternglass could tell.

"Hand on my heart," Okello said, and tapped his fingers against his chest. "He got on the radio, said he had someone lifting boxes off the loading dock behind Boost Yer Game. Said I had a box cutter and a gun, too. But before his office radioed the cops, Mr. Boston saw what was happening and came running out to tell him it was all right. That I was an employee."

"You had a gun?"

"I had a *tape* gun," Okello said. "To seal a couple of boxes. The handle was jutting out of the pocket of my hoodie. He was right on the box cutter, though. That was in the back of my pants."

The suspect rose, and I saw a flash in his hand. He leapt. I thought he was coming for me with a knife, and I fired my weapon to defend myself— that was what Officer Mooney had said when he was deposed before a grand jury. Lanternglass had read the entire statement years later. All it took to turn a CD into a knife or a tape gun into a .45 was a little imagination, a little panic, and a lot of prejudice.

"You're lucky you didn't get shot," Lanternglass said. "Why didn't he get fired?"

One corner of Okello's mouth turned up in that movie-star grin of his, although there was a certain cynicism in it now that disheartened her. "Mr. Boston had the shakes for an hour. He was so pale he looked like he had the flu. He said he was going to call the complaint line for the firm that runs mall security, but when he tried, it was disconnected. He wrote them an e-mail and it bounced back as undeliverable. They're a big southern outfit—Falcon Security? They provide the men for a lot of shopping centers. You'd think it'd be easier to get in touch with them. Mr. Boston asked if I wanted to go to the cops and file a complaint, but I figured nothing would happen, so I said skip it."

"Why didn't you quit?"

"'Cause I can't pay for college with my good looks."

"Did Kellaway apologize?"

"Yep. On the scene and then again the next day, in his office. He gave me a twenty-five-dollar gift certificate good at any shop in the mall."

"Holy shit. That was big of him. Twenty-five whole dollars. What'd you spend it on?"

"Still got it," Okello said. "I'm going to hold on to it until someone in the mall starts selling discount bulletproof vests. I'm in the market for one."

5:15 P.M.

Lanternglass watched the press conference on TV with Dorothy.

Dorothy was on her knees in front of the television, about a foot from the screen, where she liked it best. Eight-year-old black girl with a long neck and mile-long legs, wearing a hot-pink cap with rabbit ears. She was going through a hat phase, had a drawerful of them. Getting her out of the house in the morning was a daily anguish; it could take her upward of twenty minutes to find the perfect hat for the day.

"I'm missing *Kim Possible*," Dorothy said, referring to her favorite Disney Channel series.

The local news had just cut to an unnamed conference room, with the promise that the St. Possenti police were about to address the shooting at the Miracle Falls Mall and perhaps identify the heroic security guard who had stopped the killer before the rampage could go wide.

"Mama's got to see this for work," Lanternglass said from the kitchen table, where she was on her laptop banging out two thousand words on the Ocala fire. It wasn't hard to get in the right mind-set. She could smell the smoke right there in her living room, even with the blaze miles away. She wondered if the wind was shifting.

"I want a job where I get to watch TV and ride around in helicopters."

"Next time you see Mr. Chen, you can ask if he's hiring. This household could use another source of income." There wasn't going to be any bread coming from Dorothy's father. He'd been out of the picture almost since Dorothy was born, wasn't going to let a baby fuck up his music career. Last Lanternglass had heard, he was up in New York, in Queens, had two daughters by another woman, and his music career consisted of drumming on white plastic tubs in Times Square for dollars in the hat.

Cameras flashed. There was a rustling, like the wind stirring in leafy trees, the sound of an unseen audience murmuring and settling. Chief Jay Rickles and the slim Cuban D.A. took seats behind a folding table arrayed with microphones. They were followed by a third man in a baggy hoodie that said SEAWORLD and showed a jumping killer whale. This third man was in his forties, guy with a graying mustache and a military haircut. He had the thick neck of a marine or a boxer and big, bony hands, and he regarded the cameras with oddly colorless, indifferent eyes.

Chief Jay Rickles waited for everyone to quiet down and then waited some more, because he enjoyed a long, dramatic silence. Dorothy hopped a little closer to the TV.

"That's too close, Button," Lanternglass said.

"I like to get right up next to the screen so I can see if anyone is lying."

"Your hat is blocking my view."

Dorothy crept back an imperceptible centimeter.

"Hello and good evening," Rickles began. "I'm Chief Jay Rickles, and I'm going to open with a brief statement, summarizing the events of this morning at the Miracle Falls Mall. At approximately ten-thirty A.M., a shooting occurred in Devotion Diamonds, on the second floor. We have now positively identified the shooter as Rebecca Kolbert, twenty, of St. Possenti, who was a salesgirl at the store. We believe that Ms. Kolbert entered the store, where she shot Roger Lewis, forty-seven, the manager of the Devotion Diamonds retail chain, Yasmin Haswar, a customer, and Yasmin's infant son, Ibrahim. At that point Ms. Kolbert was confronted by Randall Kellaway, the head of security at the mall, an officer with Falcon Security, and a former military policeman in the U.S. Army." At this, Rickles leaned forward and aimed an admiring glance down the length of the table toward the big man in the hoodie. "Mr. Kellaway instructed Ms. Kolbert to put down her firearm. Instead she raised her gun to fire, and at that point he shot her. Believing he had killed her, he hurried to Mrs. Haswar to offer medical aid. Another man, Robert Lutz, entered the store to try to offer his assistance, and he was shot by Ms. Kolbert. At that point Mr. Kellaway disarmed the shooter. Shortly afterward SWAT and emergency personnel swarmed the scene. Ms. Kolbert was pronounced dead at eleven-sixteen A.M." His hands were folded together in front of him. Rickles had the serene look of a man admiring a sunset while he sat on his porch with a can of beer. "Some of you are already aware that my daughter and her two children were in the mall at the time of the incident. There is no reason to believe they were ever in physical danger. There is also no reason to believe they *weren't*. Ms. Kolbert was indiscriminate in claiming innocent life, and we cannot be certain what her final intentions might have been. Certainly she was intent on killing to her last breath. I don't like to think about what might have happened if Mr. Kellaway had not responded with such swift and decisive action. Have no doubt: This was an unspeakable tragedy. In the space of a few minutes, we lost a beloved local employer, an innocent bystander who'd entered the store in an act of fearless compassion, a mother, and her infant. *Her infant.* A beautiful baby boy who was a part of St. Possenti's patriotic Muslim community. We'll be unpacking our anguish for days and weeks and months to come. But today we found out what happens when a bad guy with a gun meets a good guy with a gun. Today our grief is counterbalanced by our gratitude, our pain abides alongside our pride." He paused, leaned forward, looked at the assistant D.A. "Mr. Lopez? Would you care to add anything at this time?"

"Why would anyone shoot a baby?" Dorothy asked. "Did that really happen?"

Lanternglass said, "That really happened, Button."

"I think that's stupid."

"Me, too."

On the TV, Lopez leaned forward and said, "The Flagler County district attorney's office has committed our entire resources, including two full-time investigators, to determine the motive behind today's heinous and tragic acts and to learn whether Ms. Kolbert acted alone or had the support of any confederates." He spoke for another half a minute, reciting boilerplate: if anyone had any further information, blah, blah, no charges filed at this time, blah, blah, state-of-the-art forensics, yada, yada. Then he was done, and Rickles leaned forward again.

"Rand? Would you like to make a statement?" he asked, peering down the length of the table at the big man in the SeaWorld hoodie.

A fresh round of camera flashes strafed the room.

Kellaway sat with his hands in his lap and his head lowered, looking both haunted and a little hunted. He thought for a moment, then shifted forward in his chair and leaned toward the microphone.

"If my son is watching, I just want him to know Daddy's okay," Kellaway said.

The assembled crowd responded with a soft cooing sound that made Lanternglass think of pigeons.

"He's not *that* good a guy," Dorothy announced.

"He stopped a crazy person with a gun."

"But he also goes to SeaWorld," Dorothy said, and pointed at his sweatshirt. "They keep orcas prisoner in little, *little* tanks. Like if someone stuck you in a closet and made you stay there all day. No one should go to SeaWorld."

"Yeah," Jay Rickles said gently, almost quivering with pleasure. "Daddy's okay. Daddy's okay, folks. Daddy's just fine."

A final spasm of furious camera flashes filled the room. In their stammering, almost blinding light, Kellaway's very pale skin had a blue sheen, like gunmetal.

9:18 P.M.

They were still out there, the news vans, the camera crews, choking the street in front of his house. He sat on the ottoman in the middle of his living room, with the landline in his lap. The police had taken his cell phone. He could see the broadcast vans through a gap in the drapes pulled across the big picture window. CNN. Fox. His TV was on, the only light in the room, the volume turned off. They were playing that same clip of Jay Rickles saying his thing about the bad guy with a gun meeting the good guy with a gun.

Kellaway felt like a bullet in a gun himself, felt charged and ready to go off, to fly toward some final, forceful impact. Loaded with the potential to blow a hole in what everyone thought they knew about him. When a gun went off, everyone turned their heads to look, and they would look at him now, too. *At* him instead of *past* him or *through* him.

He expected the phone to ring, and it did. He lifted the receiver to his ear.

Holly's voice was breathless and small. "You're home. I wasn't sure you'd be home. I was just watching you on TV."

"They recorded that hours ago. You're just seeing it now?"

"Y-yes. Just seeing it now. You're all right? You aren't hurt?"

"No, love," he said to his wife. Still his wife, even now. On paper anyway.

A little indrawn breath. "You shouldn't call me that."

"Love?"

"Yes. You shouldn't even think it."

"I would've been thinking it if she killed me. If she shot me today, it would've been my last thought."

Another shuddering breath. She was trying not to cry. She cried so easily: at the ends of TV movies about Christmas, at ASPCA commercials, when movie stars died. She was always clothed in the sheer velvet gown of her emotions, the fabric of it rippling with every step into the world she took, clinging to her wherever she went.

"You shouldn't of gone in there. You should've waited for the police. What if she shot you? Your son needs a father," she told him.

"Your lawyer didn't seem to think he does. Your lawyer thought it would be just fine if I only saw George once a month, with a chaperone there to spy on me."

She took a sniffling breath, and he knew for sure she was crying now. It was several seconds before she could speak again, and then her voice was frail with emotion. "My lawyer didn't just push *you* around. She pushed *me* around, too. She threatened to quit if I tried to negotiate with you. She made me feel so stupid when I told her I knew you'd never hurt us, that you'd never—"

Holly's sister squawked in the background, a harsh, unintelligible sound that reminded him of the adults talking in a Charlie Brown cartoon. Holly didn't know how to stand up for herself. The expectations of other people were like a blasting gale and Holly just a sheet of newspaper, flapping this way and that under their influence. It was Rand Kellaway's opinion that Holly's sister Frances was a closet lesbian and that the man she was married to was, in all likelihood, a queer. The dude wore bright shirts in suspicious colors (tangerine, teal) and enthusiastically watched figure skating on television.

"What's Frances saying to you?" Kellaway asked. He felt something flare inside of him, like a stroked match hissing into flame.

But Holly wasn't listening to him anymore, she was listening to her sister. Holly said, "Yes." More squawking. "No!" And then again, *"No!"* in a pleading, whining tone.

"Tell her to mind her own business," Kellaway said. He could feel

Holly slipping away, out of reach, and it maddened him. "Don't listen to her. Whatever she's saying doesn't matter."

Holly turned her attention back to him, but her voice was flustered, hitching with emotion. "G-George wants to speak with you, Rand. I'm going to put him on. Fran says I can't talk to you anymore."

When they had lived together, it had been one of Kellaway's rules that Holly could talk to Frances only when he was in the room, for exactly this reason. He had not wanted Holly to have a cell phone because of the danger of Frances texting her. He had refused to let Holly buy one, but then the fucking company she worked for *gave* her one, *insisted* she carry one.

"You tell that hairy cunt—" he began, but then the phone clattered, and it was George.

"Daddy," George said. He had his mother's rushing, breathless, excitable voice, the same soft, sweet slur. "Daddy, you were on TV!"

"I know," he said. It took a great effort of will to steady his voice and inject some warmth into it. "I was in TV Land all afternoon, where all the TV people live. The hardest part is getting there. They have to shrink you down, very, very small, so you can fit inside the television set."

George giggled. The sound of it was so lovely it made Kellaway ache. He wanted to hold his son in his lap and squeeze him until he shouted and tried to wriggle free. He wanted to take George to the beach and shoot bottles for him. George would clutch his fists and dance every time a bottle smashed. Kellaway would smash the world to see George dance.

"That isn't true," George said.

"It *is*. First they make you very, very small, and then you get a ticket and ride to TV Land on Thomas the Tank Engine. I sat right next to one of the Teletubbies on the trip."

"No you didn't."

"I did. *Really*."

"Which one?"

"The yellow one. He smells like mustard."

George giggled again. "Mom says you saved people from dyin'! She says there was a bad person and you shot her down just like—*pow!* Is that what happened?"

"That's what happened. Just like that."

"Okay. That's good. I'm glad you shot that bad person." The squawking sounds began in the background, Fran getting going again. George listened to her, then said, "I've got to eat my Eggo and go to bed."

"You do. Go on, now. I love you, George."

"I love you, too."

"Put your mom back on."

"Aunt Fran wantsa talk to you."

Before he could reply, the phone clattered again. Then someone new was on the other end of the line. Even her breathing was unpleasant: thin and slow and deliberate.

"Hey, Randy," said Frances. "You got a court order not to talk to my sister."

"She called *me*," he said patiently. "There's no court order says I can't answer my own phone."

"That same court order says you can't own a gun."

"The gun," he said, "was behind the counter at the Vietnamese restaurant in the food court, and I asked for it. It was Mr. Nguyen's gun. And the cops are keeping that part out of the news, not to protect me but to protect *him*. He's here on a visa, and owning that gun could get him in hot water with immigration. But go ahead. Make a fuss. Force the police to deport a guy who gave me the weapon I needed to stop a mass shooting. What a hero you'll be. I want to talk to my wife." He had thought this lie through carefully and felt it was beyond Frances's limited powers to assault.

And he was right—she didn't even try. Instead she went for the easier attack. "She's not your wife anymore."

"She is until I see the divorce papers."

Frances inhaled. He could picture her perfectly, the slits of her nostrils narrowing at the end of that long, bent nose of hers. She had Holly's features, subtly distorted so that she was utterly lacking any of Holly's beauty. Holly had a soft, pliant mouth and eyes that shimmered with emotion and an innate desire to please. Frances's eyes were dull and tired, and she had deep creases bracketing her lips. Holly hugged easily. No one would want a hug from Frances; the steely points of her hard little tits would probably leave bruises.

"Maybe you think you can use this somehow to get them back," Frances said. "But it's not happening. She's not coming back, and neither is he. Not after what you did to them."

"What I did *today*," he told her, "is save lives. What I did *today* is shoot a madwoman before she could go on a killing spree."

"You'll have to shoot another madwoman before you get anywhere near either of them. Because you'd have to kill *me* to take them away."

"Well," he said to her, "that would definitely be a bonus, wouldn't it?"

He hung up.

He didn't expect her to call back, but the phone shuddered in his hand a moment later, before he even had time to let go of the receiver. Frances couldn't stand letting someone else have the last word.

"Why don't you rest your tongue," he said, "for eating pussy later?"

There was an awkward silence on the other end of the line. Then a young man said, "Mr. Kellaway? My name is Stanley Roth, I'm a producer with *Telling Stories*, on NBC? Wow, it has *not* been easy to get your number. This *is* Randall Kellaway, yes?"

It took him a moment to recalibrate. "I watch your show. You did that one about the watermelons full of meth in Orange County."

"Yes. Yes we did. Definitely our greatest claim to fame. Meth Watermelon is also the name of our office softball team. We beat the guys from *20/20* to win our league last summer, and I'm hoping to beat them again—in this weekend's ratings. I'm sure they're trying to get in touch with you to invite you on their show and talk about what happened today. I would be a very happy man if I were fortunate enough to get to you first."

Stanley Roth spoke in such an exuberant flurry that Kellaway needed to go back over it in his head to figure out the guy was making an offer.

"You want me to come on your show?"

"Yes, sir, we do. To tell your story. The story of the good man with the gun. You're Clint Eastwood, only for real."

"Clint Eastwood *is* real. Isn't he?"

"Yeah, well . . . *yeah*. But he gets paid to pretend to be what you actually are: someone who knows how to fight back. People feel so powerless most of the time, so overwhelmed by the forces lined up against them. They need these stories like they need food and drink. Stories about people who made the best, bravest choices when it would've been easier to fold, and who made a fucking difference. I hope you'll excuse my language, sir, but I get really amped up about this stuff."

"Would I have to go to New York?"

"No, you'd do it from there. We can get a local studio and tape the interview remotely. If it helps to nudge you in the right direction, I should add that Chief Jay Rickles has already agreed to talk with us as well and would join you in front of the camera. That guy loves you. I think he wants to adopt you. Or marry you to one of his daughters. Or maybe marry you himself. He talks about you in exactly the same awestruck way my son talks about Batman."

"Maybe you ought to stick with him. He seems like he knows what he's doing when he talks to the press. I'm not a public speaker. I've never been on TV."

"You don't *have* to be a public speaker. You just have to be yourself. Nothing to it, as long as you don't think about the three million people watching and hanging on your every word. Which has still got to be less scary than running into a shop where a woman is killing people indiscriminately."

"It wasn't scary. There wasn't time to be scared. I just ducked down and got moving."

"Perfect. Oh, my God. That's perfect. Get ready to duck again, because women are going to be throwing their panties at you."

"I'm married," he said with a certain edge. "And I have a little boy. An amazing six-year-old."

There was a respectful pause. Then Stan said, "Did you think you'd ever see him again?"

"Not really," Kellaway said. "But I'm still here. I'm still here, and I'm never going to let him go."

They were another twenty minutes on the line, doing what Stan called the "pre-interview" and the producer filling him in on what the

on-air discussion would be like. They would record on the afternoon of
the tenth and air it that evening. "If you snooze, it ain't news," Stan said
several times. Stan gave him some advice for looking good on camera,
but it all washed over Kellaway without registering. When he hung up,
the only thing he could remember was Stan's forceful directive not to
eat blackberries, because the seeds would get between his teeth and
make him look like a guy who never flossed.

Once again the phone rang almost as soon as he hung up. He thought
it would be Stan again, calling with some last urgent, overlooked piece
of trivia. Or maybe it would be someone from ABC or NBC, hoping to
book an interview for one of their shows.

But it wasn't Stan at all, and it wasn't CNN, and it wasn't Frances. It
was Jim Hirst. The call was grainy with hiss, and his voice sounded far
away, as if he were calling from the other side of the world, or maybe
the other side of the moon.

"Look who got famous today," Jim said, and issued a dry, hacking
cough.

"More like look who got lucky," Kellaway replied. "I figured if someone was going to blow my head off, it would be over in the suck, not
here at the mall."

"Yeah, well, sounds like some crazy bitch shopped for trouble at the
wrong place today. Got more'n she paid for, huh?" He coughed again.
Kellaway thought he was a little drunk.

"You having some of that scotch I gave you?" Kellaway asked.

"Yeah. I might've had a sip or two. I raised a glass to you, my brother.
I am so glad you're alive and she's dead and not the other way around.
I want to put my arms around you, man. If she killed you, it would've
killed *me*, you know?"

Kellaway was unaccustomed to strong emotion, and the prickling in
his own eyes took him by surprise. "I wish I was worth half what you
think I'm worth." He shut his eyes, but only for a moment. When he
shut his eyes, he saw the woman, Yasmin Haswar, rising up from behind the glass counter, her eyes wide and frightened, and he turned and
shot her all over again. Straight through the baby strapped to her chest.

"Don't get down on yourself. Don't you do it. You fucking saved a whole mess of lives today. And you made me proud. You made me glad, for once, that I survived and came home. I'll tell you what, man. It was never my childhood dream to live for fifty or sixty years as a useless drain on society. Today, though, I've been thinking, I guess I'm not a complete waste. When my best friend, Rand Kellaway, needed a gun . . . well. You weren't empty-handed today, and that's my piece of this. That's my little taste of glory."

"That's right. You had my back this afternoon. Even if no one will ever know it."

"Even if no one will ever know it," Jim repeated.

"Are you okay? You sound sick."

"Ah. It's the fucking smoke. It's right on top of the house tonight. It's burning my eyes, man. They say the fire is still two miles off, but I can't hardly see to the end of the hall."

"You should go to bed."

"Soon, man. Soon. I wanna stay up and watch the news loop around one more time. That way I can toast you again."

"Put Mary on. I'm going to *make* her send you to bed. I don't need another toast. I need you to take care of yourself. Get Mary."

And Jim's voice changed, became suddenly morose and querulous. "I can't, man. She's not here."

"Well, where is she?"

"Beats the fuck out of me," Jim Hirst said. "I'm sure I'll see her again sooner or later. All her stuff's here!" And he laughed—until it turned into the broken, hacking, rattling cough of a man choking on blood in his deathbed.

July 8, 8:51 A.M.

LANTERNGLASS REACHED OUT TO THE Lutz family first. When you had a bad job to do, it was best to do it first thing and get it out of the way. She hated calling the family of the deceased. It made her feel like a crow, pulling strands of gut out of roadkill.

The Lutz family was unlisted, but Bob Lutz, who'd died at just twenty-three, had offered one-on-one piano lessons to kids at Bush Elementary, according to the school Web site. As it happened, the vice principal at Bush was a Brian Lutz. Lanternglass called his office number and got a recording saying that he would be checking messages throughout the summer session, but if it was urgent, he could be reached at his cell, followed by the number.

She made the call on the sidewalk in front of a Starbucks, just down the street from Possenti Pride Playground, where Dorothy had tennis camp. Lanternglass had an iced coffee that was so cold she broke out in goose bumps when she had her first sip. She was almost too nervous to drink it, didn't need the caffeine to amp her up. There was no reason to think Brian Lutz would answer his cell, but he did, on the second ring, as somehow she had known he would.

Lanternglass introduced herself in a quiet, gentle voice, said she was with the *St. Possenti Digest*, and asked how he was doing.

He had a deep baritone with a very slight crack running through it. "My little brother got shot in the face two days ago, so I guess not so hot. How are you?"

She didn't reply to that. Instead she told him she was so sorry, that she hated to intrude when he was struggling with his grief.

"But here you are, intruding anyway," he said, and laughed.

Lanternglass wanted to tell him about Colson. She wanted to tell him she understood, that she had been on the other end of this herself. In the days after Colson died, journalists parked in front of the two-family house Aisha lived in with her mother and waited for them to come out. When Aisha's mother, Grace, walked her to school in the morning, the reporters would flock around them, waving tape recorders. Grace gripped Aisha's hand and stared straight ahead, and the only reply she ever made was a sound: *Nmm-nm!* That noise seemed to mean, *I don't see you, and I don't hear you, and my daughter doesn't either.* Lanternglass knew now that her mother had been sick with fright, was afraid of the attention, afraid to be looked at too closely. Grace had been to jail three times—had in fact been pregnant with Aisha on her second stint in county—and was scared the reporters would publish something that would get her sent back. Aisha herself wanted everyone to know what had *really happened.* She thought they should tell all the reporters how Colson was shot to death and he DIDN'T EVEN DO ANYTHING except take a stupid CD. She wanted to explain how Colson was supposed to go to London and meet Jane Seymour and be in *Hamlet.* She wanted everyone in the world to know.

Ain't it enough you lost him? Grace had told her. *You want to lose me, too? You want me to get locked up again? You think the police won't come down on us, we try to make them look bad?*

In the end Aisha Lanternglass did get to tell the world all about it. She just had to wait fifteen years. The *St. Possenti Digest* had published Colson's story in five parts over a single week. Those stories had been nominated for a Pulitzer Prize in local reporting, which was why Lanternglass still had a job when almost all the other full-time reporters with the *Digest* had been laid off in the recession.

But she didn't tell Brian Lutz about Colson, because she had promised herself a long time ago that she'd never use his death as a way to get a story. Even after you lost someone, it turned out you still had a relationship with that person, one you needed to tend to as you would tend to a relationship with any living friend or relative. Colson was, even now, someone she cared about and was at pains not to misuse.

So she said, "I just wanted to ask if there was a photo of Bob your family wanted to share. I don't want to make things any more awful than they are. Your brother did something really special, you know? When a lot of folks would've run in the other direction, he went into Devotion Diamonds to try to help people. I want to acknowledge his bravery when we write about what happened. I also want to respect your feelings and do right by your family, but I'll let you go this minute if you don't want to deal with a prying journalist. My paycheck is not big enough to put grieving people through the emotional wringer."

For a long time, he didn't speak. Then he laughed again, a corrosive, broken sound. "You want to acknowledge his bravery? Man, that's hilarious. You don't know how hilarious. I know only one person who's a bigger pussy than Bob, and that's me. Our uncle made us ride a little baby roller coaster once, a thing for tots at a county fair, when I was thirteen and Bob was eight, and we both fuckin' cried the whole way. There were five-year-olds on that ride who looked embarrassed for us. I don't know why the fuck he'd go in there. It's completely out of character."

"He thought the shooting was over," Lanternglass said.

"He would've had to have been pretty fuckin' sure," said Brian Lutz, and when he laughed again, it sounded closer to a sob. "We cried on the Little Zoom-Zoom coaster! I even wet my pants a little! After we got off, our uncle couldn't look at us, either of us. Just took us straight home. I'll tell you about my baby brother. He would've *died* before he walked in someplace where he coulda been *killed*. He would've just fuckin' *died*."

9:38 A.M.

Lanternglass had two e-mails speaking for Alyona Lewis, Roger Lewis's wife. The first came through her lawyer, at 9:38. Lanternglass read it at her desk in the open-plan office of the *Digest*.

"Today Alyona Lewis grieves the loss of her beloved husband of twenty-one years, Roger Lewis, killed in the senseless mass shooting at the Miracle Falls Mall; Margot and Peter Lewis grieve the loss of their beloved son; and St. Possenti grieves the loss of a lively, good-humored, and generous community member."

The e-mail went on for another eight hundred words, all of it just as formal and forgettable. Alyona and Roger had opened their first jewelry store in Miami in 1994, attended the Next Level Baptist Church, owned three Brussels griffons, wrote big checks to the Special Olympics. Flowers might be sent to the Lawrence Funeral Home. It was a tidy, professional public statement, and there wasn't a single thing in it that Lanternglass could use for a quote.

10:03 P.M.

The second e-mail came from Alyona herself, a half hour after Lanternglass went to bed but while she was still awake, lying under a single sheet and staring at the ceiling. Her phone pinged, and she rolled over to have a peek. Alyona's personal e-mail address was Alyo_Lewis _Gems@aol.com, and her message was just a single sentence long:

I bet he was fucking her.

Lanternglass didn't see how she could quote that e-mail either.

July 9, 5:28 A.M.

RASHID HASWAR DIDN'T HAVE A listed landline; he didn't have a Twitter handle or an Instagram profile; his wife's Facebook account was private. He had a job at the Flagler-Atlantic Natural Gas Corporation, in the accounting department, but the receptionist refused to give Lanternglass the number for his cell.

"If he wanted to talk to you, to *any* of you newspeople, he'd call you," the receptionist said in a thin, indignant tone. "But he hasn't, because he doesn't."

Lanternglass had one other idea, though, so Tuesday morning she woke Dorothy before dawn and walked her out to the car. Dorothy was still about two-thirds asleep, her eyes partly shut as she tramped across the dew-soaked grass. Today she had on a thick white fluffy cap with a polar bear's face on it. She fell back to sleep in the rear of the car, on the drive across town.

The Islamic Center was in the Black & Blue, in a low and ugly concrete building, across the street from a strip mall that contained a Honey Dew Donuts, a bail bondsman, and a discount shoe store. The last worshippers were already going in for morning prayers, women through a door in the side of the building, the men through the double doors in the front. A lot of them were brothers in dashikis and kufis, although there were a few Middle Easterners among them. Lanternglass parked herself in the Honey Dew, found seats at a counter by the window where she could keep an eye on the street. Dorothy got up on a high stool beside her with a glazed and a big bottle of milk, but she had only one bite and then put her head down. Outside, the sky was a shade of royal purple, the clouds kissed with gold. The wind was freshening, and the palms rattled their fronds.

Lanternglass had been watching the mosque for ten minutes when she noticed a slender, wiry man in a black baseball cap, his arms crossed over his sunken chest, standing just inside the doughnut shop's door. He was watching the street, too. The first time she looked at him, she noticed dark circles under his bloodshot eyes. He looked like he hadn't slept in days. What made her glance at him a second time were the words FLAGLER-ATLANTIC NGC embroidered on the breast pocket of his blue denim shirt. Lanternglass kissed Dorothy on the cheek—her daughter didn't seem to notice—and slid three stools to the right, taking her doughnut and coffee with her, so she was almost right next to the guy.

"Mr. Haswar?" she said gently.

He twitched as if he'd been stung with a fizzle of static electricity and looked around, his eyes wide and surprised and a little frightened. She almost expected him to dart out the door and away from her, but he didn't, only stood there holding himself very tightly.

"Yes?" he asked, no accent.

"You're not praying?"

He blinked at her. When he spoke again, there was no anger, no defensiveness, just curiosity. "You with the press?"

"I'm afraid so. I'm Aisha Lanternglass from the *Digest*. We've been trying to reach you. We were hoping you might share a photo with us, of your wife and baby. We'd like to do our best to honor them. And you, your loss. Your family's loss. It's awful." She thought she had never sounded more phony.

He blinked again and rotated his head and looked back out at the mosque. "I read your piece about the massacre."

He didn't go anywhere further with this statement, didn't seem to feel the need to add to it.

"Mr. Haswar? Do you know why your wife was there that morning?"

"For me," he said, not looking at her. "I asked her to go. My boss, Mrs. Oakley, was retiring. I was being promoted to her position. Yasmin ran by the mall to pick something out that I could give to Mrs. Oakley at the party. Yasmin . . . always got excited when she had a chance to buy something for someone else. Giving gifts was her favorite thing. She was excited for Ibrahim to be older so we could give him things on Eid. You know Eid al-Fitr?"

"Yes," Lanternglass said. "It's when Ramadan ends."

He nodded. "And you know today is the first day of Ramadan?" Then he snorted with amusement—although there was no real humor in it—and added, "But of course you know. That's why you're staking out the mosque." He did not say it angrily, like an accusation. In some ways his mildness was worse. She wasn't sure how to respond. She was still trying to think what to say when he added, "I walked Yasmin's mother here. She's inside with the other women. She doesn't know I am not praying myself, because the men and women pray in different rooms. You know that?"

She nodded.

"Yasmin's father couldn't walk her to the dawn prayer. He's in the hospital for observation. He's fainted several times since he heard the news. We're all scared to death for him. He had a bypass operation last year." Tapping his chest with his thumb. "She was his only child." He stroked his breastbone with the edge of his thumb, rubbing the place where his wife had been shot. He gazed blankly out at the temple and added finally, "Do you think it was because she was Muslim?"

"What?" Lanternglass asked.

"That she was shot. That they were both shot."

"I don't know. We may never know."

"Good. I don't want to know. I dreamed last night my son said his first word. It was 'cake.' He said, 'Mm, cake!' Probably not a very realistic first word. I haven't dreamed about Yasmin yet. But then I'm not sleeping much," he said. "You're not eating your doughnut."

"I hate these things," Lanternglass said, pushing it away from her. "I don't know why I got it."

"Shame to let it go to waste. Smells lovely," he said, and picked her doughnut off her plate without asking and, making steady eye contact, took a large bite. "Mm. Cake."

July 10, 5:40 P.M.

AFTER THEY RECORDED THE INTERVIEW for *Telling Stories*, Jay Rickles said why not come to his house for supper. He wanted Kellaway to meet the family. They could open some beers and watch the show when it aired at nine. Kellaway didn't have anything else to do.

Rickles lived on Kiwi Boulevard. It wasn't a mansion. No fountain out front, no white stucco wall enclosing the property, not even a swimming pool. But it was pretty nice all the same, a big hacienda with a red Spanish-tile roof and an enormous courtyard of crushed white shells. The front steps were flanked by a pair of green copper koi statues the size of Welsh corgis.

Inside, the house was like a Tex-Mex restaurant, with lassos and bleached longhorn skulls mounted on the walls. It was crowded, too, with willowy young women in tooled-leather boots and denim skirts and squads of little kids who crashed from room to room. At first Kellaway thought Rickles must have decided to throw a party and had invited half the neighborhood. He was there for most of an hour before he gradually realized the girls with golden hair were all his daughters and the small children were his grandkids.

They rooted themselves on a couch the size of a Cadillac, done in tribal patterns, in front of a television as large as a Cadillac's hood. There was already a big steel bucket full of ice and Coronas on the coffee table, next to a dish of salt and a bowl of lime wedges. Rickles helped himself to a beer with one hand. The other snaked around the hip of a tall, leggy woman in a pair of Wranglers so tight they were close to obscene. At first glance Kellaway thought Rickles was patting one of his daughters on the butt. At second he saw that the woman next to Rickles was maybe as old as sixty, thick makeup covering the finer creases at the corners of her mouth and eyes and the yellow of her hair almost certainly a dye job. She had the toned beauty of someone like Christie Brinkley, of someone who had always been beautiful and always would be, was beautiful almost by habit.

"Is it *Mr.* Kellaway?" she asked. "Or *Deputy* Kellaway?"

Rickles cracked her rear with one hand, and she jumped away, laughing and rubbing her bottom. "You hush up, woman. You ruin everything."

"Ruining men's plans is my life's work," she said, and wandered off, swinging her hips in a provocative sort of way. Or maybe that was just how she walked.

When she'd gone, Kellaway looked at Rickles and said, "Deputy?"

The police chief's eyes glittered damply with emotion. "That's supposed to be a surprise. We're going to make you an honorary deputy next month. Give you a key to the city, too. Big ceremony. When we announce it, try and pretend you didn't know."

"Do I get my very own badge?"

"Bet your ass," Rickles said, and laughed a husky, beery laugh. "What I wonder, how come you're not a deputy for real?"

"I applied. You turned me down."

"Me?" Rickles put a hand to his chest and opened his eyes wide in stunned disbelief.

"Well. The department anyway."

"Didn't you serve in Iraq?"

"Mm-hm."

"And we turned you down? Why?"

"One position, fifty applicants, and I came up short in the melanin department."

Rickles nodded sadly. "Christ, isn't that always the story. Though, no matter how much you do to show you care about diversity, it's never enough. Did you read that hit piece the *Digest* ran, about the drama student? No? So twenty years ago, there's an APB out for a deranged African American with a knife who cut up a white couple and stole their Miata and a Hermès purse full of loot. Wife died, husband pulled through. Cops traced the Miata to a parking lot in the Black & Blue and saw a guy matching the description walking away from it, holding a knife, purse over his shoulder. They tell him to get facedown, he runs instead. He goes around the corner of a little shopping plaza— then changes his mind and turns back. When the cops come around the corner, they run smack into him. They think he's charging, and one of them blasts his black ass. Well, turned out he wasn't holding a knife. It was a CD. The Hermès purse over his shoulder? It was a Little Mermaid backpack he was carrying for a cousin of his. He was a seventeen-year-old slickster who did summer-stock theater and who was applying to the London School of Drama. He ran because he'd been wandering around opening cars, grabbing stuff, petty thievery. Basically, he died of a guilty conscience."

In his mind Kellaway shot the Muslim woman all over again. It made him angry, thinking about her, trying to figure out why the bitch had stood up, why she didn't stay still. He resented her for making him shoot her.

"Adrenaline gets pumping," Kellaway said. "It's dark. You know the guy you're hunting has already sliced some people up, that he's crazy. I don't see how you blame the cops for shooting."

"You don't, and a grand jury didn't. But it was a scandal and a heartbreak. The cop who shot the kid developed a serious drug and alcohol problem, poor guy, and later had to be fired for domestic abuse. Anyway. The cousin with the Little Mermaid backpack witnesses the shooting. Fifteen years later she's working for the *St. Possenti Digest,* and she writes this great big goddamn exposé about it. All about systemic racism in Florida policing and the reflexive tendency to protect officers who abuse the badge. Anyway. I sat down with her, gave her an interview, said all the things I had to say. I bragged on our hiring of minorities, said 1993 was literally a different century, said that it's our job to make certain the black community sees us as an ally, not an occupying power. I made sure there were nothing but black faces in the typing pool when I led her to my office. I even had our IT guy sitting at one detective's desk. I had the dude who cleans our windows at another. It was so black in there you'd think she walked into a Luther

Vandross concert instead of a police station. You do an interview like that, you got two choices. Either you say what they want you to say or you get smeared by the press for committing a thought crime. I didn't like doing it, but I got through it. You might want to remember that when she talks to *you*."

"What do you mean, when she talks to me?"

"She's on *your* ass now, partner. Aisha Lanternglass. The girl who wrote up the story of the dead drama student and who made my whole department look like the local chapter of the KKK. They've got her covering the mall story. You want to watch out for her, Kellaway. She does hate whitey."

Kellaway sipped his Corona and thought it over.

"They ever get the guy who sliced up the couple?" he asked finally. "The black dude with the knife?"

Rickles shook his head ruefully. "There was no black dude with a knife. Turned out hubby had a girlfriend. He murdered his wife, then had his honey stab him a few times to make it look like he'd been attacked as well. Then he had her drive off in the Miata and park it in the Black & Blue. We got the girlfriend on a security camera, abandoning the car in the lot." He sighed. "Shit, I wish we had more security footage of what happened in Devotion Diamonds. We've got her going in, but nothing from what went down in there. I wish we did. I know *Telling Stories* would sure as shit like to have it."

"So you can't lift it off Roger Lewis's computer?" The security footage for Devotion Diamonds fed to the big iMac in Lewis's office, and at some point the computer had toppled off the desk. Kellaway had made sure it couldn't be turned on again by giving it his boot a time or two.

Rickles wiggled one hand in a gesture that seemed to mean maybe yes, maybe no. "The tech guys think there's a chance they can rescue the hard drive, but I'll believe it when I see it." He sipped his beer and said, "Maybe if we can save it, *Telling Stories* will want to have us back on."

If the tech guys rescued the hard drive, it would show Kellaway putting a bullet through a six-month-old and his mother, then using Becki Kolbert's gun to kill Bobby Lutz. Kellaway hoped that if such a thing did come to pass, he had another gun by then. He could imagine quite calmly sitting on the toilet in the master bathroom and putting the snub nose of a .38 against the roof of his mouth while cops shouted in the next room. He could do it. He knew he could do it—swallow a bullet. Better to die his way than to live life mocked by the tabloids, loathed by the public, and separated from his child. To say nothing of what would happen to him if he wound up in prison.

The thought of sitting on one toilet brought to mind another, and he said, "When do you think I'll be able to get back into the mall? I'd like to collect some of my things. And maybe . . . I don't know. Walk the scene."

"Give it a week. After they open again. We'll walk the scene together, if you want. I'd like that myself. See it again, through your eyes."

Kellaway wondered if Rickles was going to move in with him, if he should buy bunk beds.

When Kellaway looked around, a perfect ten was standing in front of him, a blonde who had to be at least six feet tall, wearing a flower-print pencil skirt and a satiny white silk blouse and a straw cowboy hat. She held the hands of two small children, one on either side of her. One of them was a profoundly ugly fat girl with an upturned piggy nose, her pink Hannah Montana shirt riding up her bulging belly. The boy looked like the Mini-Me version of Jay Rickles, a towhead with narrow blue eyes and a stubborn, mulish expression on his face. Their mother was so tall they had to stretch their arms up to reach her hands.

"Mr. Kellaway," said the perfect ten. "I'm Maryanne Winslow, Jay's daughter, and my children would like to say something to you."

"Thank you," the children recited together.

"What for?" Maryanne said, pulling one arm, then the other.

The girl with the porcine features said, "For saving our lives," and began to pick her nose.

The boy said, "For shooting the bad guy."

"They were in the mall," Rickles said, turning his head and giving Kellaway a watery-eyed look of wonder and gratitude. "Bullets flying a couple hundred feet away from them. They were on the carousel."

"Oh, Dad," Maryanne said. "We didn't even get inside. We were *going* to ride the carousel, but when we reached the doors, a security guard sent us back to our car. It was all over by then. We missed the action by ten minutes."

Rickles told Kellaway, "But for the grace of God," and held out his bottle. They clinked longnecks.

"What'd you shoot her with?" the little boy asked Kellaway.

Maryanne jerked his arm. "Merritt! Rude!"

"A .327. Ruger Federal," said Kellaway. "You know about guns?"

The boy said, "I got a Browning Buck Mark .22."

"Merritt! You do not 'got a Browning Buck Mark.'"

"I do too!"

"You *have* a Browning Buck Mark," Maryanne said, and rolled her eyes at her son's disgraceful indifference to proper grammar.

"You like guns?" Kellaway asked, leaning forward, resting his elbows on his knees.

Merritt nodded.

"I have a boy only a bit younger than you. He likes guns, too. Sometimes we go fishing together, and then afterward we'll walk along the beach and find bottles to shoot. Once we found a smelly old pair of boots and shot them. We were trying to make them dance."

"Did you?" Merritt asked.

Kellaway shook his head. "No. We just knocked them over."

Merritt stared at him with his deep blue eyes for another moment, as if in a trance, then jerked his head up and looked at his mom. "Can I play Xbox now?"

"Merritt Winslow! So rude!"

"It's all right. Old people are boring," Kellaway said. "My own son told me so once."

Maryanne Winslow mouthed the words "Thank you" and walked the children away, still holding their arms up over their heads so they had to skip and hurry to stay on their feet.

Rickles sighed and leaned back into the couch. He was staring absently at the TV when he said, "I keep meaning to ask you about the gun."

"Hm?" Kellaway asked. The back of his neck prickled.

"Just I did a search, and you don't have any guns registered to you in this state." Rickles scratched an eyebrow, didn't look at him. "That might be a problem, you know."

"Oh. It's registered to Falcon Security. It's their gun. You want me to see if I can get someone to find the paper on it? They're based in Texas. It might be registered there, or maybe—"

But Rickles didn't care and wasn't listening. He swatted Kellaway's shoulder in excitement and leaned forward. On the TV there was a shot of the Miracle Falls Mall, the entrance to its parking lot blocked by a police cruiser.

"It's the new national normal," intoned a deep male voice. "You know the story. A disgruntled employee walks into her workplace with a gun and a heart full of malice and begins to kill. But what happened next, at this shopping center in St. Possenti, Florida, will surprise and inspire you."

"Here we go," said Rickles. "I'll tell you what, boy. I do like to see myself on TV. Hey. Did you get a call from Bill O'Reilly's people?"

"Yeah. And *20/20.*"

"We going to do them, too?"

"I guess."

"Good," Rickles said, and sighed. "I have days when I think about being killed in the line of duty, and you know what haunts me? The idea that I'll miss all that sweet, heartbreaking coverage when I'm gone."

"What if you die in your own bed at seventy-five after an early-morning screw?"

"I'd rather get blown away," Rickles said, and took another pull on his beer. "I'd prefer to die a legend, but I doubt I'll be that lucky."

"I'll keep my fingers crossed for you," Kellaway said.

July 11, 10:00 A.M.

WHEN JAY RICKLES TOLD KELLAWAY that he had once stocked his office with black faces to put a black journalist at ease, he was guilty of exaggeration. He hadn't really planted his window washer at a desk and told him to pretend to be a detective. The window washer was Cambodian and wasn't even working that day.

But it *was* true that Shane Wolff, an IT guy from Atlantic Datastream, had been in the office on the morning Lanternglass arrived to interview Chief Rickles about the tragic death of an unarmed black youth in 1993 at the hands of the police. Shane was usually at the St. Possenti Police Department two or three times a week, to rebuild their office network, which was still improbably running Windows XP. And it was also true that Rickles had planted Shane at an empty detective's desk, close to the front door, so Aisha Lanternglass would spot a black man in a tie as soon as she walked in.

At the time Lanternglass had nodded to Wolff, and he had mildly nodded back, and from that moment on they had studiously ignored each other. She knew him right away, of course, would've known him even if he didn't also service the computers at the *Digest*. Wolff and Colson had gone to school together, had dated some of the same girls. But it wouldn't have served to acknowledge him openly. As it happened, Shane Wolff's frequent jobs for the St. Possenti police were his highest-paying gigs. First the cops paid him—and then Aisha did, if he came across anything she could use.

On Thursday, Wolff showed up at the *Digest* just as Aisha was finishing her morning workout. She was running steps, two flights up and then back, forty-eight steps in a complete circuit. She kept her free weights tucked in the shadows under the staircase. There was no space for them in the four-room apartment she shared with Dorothy, and Tim Chen didn't mind.

"How many times do you go up and down?" Shane asked her, his voice echoing in the concrete stairwell.

She trotted to the bottom of the steps. "Fifty rotations. Almost done. Five left. Are you crying?"

Shane Wolff leaned into the open metal door that led to the parking lot. He didn't look like a tech nerd. He was six foot three, maybe two hundred pounds, his neck as thick as his head. His eyes were bloodshot and streaming and tragic.

"It's the smoke. I drove through a big cloud of it on the way here. I've never used my windshield wipers to brush away sparks before. They had me over to the PD yesterday to scrub the hard drives in Vice. About once a week, they go looking for online porn and find Russian malware instead. Anyway, while I was over there, I saw the ballistics report on the mall thing."

She started running upstairs again. Her calves throbbed. "Hold that thought. I'll be back."

"Hey," he said. "Is that good for your glutes? All those stairs? Must be."

She hesitated, almost missed a step, kept going, didn't answer him.

Tim Chen was waiting for her at the top of the steps. He had pushed open the *Digest* office's fire door and sat on the landing, leaning against it, with Aisha's battered old MacBook in his lap. He was editing her piece.

"I gotta cut these two paragraphs at the end," he told her in a remote, distracted sort of way. "You're five hundred words over, and this stuff isn't important."

"The hell I'm five hundred words over." She slowed at the landing, put her hands on her knees, and inhaled deeply. Lanternglass craned her head to see what he was cutting. "Oh, come *on*, Tim. Don't cut that. Why would you cut that?"

"You make it sound like Kellaway got kicked out of the army. He didn't get kicked out. He served his country for a full tour in Iraq. Then he came home and stopped a mass shooting."

"He was AdSep'd, administratively separated. That's kicked out."

"Don't you have terrible things to do to your body?" Tim asked.

"Jesus," she said, and trotted away down the steps.

Wolff watched her approach, his reddened eyes streaming. He looked like a mourner at the edge of a grave.

"Okay," she said. "Give it to me. 'Sources close to the investigation say . . .'"

"Becki Kolbert shot Roger Lewis three times with a .357 Mag. The first one nailed him in the chest while he was facing her. He turned to run, and she tagged him in the back and the left buttock. At that point Becki Kolbert probably tried to leave the office and was surprised by Mrs. Haswar. The way it looks, she slew the baby and Yasmin both with just one shot, right to the center mass."

"'Slew'? That's a very Old Testament way of putting it," she said. "Maybe you should be a writer."

"Shortly after Kolbert killed the Haswars, Mr. Kellaway entered Devotion Diamonds. She retreated into the office, they exchanged words, boom, boom, he fires two shots. One missed, the other caught her in the left lung. She went down, and he turned away to attend to Mrs. Haswar. Bob Lutz walked in and approached the shooter to see if she was still alive. Unfortunately for him, she was. Becki Kolbert shot him right between the eyes, military precision. At that point Kellaway disarmed her, but it's pretty much over anyhow. She bled out shortly after Emergency Services arrived on the scene."

Lanternglass was running up the stairs by then and was too out of breath to reply. She climbed twenty-four steps to where her editor sat on the concrete landing.

"You almost done?" Tim Chen asked. "You're making me tired, and I'm only watching."

"Why are you cutting the stuff about his military service?" she gasped.

He read her own article back to her: "'Kellaway may have missed his chance at heroic distinction in the Gulf—his tour of duty was troubled, and he did not receive an honorable discharge—but following the events at the Miracle Falls he'll be celebrated for his service at last.'

Why would you write that? His army record a decade ago isn't relevant. You're taking a perfectly satisfying feel-good story and stapling on this strange catty ending."

"Catty?"

"I was going to say bitchy, but it isn't politically correct."

"He was dismissed from the army for excessive use of force as an MP. He routinely drew his firearm in nonthreatening situations and once punched a handcuffed prisoner. Look at the record. This guy is *not* a war hero, no matter how they made it sound on *Telling Stories* the other night."

"Out of curiosity," Tim Chen said. "This guy Kellaway punched, back when he was an MP? The handcuffed prisoner? Was he a black guy?"

"Oh, for fuck's sake," she said, and ran back down the stairs to Wolff.

Wolff dabbed at the corners of his eyes with a white handkerchief. "I can show you some good stretches."

"For what?" she said.

"For your glutes. You want to stretch them out before you abuse them like that."

She slowed again as she approached the bottom of the steps. "You said something funny a minute ago. You said, 'The way it looks,' she slew the baby and Yasmin Haswar with one shot."

"Yeah, and you made fun of me."

"No, hang on. What do you mean, '*The way it looks*'?"

He wiped under his eyes. "That's the only theory that fits the facts. They're still digging around for the bullet. It went through a mirror and the drywall behind and disappeared into the bowels of the Miracle Falls Mall."

"Slew. Bowels. Glutes. You're full of interesting words, Shane. Can I make a suggestion?"

She started back up the stairs.

"What?"

"Verbally admiring a woman's glutes isn't the right way to lean into asking her out. Say something about her laugh."

She was twenty steps up when he shouted after her, "You'd have to laugh for me to say something nice about it. I work with what I have."

Chen was still sitting there at the top of the steps.

"Yeah. All right," Lanternglass said. "When he was with the military police, Kellaway handcuffed a black private in front of his girlfriend and then punched him. And *last year* he pulled a gun on a black teenager who he thought was stealing from the mall. Turned out the kid was an out-of-uniform employee moving stock from one store to another. And what matters here *isn't* that they were both black. What matters is that Kellaway has a history of going Rambo, acting violently without thought."

"There's nothing in the article about him harassing employees."

She jogged in place in front of him. "No. My source asked me not to print that story. Point is, I don't think it would be the worst thing for this paper to at least *hint* at the possibility that Randall Kellaway is predisposed to using excessive force. Just in case the cops recover the security footage on the conveniently destroyed iMac and we find out he shot Becki Kolbert when she was trying to surrender."

"Like the way Colson got shot?"

She quit jogging and gripped her knees and lowered her head. When she inhaled, it felt like there was a cactus in her chest where her heart belonged, needles bristling against her lungs.

"Jesus," she said. "That's a low fucking blow, Tim."

"Is it?" he said calmly. "You hear this story about Randall Kellaway harassing a black kid. You hear about him assaulting a black soldier in the army. Now he's a hero and he's got Jay Rickles hugging him on TV and calling him the good guy with a gun. If Kellaway's story came apart, you could humiliate the both of them. You could take out two with one shot."

"No, Tim. Words aren't bullets. When Yasmin Haswar and her baby hit the floor, *that* was two taken out with one shot."

Tim Chen firmly and forcefully tapped two keys. One of them was Delete. "Give me a reason to trash his military record and we'll put it in the very next story. But your personal issues don't count as a reason."

She was surprised at the sudden deep stab of hurt in her stomach. It was on her lips to say, *Fuck you*, but she didn't say it. It was on her lips to say, *That's so fucking unfair, Tim,* but she didn't say that either. She turned and ran away, ran back down the steps, because the thought was in her mind that it wasn't unfair at all, and maybe if she moved quickly enough, she could leave her shame behind, up on the top landing with her friend and editor.

When she got to the bottom of the stairs, Shane Wolff said, "Smoke is bothering you, too, huh?"

"What?"

"Your eyes," he said, and pointed. "You're crying, too. Want my hankie?"

She snatched it away from him and wiped her face. "Thank you."

"I know a pretty good rooftop bar," he said. "It's up five stories. I could take the elevator and you could run, and we could meet at the top for a beer. It'd be great exercise."

"It's hard to go out when you have an eight-year-old," she said. "I can afford to pay you for the ballistics report or I can pay for a sitter, but I can't pay for both."

"So? The report's on me, then. The beers, too."

She very gently punched him in the chest. And turned. And started back up the stairs. "That's sweet, Shane, but I don't want to take advantage. And stop staring at my glutes."

Lanternglass was a dozen steps up when she paused and looked back. Shane Wolff stood in the open door to the parking lot, covering his eyes to shield them from the sight of her glutes.

"So . . . wait," she called down to him. She stopped running, stood there with her fists balled on her hips. "Four shots when she killed Lewis and the Haswars. A pause. Then two more when Kellaway enters the store and shoots her. Another pause. Then one more, when Becki Kolbert executes Bob Lutz. Seven shots in . . . what? Five minutes?"

"That's about it," he said.

"Huh," she said, turning to climb on.

When she got to the top of the stairs, Tim Chen was still sitting there, back to the open fire door, holding her laptop.

"I want to apologize," he said. "For what I said a minute ago."

"Don't apologize," she said. "Just stick it back in."

He sighed heavily. "I can't think of one good reason to even play footsie with defaming the guy."

"How about this?" she said. "The cops say Kolbert fired four times, three into Rog Lewis, one into Yasmin and her baby. A minute later Kellaway enters the store and fires twice, hits her once, misses once. Finally, about a minute after that, there's the last shot, the one that kills Bob Lutz. That's what the forensics report tells us."

"Okay."

"But there's an eyewitness—really an *ear*witness—who heard the whole thing. And he said it was *three* shots, a pause, then *two*, a pause, then *two* more."

"So? Your earwitness was scared to death and got it wrong. Happens all the time."

"He was texting his girlfriend. He texted her after each burst of gun-fire. He was sure: three, two, two. Not four, two, one."

"I don't even know what that means."

"It means there was *another* shot after the one that killed Bob Lutz. Explain that."

Tim Chen couldn't. He sat there tapping one finger against the edge of the laptop. "Did your earwitness show you the text messages, prov-ing he heard what he says he heard, when he heard it? Did you *see* the time stamps?"

"No," she admitted. "I had to pick Dorothy up from tennis camp. I didn't get a chance to look at the texts. But I'm sure he'd share them if I asked."

Tim nodded and said, "Okay. Well. That might be interesting. But I don't see what it has to do with Randall Kellaway's piss-poor military record."

"Nothing."

"So why denigrate his service at all? Even casually?"

"To fuck with him and see what happens. You can find out a lot about someone by fucking with them."

"Yeah? You learn that in journalism school, Aisha?"

"That ain't J-school, brother," she said. "That's old-school."

July 12, 6:13 P.M.

THEY TAPED FOR *THE O'REILLY FACTOR* at the same local TV studio where they'd recorded their bits for *Telling Stories* and *20/20*. When Rickles and Kellaway came out into the warm, smoky evening, Aisha Lanternglass was waiting for them. She cut them off before they could get to Rickles's pickup.

"Hey, guys," she said. "What do you say about giving your local paper ten minutes? Or do I gotta have a TV show for you to talk to me?"

She grinned to flash her very white teeth, razzing them, just one of the guys. She was trim and fit in a pair of blue jeans and a sleeveless black top, strappy sandals. She'd brought her daughter with her, which was cheap manipulation in Kellaway's opinion. The little girl sat on the hood of the world's crappiest Passat. Her daughter wore a crocheted beanie with a cat's face on it, gray cat ears poking up. The kid ignored the grown-ups, leafing through the pages of a picture book.

Jay Rickles beamed, creases deepening in his seamed face. He hitched his belt up. "Aisha! I got your voice mail. Getting back to you has been on the top of my list of things to do for about three days now. You want my secretary to give you a ring, see if we can pencil something in?"

"That's great," she said. "If you could give me ten minutes right now, and then if we could follow up in a couple of days with a longer sit-down, that would be perfect."

Rickles glanced at Kellaway. "We better give her her ten minutes. I'm afraid if I try to climb into the truck, she'll tackle me."

Kellaway found it difficult to look her directly in the face. His insides were hot, sick and inflamed. He had heard all about her article, trashing his military service first thing in the morning. They'd hashed it out on the morning news shows.

"New details have emerged about Rand Kellaway, the hero of last week's Miracle Falls Shooting," said the newsboy, a kid who looked like he ought to be bagging groceries, not blabbing on TV. "The *St. Possenti Digest* is reporting today that Mr. Kellaway was released from the U.S. military in 2003 after repeated allegations that he was guilty of using excessive force in his time as an MP. Gun-control activists have already seized on the piece to argue that Kellaway escalated the situation by entering with a loaded . . ."

Later Kellaway found a wrinkled copy of the *Digest* in the green room at the TV studio and read the article for himself. There was nothing new in the whole story until the last couple of paragraphs, where they made him sound like a Third World torturer instead of a soldier. A postage-stamp-size photograph of Aisha Lanternglass ran alongside the piece, grinning just the way she was grinning now.

His first thought was that George would hear all about it. Holly had e-mailed a couple days before to say that George never missed the local news now, watched the morning show before school and the evening show at dinner to see what they were going to say about his father today. Now George would hear that the army had thrown his father out because he couldn't control his temper. George would hear that his father wasn't good enough to serve his country. It had been all Kellaway could do to maintain his composure during the Bill O'Reilly taping.

The parking lot in front of the local studio was a wide expanse of brand-new blacktop, soft in the lingering heat of the day. The sun was still up, but it was impossible to see it. The horizon was an ocher thunderhead of smoke. Lanternglass held her phone out to record their conversation, stabbing it at Kellaway like a knife.

"Mr. Kellaway, it's been almost a week since the shooting. I think what most of our readers want to know is—how are you doing?"

"Just fine. No trouble sleeping. Ready to go back to work."

"When do you think that might be?"

"Mall's opening tomorrow. I'll be there for the first shift."

"That's dedication."

"It's called a work ethic," he said.

"I wonder if you've had a chance to speak with the families of the be-reaved. Have you been in touch with Mr. Haswar, Yasmin's husband? Or Bob Lutz's parents?"

"Why would I do that? Just to say I'm sorry I didn't save the people you love?" Biting off his words a little.

Jay Rickles patted his shoulder. "There'll be a time to reach out to them, for sure. Maybe after they've had a chance to begin the healing process—and after Mr. Kellaway has had a chance to heal himself."

Kellaway thought there was something cautionary in the way Rick-les was petting him like a dog. *Down, boy*. He shrugged so Rickles would stop doing it.

"I'm sure after what you've been through, your own family has been a source of strength," Lanternglass said. "You have a son, yes?"

"Yes."

"And he lives with his mother? Where is that? I'd love to know a little more about your family situation. I gather you're separated. Are you seeking a divorce? I checked the county records—"

"Did you? Looking around for a little dirt? Who told you to start digging into the separation?"

The little girl, over on the hood of the car, lifted her chin and stared at them, her attention drawn by Kellaway's raised voice.

"No one. We always talk to the family after something like this."

"Not this time. Stay away from my wife and my boy."

"Mom?" asked the little girl sitting on the Passat, her voice queru-lous and uneasy.

Lanternglass darted a look back at her, waved. "Just another minute, Dorothy." She regarded Kellaway again, smiling in a puzzled sort of way, and said softly, "Hey. We're all pals here. Let's not upset my kid with a lot of shouting."

"Did you worry you might upset *my* kid when you smeared my mil-itary record in your article this morning? Did that thought ever cross your mind?"

Rickles wasn't smiling anymore. He patted Kellaway's shoulder again and said, "All right, now. All right. Rand has been under a lot of strain. Aisha, I'm going to ask you to show some consideration and go easy on him."

She nodded, took a step back. She wasn't smiling anymore either. "Okay. Sorry. I know it's been an exhausting week. Jay, have your office call me. We'll make an appointment to talk about the police response."

"Will do," Rickles said. He had Kellaway by the arm now, gripping him just above the elbow, and began to steer him toward the truck.

"Oh, hey," Lanternglass said. "One more thing, while I've got you. The security department at Miracle Falls Mall isn't supplied with guns. Was your firearm your own personal weapon?"

Kellaway knew a trap when he heard it, knew she wanted him on record admitting he owned a firearm in defiance of the restraining order.

"Wouldn't you like it if it was?"

His stomach hurt like cancer.

As the two men drove out of the parking lot, they passed Lanternglass, sitting on the hood of her Passat, rubbing her daughter's back and staring at the truck. Eyes narrowed in speculation. Rickles pulled out so fast the rear tires spit pebbles. He accelerated north up the highway, toward St. Possenti.

"The hell was all that about, partner?" Rickles said. For the first time ever, he sounded clipped and a little cross.

"My kid watches the news morning, noon, and night to hear the latest about his old man. She made it sound like I left the army in disgrace, and he's going to hear that."

"He's also going to hear about you getting made special deputy soon enough. Lanternglass is a rinky-dink reporter for a rinky-dink local paper. Most of what she writes is there to fill space between ads and wedding announcements. But you go making a lot of smoke, she's going to think there's fire. Speaking of," he said, scowling. They drove into a thick, fluffy cloud of it. The smoke burned Kellaway's eyes.

They drove another half a mile, and then Rickles said, "Is there anything I need to know about that gun?"

"Yeah," Kellaway said. "If I didn't have it, there'd be a whole lot more people dead."

Rickles didn't reply. They went on in an uncomfortable silence for one minute, and then two, and finally Rickles said something obscene under his breath and turned on the radio. They listened to news the rest of the way back, didn't say a word to each other. Bombs in Iraq. Sanctions against Iran. And in bad news for the firefighters trying to tamp down the Ocala blaze, the wind was shifting toward the east. With moderate gales expected, the fire now endangered homes and businesses on the western edge of St. Possenti.

More on that story, the anchor promised, as it developed.

6:27 P.M.

"Are we going?" Dorothy asked. "Or are we just going to sit here?"

"Just sit here for a minute," Lanternglass said. "Mama might need to make a call."

They idled in the car in front of the TV station with the windows down and the music low. Lanternglass went over it again in her mind, playing back what Kellaway had said and how he'd said it.

Kellaway hadn't wanted to look at her, but when he did—when he met her eyes—she'd felt him hating her. She had wanted to fuck with him, wanted to see how he'd respond. Now she knew.

What he made her think of was a gun: a big cocked pistol, the kind of thing Wyatt Earp carried around. In her mind Lanternglass pictured this enormous cannon with the hammer pulled back, resting on the passenger seat of a car as the vehicle sped along a bumpy, rutted dirt road. When the car jolted, the gun shimmied and slid a little farther across the seat, toward the edge. Any fool could see what would happen if it was knocked down. It would go off. She had the nasty idea that if Kellaway were knocked down, he would go off, too.

She'd asked if it was his gun, and he'd said, *Wouldn't you like it if it was?* Why would she like it?

"Mom! I have to pee!"

"You always have to pee. You got a bladder about the size of a walnut," Lanternglass said, and she picked up her phone and dialed Richard Watkins at the state police.

Watkins answered on the second ring, "Flagler County Sheriff's Department, this is Richard Watkins, Victim Services, how can I help you?"

"Richard Watkins! It's Aisha Lanternglass, *St. Possenti Digest*."

She had done a piece on Watkins the year before, after he started a trauma support group for children, busing the kids to Orlando so they could swim with dolphins. Aisha thought it was sweet (and big-time clickbait), but Dorothy disapproved, said the dolphins probably needed a trauma support group of their own, since they were prisoners who had to entertain tourists if they wanted to eat.

"Hey," Watkins said. "If you're calling about the mall shooting, you wanna stick to St. Possenti PD. That one is theirs, not ours. And if you're calling about the fire, hang up, drive to your office, and pack all your junk before that place goes up in smoke. The blaze is turning your way. There might be an evacuation order issued tomorrow morning."

"No shit?" she asked.

"No shit."

"Ugh."

Dorothy kicked the back of her seat. "Mom!"

Lanternglass said, "Hey, Watkins, I'm actually calling to see if you know who at the sheriff's department serves papers. Divorce, subpoenas, that kind of thing."

"We got a few people do that, but Lauren Acosta is our head process server. If you want to find out about someone who had papers served on them, either she did it herself or she can tell you who did."

"That's great. Can I talk to her?"

"I can give you her cell. I don't know if she'll answer. She's in Alaska. She's doing a cruise with her sisters. They're taking pictures of icebergs and reindeer and other shit you could get frostbite from just thinking about. She's got a North Pole fetish. In December she goes out to deliver subpoenas wearing a Santa cap."

"Wow," Lanternglass said. "Nothing gets a guy into the Christmas spirit like a woman in a Santa cap handing him divorce papers. Yeah, please, let me have her number. I just want to have a quick word if she has a minute."

Dorothy kicked the back of her mother's seat again just as she thanked Watkins and hung up.

"You want to cut it out?" Lanternglass said.

"You want me to pee all over the backseat?"

"There's a McDonald's up the road. We can use the restroom there." She put the Passat in gear and made a 180 so the car was pointed toward the street.

"Somewhere else," Dorothy said. She plucked at one ear of her kitten cap. "McDonald's falls short of my ethical standards. Meat is murder."

"You want to learn about murder," Lanternglass said, "kick the back of my seat one more time."

8:11 P.M.

Rickles took them to his hacienda on Kiwi Boulevard, where Kellaway had left his car. The police chief told Kellaway to swing back by the house tomorrow, just before eleven, and they could go to the mall together.

"I can meet you there," Kellaway said. "That'd be easier."

He dropped out of the truck, his shoes crunching on crushed shells.

"We better go together. For the candle-lighting ceremony. The newspeople want to photograph your return to the mall." There was going to be a candle-lighting ceremony in the food court out in front of the carousel, to honor the fallen. Afterward the mall was celebrating a special Day of Remembrance, with 20 to 40 percent off selected items in every store.

"Who cares what the newspeople want?" Kellaway stood in the courtyard, peering up into Rickles's truck.

Rickles slung one arm over the steering wheel and leaned across the passenger seat toward Kellaway. He was smiling, but his eyes were cool, almost unfriendly. "*You* ought to. Lanternglass is a tiresome little race activist, kind of person who believes every cop can't wait to take a fire hose to a crowd of black people. But she's nobody's fool, and you just about begged her to go poking around in your past. I don't know what kind of embarrassing shit you've done, but I'm sure I'll be reading all about it by the end of the week, if not sooner. You got any sense at all, you'll give yourself a good shave first thing tomorrow morning, slap on your best cologne, and be ready to light candles with me at eleven A.M. The press is lazy. If you give them a feel-good story on a silver platter, they'll eat it. And you want to keep them well fed. Otherwise they might turn their forks and knives on you, *capisce*?"

Kellaway didn't want to go back to the mall with Rickles. He wanted to get there ahead of him, ahead of everyone, early enough to visit the little employees' bathroom behind Lids. He wanted to argue, to say— truthfully—that he had never once arrived at work as late as 11:00 A.M. But then he observed again the icy way Rickles was watching him, above a thin, no-longer-friendly smile, and he nodded.

"Sounds good," he said, and slammed the door of the truck.

He pulled out of the driveway in his Prius, hooked left when he should've turned right. He didn't want to go home, didn't want to see the TV vans parked out front, didn't want the TV people to see *him*. Instead he turned the car out of town, nosing into the smoke and gathering night.

Jim Hirst's farmhouse was dark, an angular arrangement of black boxes against a sky the color of cinders. The only light in the whole place was the television. It cast a sickly blue glow, visible through the holes where the windows were missing on the western side of the house. The big sheets of plastic draped over that end of the building rippled in the gusting wind, making slow, heavy, ominous slapping sounds.

Kellaway got out of his car and stood beside it and listened to the tidal shush of the wind. He couldn't hear the TV. Sound had to be off.

He started toward the house, his feet crunching in the gravel—and then stopped moving, froze to listen. He had heard footsteps, he was almost sure of it. It seemed to him there was a man on the other side of his car. He could see him in his peripheral vision. Kellaway found he was afraid to look at him directly, couldn't will himself to turn his head.

It was Jim Hirst—Jim, who had not walked for more than a decade. Jim walking easy in the night, ten feet away, on the other side of the car. He would know Jim anywhere, knew him by the way his arms hung at his sides. He recognized the curve of his bare skull against the smoky night.

"Jim!" Kellaway cried, in a voice he hardly recognized as his own. "Jim, that you?"

Jim took a slow, heavy step toward him, and Kellaway had to shut his eyes, could not bear to see the man in the darkness at the edge of the road. His fear drove the breath out of him. He had not been half as scared when he'd crawled into Devotion Diamonds toward a woman with a gun.

He heard Jim take another step toward him and forced himself to open his eyes.

His eyes had adjusted to the dark by then, and he saw in a moment that what he'd taken for a man was a stunted black mangrove. The curve he'd imagined to be Jim Hirst's bare skull was nothing more than a smooth knob where a branch had broken away long ago.

The plastic hanging off the house flapped heavily again, sounding like a man taking slow, heavy steps.

Kellaway exhaled. A crazy thing to think, that Jim was walking with him in the dark. And yet even as he continued toward the house, he could not quite escape the feeling of having company. The night was in restless motion, branches flinging themselves frantically back and forth. The grass hissed. The wind was rising.

He rapped at the doorframe and called for Jim, called for Mary, but he was not surprised when no one answered him. For some reason he had not expected a reply. He let himself in.

Beneath the campfire smell that was on everything, Kellaway caught the odor of stale, flat beer and urine. He flicked on the light in the foyer.

"Hello?"

He looked into the living room. Monster trucks were racing on the TV, lunging over great muddy hills. No one there.

"Jim?" he called again. He peeked into the kitchen. Empty.

By then he knew what he was going to find before he found it. He could not have said why. Maybe he'd even known out in the driveway, when he sensed Jim close to him in the darkness. He did not want to look into the master bedroom but couldn't help himself.

The lights were off. Jim was lying on the bed, his wheelchair parked beside it. Kellaway clicked on the light, but only for a moment. He didn't want to look. He flipped the switch, and it was dark again.

After a moment Kellaway walked over to the bed and sat down in the wheelchair. The room was fragrant with the sharp copper reek of blood. It was a filthy place to die: diapers stuffed into a plastic trash pail, beer cans on the floor, orange pill bottles and pornographic magazines on the bedside table. Just a few feet from the bed was a closet. Kellaway switched on the closet light. That made it possible for him to see, while casting a more merciful glow on the man under the sheet.

Jim Hirst with a .44 in his mouth and his brains sprayed all over the headboard.

He'd died with some of his birthday scotch left, the bottle still a quarter full. Jim had set it on the pillow next to him, as if he knew Kellaway would be by later and wanted to return it to him. He'd clothed himself in the jacket of his dress uniform, his Purple Heart pinned to his breast. He hadn't bothered with a shirt, though, and the sheets were pulled up to just below the big slope of his belly.

When Kellaway reached across Jim's body for the scotch, his sleeve brushed a sheet of ruled paper. He caught it, sat back, held it up to read it by the closet light. He was not at all surprised to see that the note was addressed to him.

> Rand—
>
> Hey, brother. If you're the one who finds me—and I hope you are—I'm sorry about the mess. I just couldn't hang in there anymore.
>
> About three months ago, I dropped in on my doc for a routine checkup, and he didn't like the sound of my chest. The X-ray spotted a shadow in my right lung. He said we should follow up. I said I'd think about it.

And I did think about it, and what I thought is: *Fuck it.* I can't stand the smell of my own piss anymore, there's nothing good on TV, and Mary's gone. In a way she's been gone for almost a year. She was still spending the days here, so she could look after me, but she'd take off at bedtime to visit a guy she met at work. She spends most nights with him, and when she comes home, I can smell it on her. I can smell she's been fucking him. Couple of days ago, she made it official, told me it was time for her to move out.

No one ought to live this way. Sometimes I put the gun in my mouth and I'm surprised how good it feels. How much I like the taste. I've eaten Mary's pussy a thousand times, and I'll tell you what, I'd rather go down on a .44.

It's like that joke for teasing vegetarians: If God didn't want us to eat animals, he shouldn't of made 'em so tasty. If Colt didn't want us to eat a pistol, they shouldn't of made gun oil so tasty.

I think it was what happened at the mall, finally made me brave enough to do this thing. When it mattered, you had the balls to stand up and put a bullet where you knew it could do some good. You were ready to die to stop something that needed stopping. And that's how I feel, too, man. I can't live like this anymore. It needs to stop, and I need to be brave enough to stop it. To put a bullet where it can do some good.

I couldn't of done this if I had to figure out how to hang myself or if I had to cut my wrists and bleed out slow. I know I couldn't. I'd lose my nerve at the last minute. My brain is my enemy. Thank God there's a way to switch it off quick.

Oh, hey, if you want any of my weapons, they're all yours. I know you'll appreciate them and take care of them. Ha ha ha why don't you test them out on Mary! You make it look like I killed her in a murder-suicide, and I'll gay-marry you in heaven.

Not being gay at all when I say I love you, Rand. You were the only person who ever came to visit me. You were the only person who cared. We had some times, didn't we?
Best,
Jim Hirst

Earlier, when Kellaway was outside, it had seemed to him that Jim was close, that his old friend was somehow, impossibly, walking alongside him. Now he felt Jim near him again. He wasn't in the bed. That was just ruined meat and thickening, cooling blood. Kellaway thought he could see Jim at the edge of his vision, just outside the doorway, a big, dark shape lurking in the corridor.

Before, the idea of Jim walking alongside him had frightened him, but now it didn't bother Kellaway at all. He was instead comforted by the notion.

"It's all right, brother," he said to Jim. "It's all right now."

He folded the note and put it in his pocket. He uncorked the scotch and had a swallow. It blazed inside him.

For the first time since the morning of the mall shooting, he felt calm, centered. He was sure, if their positions had been reversed, he would've shot himself years and years before, but he was glad Jim got there eventually.

He did not think it would be best to be the person who discovered the body. Let Mary find him. Or Jim's sister. Or anyone. If the press connected him with yet another gunshot victim . . . well, what had Rickles told him? They'd make a meal out of him for sure.

But Kellaway was in no rush to leave. No one was coming by Jim Hirst's house at nearly ten in the evening. No one was going to bother the two of them. It was good scotch, and Kellaway had slept on Jim's couch before.

And besides: Before he left in the morning, he could step into the garage and have a look at Jim's guns.

9:32 P.M.

She heard her cell phone ringing and kissed Dorothy on the nose, stepped out of her daughter's dark bedroom and into the hall. She got it on the third ring, didn't recognize the number.

"Lanternglass," she said. "*Possenti Digest*. What's up?"

"I don't know!" called a merry voice with a faint Latin accent through the hiss of a signal bouncing off a satellite a third of the way around the world. "You called me. Lauren Acosta, sheriff's department. *Whoo!*" That *whoo!* didn't seem to be directed at her. Other people were *whoo*-ing in the background.

"Thanks for returning my call. You're in Alaska?"

"Yeah! We've got whales breaching here! *Whoo!*" Off on the other end of the line, from up in the Arctic Circle, Lanternglass heard yells and scattered applause and a sound like someone playing ugly notes on a tuba.

"I hate to interrupt your vacation. Do you want to watch your whales and call me another time?"

"No, I can talk and still admire a thirty-ton sexy beast doing back-flips."

"What kind of whales?" asked Dorothy. She had crept to her bed-room door and stood holding the doorframe, staring into the hall, her eyes glittering at the bottom of dark hollows. She was wearing a red-and-white-striped nightcap that looked like it had been swiped from Waldo.

"None of your business," Lanternglass said. "Get back in bed."

"What did you say?" Acosta asked.

"Sorry. I was speaking to my daughter. She's excited about your whales. What kind?"

"Humpbacks. A pod of eighteen."

"Humpbacks," Lanternglass repeated. "Now, scoot."

"I have to pee," Dorothy announced primly, and sashayed past her mother, down the hall, and into the bathroom. She clapped the door shut behind her.

"Lauren, I'm calling about Randall Kellaway. You've probably heard—"

"Oh, *that* guy."

Lanternglass stiffened, felt a curious crawling sensation up her spine, as if someone had breathed on the nape of her neck.

"You know him? Did you serve papers on him?"

"Yeah, I delivered the restraining order. I had to collect up about half his arsenal. My partner, Paulie, got the rest out of his house. Guy owned a fully automatic Uzi. He drove around with it! You know what kind of person drives around with an Uzi in his car? The evil henchman in a James Bond movie. What's up with Kellaway? I hope he didn't shoot anyone."

Lanternglass leaned against the wall. "Holy shit. You don't know."

"Know what? Oh, no," Acosta said, all the pleasant hilarity draining from her voice. In the background someone blew that awful note on a tuba again. "Please tell me he didn't kill his wife. Or his little boy."

"Why . . . why would you think that?"

"That's why we took the guns. He had a bad habit of pointing them at people in his family. This one time his wife took their son over to her sister's house to watch a movie. She left a note for him, but it fell off the fridge, so Kellaway didn't find it when he got back from work. He began to think maybe she took off on him. When she finally got home, Kellaway pulled his little boy up into his lap and asked her if she knew what he'd do if she ever really left him. And he pointed a gun at his son's head and said, *'Bang.'* Then he pointed the gun at her and winked. He's a grade-A fucking psycho. The kid isn't dead, is he?"

"No. It's nothing like that." Lanternglass told her about the mall.

By the time she finished, Dorothy was out of the bathroom, leaning against the wall beside her, cheek resting against her hip. "Back to bed," Lanternglass mouthed. Dorothy didn't move, pretended she didn't understand.

Acosta said, "Huh."

"Did he have an exception that would've allowed him to carry a gun in his place of work? For his job?"

"Not a mall cop. If he was a real cop maybe. Or a soldier. I don't know. You'd have to track down the transcripts of his hearing."

"I checked the public-records Web site, and there was nothing in there about a divorce order."

"No, there wouldn't be. He never got divorced. The wife is very timid, got a case of Stockholm syndrome. He didn't allow her to have her own cell phone for years. Or her own e-mail account. The only reason she left him is that she's more scared of her sister than she is of her husband. And a restraining order would be filed with the courthouse.

You can't pull that offline. I can get someone to e-mail you a copy of the injunction if you want. Tomorrow, day after?"

Lanternglass was quiet, thinking it through. She'd need to see a court transcript before Tim would let her run with the allegation that Kellaway had pointed a gun at his wife and child. But she could at least get something in tomorrow's edition about the restraining order, get it out that he'd been forbidden to carry a weapon after . . . what? Menacing his wife and child? "Menacing" was a safe verb, she thought. Tim might let her have "menacing."

"Yeah," Lanternglass said. "I'd appreciate that. But if it's all right, I'd like to squeeze something into tomorrow's edition about this. 'A source within the sheriff's department says . . .'"

"Oh, the hell with that. Use my *name*. Even better, see if you can get my picture. I love to see my face in the paper."

"It's all right to directly source you?"

"By all means. Kellaway and I really hit it off, the one time we met. I'm sure he'll be delighted to hear I'm still thinking about him."

The tuba wailed.

"Is that a foghorn?" Lanternglass asked.

"That's a whale!" Acosta yelled. There was more cheering in the background. "They're serenading us!"

Lanternglass didn't know how Dorothy heard what Acosta was saying, but all at once she was jumping up and down.

"Can I *hear*? Can I *listen*?"

"Ms. Acosta? My daughter is wondering if you'd hold your phone up so she can hear the whales."

"Put her on!"

Lanternglass lowered her phone and pressed it to Dorothy's ear. And stood and watched her daughter. Eight years old. Eyes very large, face calm, attentive. Listening while the world sang to her.

July 13, 8:42 A.M.

KELLAWAY WOKE BEFORE NINE, PEELED himself off the couch, and padded into the bathroom to take a leak. When he came back, ten minutes later, with toast and coffee, his own wide, bristly, impassive face was on the TV, above a chyron that said GUNNING FOR TROUBLE? He had passed out with the television going and the volume turned all the way down, had slept heavily and well in that silent flicker of uncanny light. He had felt easier with a gun again, had drifted off with Jim's British Webley & Scott on the floor beside him.

He sat on the edge of the couch now, unconsciously holding the gun in one hand and the remote in the other. He turned up the volume.

". . . heels of the story that Randall Kellaway was released from the army after *allegations* that he repeatedly used excessive *force* in his stint with the military police," said the morning news anchor. He talked in the style popularized by Wolf Blitzer: in fragmentary sentences, with emphasis on any word that was reasonably dramatic. "Now, the *St. Possenti Digest*, out with a *shock report* that Kellaway was *forbidden* to possess a *firearm* because of threats he made against his wife and young son. Sheriff's Sergeant Lauren Acosta *confirming* to the *Digest* that Kellaway would not have been granted an exception to carry a weapon because of his job as a mall security guard, and that possession of the .327 would've been a clear *violation* of the injunction against him. No word yet why Mrs. Kellaway applied for the injunction, or the nature of the *threats* leveled against her by her husband. Mr. Kellaway and the St. Possenti police have yet to return our calls for comment, but we expect Chief Rickles to make a statement today, when he appears at the Miracle Falls Mall for an eleven A.M. candle-lighting ceremony to remember the fallen in the recent attack. Randall Kellaway is scheduled to light the first candle and may also comment, we don't know, but we'll be there, live, to cover . . ."

It was *her*, of course. It was the black, Lanternglass, who had turned up yesterday evening to ambush him when he walked out of the local TV studio. She couldn't leave him alone. She didn't care if he ever saw his kid again. For her he was just a character in a nasty story that she could use to sell some papers.

He had not dared to admit to himself until now that a part of him had begun to believe he could leverage his sudden unexpected celebrity into getting it all back: Holly and George, sure, but something else, too. "His *rights*" were the words that came to him, but that *was* and *wasn't* quite it. It wasn't his right to have a gun, or not *just* his right to a gun. That was only part of it. It seemed to him that there was something obscene about an America where a grinning Latina could tell him to stay away from his own son, and never mind he worked fifty hours a week, never mind what he had sacrificed as a soldier representing his nation in a hostile, foreign land. The thought of the tiny black woman grinning at him while she poked her cell phone in his face, asking him her loaded questions, made him feel feverish. It seemed grotesque that he lived in a society where someone like that could make a living out of humiliating him. She didn't care that George would hear on the TV that his father was a sick man who pointed guns at his own family. She didn't care what kids said to George at school, if he got teased and harassed. Lanternglass had decided he was a criminal from the moment she laid eyes on him. He was white and male. Obviously he was a criminal.

Kellaway clicked off the TV.

Tires ground on gravel outside.

He rose, twitched aside the curtain, and saw Mary, pulling into the drive in a banana-colored RAV4 that he didn't recognize. Coils of smoke unwound from the tops of the palms, turned to golden froth in the early light.

Kellaway left the Webley on the couch. He opened the door as she drew to a stop and shut off the RAV.

"What'chu doing here?" she asked.

"Could say the same to you."

She stood at the front end of the RAV, scrawny and sinewy in a pair of cutoff jeans and a man's flannel shirt. She held one hand over her eyes as if to shield them from the sun, although there was no particular glare.

"Get a couple of my things," she said. "He told you?"

"I know about it," Kellaway said. "You took it easy living off his insurance money till it was all used up, then figured you'd jump ship, huh?"

She said, "You think changing his diapers and pumping up his cock every night is taking it easy, *you* do it for a while."

Kellaway shook his head and said, "I don't know about changing his diapers, but can you come in here and show me where the urine bags are? The one he's got on now burst, and there's piss all over the place."

"Oh, Jesus," she said. "Jesus Christ. How much did you let him drink last night?"

"Too much, I guess."

"Hire the fucking handicapped. I'll fix it."

"Thanks," he said, stepping back into the house. "I'll meet you in the bedroom."

9:38 A.M.

After it was done and she was on the floor with a hole where her right eye had been, Kellaway put Jim's .44 in Mary's own hand. He sat for a while on the edge of the bed, his wrists resting on his knees. The ringing echo of the shot seemed to throb inside him, to reverberate long after it should've faded. He felt switched off inside. Blank. She'd been crying as she stared into the barrel. She had offered to suck his cock, snot bubbling out of her nose. Some tears and snot were good. It would look like she'd been weeping when she shot herself.

How would the cops take it? Maybe they'd figure that after discovering the body of her former lover, she decided to join him in the afterlife, a shabby, scrawny Juliet racing after her disabled, diabetic Romeo. Then again, maybe her boyfriend couldn't swear she'd been in bed with him all night. Maybe they'd hang Jim's murder on her. It wasn't like they were going to find Jim's suicide note. Kellaway would take it with him and get rid of it somewhere.

Or maybe the police would smell a put-up job, but who gave a fuck if they did? Try to prove something. Let 'em come fishing. He had wriggled off the hook at the mall, he could wriggle out of this.

He needed some fresh air and went outside to find some. Only there wasn't any. The day stank like an ashtray. It had almost been better inside.

Kellaway's thoughts spun like sparks rising from a collapsing fire. He was waiting for them to settle when he heard—almost *felt*—a faint throb in the air. Fine-grained particles of smoke shivered all around him. The morning was full of strange vibrations and tremors. He tilted his head and listened, heard the distant ringtone of his cell.

He tramped to his car, plucked the phone out of the passenger seat. He had missed seven calls, most of them from Jay Rickles. It was Jay now.

He answered. "Yeah?"

"Where the hell have you been all morning?" Rickles sounded bent.

"I went for a walk. Needed to clear my head."

"Is it clear now?"

"I guess."

"Good, because you got a goddamn mess to figure out. In the next hour every news channel in this state is going to be running with the story that you pointed a gun at your toddler and threatened to shoot him if your wife ever left you. Do you know how that looks?"

"Where'd you get that story?"

"Where do you *think* I got the story? I read the fucking transcript from your fucking court proceedings, two hours ago. I got to it before anyone else did so I could find out what I'm up against. You didn't feel like mentioning any of this to me at any time?"

"Why would I mention something like that? Something humiliating like that?"

"Because it was going to come out anyway. Because you sat next to me on TV to tell the world what a big hero you were, taking out a shooter with a gun you had no right to possess."

"Think how lucky it is I didn't follow the injunction. Becki Kolbert was just getting started when I walked in."

Rickles took a long, unsteady breath.

"I came back from Iraq with PTSD. I didn't take antidepressants because I didn't want to solve my problems with medication. I *never* pointed a loaded gun at my son, but I did do things I regret. Things I wish I could take back. If I hadn't done them, my child would still be living with me." A lot of it was true. He had pointed a gun at George once, to make a point to Holly, but it wasn't loaded at the time. And for all he knew he *might* have PTSD. More came back from Iraq with it than not. He wasn't lying when he said he'd never gotten on antidepressants. He'd never been offered any.

For a long time, Rickles didn't reply. When he did, his voice was still husky with emotion, but Kellaway could hear he had calmed down. "And that's what you're going to tell the press today at the candle-lighting. You say it just like that."

"You know it's that reporter trying to stir shit," Kellaway said. "The black one. Same one who tried to make your department look bad. People don't believe the blacks can be racist, too, but they can. I could see the way she looked at me. I'm a white man with a gun, and to them we're all Nazis. To the blacks. She looks at you the same way."

Rickles laughed. "Isn't that the truth. Doesn't matter how many toys for tots I've handed out to little pickaninnies with food-stamp mamas and daddies in jail. Black people feel bad about all the things they don't have, and they resent everyone who's made out better. It's never your hard work that got you where you are—it's always the racist system."

"You sure you even still want me to go to the candle-lighting?" Kellaway said. "Maybe it might be better for you to put distance between the two of us."

"Fuck that," Rickles said, and he laughed again, and Kellaway knew it was all right. "Too late anyway. We've been on cable news together every night all week. You don't know this yet, but I got an e-mail from a top man at the NRA, and they want us both to deliver a joint keynote speech in Las Vegas next year. Hotel rooms, tickets all paid, ten-thousand-dollar speaking fee. I spoke to them about the restraining order, and it don't bother them at all. Far as they're concerned, it just proves the state puts people at risk when they step in to deprive them of their rights." He sighed and then said, "We'll get through it. You're still the good guy in this. Just . . . no more surprises, Kellaway. All right?"

"No more," Kellaway said. "I'll see you at your house in half an hour."

He ended the call and breathed in the scent of char, of sizzling pine-cones, stood tall in the smoke of a burning world. After a moment he tossed the phone back into the passenger seat. He thought that before he got on the road, he might like to grab the Webley and put it in the trunk. Jim didn't need it anymore.

Jim didn't need the guns in his garage either. Kellaway decided to take a minute to hunt around, see if there was anything he might want. Jim had said he ought to help himself.

9:44 A.M.

"Right here," Okello said, pointing at his feet.

They were halfway up the great, curving staircase at the center of the Miracle Falls Mall, in a deep well of sunlight, beneath a banked roof of skylights.

"I got low and stayed here," Okello said. "Sarah had me texting her every thirty seconds to let her know I was still alive."

"I've been meaning to ask about that," Lanternglass told him. "Let's walk up the rest of the way. I want to have a look at Devotion Dia-monds."

They climbed to the top, all three of them: Okello, Lanternglass, and Dorothy. Lanternglass had called Okello over breakfast to ask if she could read and possibly quote from his text messages to his girl-friend. She did not mention she wanted to look at the time stamps on his messages and see if they revealed when each of the shots had occurred. Okello had offered to do her one better.

"The mall is reopening this morning. Going to be a candle-lighting ceremony at eleven."

"I know," Lanternglass had said. "I was planning to be there to cover it."

"So come by at nine-thirty, before the stores open up. Meet me at the entrance to Boost Yer Game. I can show you my texts and walk you through what I did and what I heard."

"That's no problem?"

"You kidding? My little sisters are going nuts about me being in the paper. Total strangers have been asking if they can take selfies with me. I might be getting a taste for fame. I think it suits me."

She'd smiled at that but had felt a kind of gentle twisting in the chest as well. In that instant Okello sounded very like Colson.

The entrance to Devotion Diamonds was still blocked off by yellow crime-scene tape. On the other side of the tape, the doors had been slid shut and locked. The rest of the stores along the gallery were busy, prepping for the eleven o'clock ceremony and the expectation of a curious crowd. Voices yelled and echoed in the big open space of the central atrium. The gate was rolled up at Lids, the hat store next to Devotion Diamonds, and a sleepy-looking stoner with bushy, shoulder-length yellow hair was using a sticker gun to put 20-percent-off tags on baseball caps.

"Hats!" Dorothy cried, squeezing her mother's hand. Dorothy wore a fuzzy yellow chicken-headed hat today, tied under her chin. "*Hats!* Mom!"

"Mm-hm," Lanternglass said. She craned her neck and raised her voice to be heard by the stoner. "Hey, you mind if my daughter has a wander around?"

"Huh? Sure. Go for it," said the stoner, and Dorothy squeezed her mother's fingers again and went leaping into the aisles of Lids.

Okello said, "Sorry—there isn't really anything to see. But you want to look at my phone?" He held it out to her. "I scrolled back to my texts from the day of. Um, don't go back any further, okay?"

Lanternglass said, "Pictures?"

"You know it." Okello grinned.

"She's out of high school, isn't she?"

Okello scowled, looked offended. "She's a year older than me!"

"Are *you* out of high school?"

"I told you I'm in college. College is the reason I work this job. Books don't pay for themselves."

"They pay you plenty eventually, if you keep at 'em," Lanternglass said, and accepted his phone.

Holy shit, this girl just walked into
Devotion Diamonds and started
shooting.
10:37

For real. Three shots.
10:37

WHAT????? Where are you?
Are you okay?
10:37

On the big staircase, about halfway
down. I'm flat on the steps. I'm practically close enough to see what's
happening.
10:38

STAY DOWN. Can you7 get
away? OMG OMGOMG I'm
freakingo ut
10:38

If I go down the stairs I'd move into
sight of anyone standing in the hallway above.
10:39

I love you.
10:39

I love you too.
10:39

Don't move. Stay where you
are. Oh Jesus God. Praying
so hard right now.
10:39

You said the person with a
gun is a girl you saw her?
10:40

Another hots.
10:40

"shot" not "hots"
10:40

ohgod oh god please please
please I don't want you tog
et shot
10:40

Im kinda hoping not to get shot too
10:40

you idiot I love you
10:40

Something fell over and then there
was another shot.
10:41

r u all right? you havent
texted
10:42

I'm fine
10:42

whd you stop texting
10:42

I didn't it's only been a minute.
10:42

You cared me don't you dare
stop texting
10:42

Im all right.
10:43

Still all right.
10:44

Shit. Another shot.
10:45

Oh God. Oh God.
10:45

I'm not sure what's going on now.
10:46

And another shot.
10:46

OK maybe you should run
for it
10:46

I'm all right. I dont want to leave the
frappachinos.
10:47

THE WHAT YOU ASSHOLE?
10:47

I've got frappachinos. I cant run with
my drinks. I'll spill them.
10:48

I hate you. So much.
10:49

There was more, but Okello didn't mention any other shots. He had the cops arriving and stepping on his hand at 10:52, less than twenty minutes after the first shot was fired but way too late in the day to change what had happened.

The way the St. Possenti police had it, Becki Kolbert had put three into her boss and one into Mrs. Haswar and her child. Kellaway had entered, fired twice, nailing Kolbert once and missing with the second. Then a final shot, when Kolbert rose up again to shoot Bob Lutz. Seven shots in all.

On the time stamp, though, they clustered differently, wrongly. Three, then two a bit later (And something fell over. What? The computer maybe?), then one, and then one more. Lanternglass had some ideas about what that might suggest, but it wasn't anything she could take to press. She wasn't sure Tim Chen would even let her note the discrepancies between Okello's texts and the official report.

She gave Okello back his phone and dug her own out of her pocket.

"You want screen captures of any of these, that's no problem," he said.

Lanternglass said, "I might. Let me talk to my editor and run a couple of possibilities by him."

Dorothy skipped to the threshold of Lids and stopped just inside the security barrier, wearing a raccoon hat with raccoon paws and a raccoon face. Not a Davy Crockett–type cap—more like a raccoon hand puppet that fit on a person's head.

"No," Lanternglass said, and Dorothy's grin vanished, replaced by an ugly scowl.

"Twenty percent off," Dorothy said.

"No. Put it back." Lanternglass dialed the office.

Dorothy said, "I have to pee."

"In a minute," Lanternglass said.

"They've probably got an employee bathroom out back of Lids," Okello said. He jerked his head at the stoner with bushy hair. "Hey, bruh. You mind if pokey here runs into your bathroom?"

The stoner blinked slowly and said, "Sure, man. Go fur it."

Dorothy began to prance back toward Lids.

"No, wait," the stoner said in a dreamy sort of tone. He looked as if he had only just been shaken awake. "Shoot. Maintenance is in there. We been asking 'em for three months to fix the flush. It only took a mass shooting for them to finally find time."

Dorothy gave her mother a wide-eyed, bewildered look: *What now?*

"Wait," Lanternglass hissed, just as Tim Chen picked up.

"Aisha," Tim said, no preamble. "You heard?"

"Heard what?"

"About the evacuation order." Tim sounded untroubled, almost mild. "Park Service fire department called forty minutes ago and made it official. We need to clear the office by ten tomorrow morning."

"You're shitting."

"I never shit," Tim told her.

"You really don't. You're the most constipated man I know."

Tim said, "I need you back here. Everyone's coming in, and I've got Shane Wolff swinging by to pack up our computers. There are trees burning less than a quarter of a mile away, and the wind is picking up."

"We going to lose the building?" she asked. She was surprised at her own calm, although her anxiety was a smooth, hard weight in the pit of her stomach, like a swallowed stone.

"Let's just say they can't promise to save it."

Lanternglass said, "What about the candle-lighting ceremony?"

"They'll cover it on TV. We can watch it when we have a chance."

"Are we going to be able to get tomorrow's paper out?" she asked.

When Tim Chen replied, his voice was forceful, almost harsh. She had never heard him say anything in such a tone. "You bet your ass we will. This paper has come out every weekday since 1937, and I'm not going to be the first editor to let down the team."

"I'll be back as soon as I can get out of here," Lanternglass promised him. She disconnected, glanced around for her daughter.

She expected to find Dorothy back in Lids, digging through the hats. But the little girl was sitting with Okello on a steel bench down the corridor—both of them planted in the very same place Randall Kellaway had settled, almost exactly a week ago, after the shooting in Devotion Diamonds.

But someone *else* had appeared in Lids: a skinny, elderly Asian man in a stained maintenance jumpsuit. He had a dripping wrench in one hand and was waving it at the stoner, muttering in a low, almost angry voice.

"Everything okay?" Lanternglass asked him.

The maintenance man went silent and turned his stern gaze upon her. The stoner gave her an embarrassed shrug.

"I'll tell you what I told him. The last person to use that toilet," the maintenance man said, wagging his wrench, "left something in it. I think *someone* needs to take a look at it."

The stoner lifted one hand in a placating gesture. "And like I said: *Dude*. Whatever it is, it *wasn't* me. Swear to God. I *never* crap at the mall."

10:28 A.M.

When Kellaway steered his Prius into the courtyard of crushed white shells, Jay Rickles was already in the cab of his pickup, sitting in the open door with his feet on the chrome running board. Kellaway got out of his ride and climbed up into the chief's.

"That the same thing you were wearing last night?" Rickles asked, slamming the driver's-side door and starting the truck.

Rickles wore a crisp dress uniform: blue jacket with a double row of brass buttons, blue uniform pants with a black stripe down the sides, Glock on his right hip in a black leather holster that looked as if it had been oiled. Kellaway had on a rumpled blue blazer over a polo.

"It's the only thing I've got I can wear on TV," Kellaway said.

Rickles grunted. He wasn't the grinning, grateful, wet-eyed grandpa today. He looked sunburned and irritable. They took off in a bad-tempered lurch of speed.

"This was supposed to be a hero's welcome," Rickles said. "You know you and I were going to lay a wreath of white roses together?"

"I thought we were each just lighting a candle."

"PR thought a wreath would look nice. And the CEO of Sunbelt Marketplace, the guy who manages the Miracle Falls Mall—"

"Yeah. I know him. Russ Dorr?"

"Yeah, him. He was going to give you a Rolex. I don't know if that's still happening now. People get skittish about pinning medals on wife beaters."

Kellaway said, "I never touched Holly in my life. Not once in my life." It was true. It was Kellaway's belief that if you reached a point where you had to use your knuckles on a woman, you had already shamefully lost control of the situation.

Rickles slumped a little. Then said, "I'm sorry. I take that back. That was uncalled for." He paused and said, "I never pointed a gun at my wife, but I used a belt on my oldest daughter, when she was seven. She wrote her name all over the walls in crayon, and I went ballistic. I snapped my belt at her, and the buckle hit her hand and broke three knuckles. This was over two decades ago, but it's still fresh in my mind. I was drunk at the time. Were you drinking?"

"What? When I threatened her? No. Sober as you are now."

"It would be better if you *had* been drinking." Rickles tapped his thumb on the steering wheel. The police scanner under the dash crackled and men talked, calling out codes in lazy, laconic voices. "I'd give anything to take it back—what I did to my little girl's hand. Most horrible thing. I was blasted and feeling sorry for myself. Defaulted on a loan. Had my car repoed. Hard times. Do you go to church?"

"No."

"You might think about it. There's a part of me that will always carry a bruised heart because of what I did. But I was redeemed through the grace of Jesus, and eventually I found the strength to forgive myself and move on. And now I have all these amazing grandchildren and—"

"Chief?" came a voice on the scanner. "Chief, you there?"

The chief snagged the mic. "Rickles here, go ahead, Martin."

"It's about the thing happening at the mall. Did you pick up Kellaway yet?" Martin said.

Rickles clapped the mic to his chest and looked at Kellaway sidelong. "He's going to tell me you're not getting the Rolex. Do you want to be here or not?"

"I guess just say you haven't seen me yet," Kellaway said. "If he tells you I'm not getting a fancy watch, I promise I won't embarrass you by sobbing in the background."

Rickles laughed, a fine web of wrinkles appearing at the corners of his eyes, and for a moment he was his old self. "I like you, Rand. I always have, from the first instant I clapped eyes on you. I hope you know that." He shook his head, barely clamping down on his mirth, then squeezed the mic. "No, the son of a bitch hasn't turned up yet. What's the story?"

They were cruising along the highway, through a fog of pale blue smoke, maybe ten minutes from the mall. The wind caught the high pickup and rocked it on its springs.

"Phew," Martin said. "Good. Listen, we've got a real fucking problem down here. A maintenance guy was fixing a toilet out in back of Lids, the shop next to Devotion Diamonds, and you aren't going to believe what he found in the tank. A lead slug. Looks like the one we couldn't locate, the one that took out Mrs. Haswar and her baby, over?"

"How the hell did it get in a toilet, over?"

"Well, didn't someone have to put it there? Gets worse, Chief. That reporter, Lanternglass, she was right there, she heard all about it. What's the bet it's all over TV by lunch, over?"

While Martin was blabbing, Kellaway reached across the seat and unbuttoned the chief's holster. Rickles glanced down as Kellaway pulled out the Glock and stuck the barrel in his ribs.

"Tell him to head to my house and that you'll meet him there, then hang up," Kellaway said.

Rickles held the mic in his hand, staring down with clear, surprised blue eyes at the gun in his side.

"And watch the road," Kellaway added as Rickles looked up and braked hard to keep from rear-ending a Caprice dawdling along through the smoke.

Rickles squeezed the mic. "Jesus. Okay. What a fucking mess. We better . . . we better convene at Kellaway's house. He hasn't turned up at my place, so he's probably still there. First officers on the scene should hold him. I'm putting on my party lights and heading that way now. Out." He released the mic and hung it on the scanner.

"Pull over in that gas station," Kellaway said. "The Shell up on the right. I'm going to let you out and drop you off—because I like you, too, Jay. You've never been nothing but generous to me."

Rickles touched his blinker and began to slow. His face was stiff, impassive. "Yasmin Haswar? And the boy, Ibrahim? That was *you*?" he asked.

"It was the last thing in the world I ever meant to happen," Kellaway said. "They say that guns don't kill people, that people kill people. But I feel like the gun *wanted* the both of them. I really do. Yasmin Haswar leapt up out of nowhere, like she knew there was a bullet waiting for her, and the gun went off. Sometimes guns *do* kill people."

The truck pulled in to a parking lot containing eight rows of pumps and a small central convenience store. At that time of the morning, most of the pumps were empty. A film of blue smoke rippled steadily across the lot, coursing over the roof of the tiny mini-mart. The truck's blinker was still *click-click-click*ing.

"What a pile of shit," Rickles said. "You asshole. You careless ass-hole. Guns don't just go off."

"Don't they?" Kellaway asked, and shot him.

10:41 A.M.

He unbuckled Rickles's seat belt and pulled him sideways, so the stout little man dropped across the front seat. Then Kellaway got out and went around to the driver's side and hauled himself up behind the wheel. The driver's-side window was mucked with blood and tissue, as if someone had thrown a great fistful of pink slime against the glass.

He pushed Rickles over to make more room, and the older man slipped and fell into the passenger-side footwell. Only his feet remained tangled up on the seat.

A guy had come out of the convenience store, a fifty-something dude with long, graying hair and a Lynyrd Skynyrd tee beneath an unbuttoned flannel shirt. Kellaway lifted a hand in a casual wave, and the guy nodded back and stuck a cigarette in his mouth. Maybe he'd heard the shot and come out for a look. Maybe he just wanted a smoke. No one else gave the pickup a second look. It wasn't like on TV. People didn't register what they heard, didn't process what they saw. Busy pedestrians might walk by a dead homeless man for hours, assuming he was asleep.

Kellaway steered back toward Jay's house and away from the life he'd lived for the last fifteen years. He thought his chances of escape were very slim, although he had a few things working in his favor. Those things were in his Prius. One of them was loaded with a banana clip.

He pulled into the courtyard of Rickles's hacienda and parked the truck. As he climbed down, the front door opened and the towheaded boy named Merritt stood there gazing blankly out at him. Kellaway nodded—*How ya doin'*—and walked swiftly to his Prius with Chief Rickles's Glock in his hand. He tossed it onto the passenger seat of his car and got out of there. When he looked in the rearview mirror, the kid had turned his head to stare at his grandfather's pickup. Maybe he was wondering why there was crap all over the inside of the driver's-side window.

A gust of wind tried to shove the Prius out of its lane and onto the dirt embankment, and Kellaway had to struggle with the wheel to stay on the blacktop. Smoke churned around him as he drove west.

If he moved quickly and didn't hesitate, he thought there might be time to get George away from Holly and the sister-in-law. He had a boat, a little eighteen-footer with an outboard; in happier days he'd sometimes taken George fishing in it. He had a notion to get the boy and make a run for the Bahamas. They could hide out in the rocks off Little Abaco, maybe eventually work their way south to Cuba. It was two hundred miles or more to Freeport on Grand Bahama Island, and he doubted he'd ever been more than three miles out in the boat. But he wasn't afraid of the deep swell, or of drifting off course and slow-roasting to death under the equatorial sun, or of capsizing and drowning with his child. It seemed to him far, far more likely that the Coast Guard would find him offshore and a sniper in a helicopter would blow his brains out while little George watched.

If they could hit him in the chop. If he didn't hit them first.

Besides. They might stay back if they weren't sure what he'd do to the kid. He'd never point a loaded gun at his child, but from a helicopter how could you tell if a gun was loaded or not?

The boulevards were wide and open, but the farther west he went, the less imposing the houses became. Modest one-floor ranches drifted toward him out of the haze and slipped away again. The makes of other cars were almost unidentifiable in the filthy murk. Headlights bobbed up out of the soup and sailed past, attached to shadows. In the movies the man with a license to kill pressed a button and released a cloud of smoke from the back end of his Aston Martin to blind his pursuers and make an escape. Kellaway was stuck with a Prius instead of a British sports car, but his smoke cover was much more effective.

Frances's silver BMW wagon was in the driveway, parked nose-in to the garage, so Kellaway could read the COEXIST sticker on the back end. He pulled in right behind it, blocking her, and got out. The wind sheared across the lawn, and his eyes stung in the billowing smoke. Kellaway held the Glock in one hand. He popped the hatchback of his

Prius and threw aside the sleeping bag that covered the weapons he'd
lifted from Jim Hirst's garage. He considered the Bushmaster, the Webley, and the .45, then picked up the single-barrel Mossberg with the
pistol grip. He loaded it with PDX1 rounds, squeezed five in the tube,
one in the chamber. The matte finish on the gun barrel was a flawless
black. It looked as if it had never been fired.

Kellaway cut across the front yard, headed for the door. Frances's
ranch was guacamole green, the walls all rough, spiky stucco. She had
cacti for border plantings, which he thought fit her personality. The
front door was flanked by tall, narrow sidelights with cheap white panel
curtains.

As he approached, he saw one of the curtains twitch. He couldn't
tell who'd been watching him, Holly or Frances, but just as he reached
the door, he heard the bolt turn. It was almost funny, the idea that she
thought she could lock him out.

He lowered the Mossberg and pulled the trigger, and the shotgun
went off with a thunderous slam and blew a hole through the lock and
the wood surrounding it. He planted his boot in the center of the door
and shoved, and it flew open, and he followed it in and almost stepped
on George.

Along with a fist-size chunk of the door, the Mossberg had blown
away the upper right half of George's face and a large portion of his
skull. A splinter the size of a kitchen knife had gone through his left
eye. The boy opened and closed his mouth, gurgling strangely. Kellaway could see his brain, glistening pinkly. It seemed to pulse, to *beat*,
not unlike a heart. George tried to say something but could make only
wet, smacking sounds.

Kellaway looked down at him in perplexity. It was like an optical
illusion, something that didn't make sense to the eye.

Holly stood six feet away, holding a cell phone up to her cheek. She
wore white slacks and a sleeveless green blouse, and her hair was tur-
baned in a towel. Like George, she was opening and closing her mouth
without making any sound.

The shot seemed to go off again, and then again, only inside Kellaway, in his head. He was screaming for a while before he realized it. He didn't know when he dropped to one knee. He didn't know when he set aside the Glock to put a hand gently on his son's chest. Time just skipped forward, and he found himself bent over his child. Time skipped again, and Holly was kneeling by George's head, cupping the red ruin of his skull in her hands. Blood squirted on her white pants. George had stopped trying to talk. Holly had put the phone down next to her knee, and someone on the other end was saying, "Hello? Miss? Hello?" A 911 operator, calling to them from another galaxy.

Kellaway took another deep breath and found he was done screaming. His throat was ragged and sore. He kept his hand on his son's chest, had slipped it under his shirt to place a palm against his warm skin. He could feel George's heart beating rapidly, a furious, frightened stammer in his chest. He could feel when it stopped.

Holly wept, tears plinking onto George's face. George's expression was stunned and blank.

"You told him to lock me out," Kellaway said to her. It seemed incredible to him that his son had been alive and complete less than two minutes ago and now, abruptly, was dead, his face obliterated. It was too sudden to make sense.

"No," Frances said.

Frances stood in the living room, on the other side of a pony wall. She held a vase in one hand. He assumed she had heroic notions of smashing it over his skull, but she seemed unable to move. All of them were stuck in place, shocked by the non sequitur of George dying in a single shot.

"He saw you coming before any of us. He saw you coming, and he was scared," Frances said. She was quivering. "You had a gun."

"I still do, you foolish cunt," Kellaway said.

It turned out Frances's fag of a husband, Elijah, was hiding in the bedroom. By the time Kellaway found him, the shotgun was empty. He had put three into Frances and two into Holly when she tried to run out the door. But there were still fourteen rounds in the Glock, and he needed only one before his work was done.

11:03 A.M.

He might've sat with George forever.

He went over it again and again in his head, what should've happened.

In his mind Kellaway crossed the front yard to the door and blew a hole through the lock and shoved the door in and George was there but fine, ducked down, hands over his head. Kellaway scooped him up in one arm and leveled the shotgun at Holly as he backed out the door. *You had your turn with him. Now it's mine.*

Or try this: He crossed the yard to the front door and blew a hole through the lock and Frances's stomach at the same time. She was the one standing on the other side of it, not George. Why would it be George? That didn't make any sense. Why would George be afraid of him?

He imagined crossing the yard to the front door and George threw it open before he could get there and ran to him, yelling, *Daddy!*, arms open wide. That was how it was when George and Holly still lived with him. George yelled *Daddy!* whenever he got home from work, as if he hadn't seen him for months instead of just hours, and always came running.

What brought Kellaway up and out of his thoughts was the sound of someone saying his name in the next room, in a low, distant voice. He wondered if Frances was not dead, although he didn't see how she could still be alive. Her guts were all over the carpet. Two blasts from the shotgun had all but cut her in half, just above the waist.

He'd been holding George's small hand—it was already cold, the extremities cooled off so quickly once circulation ceased—and now he folded it across the boy's small, slight chest and stood. Frances was splayed on her back on the other side of the pony wall. Where her stomach belonged was a red-and-black slime of mutilated intestines. A third shot had ripped a hole in the left side of her neck. It looked like her throat had been partly torn out by an animal. He supposed in some ways this was exactly what had happened, and he was the animal.

It wasn't Holly saying his name either. Holly had fled into the kitchen, where she was now lying facedown, arms stretched out over her head, like a child pretending to be flying. He had gotten her in the heart, which was where she had gotten him, too.

The voice he heard was coming from the TV. A stern, dark-haired news anchor was saying that a lead slug had been found hidden in a toilet and that the discovery threw Randall Kellaway's story into serious doubt. The newsman said the candle-lighting ceremony had been canceled abruptly with no explanation. He said the disturbing new evidence had been confirmed by a reporter with the *Digest*. The news anchor said the reporter's name—and Kellaway said it too, very quietly.

Why had George been afraid of him? Because Aisha Lanternglass told him to be. She'd been telling the world for days that Kellaway was a scary person. Maybe not explicitly. But it was hinted at in every line she wrote, in every gleeful insinuation. When he met her in the parking lot and she flashed her teeth at him, her bright gaze had said, *I'm going to fix you, cracker. I'm going to fix you good.* The thought gave her joy; he could see it all over her face.

He kissed George good-bye, on what was left of his brow, before he left.

11:26 A.M.

Lanternglass drove at a crawl the whole last quarter of a mile to the office, on the western outskirts of town. Smoke billowed across the road in smothering yellow heaps that the headlights could barely penetrate. The wind snatched at her elderly Passat, jolting it this way and that. Once she drove through a whirl of sparks that spattered and died against the hood and the windshield.

"Mom, Mom, look!" Dorothy called from the backseat, pointing, and Lanternglass saw a sixty-foot-tall pine tree, engulfed in a red shroud of flame, over on the right side of the road. Nothing else around it was visibly burning, just that one tree.

"Where are the fire trucks?" Dorothy asked.

"Fighting the fire," Lanternglass said.

"We just *passed* the fire! Didn't you see the tree?"

"The fire is even worse farther down the road. That's where they're trying to hold it. They want to keep it from jumping the highway." She didn't add, *And pouring down the hills into St. Possenti.*

Just before they reached the office, the smoke lifted a little. The *Digest* was in a squat, unremarkable two-story redbrick building, which they shared with a yoga studio and a branch of Merrill Lynch. The parking lot was about half full, and Lanternglass saw people she knew, other employees, carrying boxes to their cars.

She got out and started to walk toward the fire door, and the wind came up behind her and shoved. She saw more sparks, floating in the high thermals. Her eyes watered. The late morning stank of char. Lanternglass took her daughter's hand. They half ran and were half carried by the gusts to the stairwell.

They went up the cement stairs, three at a time, almost at a run, as she had so often done before. She wasn't going to be able to pack her weights, still tucked in under the stairwell. If the building burned, they'd be melted back to ingots of raw iron.

The fire door to the newsroom was propped open with a cinder block. It was a modest office space containing six desks of the cheapest quality, low particleboard dividers arranged between them. At the far side of the room was a floor-to-ceiling glass partition, looking into the only private office at the *Digest*, Tim Chen's. Tim stood in his office door, clutching a cardboard file box with some framed photographs and several coffee cups balanced on top.

Shane Wolff was there, too, sitting at a desk by the fire door, dismantling a PC and neatly setting the components into a cardboard box. Several other computers had already been removed. An intern, a wispy, nervous, nineteen-year-old girl named Julia, was pulling steel drawers from the file cabinet that occupied most of one wall and stacking them on a dolly. A short, solidly built sportswriter named Don Quigley used bungee cable to strap them in place. The atmosphere was one of quiet, industrious urgency.

"Lanternglass," Tim said, and nodded toward her desk, which was the one closest to his office.

"I'm on it. I can pack everything I've got in ten minutes."

"Don't pack. Write."

Lanternglass said, "You aren't serious."

"I think we both know I'm famously humor-deficient. I put an alert on the Web site about the bullet. The TV news is already running with it. I want the full story uploaded to the server by noon. Then you can pack," he said as he hurried past her, carrying his box.

"My car is unlocked," Lanternglass said. "Bring up my laptop? It's in the backseat."

He jerked his head in a gesture that seemed to indicate assent and hauled his file box out and down the stairs.

She slowed near Shane Wolff. "I'm going to miss this place if it burns down. Some of the most mediocre hours of my life were spent in this very room. You think you'll miss anything about coming here?"

"Watching you run up and down the stairs," he said. "Nothing mediocre about that."

"Ew," Dorothy said. "Mama, he's hitting on you."

"Who says?" Shane asked her. "Maybe I'm a fitness nut. Maybe I just admire someone who shows real dedication to staying in shape."

Dorothy narrowed one eye to a squint and said, "You hitting on her."

"Pfff," Shane said. "Don't go ragging on me now. I'm not the one walking around with my head stuck up a chicken's butt."

Dorothy touched her chicken hat and giggled, and Lanternglass tugged her hand and led her on to her desk.

A stack of flattened cardboard boxes leaned against the full-wall window looking into Tim Chen's office. Lanternglass assembled one, and she and Dorothy began to empty out her desk. The box was half full when Tim returned with her laptop bag.

She fired up her aging MacBook and opened a new document while Dorothy continued to pack the box. Lanternglass began to write, starting with her headline: CRIME-SCENE DISCOVERY RAISES QUESTIONS. Shit, that was terrible. Too general, too vague. She deleted it, tried another.

NUMBER ONE WITH A BULLET: CRIME-SCENE DISCOV— Fuck, no, that was even worse.

It was hard to think. She had a sense of the world coming apart around her, buckling and splitting at the seams. In his office Tim Chen was throwing piles of folders into a box. Shane Wolff was on the other side of the room with part of the carpet torn back. He yanked a long Ethernet cable out from under it, gathering it in loops. A file cabinet with all its drawers hanging open overbalanced and fell with a crash. The wispy intern screamed. The sportswriter laughed.

At Lanternglass's back she heard the wind whap against the windows, and suddenly Dorothy jumped to her feet, staring outside with enormous eyes.

"Whoa, Mom, it's *really* blowing," she said.

Lanternglass rotated in her office chair for a look. For a moment they all stopped what they were doing and stood still to stare through the windows. Fog roiled and foamed on the other side of the glass, all but obscuring the parking lot below. The wind roared, rushing the cloud along, the smoke a poisonous shade of yellow. Sparks whirled. For the first time, Aisha Lanternglass wondered if it had been a good idea to bring her daughter along with her to the office, if there was a chance of the flames overwhelming the fire department and reaching the building while they were still in it. But no, that was ridiculous. They didn't even have to be out of the facility until tomorrow morning. The Park Service would not have allowed them so much time to evacuate if there was any real danger. Besides, people were still arriving to help with the move. Down in the lot, she dimly saw a bright red Prius turning in off the highway. Then the smoke thickened and she lost sight of it.

"Come on," Lanternglass said. "Finish up, honey. I just need to do this, and we can go."

She began to type again, new title: A SINGLE BULLET CHANGES EVERYTHING. There, that had plenty of zing. Anyone who read that would just have to go on to the next line. Whatever the next line was going to be. Lanternglass would find her way to it in a moment. She narrowed her eyes, squinting at the screen, like a shooter taking aim.

"What the fuck?" said the sportswriter in a strangely shrill voice. He was standing in the doorway leading to the stairwell, ready to slow-walk the dolly down the steps. Lanternglass heard him but did not look over, was deep in her story space, forming the next sentence in her mind.

She did not look until the AR-15 went off with one flat, deafening crack, and then another, and then a third. She glanced around in time to see the sportswriter's head snap back, blood scattering in a fine spray across the particleboard ceiling above and behind him. He fell back-ward, bringing the iron dolly down on top of him, boxes sliding out from under the bungee cables holding them in place and crashing to the floor.

Kellaway stepped in and over the body, the Bushmaster just above the level of his hip, the strap thrown over his shoulder. Big man in a dove-colored polo already stained with blood. Shane Wolff, in the far corner of the room, rose to his full height, holding several loops of Eth-ernet cable. He lifted his free hand, palm out.

"Hey, whatever you want—" he said, and Kellaway shot him in the stomach and the chest, driving him back into the window behind him. Shane's shoulders hit the glass hard enough to put a pair of spiderweb cracks in it.

Lanternglass shoved her chair back with her rear and dropped to one knee. Dorothy had stood up to see what was happening, but Lantern-glass grabbed her wrist and pulled, hard, and the girl dropped to her knees. Lanternglass put her arms around her daughter and dragged her in under the desk.

The Bushmaster went off with more of those flat, hard reports. That would be the sound of Kellaway killing Julia, the intern. From her position in the footwell under her desk, Lanternglass could see the win-dows overlooking the parking lot and a bit of Tim Chen's private office through the wide panel of glass that served as one wall. Tim stood behind his desk, staring out into the office pool with bewildered eyes.

Beyond the windows the smoke boiled and rushed, driven by the wind. Another spinning wheel of sparks blew past. Dorothy shuddered, and Lanternglass held her daughter's head to her breast and pressed her mouth to her daughter's hair. She breathed in the deep smell of her child's scalp, of Dorothy's coconut-crème shampoo. The child's wiry arms were around her mother's waist. And Lanternglass thought, *Don't let him have seen us. Please, God, don't let him have seen us. Please, God, let this child live.*

Tim Chen disappeared from Lanternglass's view, moving toward the door of his office. He had picked up a marble bookend, a block of pink-and-white stone, the only thing he could find to fight with. Lanternglass heard him shout, an inarticulate cry of horror and rage, and the Bushmaster went off again, *chunk-chunk-chunk-chunk*, not eight feet away, just the other side of her desk. Tim Chen fell so hard the floor shook.

Her ears rang strangely. She had never held her daughter so tightly, could not have squeezed her any harder without breaking something. Lanternglass took the tiniest sip of air, was afraid that if she inhaled too deeply, Kellaway would hear. But then maybe he would not be able to hear anything after firing so many shots. Maybe after all that gunfire, he would be deaf to the small sounds of a shaking girl and a quietly gasping mother.

The wind roared, rising and rising in volume. Lanternglass stared out through the windows, into the smoke, and with a kind of horrified wonder saw a twisting rope of flame, three hundred feet tall, out in the murk: an incendiary top whirling down the middle of the highway. A slender tornado of fire, reaching up into the suffocating white sky and disappearing. If it turned toward the building, perhaps it would strike, and tear apart the bricks, and carry her daughter, Dorothy, away to some golden, burning, terrible yet wonderful Oz. Maybe it would carry them both away. At the sight of it, Aisha Lanternglass's chest filled with an awe that was like breath, swelling her lungs, swelling her heart. The beauty of the world and the horror of the world were twined together, like wind and flame. The smoke rose, filthy and dark, and pressed against the glass, and then subsided, and suddenly that blazing, twisting stairwell into the clouds was gone.

One combat boot appeared, coming down in front of their hiding place in the footwell beneath the desk. Dorothy's eyes were squeezed shut. She didn't see. Lanternglass stared out over her daughter's head, holding her breath. The other boot appeared. He was standing right in front of the desk.

Slowly, *slowly*, Kellaway bent down to look in at them. Holding the butt of the Bushmaster under his right armpit. He stared upon Lanternglass and her little girl with something very like serenity in his pale blue, almost white eyes.

"Just think. If you had a gun," he said to her, "this story might have a different ending."

ALOFT

1

HE HATED IT IN THE back of the little plane, squished in with the others. He hated the reek of gasoline and moldy canvas and his own rancid farts, and by the time they reached six thousand feet, Aubrey Griffin decided he couldn't go.

"I'm so sorry to do this, man—" Aubrey began, calling over his shoulder to the guy he thought of as Axe.

His jumpmaster's name had flown out of his head as soon as the dude introduced himself. By then Aubrey was having trouble hanging on to even the most basic information. In the half hour before they had boarded the single-engine Cessna, Aubrey's panic was making a roar of static that filled his head. People looked him right in the face and said things—shouted them, really, everyone souped up on adrenaline—but all he heard was unintelligible noise. He could grasp the occasional obscenity, nothing more.

So Aubrey began to think of him as Axe, short for Axe Body Spray, because the guy looked like he'd walked off the set of a commercial featuring hot rods, explosions, and models having pillow fights in their underwear. The jumpmaster was fit and lanky, with golden-red hair cut short and feathered back, and he possessed a coked-up energy that amplified rather than subdued Aubrey's terror. How absurd was it to have considered putting his life in the hands of someone he didn't even know by name?

"Whadja say?" Axe yelled.

It didn't seem like it should be so hard to make himself heard, especially to a guy who was strapped to his ass. They were harnessed together; Aubrey sat in Axe's lap like a child getting cozy with a shopping-mall Santa.

"I can't do this! I hoped like hell I could. I really thought—"

Axe shook his head. "That's normal! Everyone gets that!"

He was going to make him plead. Aubrey didn't want to plead, not in front of Harriet. To his dismay, he uncorked another string of greasy farts. They were inaudible over the drone of the engine, but they burned and stank. Axe had to be tasting every one of them.

It was awful to be pathetic in front of Harriet Cornell. It didn't matter that he and Harriet were never going to date, never be in love, never lie nude beneath cool sheets in St. Barts with the French windows open and the sound of the waves crashing on the reefs in the distance. He still had his daydreams to protect. It dismayed Aubrey to think this was the last memory of him that Harriet would take with her to Africa.

Harriet and Aubrey were both on their first jumps. (Or maybe it was more accurate to say Harriet was on her first jump. Aubrey had come to see in the last few moments that he was not.) They were going tandem, which meant each of them was buckled to a jumpmaster, men who did this every day. Brad and Ronnie Morris were in the plane as well. This was old hat for them, though, both boys experienced skydivers.

June Morris was dead, and they were all jumping in her memory: her brothers, Brad and Ronnie; Harriet, who had been her best friend; and Aubrey himself. June had been dead six weeks, wiped out at twenty-three by cancer. That was some odds-defying shit right there, Aubrey thought. It seemed to Aubrey you were about as likely to become a rock star as you were to die that young of something like lymphoma.

"There's nothing normal about it!" Aubrey shouted now. "I have a clinical diagnosis as a quivering pussy. Seriously, if you make me jump, I'm going to fill my pants with hot, creamy shit, man—"

At that moment the sound dropped in the hollow, roaring stainless-steel capsule of the light aircraft, and his voice carried from one end of the plane to the other. Aubrey was aware of Brad and Ronnie turning to look at him. They both had GoPro cameras screwed to their helmets. Presumably all this would be on YouTube later.

"The first rule of skydiving: Don't take a shit on the jumpmaster," Axe said.

The mindless thunder of the engine rose again. Brad and Ronnie looked away.

Aubrey didn't want to glance over at Harriet but couldn't help himself.

She wasn't staring at him, although he thought she had only just turned her face away. She clutched a small purple stuffed horse with a silver horn protruding from its brow and twee iridescent wings behind its forelegs: the Junicorn. Harriet and the Junicorn were turned to face the door, a big, loose, rattling hatch made out of clear plastic. Every time the plane tilted to the left, Aubrey was consumed by the sickening certainty that the door would flap open and he'd slide right out while Axe Body Spray hacked a maniacal, coked-up laugh. It seemed like nothing was holding it shut, fucking nothing.

The way Harriet was pointedly not looking at him was almost as unpleasant as if she'd been staring at him with a mixture of pity and disappointment. Aubrey didn't need Axe to give him permission to stay in the plane. His opinion didn't matter. What Aubrey wanted was for Harriet to tell him it was all right.

No. What he wanted was to go out the side of the plane with her—*ahead* of her. But to do that he would have had to be someone else. Maybe that was what he hated most: not his queasy stomach, not his sick farts, not the collapse of his nerve. Maybe what he despised most was being found out. Was anything in all the world more heartrending than being found out by someone you wanted to love you?

He leaned forward and thunked his helmet against hers to get her attention.

She turned her face toward him, and he saw, for the first time, that she was pale and drawn, lips pressed so tightly together that all the color had gone out of them. It came to him with something like relief that she was terrified, too. He grasped at an idea with an almost frantic hope: Maybe she would stay in the plane with him! If they were cowards together, the situation would no longer be shameful and tragic; it would be the most hilarious thing ever.

He had meant to tell her he was backing out, but now, seized by this new notion, he shouted, "How you doing?" Prepared to comfort her. Looking forward to it, in fact.

"I'm *this* close to throwing up."

"Me, too!" he cried, perhaps with a dash too much enthusiasm.

"I'm shivering like a leaf."

"Jesus. I'm so glad I'm not the only one."

"I don't want to be here," she said, her helmet resting against his, their noses almost touching. Her eyes, the cool greenish brown of a frozen marsh, were wide with undisguised anxiety.

"Fuck!" he said. "Me neither! *Me neither!*" He was close to laughter, close to taking her hand.

She shifted her gaze back to that door of clear, rattling plastic. "I don't want to sit one more second in this plane. I just want to be out there *doing* it. It's like waiting in line for a roller coaster. The wait just about kills you. You can't stop building it up in your mind. But then, when you're on the ride, you're like, 'Why was I so scared? I want to do this again!'"

A weak, small, oily fart of disappointment slipped free. The enthusiasm, the swell of sweet courage he heard in her voice, filled him with Seattle-grunge levels of despair.

Harriet's eyes widened. She pointed out the clattering door and shouted with an almost childlike excitement, "Hey! Hey, guys! Spaceship!"

"What's that?" cried the big lumbersexual spooning her from behind.

Harriet was strapped to a chunky guy with the kind of bushy beard that suggested a closetful of flannel shirts and a second job serving fair-trade espresso in an upscale coffeehouse. When it was time to pair up with a jumpmaster, Aubrey had acted quickly to claim Axe Body Spray. He didn't want Harriet leaping out a plane with the dude, her ass nestled against the guy's probable erection all the way down. The Wookiee had paired with Harriet. Unfortunately (and predictably), she and the furry fat guy had been falling around laughing from their first moments together. By lunch the two of them were dueting to an a cappella version of "Total Eclipse of the Heart," her chubby jumpmaster singing the male parts in a warm, low, surprisingly soulful voice. Aubrey loathed him. It was Aubrey's role to be soulful and to surprise Harriet with laughter. He loathed all clever, decent fat men who cozied their way into Harriet's spontaneous hugs.

"There!" Harriet cried. "There, *there*! Aubrey! You see it?"

"See what?" yelled her Wookiee, even though she wasn't talking to him.

"That cloud! Look at that weird cloud! It looks just like a UFO!"

Aubrey didn't want to look. He didn't want to go anywhere near that door. But he couldn't help himself—Axe was edging closer to see what she was pointing at and taking Aubrey along for the ride.

Harriet pointed at a cloud, shaped just like a flying saucer from a 1950s alien-invasion flick. It was wide and circular and at the center it was mounded up in a cottony dome.

"Kinda big for a UFO!" shouted Chewbackish. He was right—that cloud had to be almost a mile across.

"It's the mother ship!" Harriet cried with glee.

"I saw one that looked like a doughnut once," Axe said. "Like God blew a smoke ring. Had a big hole in the middle. We're much closer to the supernatural up here. Everything gets very surreal when you're falling from twelve thousand feet. Reality gets as flimsy as parachute silk, and your mind opens to new possibilities!"

Oh, fuck you and your flimsy parachute-silk reality—that was Aubrey's view. Fuck Axe and his promise that the experience would open Harriet to new possibilities (like maybe a post-jump three-way with Axe and Harriet's furry jumpmaster).

Harriet shook her head with satisfaction. "June would've loved that cloud. She believed 'They' walk among us. The Greys. The Visitors."

Fat-and-Furry said, "We'll get a closer look pretty soon. We're almost at jump altitude."

Aubrey felt a poke of fresh alarm, like the stick of a needle, but for an instant anyway the jump was only the *second* thing on his mind. He leaned forward, hardly aware he was doing it, surprising Axe, who had to lean forward with him. The harness joining them together creaked.

Aubrey watched the cloud for half a minute as they climbed and began to circle toward it—they would pass right above it in a moment or two. Then he looked past Harriet at the guy with the beard.

"Yeah!" he said. "Yeah, man, she's right. That cloud is fucked up. Look again."

Harriet's jumpmaster said, "It's a fine specimen of a cumulonimbus. Very cool."

"No it's not. It's not *cool*. It's *weird*."

The Wookiee gave him a glance of appraisal that seemed to mingle boredom with contempt. Aubrey shook his head, annoyed that the guy didn't get it, and pointed again.

"It's going *that* way," Aubrey said, jabbing a finger to the north.

"So what?" Brad Morris called out. For the second time in the last few minutes, everyone was looking at Aubrey.

"All the other clouds are going in the *opposite* direction!" Aubrey yelled, pointing south. "It's going the wrong way."

2

THE CLOUD HELD THEIR ATTENTION for one shared moment of respectful silence before the chubby jumpmaster explained. "It's called an air box. It's a pattern of circular flow. The air pushes in one direction at one altitude, then folds back and shoves everything in the exact opposite direction at a different altitude. When you go up in a hot-air balloon, a current like that means you can float away from your point of departure, then drop a couple thousand feet and float back to the exact same place you took off." The chubby jumpmaster did hot-air-balloon rides, too, and had offered to take Harriet up sometime for free—an evil suggestion as far as Aubrey was concerned, tantamount to inviting her to a sex club for a lazy night of cocaine and hand jobs. Aubrey supposed most men who went into skydiving and ballooning and other forms of high-altitude devilry did it for the pussy. There were all those opportunities to buckle girls into safety harnesses, to cop a feel when comforting them in a moment of high anxiety, to win their admiration with cheery shows of fearlessness. Of course, to be fair, Aubrey himself wouldn't have been in the plane if not to impress Harriet.

"Oh," Harriet said, shrugging with mock disappointment. "Too bad. I thought we were about to make contact."

Axe held up two fingers, Churchill declaring victory on VE-Day. "Two minutes!"

Harriet bopped her helmet against Aubrey's and met his gaze. "Yes?"

Aubrey tried a smile, but it felt more like a grimace.

"No," he said. "I can't."

"You can, though!" Axe shouted, finally deciding not to pretend he couldn't hear. "This whole experience is about the power of 'can'!"

Aubrey ignored him. Axe Body Spray didn't matter. The only thing that concerned him was how Harriet took it.

"I really wanted to," he told her.

Harriet nodded and took his hand. "I *have* to. I promised June."

Of course he had promised June, too. When Harriet said she would jump, Aubrey had sworn he'd be screaming all the way down right beside her. At the time June was dying, and it had seemed like the right thing to do.

"I feel like shit—" Aubrey began.

"Don't worry!" Harriet yelled. "I think it's rad you came this far!"

"I doubled up on my antianxiety meds and everything!" He wished he could stop explaining himself.

"One minute!" Axe yelled.

"It's all right, Aubrey," Harriet said, smiling impishly. "Hey, I better get myself ready, right?"

"Right," he agreed, nodding feverishly.

"I'm set to go!" Ronnie Morris shouted. "I could use the fresh air."

Brad Morris laughed, and they slapped each other five. It stung Aubrey that they could make a joke out of the cowardly farts stinking up the compartment. Bad enough that he was pitifully scared, but even worse to be betrayed by his body and then ridiculed for it.

Aubrey looked at Harriet, but her gaze was intent on the clear plastic door now. He had been dismissed from her thoughts. That felt worse than he had imagined it would. He had expected her to be disappointed in him, but she wasn't disappointed, just indifferent. He'd made himself believe he *had* to do this, had to be here for June, for Harriet, but in fact his presence one way or another was of no matter.

And now that he was sure he wasn't going, he felt listless and deflated. Harriet was holding up the Junicorn and whispering to it, pointing it out at the vast UFO-shaped cloud, just as the Cessna banked toward it.

Axe fiddled with the camera on his own helmet. "Hey, listen. Audrey, man." It was a small, bitter pleasure that the jumpmaster didn't know his name either. "If you've made up your mind, it's your right to back out. But you should know it costs the same whether you go or not. I can't even refund you the cost of your DVD."

"I'm sorry I ruined everyone's good time," Aubrey announced, but the really miserable thing was that he hadn't ruined anything for any of them. No one was even listening.

The plane tilted ever more steeply into its turn.

"We're going to circle back over the landing strip—" Axe began, which was when everything shut off.

The propeller on the nose of the little Cessna whined and clattered and stopped turning very abruptly. Wind whooshed under the wings, the soft bellow filling the sudden silence. The running lights inside the jump compartment blinked out.

The vast, whistling silence amazed Aubrey more than it frightened him.

"What happened?" Harriet asked.

"Lenny!" Axe shouted toward the front of the plane. "What the hell, man? We just stall out?"

The pilot, a curly-haired guy in a puffy headset, flipped a toggle switch, pulled a long steel stick out of the dash, and poked a button.

The Cessna floated, a sheet of newspaper hovering above a subway grate.

Lenny the pilot looked over his shoulder at them and shrugged. He wore a white T-shirt with the Kool-Aid mascot on it, that inanely smiling pitcher of red juice. He yanked his headset down around his neck.

"I don't know!" Lenny yelled. He didn't sound worried—more annoyed. "Maybe! But I also got no electric! Everything just died. S'like a connection is loose in the battery."

The Cessna quivered, wings tilting minutely, this way and that.

"No big deal to me," Brad said. "I was going to step out right around here anyway."

"Yeah," Ronnie said. "I was thinking I'd like to stretch my legs."

"Go on!" Lenny called. "Jump! After everyone is out, I'll dive and pop it. If that doesn't work, I'll have to glide her in. Hope I hit the runway. Gonna be bumpy if I don't."

"Oh, come on!" Aubrey shouted. "Come on, this is *bullshit*! I don't believe a word."

Brad scooted to the door and rotated the stainless-steel latches that held it shut, one after the other. He pushed it up and out of the way. The opening was roughly as wide as a soccer net. He put a foot onto the piping that ran under the door.

"Audrey, my friend," Axe said gently.

"No!" Aubrey shouted. "This isn't funny! Make him start the plane! You can't coerce someone to jump this way!"

"See you on the dirt," Brad said. He clung to the side of the plane, facing in toward them, one hand holding the rail above. With his free hand, he snapped off a jaunty salute—*asshole*—stepped from the plane, and was snatched away by the sky.

"Audrey! Audrey, breathe!" Axe said. "No one is running a game on you. There *is* a problem with the aircraft." He spoke very slowly and enunciated each word with care. "We would never shut a plane off to scare you into jumping. Honestly. A lot of people back out last minute. I don't care. I get paid the same either way."

"Why would the plane just stop working?"

"I don't know. But believe me, we don't want to be in it when he tries to pop the engine."

"Why not?"

"Because he's going to point it at the ground."

Ron Morris scooted to the edge of the open door, preparing to follow his brother. He sat for a moment, feet on the bar that ran along the outside of the plane, elbows resting on his knees, enjoying the view. The blast of the wind made his skin ripple, distorted the loose flesh of his chubby face. Gradually, almost like a man nodding off, he tipped forward, then dropped headfirst and was gone.

"Hurry up back there!" shouted Lenny from the single seat at the controls.

Harriet had been sitting between her jumpmaster's legs, looking from Aubrey to Axe to the pilot with a fearful fascination. She squeezed the Junicorn to her chest, as if worried someone might be about to try to snatch it away from her. The Junicorn was a stand-in for June herself, and Harriet was under orders to look after it and take it with her while she did all the things June was never going to get to do: see pyramids, surf in Africa, skydive. Aubrey had the ridiculous sense of being stared at by girl and stuffed animal alike.

"Aubrey," Harriet said, "I think we ought to go. Right now. Both of us." She looked past Aubrey to Axe. "Can we go together? Like, hold hands?"

Axe shook his head. "We'll be three seconds behind you."

"Please, if we could just hold hands. My friend is scared, but I know he can do this if we go together," she said, and Aubrey loved her so much he felt like crying. He wanted to tell her right now that he loved her, but that was even more beyond him than stepping out over a twelve-thousand-foot drop.

"It's not a good idea on a first jump. Our drogue chutes could tangle. Harriet, please go. We'll follow."

The chubby jumpmaster began to scoot across the steel floor on his butt, shifting Harriet away and closer to the door.

"Audrey?" Axe said. His voice was soothing and calm and reasonable. "If we do not go, you are risking my life as well as your own. I want to jump while we can. I'd prefer your consent."

"Oh, God."

"Close your eyes!"

"Oh, God. Oh, my God. This is fucked."

Harriet and her jumpmaster had shifted all the way over to the open hatch. Harriet's legs were hanging out. She cast a final pleading look at Aubrey over her shoulder. Then she grasped her jumpmaster's hand and they were gone.

"You'll have solid ground under your feet before you know it," Axe said.

Aubrey shut his eyes. He nodded okay.

"I'm sorry I'm so chickenshit," Aubrey said.

Axe humped them across the bare steel, sliding them toward the opening in modest increments. Aubrey thought, randomly, that he was glad Harriet wasn't sitting in Axe's lap, feeling him pump his hips against her ass this way.

"Have you ever jumped with anyone worse than me?" Aubrey asked.

"Not really," Axe said, and pushed them out the side of the plane.

It was more than ten thousand feet to the ground, one minute of free fall and perhaps four minutes of slow, gliding hang time in the parachute. But Aubrey Griffin and his jumpmaster dropped just under four stories before they struck the edge of the UFO-shaped cloud that wasn't really a cloud at all and stopped falling.

3

FEAR THICKENS TIME, TURNS IT slow and viscous. One second of deeply felt terror lasts longer than ten regular seconds. Aubrey fell for only a moment, but it was an instant that lasted longer than the whole long, circling climb into the sky on board the Cessna.

As they went through the door, Aubrey tried to turn, to stay in the plane, just as Axe was pulling them out. He plunged backward, looking up at the aircraft, with the jumpmaster beneath him. Aubrey dropped with a great tingling thrill of emotion that ran from balls to throat, a single thought beating in his mind as he fell:

STILL ALIVE STILL ALIVE STILL ALIVE STILL—

—and then they hit.

What they struck didn't feel at all like earth but much closer to raw bread dough. It was thick and rubbery and cold, and if they had dropped only ten or even fifteen feet into it, it might've been a soft, springy landing. In fact, though, they had fallen thirty-nine feet, and Axe absorbed the full brunt of the impact. The fragile hoops of his pelvis snapped in three places. The upper part of his right femur broke with a pop. Aubrey's helmet snapped back into Axe's face and smashed his nose, which shattered with a glassy crack.

Aubrey himself was not entirely unhurt. Axe kneed him in the hip hard enough to make a gruesome bruise. He also banged his funny bone so sharply he lost all the sensation in his right hand.

Dry, cold smoke erupted around them in a great puff. It had a sharp odor, like pencil shavings, like the wheels of a train, like lightning.

"Hey," Aubrey said, in a thin, shaking voice. "Hey, what happened?"

"Aaa!" Axe cried. *"Aaa!"*

"Are you all right?"

"Aaaa! Oh, Jesus. Oh, cocksucker."

All that high, singing emotion had been slammed out of Aubrey on impact. All the thought had been slammed out of him, too. He waved his arms and legs in the helpless, struggling motion of a beetle turned over on its back. He stared up into the clear blue. He could still see the plane, the size of a toy, above them but tilting away to the east. It was funny how far away it was already.

Axe sobbed.

The sound was so unexpected, so dreadful, it shocked Aubrey out of his stunned, blank, amazed state. He made a fist with his right hand, trying to work the feeling back into it.

"Can you unbuckle me?" he asked.

"I don't know!" Axe said. "Oh, man. I think I'm really fucked up."

"What did we hit?" Aubrey asked. It looked like a cloud, which didn't make any sense. "What are we on?"

Axe panted in a horrible, frantic sort of way. Aubrey thought he was working up to another sob.

"You have to unclip me," Aubrey said.

Axe groped up and down Aubrey's sides. One carabiner snapped loose, then another, then a third, and finally the fourth, and Aubrey rolled off him, wrestled his way up into a sitting position, and looked around.

He sat on the cloud, an island of churned white cream, adrift in a vastness of serene blue. They were at one tip of a mass almost a mile long, with a great central bulge in the shape of a dome. It reminded Aubrey of St. Paul's Cathedral in London.

A sense of nausea tickled the inside of his throat. His head swam.

He pressed his tingling right hand into the cloud. At first he was pushing his palm down into cool, drifting vapor. But as he sank his weight into it, the fog *stiffened* into a solid, with the consistency of cream cheese or maybe mashed potatoes or, really, Play-Doh. When Aubrey lifted his hand, the cloud melted back into mist.

"Fuck," he said. For the moment it was the most sophisticated response he could manage.

"Oh, dude. Oh, God. Something is really broken inside me."

Aubrey turned a stunned stare upon the other man, who was writhing and twisting weakly in the unsettled smoke. His heels kicked at the mist, drawing furrows in that weird, semi-solid cream. Axe's sporty goggles—the lenses were the coppery red of a Cape Cod sunset—were smashed. He probably couldn't see, was feeling around blindly with one hand. The GoPro camera mounted on his helmet gazed blankly and stupidly at Aubrey.

"Did I pull the chute?" Axe asked. "I musta, huh, if we're on the ground. What happened? Did I bang my head on the side of the door going out the plane?" His voice was strained and feeble with pain. He didn't know where they were. He didn't understand what had happened to them.

Aubrey didn't understand what had happened either. It was hard to think. Too much had occurred too quickly, and none of it made sense or seemed real.

Axe had not opened their chute—although the drogue chute had deployed automatically. This was a very small secondary chute, a little bucket of red-and-yellow silk, just big enough to wrap a Thanksgiving turkey. The wind pulled it out and straight back, and now it fluttered kitelike over the edge of the cloud, swerving this way and that. Aubrey wasn't sure what a drogue chute did. Axe had tried to explain, but at the time Aubrey had been too nervous to retain any information.

It came to Aubrey that Axe wasn't writhing and twisting after all. He wasn't kicking his feet either. He was lying perfectly still, one arm curled over his torso, the other hand clapped to his hip. His heels were making shallow indentations in the milky paste of the cloud because the drogue chute was slowly but steadily hauling him away.

"Hey," Aubrey said. "Hey, man, watch out."

He grabbed the harness around Axe's chest and tugged, and Axe shrieked in pain, a sound so piercing that Aubrey immediately recoiled and let go.

"My chest!" Axe screamed. "My fucking chest! What are you doing?"

"I just want to pull you back from the edge," Aubrey said. He reached for the harness again, and Axe elbowed his hand aside.

"You don't move someone who's been in an accident, you neurotic asshole!" Axe cried. "Don't you know *anything*?"

"I'm sorry."

Axe panted for breath. His cheeks were smeared with tears.

"Edge of what?" Axe asked at last, in a miserable, almost childish voice.

At that moment the breeze rose, churning the cloud milk around them. The drogue chute swelled, lifted, and suddenly snapped straight back, jerking upward into the bright blue sky. The wind yanked all the parachute cords taut and half lifted Axe into a sitting position. The jumpmaster screamed again. His boots dragged through the rubbery, puffy cloud stuff, making trenches six inches deep. Aubrey thought again of uncooked bread, of someone sinking fingers into raw, elastic dough.

Aubrey grabbed for one of those trailing boots, caught it with his still-numb right hand. But there was no feeling in his fingers, and he held it for only a moment before it was yanked right out of his grasp.

"Edge of *what*?" Axe screamed as he was carried away.

The wind sucked the drogue chute up and back and took him off the edge of the cloud with a sudden whisking motion, like a maid yanking a sheet off a hotel-room bed. Axe yelped, grabbed the parachute cords rising around him. He was pulled up into the sky, about six or seven feet. Then the wind flagged, and he promptly dropped, past the cloud and out of sight.

4

THE WIND SANG, A SHRILL jeering tone, barely audible.

Aubrey stared at the place where Axe had been, as if he might reappear.

After a time he discovered he was trembling helplessly, although he had left his panic behind, on the airplane. What he felt now was bigger than fight or flight. It was shock, perhaps.

Or maybe it was just the cold. In the world below, it was the third day of August, an afternoon of dry, wilting heat. Pollen coated cars in a layer of mustard-colored grime. Bumblebees droned their sleepy trancesong in the dry, baked grass. Up here, though, it was a cool morning in early October, as crisp and chilly and sweet as a bite of a ripe apple.

He thought, *This isn't happening.*

He thought, *I was so scared something snapped in my mind.*

He thought, *I struck my head on the side of the plane, and this is my last giddy fantasy as I die of a skull fracture.*

Aubrey riffled through these possibilities like a man dealing cards, but only in a remote, half-aware sort of way, barely registering them.

There was no arguing with the brisk chill in the air or with the whistle of the breeze, which was producing a sharp, clear E note.

For a long time, he remained on all fours, peering off the trailing edge of the cloud, wondering if he could move. He was not sure he dared. He felt that if he moved, gravity would notice him and drop him through the cloud.

He patted the mist ahead of him, stroked it like a cat. It firmed up into a lumpy, pliant mass at the first touch.

Aubrey crawled, his thighs quaking. It was very like moving across a surface of soft clay. When he'd gone a yard or so, he looked back. The path he was making across the cloud melted after he'd started on his way, turning back to slow, curdling fog.

When he was five feet from the ragged, trailing southern edge of the cloud, he sank to his belly and lay flat. He squirmed a bit farther on his stomach, his pulse whamming so hard that the day brightened and darkened with each beat of his heart. Aubrey had always been scared of heights. It was a good question, why a man with a dread of heights, a man who avoided flying whenever he could, would agree to jump from an airplane. The answer, of course, was maddeningly simple: Harriet.

The cloud tapered off at the edge . . . tapered off but did not give way. The very end of the cloud was only an inch thick but the firmest, hardest stuff yet, as hard as concrete, with no sense of give at all.

Aubrey peeked over the edge.

Ohio lay beneath him, an almost perfectly flat expanse of variegated squares in shades of emerald, wheat, richest brown, palest amber. Those would be the famous waves of grain mentioned with such admiration in "America the Beautiful." Ruler-straight ribbons of blacktop bisected the fields below. A red pickup slid along one of those black threads like a bright steel bead on an abacus.

He saw, to the south and west, the runway of baked red dirt, behind the hangar that housed Cloud 9 Skydiving Adventures. And there was the Cessna, just touching down. Either Lenny had gotten the plane going again or he'd done a fine job of gliding it in.

A moment later Aubrey saw a parachute, a vast, straining tent of gleaming white silk. He watched it sink to the ground and settle in a field that had been planted with something: green rows separated by lines of dark earth. The chute crumpled in on itself. Axe was on the ground then. He was on the ground, and he had been aware enough to pull the rip cord. Axe was down, and soon help would reach him, and he would tell them—

—something. Aubrey could not quite imagine what. *I left my client on a cloud?*

Below, the parachute rustled across the field, expanding and shrinking like a lung.

When Axe told them what had happened, they were going to figure him for hysterical. A bloodied, badly injured man who raved that he'd landed on a cloud was going to be met with worry and words of comfort, not belief. They were going to reach for the explanation that made the most sense. They were going to assume that Aubrey had come unclipped in some kind of freak accident, possibly after striking the side of the plane—that would explain Axe's injuries as well—and fallen to his death. Even to Aubrey this seemed a more plausible story than what had really happened, and Aubrey was actually on the cloud looking down.

It was a dreadful idea, but there was also something wrong with it. He tried to see it—spotting the flaw was as tricksy as trying to find a mosquito that whined in one ear but disappeared when you spun around looking for it. He almost had to stop searching for it, stop thinking altogether. Had to let his eyes go unfocused.

A dry, throbbing pain was building in his sinuses, behind his temples.

He reviewed his last glimpse of Axe Body Spray in the instant before the drogue chute yanked him off into the emptiness—and then he saw it. His mind's eye focused in on the stupid, glaring lens of the GoPro mounted atop the jumpmaster's helmet. The whole thing was on video. No one needed to take Axe's word for what had happened. All they had to do was watch the recording. Then they'd know.

Then they'd come for him.

5

SOMETIME LATER HE ROSE TO his knees and looked around.

The great wheel of cloud still held the pie-plate shape of a UFO, with that great dome rising in the exact center, its dominant feature. The rest was far from smooth; the surface bubbled up, ruffled into dunes and hillocks.

Aubrey searched the blue sky until he felt dizzy and had to lower his gaze. When his head stopped swimming, he realized he was still on the very edge, a bad place to be. He slid inward on his butt, putting distance between himself and the precipice.

At last he decided he was going to have to risk standing up. He pushed himself to his feet, legs still trembling.

Aubrey Griffin stood alone on his island of cloud.

It came to him slowly that the harness was uncomfortable. The straps made a tight, painful V at his crotch, squeezing his balls. Another strap was tight across his chest, making it hard to breathe. Or was that the skimpy air?

He unbuckled the harness and stepped out of it. He was going to drop it into the cloud when he saw the coatrack.

It was to his left, on the edge of his vision: an old-fashioned coatrack, with eight curved hooks, made out of sculpted cloud.

He eyed it carefully, feeling dry of throat, aware his heart was beating much, much too fast.

"The fuck is that?" he asked no one in particular.

Of course it was perfectly obvious what it was. Anyone with eyes could see what it was. He told himself it wasn't really a coatrack, that it was just a deformity in the cloud. He circled to inspect it from every angle. It looked like a coatrack no matter where he stood—a coatrack of cloudstuff, but a coatrack nonetheless.

Experimentally, he hung the olive-colored harness from one of the hooks. It should've dropped, scattering veils of fog.

Instead it dangled from the hook, rocking in the breeze.

Aubrey said, "Ha!"

It was not a laugh but the actual word, a sound of surprise, not hilarity. There was no reason to be surprised, really. The cloud was holding him up, and he weighed 175 pounds. What was a canvas harness that couldn't be all of two pounds? He unbuckled his helmet and stuck it on another hook.

The ache that had begun in his sinuses was now a skewer of pain that shot from his left temple to the right. That was the skull fracture, he thought, the one he'd picked up when he smashed his head on the side of the plane. That's all any of it was: the vivid fantasy of a brain with splinters of bone poked through it.

Beneath that notion, though, was a very different idea. Another one of those mental mosquitoes was whining around his head—the inside of his head rather than the outside. He was thinking, *How does a cloud know what a coatrack looks like?* A notion so absurd it sounded like the caption to a *New Yorker* cartoon.

He sucked at the thin, cool air and for the first time wondered what the temperature would be like in six hours, when the sun went down.

But by then he would be on CNN. He would be the biggest news story in the world. There would be a gnat swarm of TV news helicopters whirring around to get live footage of the man who walked on clouds. The GoPro video would be running on every channel in an hour, would be all over the Internet.

He wished he had not been such a shrill and pathetic panic case in the Cessna. If he'd known he was going to be on a video seen worldwide, he thought he could've at least *pretended* to have nerve.

Aubrey had wandered a few steps from the coatrack, reeling along in an only half-aware way. He paused and looked back. The coatrack was still there. The coatrack *meant* something. Was more than a coatrack. But in his headachy state, he could not work out its full importance.

He walked.

At first he walked like a man who suspected he was on rotten ice. He would slide one foot forward to be sure the cloud would remain solid underfoot, kicking puffs of mist ahead of him. The surface held, and after a bit he began—not even knowing he was doing it—to walk normally.

He stayed at least six feet from the edge at all times, but initially did not wander toward the bulge in the center of the cloud. Instead he found himself circumnavigating his desert island in the sky. He scanned for airplanes and paused once when he saw one. A jet drew a line of white smoke across the brilliant blue. It was miles away, and after a moment he stopped paying attention. He understood he had no more chance of being noticed than if that plane were passing overhead while he walked across the campus of the Cleveland Institute of Music, where he had been an undergrad.

He was light-headed, and he held up now and then to catch his breath. The third time he stopped, he bowed his head, gripped his knees, and inhaled deeply, until the vertiginous, about-to-fall-over sensation passed. When he straightened up, he was seized with a sudden, perfectly sensible realization.

There wasn't enough air up here.

Or at the very least there wasn't as much air as he was used to. How high was he? He remembered Axe telling them they were at twelve thousand feet right before the Cessna lost power. Could you even breathe at twelve thousand feet? Obviously. He was breathing now. A phrase, "altitude sickness," rose to the top of his thoughts.

He was a long time circling his vast platter of fog. For the most part, it was flat: a bit lumpy here, dipping a bit there. He climbed to the top of the occasional dune, descended into a few shallow ditches. He lost himself for a while in a confused series of gullies on the eastern rim, wandering through narrow crevasses of white fluff. In the north he paused to admire a mass of cloud boulders that bore a close resemblance to the head of a bulldog. On the western side of the cloud, he crossed a series of three swells that looked like enormous speed bumps. But in the end he walked for almost an hour and was surprised at how featureless his hubcap-shaped island really was.

By the time he made his way back to the coatrack, he was dizzy and weak and sick of the cold. He needed something to drink. It hurt to swallow.

In Aubrey's experience, dreams had a habit of making jumpy, improbable leaps. First you were in an elevator with your sister's best friend; then you were boning her on the roof in front of family and friends; then the building began to sway in a violent wind; then cyclones were touching down all over Cleveland. Here on the cloud, though, there was no narrative at all, let alone a whirl of frantic dream incidents. One moment staggered into the next. He could not dream his way off the cloud and on to something better.

He stared at the coatrack, wishing he could send a picture of it to Harriet. Whenever he saw something beautiful or improbable, his first impulse was to take a snap and send it to her in a text. Of course, if she started getting photographs of clouds from her missing-presumed-dead friend, she would probably think he was texting her from heaven, she would probably start screaming her—

And at that moment Aubrey Griffin remembered it was the twenty-first century and there was a smartphone in his pocket.

It was in his cargo shorts, under his jumpsuit. He had switched it off when the plane was taxiing down the runway, as one would on any flight, but he still had it. Now that he was thinking about it, he could feel it digging into his thigh.

He didn't have to wait for them to download the footage on Axe's GoPro. He could call them directly. If he had a strong enough connection, he could even video-chat with them.

He snatched at the zipper of his jumpsuit. The cold air knifed into the opening, going right through the T-shirt underneath. Aubrey wrestled the phone out of his pocket—and it flipped right out of his sweaty hand.

Aubrey cried out, sure it would drop through the cloud and vanish.

It didn't, though. It landed in a cup of hardened fog, shaped almost like a soap dish.

He snatched the phone back up, shaking helplessly now from the shock of sudden hope. He squeezed the button to turn it on, his thoughts running ahead to the next bit: He would call Harriet; he would tell her he was alive; she would begin to sob with relief and incredulity; he would start to cry, too; they would both have a happy cry together; and she would say, *Omigod, Aubrey, where are you?* and he would say, *Well, babe, you aren't gonna believe this, but—*

The screen of his phone remained stubbornly black and blank. He pressed the On switch again.

When it still didn't light up, he squeezed the On button as hard as he could, clenching his teeth as if he were engaged in some activity that required brute force—loosening a rusted lug nut on a flat tire, for example.

Nothing.

"What. The actual. Fuck?" he said, squeezing and squeezing until his hand ached.

His dead phone offered no explanations.

It didn't make sense. He was sure it still had a full charge, or close to it. He tried a force restart. Nothing.

He pressed the glass face to his brow and begged it psychically to be good to him, to remember how well he'd treated it over the years. Then he patiently tried again.

Nope.

He stared at it, his eyes dry and sore, hating Steve Jobs, hating his phone service carrier.

"This is not fair," he told the useless brick of black glass in his right hand. "You don't get to just die. Why would you just stop working?"

The reply he heard in his mind came not in his own voice but in the voice of jumpmaster Axe: *What the hell, man? We just stall out?* And Lenny the pilot's reply: *I don't know! Everything just died.*

A bad thought began to take shape. Aubrey had a Shinola watch, a Christmas gift from his mother, a thing with a leather strap and honest-to-God moving hands. It didn't have apps, didn't connect to his phone, didn't do anything except look good and tell the time. Aubrey pushed back the sleeve of his jumpsuit to stare at it. The hands read 4:23. The second hand wasn't moving. He stared at the watch face without blinking until he was convinced the minute hand wasn't moving either.

The cloud had done something to the Cessna when they flew over it. It emitted some kind of electromagnetic force that could zap the battery in a light aircraft, or a watch, or a smartphone.

Or a GoPro camera.

The idea was so woeful he wanted to shout in dismay. The only thing that stopped him was fatigue. Shouting up here in the cool, dry air seemed like a lot more effort than he could manage.

He saw clearly now: No one was going to upload a video of him lost on an island of cloud, a Robinson Crusoe of the sky. He was not going to go viral. News helicopters were not going to crowd around the man who walked in the heavens. If they got close, their cameras would record nothing and the helicopters would drop like cement blocks. But no one was going to come, because his jumpmaster's helmet cam had fried along with the battery under the plane's hood. The video might have recorded a few unpleasant minutes of Aubrey growing nauseated with anxiety, but it had certainly lost power well before they took the plunge.

The unfairness of it toppled him. He dropped heavily onto his rear, arms crossed over his knees. But even just sitting up required too much effort. He curled on his side, going fetal. Clouds puffed and settled around him. He decided to shut his eyes and wait awhile. Maybe when he opened them, he'd discover he had passed out before even getting on the plane. Maybe if he took deep breaths and rested, when he next lifted his head there would be green grass beneath him and concerned faces—Harriet's among them—bent over him.

It was just cool enough to make him a tiny bit uncomfortable. At some point, nestled in a soft, slightly elastic nest of cloud stuff, he reached out absently, found the corner of a blanket, drew a thick quilt of churning white smoke across his body, and slept.

6

THERE WAS ONE GOOD MOMENT, just as he woke, when he didn't remember any of it.

He gazed into a bright, clean sky, and he felt that the world was a kind place. His thoughts turned naturally to Harriet, as they often did when he first awoke. Aubrey liked to imagine rolling over and finding her beside him. He liked to imagine her bare back, the sharp, clean lines of her shoulder blades and spine. It was his favorite morning thought.

He rolled over and looked out across barren cloud.

The shock of it jolted through him, knocked the lazy, rested, in-no-rush-to-get-up feeling right out of him. He sat up and found he was in a large bed, a four-poster shaped out of white cotton. Blankets of creamy smoke had been pushed down around his waist. Pillows of vanilla custard were mounded beneath his head.

His coatrack kept a lonely watch a few feet away, helmet and harness dangling where he'd left them.

It was close to dusk now. The red coal of the sun stood off to the west, almost level with him. His shadow stretched to the far edge of the cloud island. The shadow of the bed was harder to see, a shadow cast by a ghost.

He did not give the bed much thought, not then. It was like the coatrack, just on a larger scale, and at the moment he was still too drowsy to manage much in the way of amazement. He slipped from under the blankets and crossed to the trailing edge of the island, keeping only about four feet between himself and the drop.

The country below was drenched in crimson glare. The green fields were shading to black. He did not see the runway, did not recognize any of what was below him. How fast was the cloud moving? Fast enough to have left the headquarters of Cloud 9 Skydiving Adventures far behind. He was surprised, and also surprised at his surprise.

Aubrey studied the darkening map of Ohio below. Or at least he *assumed* it was still Ohio. He saw forest. He saw ruddy rectangles of sun-roasted earth. He saw aluminum roofs flashing in the dying furnace light of the day. He spotted the broad, dark stroke of a state highway almost directly below, but who knew which one it might be?

He thought he was still being carried north and east, at least based on where the sun was going down. What was ahead? Canton? They might've skirted by Canton while he dozed. He couldn't even begin to estimate how fast the cloud was moving, not without some way to keep time.

It unnerved him, looking over the edge of the cloud. With the help of a therapist, Dr. Wan, he'd made good progress, had come to feel he was well past his fear of heights—one of a dozen neurotic anxieties she'd been working on with him. At the end of their sessions, she would push open her office window and they'd both stick their heads out to peer at the sidewalk six stories below. For a long time, he could not look without being nearly overcome by vertigo, but eventually he got to the point where he could nonchalantly lean on the sill and whistle Louie Armstrong numbers into empty space. Dr. Wan was a big believer in "testing the anxiety," in steadily diminishing its power by confronting it. But a sixth-floor office was one thing and a platform of smoke located almost two miles above the ground was another.

He wondered what Dr. Wan would've made of his plan to attempt skydiving. He hadn't told her because he suspected she would be skeptical of his ability to do it, and he didn't want skepticism. Besides, if he told her he was going to jump out of a plane, she would've asked why, and he would've had to say something about Harriet, and for the purposes of therapy he was over his Harriet fantasies.

He turned and considered his four-poster bed of cloud, his coatrack, and his likely fate.

It did him no good to disbelieve his situation, to argue with his circumstances. He was here, and he accepted he would go on being here, no matter how hard he tried to talk himself into denying the reality around him.

And that was fine and that was right. Aubrey was a musician, not a physicist or a journalist. He didn't know if he believed in ghosts, but he liked the idea of them. He had enthusiastically participated in a séance with June and Harriet once (holding Harriet's hand for half an hour!). He was pretty sure Stonehenge was a landing pad for aliens. It wasn't in Aubrey's nature to ruthlessly interrogate reality, calling bullshit on every unproved notion and improbable hope. Acceptance was his natural state. Running with the situation was the first rule of a good jam.

His throat felt cracked and sore, and it was killing him to swallow. The fatigue was returning already, and he wished he had a comfortable place to sit and think. Could his exhaustion be a simple matter of altitude sickness? Aubrey's mind, which had a knack for generating worst-case scenarios, snatched at a new idea: He was standing on some lighter-than-air cloud of radiation. Whatever had killed the electrical power in the plane and his phone would soon wipe out the electrical impulses that governed the beating of his heart. The cloud might be producing as much atomic poison as the overheated reactors in Fukushima that had made a few dozen miles of Japan into a zone inhospitable to human life.

The idea turned his kidneys into cool, stagnant water. His legs felt suddenly wobbly, and he reached thoughtlessly for something to steady himself on, and his hand fell upon the armrest of a fat easy chair.

It had boiled up from the cloud behind him while he wasn't paying attention. It was a great soft-looking throne, tinged a pretty shade of coral by the last of the day's light.

He considered it with interest and suspicion, forgot all about lethal doses of radiation for a moment. He lowered himself tentatively into it. He still half expected to fall through, but of course he didn't. It was the soft, plump easy chair that other easy chairs dreamed of being.

A coatrack, a bed, a chair. What he needed, when he needed it.

When he thought of it.

He held this notion in his mind, turning it over, considering it.

This was not a cloud. He had to stop thinking of it as a cloud. It was . . . what? A device? A machine? Of some kind, yes. Which raised the next obvious question: What was under the hood? Where the hell *was* the hood?

His gaze drifted uneasily to the vast central mound, the one part of the island he hadn't explored. He would have to go take a look. Not yet, though. He wasn't sure if it was strength or courage he lacked. Maybe both. He had slept at least an hour but was still exhausted, and the sight of that huge, creamy white dome oppressed him somehow.

He lifted his head, searching for his next insight, and saw a cherry-colored sky scattered with the first stars. The astonishing clarity of the early night stunned him. For a moment he felt a flicker of something dangerously like gratitude. He was not dead, and the stars were coming out in all their glittering profusion. He watched while the sky dimmed and constellations mapped the darkness.

When the lid of night had fastened itself over the Midwest, he became aware that he was very cold. It was not unbearable—not yet—but it was disagreeable enough to make him turn his thoughts to the immediate problems of survival.

It seemed to him important to take an inventory. He wore a jumpsuit and one Converse high-top. He'd been told to leave his right shoe on the ground but no longer remembered why. It seemed silly now. Why did you jump in only one shoe?

Beneath the jumpsuit he wore knee-length cargo shorts and a tee made out of chunky cables of knitted cotton. It was his favorite shirt, because once Harriet had stroked it and said she loved the fabric.

He was hungry, in a distracted sort of way. That at least could be managed for now. He remembered tucking a granola bar into his shorts earlier that morning, wanted to have something on him in case of low blood sugar. It was still there. His thirst was going to be a bigger issue. He was so thirsty his throat ached, and at the moment he didn't have any idea what he was going to do about it.

Back to the inventory. He had his harness, and he had his helmet.

He unzipped his jumpsuit and shivered at the wind's cold touch. He worked his hands over the pockets of his shorts, itemizing his finds.

The phone: a dead slab of steel and glass.

His wallet: a leather rectangle with a few cards tucked into its pockets and his student ID. He was glad for the identification. If he were blown off the cloud, or if its miraculous powers of support suddenly gave out, the smashed turnip of his body would have a name. Wouldn't that shock the shit out of some people, if his pancaked corpse turned up in northeastern Ohio—or southern Pennsylvania!—a hundred miles away from where he'd last been seen, leaping from a plane? He took out his wallet and phone and put them on the end table.

In another pocket he—

—he jerked his head around to look at the end table.

In the summer darkness, the cloud was all silver and pearl, vivid by the light of a quarter moon. After the coatrack and the bed and the chair, he was not terribly surprised to be offered an end table in response to an unarticulated wish, although it was still a jolt, the way it had snuck up on him. But what interested him most is that he *knew* this end table. There'd been one just like it in between the couch where his mother stretched out and the chair he usually sat in when they watched TV together (usually something like *Sherlock* or *Downton Abbey* on PBS). It was where they put the popcorn.

He imagined Harriet calling his mother to say he'd been killed in a skydiving accident, then immediately pushed the thought aside, couldn't bear it. The vision of his mother screaming and collapsing into agonized sobs was more than he could take right now.

No. What interested him was that this end table—which had a wide circular top and a long beaded column—was a twin of the one he remembered from childhood. The only difference being that it was made out of cloud instead of cherry. And that meant something—didn't it?

His hand was still burrowed in one pocket of his cargo shorts, and his fingers fumbled at a few small, waxy blocks. He plucked one out and squinted at it in the opalescent light. When he realized what it was, his body responded with a throb of pleasure and need.

In the little flight office inside the airplane hangar, there'd been a glass dish on the reception desk full of individually wrapped Starburst candies. He'd furtively gone through them, picking out all the pale pink strawberry-flavored pieces. He had a weakness for them and had imagined they might come in handy—if he started panicking on the plane, he could stick one in his mouth and let sweetness infuse him. Plus, with his mouth full, he would be less likely to say cowardly, desperate things.

But of course the Starbursts had been in the pocket of his shorts, beneath the jumpsuit and harness, where he couldn't get at them, and besides, by the time they were in the sky, three hours later, he was so distracted by his own alarm that he'd forgotten about them.

How many did he have? Three. There had been five, but he'd chewed two to calm his nerves while he read over the preflight waivers.

His throat ached for one, and his fingers trembled as he unwrapped it and popped it into his mouth. He shuddered with physical pleasure. It wasn't as good as a bottle of water, but it would keep his thirst in check for now, and he had two more for later.

If his kingdom of clouds could provide him with an easy chair and an end table, couldn't it give him a pitcher of water?

No. He didn't think so. If it could've, it would've already. It was responsive to his immediate needs, providing as soon as the thought occurred. So it was—what—telepathic? Well, wasn't it? How else could it know what an end table looked like? It had offered up not just any piece of furniture but Aubrey's own Platonic ideal of an end table. That had to mean it could, in some way, read his memories and beliefs like a reference guide: *Life Among the Humans.*

So why couldn't it give him water? he wondered, sucking thoughtfully on the last sliver of his Starburst. Wasn't cloud stuff just water in the form of a gas?

Perhaps—but not *this* cloud stuff. When it hardened into the shape of a bed or a chair, it was not turning into snow.

In Dr. Wan's waiting room, there were magazines on a coffee table: *The New Yorker, Fine Cooking, Scientific American.* Aubrey's thoughts flashed to a photo he'd seen in an issue of *Scientific*: what looked like the ghost of a brick, a semitransparent cube of palest blue, improbably resting atop a few blades of grass. It had been something called aerogel, a block of solid matter that was lighter than air. Aubrey had an idea that the stuff beneath him now was similar in composition but vastly superior.

The last of his fruit chew melted away, leaving his mouth sticky sweet. He wanted water more than ever.

He thought he should try to visualize a pitcher of water anyway, before ruling it out. God knew it would be easy enough to imagine a jug of fresh water, blocks of ice clicking off each other inside the sweating glass. But before he could so much as close his eyes and concentrate, it came to him it was already there, sitting on the end table. It had fashioned itself while his thoughts were elsewhere—a perfect pitcher, made of fog, not glass, with a tumbler right beside it.

He lifted the pitcher by the handle and poured. A bubbling trickle of vapor and little cubes of hardened smoke poured slowly, dreamily into his cup.

"Well, that's fucking great, thanks," he said, surprised at his own bitterness.

The pitcher, ashamed, melted in his hand and drifted away. The cup puddled into fog and foamed silently off the end table, rejoining the cloud.

Aubrey shivered, fumbled about at his feet, and drew a blanket of billowing fumes across his legs. Better. He had lost his train of thought, tried to recall where he'd been and where he was going.

An inventory. He had been making an inventory. He had completed his examination of his physical supplies. Now he turned his attention to his psychological resources, whatever they might be.

He was Aubrey Langdon Griffin, single male, only child, twenty-two going on twenty-three. He was an accomplished Rollerblader, could speak with great fluency about MLB and the NBA, and could play the cello like a motherfucker.

Aubrey had never, in all his life, been so struck with his own near-total lack of survival skills. In grade school he'd had a friend, Irwin Ozick, who could make a compass with a needle and a cup of water, but right now if Aubrey had a cup of water, he'd drink it, and besides, how the fuck was a compass going to help him? Did it matter what direction he was moving in? After all, he couldn't steer the goddamn thing.

"Can I?" he wondered aloud.

It had offered a bed when he was weary. It provided a coatrack when he had something that required hanging. It *responded*.

Could he turn it back around toward Cleveland?

No sooner had this notion occurred than he was pricked with another, more thrilling possibility. Could he just close his eyes and concentrate on descent? Why not just wish it down?

He closed his eyes and drew a long, chilly breath, and with all his heart told the cloud—

But he had not even completed mentally announcing what he wanted when he felt something *push back*. It was more a physical sensation than a psychological impression. His mind was filled, suddenly and forcefully, with the image of a smooth black mass, glassy and dense. It drove itself back into his thoughts, crushing ideas just as a boot heel might stamp a beer can flat.

He recoiled in his chair, hands flying to his brow. For a moment he was blind. For a moment there was nothing but the black block (*no, not a block . . . a* pearl) filling his head. His ears popped from the pressure. An unpleasant tingle shot through his nerve endings, a rashy sensation of prickling heat.

When his vision cleared, he was standing again. He didn't recall leaping to his feet. He had lost a slice of time. Not long, he believed. Seconds, not minutes.

The dark, thought-flattening block (*the pearl*) had withdrawn but had left him feeling drained and woozy. He reeled unsteadily to the bed, climbed under the thick, snowy covers. The stars wheeled against the immense, crystal blackness of the night. The sky was a glassy black circle (*a pearl*) pressing down on him, squeezing him flat.

He shut his eyes and fell and fell and fell into the bottomless darkness of the unconscious.

7

HARRIET AND JUNE PLAYED THE open mics on Saturday nights in a pub called the Slithy Toves. Mostly they shared a mic and played ukuleles together and looked good in sweaters and pleated skirts and cute hats. June wore a top hat, purple velvet, with a little brown taxidermied woodcock peering down from the brim. Harriet wore a shockingly loud plaid bowler. They did covers of Belle & Sebastian and Vampire Weekend, mixed in with a couple of their own tunes. Now and then June ran behind a piano and played.

Aubrey saw them perform lots of times. He was in a consort that made chamber music out of video-game soundtracks and they played the Slithy Toves too.

One night his group (they were called Burgher Time, a joke absolutely no one got) was scheduled to go on right after Harriet and June's duo, Junicorn (a joke absolutely everyone got—Harriet's last name was Cornell). He was in the dark, at the edge of the stage, already had his cello out so he could rosin the bow. Junicorn was finishing their worst set ever. Harriet fucked up the opening of "Oxford Comma," and the thing turned into an incoherent mess. It didn't finish so much as stagger to a halt. Then they had a little whispered fight after it became clear that Harriet had forgotten her banjo, which they needed for their cute showstopper (they played a Monty Python number, "Always Look on the Bright Side of Life," coaxing the audience into a sing-along). There was a good crowd, but no one was listening. Harriet had angry red blotches on her cheeks and was trying not to brush her eyes, didn't want anyone to see how hard she was fighting not to cry. When June had finished chewing her out in a whisper that was probably audible out in the street, she sat down behind the piano, unable to look at Harriet or the crowd. They argued about what to play without making eye contact, Harriet hissing over her shoulder. A drunk in the crowd began to howl suggestions.

"Play some Kiss!" he shouted. "'Lick It Up'! Hey, girls! Girls! 'Let's Put the X in Sex'! C'mon!"

Finally Harriet and June agreed on "Wonderwall." The noise of the crowd dipped into a brief lull, and in that moment of near silence everyone close to the stage could hear June say, "F-sharp! F, *F*, as in 'Don't *fuck* it up.'" The people closest to the stage tittered.

Harriet began to strike the chords of an acoustic guitar while June found the melody on the keys. They sang, both of them sounding fragile and heartsick, but the crowd didn't really start to listen until Aubrey began to play offstage, drawing bow across string, deepening the melody with an almost tidal sound of yearning. The girls themselves didn't notice at first, didn't realize they'd just become a trio. But they knew when they were winning the crowd back, and they straightened, their voices strengthening and twining together. The chatter fell away, and the song filled the room. The drunk wailed, "I want some fuckin' *Kiss*! 'Lick It *Uuuuuuuup*'!" and then was silenced when someone else said, "You're gonna be lickin' up whatever's on the floor, you don't shut your fuckin' mouth."

When they sang the final chorus, their voices were brave and happy and they knew they'd been saved, and that was when Harriet heard the cello. She turned her head and saw Aubrey in the wings. Her eyes widened, and her eyebrows flew up, and she looked like she wanted to laugh. When the song was over and people began to hoot, she didn't linger to enjoy the applause but bounced off the stage, took off her bowler, and put it on his head. She kissed him fiercely on the cheek.

"Whoever you are, I want you to know I will love you forever. Maybe longer," she said to him.

June played three bars of "Lick It Up," then jumped to her feet, slid across the top of the piano like a cop in an eighties action show sliding across the hood of his Ferrari, and shouted, "Hey, who's in the mood for a threesome?" And then she was planting a kiss on Aubrey's other cheek.

She was joking, but the funny thing was, by the summer they were one. That May, Aubrey declined a seat with the Cleveland Orchestra so he'd be free to play East Coast gigs with Junicorn.

8

HE WOKE TO A RAGGED, cold wind and his belly cramping with hunger. A sharp stab of pain lanced him in the throat every time he swallowed.

Aubrey huddled, dazed and weak, beneath the sheep fluff of his cloud blankets. They were feathery soft to the touch and held a capsule of lovely, cozy warmth. His head, though, was exposed to the elements, and his ears were full of sick pain from the chill.

He found his granola bar, pulled back the wrapper, and allowed himself a bite: sticky coconut, salted almonds, a sweet caulk of chocolate. He was half frantic to gobble the rest, but he folded it back into the wrapper, returned it to his pocket, and zipped up his jumpsuit to put an extra barrier between the bar and himself. Maybe he did after all have a single survival skill: his restraint, which he had honed over the course of a hundred nights spent in the backseat of June's car with Harriet. Sometimes Harriet dozed off with her head on his thigh, murmuring, "G'night, love muppet," her mouth almost against his stomach. His self-control was second to none. As badly as he wanted to eat, he had wanted Harriet far more, but he never kissed her, never stroked her face, took her hand only when it was offered. Except for that one time at Sugarloaf, of course, and then she had initiated the touching and the kissing, not him.

He sucked on a Starburst to get some liquid into his throat. He made it last a long time, while he woke up and his wits returned to him. The sky above was clouded over, a rumpled argent landscape of lead-colored hills and pewter valleys.

When he cast aside his blankets and stood, the wind took a swipe at him and his weak legs almost buckled. The gusts threw his hair every which way. He staggered to the trailing aft end of the cloud.

Masses of hill lay below, thickly forested. He spied the pale brown thread of a little stream. Patches of green, squared-off farmland. Some roads scrawled here and there. Who the fuck knew what he was looking at? Maryland? Pennsylvania? *Canada?* No. Probably not Canada. He didn't believe he could've crossed the vast expanse of Lake Erie while he slept. It was hard to say how fast they were moving, but slower than the cars he saw gliding along the roads below.

"Where are you taking us?" he asked, shivering, feeling feverish.

He half expected the glassy blackness—*the pearl*—to stamp itself into his mind again, but nothing of the sort happened.

What had that been? he wondered. But he already knew. It had been an answer, an emphatic *no*. It was refusal in the cloud's own psychic language.

The castaway cast his woozy gaze around his island. He soon found himself staring again at the central mound, as big as St. Paul's dome and shaped much the same.

He drew a soft, downy robe of fog out of the smoke at his feet, and a scarf, too, a ten-foot streamer of haze. He swooped a hand through the cloud and came up with a hat. When he was all bundled up, he set out for the center of the cloud, looking like a snowman brought to life.

He trod across a vast, creamy meadow, through a profound hush and peace. That silence was unnerving. One didn't realize how much bustle and noise the world made until one was miles away from it, away from any other human.

Aubrey had just reached the milky white dome at the heart of the cloud, when a black flash filled his head, staggering him. A hand flew to his head and he put a knee against the side of the dome. The pain (*the pearl*) subsided, leaving a sore space in his mind. He waited, temples throbbing, for another black psychic blast, a human bowling pin preparing to be knocked off his feet by that rolling obsidian pearl. Nothing.

Aubrey thought he knew what would happen if he went on. He

began to haul himself up the side of the dome. It was a steep climb, and he had to dig hands and toes into the cloud itself. It had a clammy, custardy texture to it. He might've been climbing a lump of semi-solid pudding.

Aubrey climbed two yards and was hit by another pulverizing black crash. It was like a branch snapping into his face. His eyes watered. He stopped, went still. That obliterating mental explosion was worse than unconsciousness. It was *unbeing*. For an instant, Aubrey was gone.

"What don't you want me to see up there?" he said.

The cloud did not reply.

He decided to keep climbing, just to see what would happen—how intent it was on psychically kicking the shit out of him if he persisted. He made another handhold and another and

A dark weight dropped on his conscious mind like a falling chandelier.

But when his wet, leaking eyes cleared, he found he had continued to ascend, even in those blank moments when it seemed to him he simply ceased to be. He was midway up the dome, no longer climbing but crawling on all fours, as the curve became more gradual. The apex was maybe another ten minutes of struggle away, assuming his host didn't decide to squash his mind like a man splitting a tick between his thumb and index finger.

He shut his eyes and rested, face damp from the effort of pulling himself up the slope.

Aubrey felt it then. Something held in the very center of the cloud (*the pearl*), like a marble held in one's mouth. It hummed, very faintly, a low, muted drone, although Aubrey detected it right away. Maybe that was another survival skill—he had acute, sensitive ears, could hear a single off-key violin in a fifty-person string section. And with that gentle thrumming noise, he sensed a kind of *ache*. Could one person sense the ache in another? He was seized by a disconcerting, nonsensical idea. He stood before the closed, locked door of a dark house. A family mourned within. A dead grandfather lay stiff in the sheets of his bed.

Aubrey wondered if he dared knock on that door and ask for directions home.

He believed that if he continued to climb, he would soon be met with another black thump, this one maybe as bad as the one that had swatted him the night before when he'd asked the cloud to take him home. He turned and sat on the side of the hill and looked upon his domain, a great white fiefdom of fluffy, barren cloud. From up here, maybe four stories above the rest of his island—but still far from the peak of the dome—he could no longer make out his cumulonimbus bed, his chair, his coatrack. They were lost against the pale background, impossible to make out amid the other irregularities of the cloud.

The castaway sat while the chill breeze cooled the sweat on his face.

Perhaps a mile off, he spied a jumbo jet, a 747, climbing into the higher ceiling of cloud above. He leapt up and waved his arms, pointlessly. He was no more visible to them than his bed was visible to him. Nonetheless he yelled and leapt.

The third time he jumped, he lost his footing and went sliding back down the dome on his ass. At the bottom he tumbled face-first into the drifting paleness. His face thumped on something fluffy and soft in a way that was different from the cloud's spongy softness.

He felt around for it, frowning to himself, found it, and lifted it out of the haze—a stuffed purple horse with a silver horn and twee little wings behind its forelegs. Harriet had gone out of the plane with it, but hadn't kept hold of it, and so he wasn't alone on the cloud after all.

There was also the Junicorn.

9

JUNICORNS WERE HARRIET'S IDEA, SOMETHING to sell along with T-shirts and their locally produced CD, and it turned out to be an inspired business decision. Dudes bought them for their girlfriends; girls bought them for themselves; parents bought them for the kids. They sold so much horse, June said, they were practically heroin dealers.

Aubrey was in the conservatory at the Cleveland Institute of Music and had arranged access to their recording studio. On their little sheet of liner notes, Harriet was credited with one song, June with two. There were a pair of covers. Everything else was Cornell-Griffin-Morris. Aubrey brought in the melodies and figured out the arrangements and worked out the choruses, but as far as he was concerned, Harriet's additional lyrics and June's piano fills qualified them for equal credit. He was very good at talking himself into believing these were genuinely collaborative works. In some ways he believed it more than anyone.

"Am I the only one who thinks it's stupid we're called Junicorn when Aubrey is the musical genius?" Harriet asked one day when they were recording in the spacious studio with the exposed rough wooden beams. "We oughta call the band Griffin. We could sell stuffed Griffins."

"Don't give him ideas," June said, and tinkled a bit of one of her songs, "I Hallucinate You," on the piano. Either that or it was Coldplay's "Princess of China." All June's songs sounded like other songs. One of them sounded so much like "Shadowboxer" that June had once embarrassed herself by forgetting her own lyrics and singing Fiona

Apple's lines when they were onstage. No one in the crowd noticed, and Harriet and Aubrey pretended not to notice either.

They rolled to the gigs in June's battered old Volvo, but the boxes of Junicorns came along behind them in a dismal red Econoline driven by Ronnie Morris. The Morris brothers went to all the gigs as roadies, hauling the gear and the merch. They had learned that if you were with the band, there were frequently offers of free beer and always decent odds of meeting skanks. Along with the instruments and Junicorns and boxes of T-shirts, Ronnie and Brad almost always brought along the Pen Pal.

The Pen Pal was how Aubrey thought of Harriet's boyfriend. When Harriet was nine, her father had taken her to San Diego on a business trip, which he stretched into a long weekend so they could catch a baseball game and visit the zoo. On their last morning, Harriet's dad took her down for a wander along the waterfront and bought her a soda. When her Coca-Cola was gone, Harriet tucked a note into the bottle, with her address in Cleveland, a dollar bill, and a promise that there would be more money if whoever found the bottle would be her pen pal. Her father launched the sealed bottle a good hundred feet out into the sea.

Two months later, she received an envelope from someone named Chris Tybalt. He had returned her dollar bill, along with a photo of himself and an informative note. Chris was eleven, and his hobby was building and launching model rockets. He had gone to Imperial Beach, just south of San Diego, to launch his new CATO rocket, and the Coca-Cola bottle had been sticking out of the sand. He let her know that his favorite president was JFK, his lucky number was sixty-three, and he had only four toes on his right foot (accident with a firecracker). The photo, standard school issue, with a cloudy blue backdrop, showed a boy with reddish-blond hair, dimples, and braces.

They wrote letters for another three years before they met in person, when the Pen Pal was on his way across country with his grandmother. Tybalt spent a weekend at Harriet's house, sleeping with his gram in the guest room. Harriet and the Pen Pal launched a rocket together, an Estes AstroCam that snapped a picture of them from six hundred feet up: two pale spots in a green field, a dreamy beanstalk of pink smoke leading down to their feet. By Harriet's sophomore year in high school, they were "dating," had switched to e-mail, and agreed they loved each other. He applied to the Kent State aeronautics program just to be near her.

Aubrey thought the Pen Pal looked like a freckled junior investigator from a young-adult novel, and never mind he was in his early twenties. He played golf with unnerving grace, looked like he'd never had acne, and had a habit of finding injured birds and nurturing them back to full health. June's brothers loved him because he was easy to get drunk, and when he was drunk, he would try to kiss them—he called them bro kisses. Aubrey desperately wanted him to turn out to be a closeted homosexual. Unfortunately, he was just Californian. When Harriet and the Pen Pal talked about what they would name their children— Jet if it was a boy, Kennedy if it was a girl—Aubrey felt that his own life was hopeless.

There was room for Harriet in Ronnie Morris's van, but she always went to the shows with June and Aubrey in the Volvo. The Pen Pal insisted.

"Chris says I have to," she told Aubrey on one of these rides. "He says he doesn't want to be our Yoko Ono."

"Ah," Aubrey said. "So we're keeping lovers apart. Riding in the backseat with me is almost a form of punishment."

"Mmm," she said, closing her eyes and rolling her head around to get comfortable in his lap. "Like a weekly spanking."

June cleared her throat in the front of the car in a funny way, and after a moment Harriet made a low sound of discontent and sat up, then shifted around. Harriet had a Junicorn of her own, and she made a pillow of it, dozed off with a foot of space between herself and Aubrey.

10

IN THE LATTER PART OF the afternoon, the wind picked up, whipping the surface of the impossible island into a series of rough wavelets. His island, like a cutter, was beating right into the blow, tacking this way and that. Aubrey smelled rain.

His cloud vessel fought its way toward lowering, ugly clouds, straight into a downpour like a black scarf, miles across. The first rattling pellets hit Aubrey sideways, tearing at his coat of cloud. He flinched, hugging his stuffed Junicorn protectively, as a mother caught out in the rain might've protected an infant. He retreated, looking for cover. An umbrella handle of white fog protruded from a bucket of cloud, next to the coatrack. He grabbed it and threw it open, and a vast spreading canvas of hard cloud opened above him.

Now and then he turned the umbrella aside to shut his eyes and open his mouth. Icy pellets of water stung his lips, tasted cold and good, tasted like licking the blade of a knife.

More rain fell into a claw-foot bathtub of dense cloud. A great pool of water, suspended in a chalice of ice. A deep puddle hanging in smoke.

They were three hours in the pelting rain before his vast ship of cloud veered off to the east and raced away from the storm. Aubrey lay flat in the day's last dazzle of sunlight, head hung over the edge of the cloud, to watch the mile-wide shadow of his sky island racing across the green map of the world below.

By then his belly hurt from all the water he'd drunk, using a dipper as big as his own head to collect the rain from his deep tub. By then he had taken a nearly thirty-second piss off the side of the island, a golden parabola leaping into the brilliance of the afternoon. By then Aubrey Griffin had forgotten he was terrified of heights. It had, for the moment, slipped his mind.

11

THE ONE TIME SHE SLIPPED into his arms was the night they played Sugarloaf Mountain in Maine, a gig at a gastropub right off the slopes. The Pen Pal wasn't along that time. Harriet said he had to stay at school and study, but Aubrey learned from June that there'd been a fight: ugly sobbing, terrible things said, doors slammed. Harriet had come across e-mails from a West Coast girlfriend the Pen Pal had never bothered to mention. He swore they weren't still together, but he hadn't seen any reason to get rid of the photos. The half-naked selfies weren't the worst of them. The one that had really turned Harriet's stomach was a picture of Imperial Beach from five hundred feet up, shot from an AstroCam, the Pen Pal and his West Coast Sally staring up at it together. The West Coast Sally called him "Rocket" in her e-mails.

Aubrey was sick at the news—sick with excitement. In three weeks he was due to fly to Heathrow Airport. He was doing a semester at the Royal Academy of Music, beginning right after Christmas break. He had already put half a year of savings into the flat he was renting, money he couldn't get back, but he had a wild notion to stay, to make an insane leap, grab at a moment with Harriet.

She was stiff and uncommunicative the whole twelve-hour drive to the show, where they were opening for Nils Lofgren. Privately, Aubrey calculated that the pay would not quite cover the gas money, but they had free rooms in the resort, meal vouchers, and the lift tickets were on the house. In happier times Harriet and the Pen Pal had made plans for a full day of skiing. In a sign of how things were now, she had not even brought her skis, muttering that she'd pulled something.

"Actually, it was Rocket who pulled something, wasn't it?" June asked as they were loading the car. Harriet replied by slamming the trunk.

Harriet spent the drive up chewing her thumbnail and glaring out at snowy rises, firs humped under powder. It had snowed heavily all the week before, and they might've been driving through a tunnel in the clouds, sculpted white cliffs rising along either side of the road.

That night they played to a room packed to the walls, people older and wealthier than they, looking for some good noise on a Saturday night after a hard day of skiing and exercising their credit cards. The room was hot and stank of hops, wet wool, wet hair, and woodsmoke. Harriet wore a pair of low-slung blue jeans, and when she crouched over her acoustic, Aubrey could see the top of her emerald thong. She was especially good that evening, careless and funny, her usually clear voice pleasantly hoarsened, as if she were recovering from a cold. They played and they drank, Belgian beer with a pink elephant printed on the label. Aubrey was on his fourth and feeling dizzy when he discovered that it was 8.5 percent ABV.

There was no room in the tiny elevator for all of them and Aubrey's cello, so Aubrey and Harriet rode up together, leaving June behind with her brothers. When they got out on the third floor, Harriet looked one way, then the other, squinting at the white-numbered doors. She swayed and took Aubrey's arm.

"Where's my room?" Harriet asked. "Do you remember?"

Aubrey asked to see her key card, but it was just a featureless black rectangle, revealing nothing.

"We'll call down from my room," Aubrey said, but they never did.

12

THE STARS CAME OUT, a swarm of bright sparks in the wintry dark. It felt like winter up here, ten thousand feet above the soil. Aubrey ate the last of his granola bar and huddled in his piles of blankets with the Junicorn, pushing it into his face, trying to smell Harriet on it, remembering the way her hair smelled that night in Maine, like pine trees, like juniper.

Thinking about Maine, remembering the way they yanked at each other's clothes, kissing almost desperately, Aubrey felt the need for Harriet as intensely as he had ever wanted water. And in the deepest part of the night, she pushed the blankets back and climbed carefully, almost shyly, to his side: a Harriet made of cloud, pillowy white breasts, cool flowing silk for hair, lips of dry fog, tongue of cool vapor.

He sobbed gratefully, drew her to him, and fell into her, a long, sweet plunge without a parachute.

13

IF AUBREY WOKE UP FIRST, he believed his whole life might have been different. He didn't know what that would've been like, to awake bathed in sunlight, amid the pillows and piles of white sheets, with Harriet naked beside him. How he would've liked to see the light on her bare back. How he wished to wake her with a kiss on her shoulder.

But when he clawed his way up out of sleep, Harriet had already left. She didn't answer the knock on her hotel-room door. She wasn't at the breakfast buffet. He did not see her all the rest of the time they were at Sugarloaf, except once, briefly: She was in the courtyard in front of the resort, shivering in a too-flimsy denim jacket, eyes streaming while she had it out with someone on the phone. The boyfriend, he was sure, and he felt a great throb of hope. *They are breaking up*, he thought. *She is breaking up with him, and now it will be our time.*

He was watching through the tinted front windows of the hotel lobby, and he would've gone to her—wanted to be close to her if she needed him, if his silent presence would help her get through it. But he'd arrived in the lobby with June, who was in a lot of pain. She was having nasty cramps, she said, or maybe a reaction to something she'd eaten. She was hanging on to Aubrey's arm, and after they had both looked out on the scene in the courtyard for a moment, she tugged him toward the reception desk.

"Let her be," June said. "I need you more than she does. I'm bleeding so bad it's less like menstruation, more like afterbirth. I could not have more stuff spilling out of me without giving it a name and buying it diapers."

June was in such a bad way that she asked Aubrey to do the driving. By the time Aubrey got his cello downstairs, Harriet was already gone. She had split with the Morris brothers. June said it was because Harriet had an obliterating headache and wanted to sleep on the bed in the back of the van, but Aubrey was disturbed. It felt less as if Harriet had departed, more like she'd fled.

"I think that pink-elephant stuff we drank last night might be aggravating my period," June said. "It sure isn't helping. We all drank *way* too much. I wish I could have last night back. I bet Harriet does, too. Like Reagan said: Mistakes were made."

Aubrey wanted to ask what she meant by that, wanted to know what June knew, if she was talking about more than beer, but he lacked the courage, and soon June was asleep and snoring in a very unlovely way.

When he was back in his apartment, he texted Harriet almost a dozen times, beginning with Wow! So THAT happened, continuing on to I really want to give this a chance, and finishing with Are you there? Are you okay? She didn't reply, and her silence made him sick with dread. He couldn't sleep, couldn't even get into bed. He paced his little bedroom, his stomach upset, playing games on his phone so he wouldn't have to think. Finally he dozed off on his threadbare second-hand couch, which smelled faintly of rancid pizza.

His phone finally plinked with a message at four-fifteen in the morning.

I'm a horrible person I'm so sorry. I shouldn't have done that it wasn't fair to you. I need to be alone for a while. I've had a boy in my life since I was nine and now I need to figure out who I am without one. Please don't hate me. Please never hate me my friend Aubrey.

Beneath that was an emoji of a heart being torn in two.

Three weeks later he was putting his bags down in a flat in the East End. He didn't hear from Harriet again until March, and then it was another text:

June is really really sick. Can you call?

14

HE THOUGHT HIS CLOUD HARRIET would be gone when he woke, but she was cuddled against his chest, the gossamer specter of a girl with the blind, smooth features of classical statuary. Her hair streamed and curled in the breeze, feathers of white silk. His cock was chapped from screwing her. It had been a little like fucking a pail filled with cold porridge.

He didn't tell her that, though. Aubrey liked to think he was a gentleman. Instead he said, "You're a good kisser."

She gazed at him adoringly.

"Do you understand me?"

She knelt on the bed, hands on her thighs, studying him with a rapt and vaguely idiotic devotion.

He took her hands of smoke and squeezed, squishing them a tiny bit out of shape.

"I have to get down to the ground. I'll starve up here."

Her hands spilled out of his as effortlessly as water dribbling through his fingers. She seemed, briefly, diminished and disheartened. Her slumped shoulders implied he was a buzzkill.

"You *must* care about me," he tried again, "or you'd let me fall. But you have to understand. I'll die if I stay up here. From exposure or hunger."

Cloud Harriet gazed at him with a blind look of desperate concern, then spun away, dropped her slender legs over the side of the bed. She cast a sly, beckoning glance over her shoulder and nodded out across the cloud, to point his attention to what waited there.

A palace of cloud, like something from the *Arabian Nights*, loomed beyond: a soaring mass of minarets and arches, courtyards and walls, staircases and ramps. The magnificent structure swelled high into the sky, dazzling in the early-morning light, as opalescent as a pearl (*the pearl!*). It had sprung up overnight and crowded around the towering dome at the center of his floating island.

He rose to follow her and staggered and nearly went to one knee. He was weak, felt as light as a cloud himself. He was a long way from starvation—that would take weeks—but his hunger left him dazed, and when he moved too quickly, his head swam.

She took his hand, and soon they came to a moat. His heart lunged. A ring of open sky encircled the castle. He could see folds of green earth a couple miles below, ravines and shadowed, fir-covered slopes. She tugged his arm and led him across a wide drawbridge of smoke and through the palace gates.

When they were on the other side, he pulled his hand free and turned in a slow circle, taking it all in. They had entered a grand hall, with lofty arched ceilings the color of snow. It was like standing beneath a giant's wedding dress.

He got so dizzy turning around and around that he almost fell again. Harriet caught his elbow and steadied him, then guided him to an immense white throne. He sat, grateful to be off his wobbly legs, and she sank into his lap, all cool, slender waist and round hips. He shut his eyes and rested his head on her chill, comforting shoulder. It was a relief anyway, to be held.

But when he opened his eyes, he discovered he was holding a cello of cloud. Her smooth, perfect ass, slender waist, and pale bosom had become the body of the instrument.

His Harriet of the troposphere now sat a yard away, in a silky pale gown, watching him with the adoration of a dog regarding a man holding a hamburger.

Aubrey reached into the cloud at his feet and drew a bow, whip thin and the translucent white of a fish bone. He was hungry and from the first stroke played the music of hunger: Mahler, Symphony no. 5, the third part, a meditation on doing without, on realizing what wasn't and couldn't be. A cloud cello did not sound like a wooden cello. It had the low, haunting sound of the wind beneath the eaves, of a gale blowing across the spout of an empty jug, but for all that the song was distinct.

Sky Harriet rose from her stool and swayed and turned. He thought of a sea frond pulled by the tide, and when he swallowed, his throat clicked.

She revolved like a ballerina in a music box, a stem of a girl, with a complexion of unearthly smoothness. It was as if he spun her himself, as if she were a lathe powered by song. She lifted from the cloud beneath her feet and rose on spreading wings of hallucinatory beauty and began to sail in circles above him.

He was so entranced he forgot to play. It didn't matter. The cello played on without him, standing before his knees while the bow floated there, stroking strings he'd been able to feel but not quite see.

The sight of her drew Aubrey to his feet. He reeled, reaching for her. He wanted to be held—to fly.

She dipped, caught his hand, pulled him into the great heights beneath the palace roof. He left his stomach behind. Air whistled, and the cello yearned, and he cried out and seized her to him, her hips to his. They fell, swooped, rose again, his blood heavy and his head light. He was already hard.

His Harriet of the mists carried him to a landing at the top of a dizzying staircase. They collapsed there together. Wings became honeymoon sheets, and he took her again, while the cello played a lewd, strutting cabaret number below.

15

JUNE GOT BETTER, JUNE GOT WORSE. There was one good month when she was getting around on aluminum crutches, her head wrapped in a scarf, and she was talking about adjusting to her new reality. Then she stopped talking about adjusting and took a bed in the cancer ward. Aubrey brought her a ukulele, but it never moved from its spot between the spider plants on her windowsill.

One day when Aubrey and June were alone together—Harriet and June's brothers had gone down to the gift shop to get candy bars—June said, "When we're all done here, I want you to move on, as quickly as possible."

"Why don't you let me worry about how to deal with my feelings?" Aubrey said. "This may come as a surprise to you, but I can't just . . . be done with you without a thought. Like you're an umbrella I left at a hotel."

"I'm not talking about *me*, dummy," June said. "I expect you to grieve for *me* for at least a decade. I want a prolonged period of grim desolation and at least a little unmanly crying in public."

"So what are you—"

"*Her*. Harriet. It's not happening, dude. You played in our shitty band for almost two years hoping to tap that."

"It *already* happened."

June looked away, past her dusty ukulele, out the window at the parking lot. Rain pricked at the glass.

"Oh. That." June sighed. "I wouldn't make too much of that, Aubrey. She was having a really bad week, and you were safe."

"Why was I safe?"

June looked at him blankly, as if the answer were glaringly obvious. And maybe it was. "You were going away for six months. You don't start a relationship with someone who has his suitcases packed and one foot out the door. You were safe, and she knew there was nothing she could ever do that would make you hate her."

Ever since June was first diagnosed with lymphoma, she'd been parceling out nuggets of gentle wisdom, pretending she was Judi Dench or Whoopi Goldberg playing the tragic mentor in a heart-affirming movie about what really matters in life. It wore on him.

"Maybe you should try to sleep," he said.

"I was pissed off at her, you know," June told him, as if he hadn't spoken.

"Because we got drunk and fooled around?"

"No! Not because of that. Because of everything before that. All those nights she put her head in your lap on long, dark rides. Introducing you to people as her love muppet. You can't do things like that to people. They might fall in love with you."

"Okay," he said, in a tone that meant it wasn't.

"No, it's not," she said. "It was very unfair to you."

"I've had some of the best and most important conversations of my life with Harriet."

"Of *your* life. Not hers. You wrote that song about wearing each other's favorite sweaters and she sang it, but Aubrey—*Aubrey*. Those were *your* lyrics. Not hers. She was just singing the words you wrote for her. You need to break up."

"We're not together."

"You are *in your head*. You need to break up with imaginary Harriet and fall in love with someone who will love you back. Not that real Harriet doesn't love you. She just doesn't love you like *that*."

"Where the fuck *is* the real Harriet?" he fumed. "I think she walked all the way to Hershey, Pennsylvania, to get this candy bar." She was always going off on these quests with June's brothers, determined to find June the weird chocolate or weird soda or weird T-shirt that would make another day with cancer less depressing.

June sighed in a very heavy sort of way and turned her head to look out the window. "Why are there so many romantic songs about the spring? I hate the spring. The snow melts, and everything smells like thawing dog shit. Don't you dare write any romantic songs about springtime, Aubrey. It would kill me, and dying once is bad enough."

16

FOR A LONG TIME AFTERWARD, he lay panting, happily exhausted, and slicked with cool sweat. His head was spinny from the combination of hunger and exertion, but the sensation was not entirely disagreeable, came with the endorphin rush that might accompany a whirl on a fairground ride.

She had slipped away—melted in his hands when his orgasm was complete—flowed across the floor in a shuddering blanket of fog. He liked to think it had been good for her, too. When he looked about for her, he saw her waiting through a high archway, at a ghost-colored table.

He wriggled back into his jumpsuit and walked into a grand dining room. He looked upon the immensity of the table, set with spectral goblets, a cottony-looking white turkey, and a bowl of cloudfruit.

Aubrey was famished—more than famished, almost shaky with hunger—but the sight of the smokefood wasn't promising. He couldn't smell it. It was sculpture, not dinner.

She carved him a slice of nothing, put it on a platter of sky, next to a prickly-looking cloudfruit. She regarded him with an almost childlike desire to please.

"Thanks," he said. "Looks delicious."

He used a pale knife to cut a long, canoe-shaped slice of the cloudfruit. Aubrey speared it with his fork, considered it in the muted light, then decided what the fuck and took a bite.

It crunched and splintered, not unlike rock candy. It tasted of rain, coppery and cold. He had been in error. Close up, it *did* have a scent. It smelled faintly like thundershowers.

He tucked in.

17

IT STARTED TO HURT ON his second slice of phantom turkey breast—a sharp, lancing strike of pain through his abdomen. He grunted, clenching his teeth together, and bent over in his smoky chair.

His mouth had a silky residue in it, a bad flavor like he'd been sucking on a handful of grimy pocket change. Another sewing needle pushed itself through his intestines. He cried out.

Sky Harriet, sitting catty-corner to him, reached for Aubrey in alarm, taking his hand in hers. With her free hand, she passed him a goblet of white smoke. He drank the froth in desperation, two big swallows before he realized it was just more of God knew what toxic foam. He flung the goblet away.

Bumblebees crawled frantically through his insides, stinging haphazardly.

He lurched to his feet, accidentally tearing Sky Harriet's hand off. She didn't seem to mind. He hurried through the archway as he was stricken with another shooting burst of pain. His bowels cramped. Oh, God.

Aubrey went down the stairs in a kind of controlled fall, a fast, reckless stumble, not at all sure where he was going. It felt as if his intestines were wrapped in a throttling coil of steel wire, drawing ever tighter with each passing moment. He had never before felt so desperately close to filling his pants. It was like losing an arm-wrestling match, only with his sphincter.

He flung himself through the gates and raced across the bridge spanning the moat. A toilet abided beside his Cadillac-size bed. He ran the last five steps with his jumpsuit around his knees, shackling his legs. He sat.

There was an eruption. He groaned. It felt like he was passing a lump of glass splinters. His guts squeezed again, and he felt the shock of pain down into his knees. His feet tingled, the circulation draining out of them. The third time his bowels convulsed, he felt a stab of pain behind his breastbone. An intense wavering shock radiated through his chest.

His high-altitude Harriet watched from a few yards away, her Greek-goddess features set in an expression of transcendent mourning.

"Excuse me, *please!*" he cried, straining at a fresh mass of stainless-steel slivers. What he really wanted to scream was *Get the fuck away from me!* Or maybe, *You just killed me, bitch.* But he didn't have the courage for cruelty, it wasn't in his nature. "I need to be alone. I'm sick."

She dissolved into gossamer streamers, a silken waterfall that was absorbed into the cloud at her feet.

18

WHAT A THING TO ASK of her, *I need to be alone.* There was no alone. For that matter, there was no *her.* There was only the cloud. He knew, from the first moment he looked into her face, she wasn't looking back at him. Not with her eyes anyway.

Maybe, in a sense, *all* of the cloud was looking back at him. If "looking" was really the right term. "Monitoring" was perhaps more accurate. Monitoring what he did, but also what he thought in some fashion. How else did it know what his idea of an end table looked like? Or a lover? His ideal lover?

And when he spoke to himself in the language of conscious thought—did it understand that?

The idea made him woozy with anxiety. But he wasn't sure it did— that it could read him with such precision. He had a notion it was turning through his thoughts the way an illiterate child would flip through a magazine with a lot of pictures in it. He wondered if it was possible to keep anything to himself, if he could push the psychic eye of the cloudmind out of his head if need be. Much might hinge on the answer to that question.

The pain was letting up, although his insides felt torn and raw. He didn't think that what he'd eaten was going to kill him directly. If it was any kind of concentrated poison, he never would've even made it out of the palace. But it wasn't food either, and he couldn't afford what it had done to him. He couldn't afford to be carved up from the inside, not when he was already enervated, exhausted by a walk of ten steps.

Anything that required physical effort cost him calories he didn't have to waste.

Which turned his thoughts back to Sky Harriet's visit in the night, and then their second, more strenuous exertions before the banquet of broken glass. Was she— But there was no *she*, he reminded himself. He forced himself to begin again. Was the cloud *trying* to exhaust him? Was it trying to use him up, deplete whatever reservoirs of fuel he was running on? But if it wanted to wipe him out, it seemed to Aubrey it would be so much easier to simply turn to insubstantial smoke and let him fall.

No. He didn't think it meant him any deliberate evil. It wanted him to have things that would make him happy, that would comfort and reassure. It would do its best to give him everything and anything he longed for, denying him only a single desire: It would not let him go.

Perhaps it couldn't even entirely help responding to his unconscious wishes. Proof of this hypothesis was close at hand, quite literally. While he wasn't paying attention, a roll of cottony white toilet paper had materialized on a rod, rising out of the cloud. He collected a fistful and wiped and had a glance. Blood. The great wad of smoke stuff was saturated with it.

He cleaned himself as best he could. He had blood down the insides of his thighs, had been bleeding even before he got to the toilet. One good thing—no matter how much toilet paper he used, the roll never got any smaller. When he was done, he gathered a fistful of the cloudcotton and wadded it inside his underwear before zipping up the jumpsuit.

Aubrey hobbled to his bed and pulled himself into it. He fumbled for the blankets, and his hand found the stuffed Junicorn. He clutched it to his face. Held it to his nose and smelled detergent and dust and polyester. The Junicorn was bedraggled and worn, which made it all the more precious. He was grateful for anything that lacked the smooth, chilly perfection of the objects made from the cloud, grateful for anything he could hold on to that was real. You knew what was real not by its qualities but by its imperfections.

He stared blearily at the great white egg rising from the center of the palace, considering that one consistent, improbable feature of his cloud island. The one consistent feature he had *noticed* anyway. Sudden uncertainty gnawed at him. It seemed to him there'd been at least one other irregularity that was not quite irregular enough to be completely accidental, but he could not for the life of him summon what it might've been.

So. Leave it. Come back to it later.

For now he considered the dome, the pearl, at the heart of the palace. When he'd tried to climb it, it had brought a black, glassy sledge down upon him, hard enough to knock all the thought out of his head. He had surrendered, gone back down, and what had happened then? It had dreamed a girl into being. The girl he wanted as he'd never wanted anyone else in his life.

We shouldn't fight, the cloud had all but said to him. *Here. Let me have my secrets and you can have Harriet. Let what's buried stay buried and—*

Aubrey's thoughts snagged on this final notion. His flesh responded, fine hairs standing up on his arms. He wondered again if he'd seen anything on the island that didn't look completely random and was met with an idea, a very bad idea.

He knew he had to climb the great white hill at the center of the cloud. There was no getting around it. When he went, it would try to drive him back, as before, would lash out at him with whatever it had.

And did it *know* he was planning another climb? Could it see that in his mind? He redirected his thoughts toward the first image that occurred to him: the Junicorn in his hands, his purple stuffed Junicorn with its bent horn and twee little wings. It troubled him to think he needed to hide his own thoughts, even from himself.

He closed his eyes, burrowing his head into the pillows. He wasn't ready to take a pass at the hill now. He was too frail, too wiped out, needed to recover some energy. He might've slept if he hadn't felt something brush his cheek. His eyes sprang open, and he looked up into the face of an enormous horse, shaped from cloud.

Aubrey cried out, and the horse took a nervous step back. No. Not a horse. There was a spear rising from the center of its head and absurd little wings fluttering behind its forelegs. Its blind gaze was morose and stupid and shy. A Junicorn.

He sat up and grimaced, needles of pain bristling in his stomach. The Junicorn stood beside the bed, watching him with dubious eyes. He stroked a hand over one alabaster flank. It felt as cool and smooth as a horse made out of plaster. He had concentrated on a Junicorn, and now, predictably, one awaited his command.

As long as he didn't command it to fly him back down to earth or ride him up to the top of the great white dome. He already knew that shit wasn't happening. But maybe he could make use of it anyway. He was too weak for a hike, but he thought he could ride, and the Junicorn was already saddled.

He caught a foot in the stirrup and pulled himself up. His shredded insides shrieked. He gasped and fell across the Junicorn's neck. Sweat prickled on his flushed cheeks. He felt for reins, found them hanging loose, and gave them a tug. It had been a few years since he'd ridden, but his mother's side of the family were all farming stock, and he was not unfamiliar.

The Junicorn turned and trotted along the edge of the cloud, bouncing him in the saddle. At first the going was hard. Each jolt filled his stomach and bowels with pinpricks of pain, as if his guts were full of steel shavings. He soon found, though, that if he stood in the stirrups, it wasn't so bad. The throbbing in his abdomen subsided to a weak pulse, and he began to breathe easier.

He rode along the shores of his island, over low dunes and across barren strands. It was all both familiar and completely new at once. The landscape was continuously being remade by the wind, and yet somehow it was always the same, acre after acre of mashed potato.

The last time he'd traveled the circumference of his little fiefdom, he lost himself in a maze of crags and gullies in the east, but those were gone now, the land blasted almost flat. He remembered some fluffy boulders that looked like a bulldog. Also gone.

He saw nothing he remembered from his earlier journey until he'd made it three-quarters of the way around the isle. He was half dozing in the saddle by then, the rock and roll of the Junicorn a natural soporific. A sudden ugly jolt thudded him out of his trance, the ache flaring through his clawed-up insides. He cast his gaze around and saw they had just come down off a snowy bulge shaped almost exactly like a speed bump. They were about to go over another, and a third lay just beyond. Three tablet-shaped mounds in parallel rows. He grimaced, yanked on the reins, and pulled the mare to a halt.

Slowly, gingerly, he slid out of the saddle and down to his feet. He leaned against the horse to steady himself, waiting for the world to stop whirling. When it did, he took a breath and considered where he found himself.

He had missed the marker the last time he'd passed through this way: a large, tilting, square block at the head of the central mound. It didn't have RIP carved into its bland, blank face, but he supposed it served well enough as a gravestone. Now that Aubrey was on his feet, looking around, it was hard to imagine how he hadn't realized the first time he saw it that this was a place of burial. But then he supposed he was often guilty of trying not to see what was right in front of him.

He sank to his knees, pushed his fingers into the cold, stiff paste of the first grave. He was tired and didn't want to have to dig with his hands. The work would be easier with a shovel. He shut his eyes and bowed his head and tried to visualize one, a perfect three-foot spade. But when he opened his eyes, there was no shovel conveniently to hand and the Junicorn had moved off a few yards to stare at him with unmistakable disdain. Aubrey thought it was the first time the cloud had denied him anything. He was almost glad. He took it as a sign he'd found himself some work worth doing.

He yanked at the zipper of his jumpsuit. His smartphone was in one pocket of his cargo shorts. It was less a shovel, more a blunted garden trowel, but it was better than nothing. He chipped and dug. Pieces of cloud fell away, and more billowed in to fill the holes, like mud sliding into a ditch on a rainy day. But for all that, the cloud stuff seemed to need half an instant to flow into place and set, and it couldn't keep up with him. As he worked, he shed his fatigue. The steady prickle of pain in his abdomen sharpened his focus.

He pried loose a tumbling heap of soft white rock to reveal a swatch of faded black cotton and a splash of bright yellow silk—and at that moment the cloud seemed to surrender to him. The burial mound collapsed and spilled away in every direction, and a body emerged from the fog. White vapor smoked from empty, staring eye sockets.

The skeleton wore a handsome antique suit, a three-piece with tails. A canary-colored handkerchief was folded neatly into the breast pocket. The vivid yellow of it was a shock to Aubrey, and as refreshing in a way as it had been to plunge his head into cold water. In the cloud world, everything was the white of monuments, of marble, of bone. Those folds of yellow were like a shout of childish laughter in a mausoleum.

It was not hard to see how the man had died. The skull had been staved in on one side by the hammer blow of some great force. The dead man didn't seem too upset about it. He grinned up at Aubrey, his little gray teeth as delicate as kernels of corn. One skeletal hand clutched the brim of a stovepipe hat.

Aubrey turned to begin on the next grave, but the smoke had already melted away, the cloud giving up its dead. A woman. She'd been buried with her parasol. Tiny black leather boots protruded from beneath her dress and petticoats. The bridge of bone between her eyes had collapsed. Aubrey didn't know if that was a natural result of decay or a sign of injury.

On the other side of the woman was a second man. He must've been a fat man in his life. His bones swam in a voluminous black suit. One claw clutched a King James Bible. The other held a pistol with big iron barrels. He must've put it in his mouth before he fired. That was the only way to explain the great hole right in the top of his skull.

Aubrey's breathing slowed. He was headachy, and his insides stung, and he wanted to lie down with these three skeletons and rest. Instead he crawled around to the fat man and tugged the Bible free. It fell open to a place just inside the cover, bookmarked by an ancient burgundy ribbon.

On the verso it read, *"To Marshall and Nell on their wedding day, February, 4th, 1859. Love never fails, Corinthians. With love from Aunt Gail."*

The words on the recto had been written in a dark brown ink, blotted there with a shaking hand.

"They would've left me—the balloonist and Nell—so I killed them both. This is the closest I shall ever come to heaven now! Not that I still believe in Our Lord. Not one word of this foolish book is true. There is no God, and the skies belong to the Devil."

The Bible felt very heavy in Aubrey's hand, a brick, not a book. He set it back on the fat man's chest.

Murder and then suicide. Marshall had shot the one in the stovepipe hat—the balloonist, no doubt—and then his bride, and finally himself. Their bones had been floating around on this cloud ever since, almost a hundred and sixty years now judging by the date in the Bible. Nell wasn't wearing white, so they hadn't gone up on the day of their wedding, but maybe they'd decided to make a romantic ascent at some point on their honeymoon. Aubrey turned over Marshall's other hand, the one clutching the pistol, for a look at his wedding ring, a simple gold band that had dulled with age.

He loosened the pistol from its nest of bones. It had not one, not two, but *four* barrels, etched with whorls and feathers, and a curved handle of black walnut. The words CHARLES LANCASTER NEW BOND STREET LONDON had been stamped into the groove between the top two barrels. New Bond Street. Aubrey had walked past it almost every day when he left the Royal Academy of Music to find himself lunch. It gave him a shock of wonder, to find some of the world he knew, up here, in heaven's own bewildering country.

He broke the gun open. The cartridges looked less like the usual ammunition for a pistol and more like shotgun rounds. Aubrey shook out the bullets. Three of the copper casings were spent, but a fourth held a bullet the size of a blue jay's egg, so big it was almost funny. Almost—but not quite.

Left one for you, kiddo, he imagined the fat man telling him. Marshall's skull grinned with small, sharp, slanting teeth. *Might come in handy. You never know. In another couple days, when you're too weak to stand, it might be just what the doctor ordered. Swallow one as needed for pain and call me never.*

When Aubrey came to his feet, all the blood rushed away from his head and the afternoon went dim. He swayed, almost sat back down. *Bed,* he thought. *Rest.* He could ponder the tragic fate of the balloonists when he felt better. He even took a step toward the Junicorn, which was pawing restlessly at the puffy ground, before he noticed he was still holding the four-barreled pistol. That gave him another chill. It felt like he'd made a decision of some kind without even consciously realizing it. No reason to take the gun with him unless, on some level, he was open to using it.

He turned and considered putting it back. The bodies lay exposed to the day, the girl's head at the foot of the big, blocky grave marker.

Aubrey made a rapid series of associations then, threading half a dozen beads of trivia onto a single shining thread.

They had come and been stranded here and died, but the important thing was they had *come,* not by parachute but by balloon. They'd wound up on the cloud somehow, and at least two had planned to leave, and how were they going to do that? And was it odd that the cloud had disinterred the bodies but the gravestone remained, that big square, featureless block? He thought it was. He also noticed, for the first time, that the monument wasn't much shaped like his idea of a traditional gravestone, or anyone else's either. When the cloud generated something—a bed, an end table, a lover—it always worked from a template seized from the minds of its guests, but this wasn't a template of anything. It was camouflage, and not very good camouflage at that.

Aubrey walked a woozy line between skeletons and stood before the gravestone that wasn't a gravestone. He kicked it, once, twice, harder each time. Ivory shards of cloud stuff flew. When that wasn't good enough, Aubrey dropped to his knees and tore with his hands. It didn't take long.

At the center of the odd, cube-shaped monument was a wicker basket, large enough to hold a family of five. It was filled to the brim with silk the colors of the American flag. The wood of the basket was so old and dry it had lost most of its color. The silk was just as bad off, worn and bleached with age, the blues paler than the sky, the whites paler than the cloud.

He pulled it out in a big, shivering mass. That pile of silk—Aubrey remembered that balloonists called it the envelope—was no longer attached to the basket or the rusted-out burner but had been deliberately folded up and put away. A dozen slender ropes ran from rings around the skirt of balloon silk, but they were wound up into a neat bundle, all the iron D-rings carefully collected into one place.

With the silk removed, Aubrey could see that the basket was badly damaged. The bottom had been torn away, pulled right out. The basket itself was square in design, but the rattan had come apart at one corner, nothing holding it together. It had taken a savage blow, and Aubrey was gripped with a mental image of the balloon striking the hard cloud at high speed and dragging across it for a couple hundred yards, the wicker coming apart in a series of shattering cracks.

"They would've left me," fat Marshall wrote forlornly, but no one had ever been going to depart in the wreck of the hot-air balloon. If someone had tried to fire up the burner, the balloon would've torn it right off what little remained of the basket.

Aubrey pinched some of the slippery old silk, rubbed it between his fingers. He unfolded it with care, spreading it out before him. He was aware of strenuously keeping his own mind blank, his head as clean and empty as the high blue sky. It took him almost twenty minutes to lay it all out, the immense envelope of silk, big enough to cover a small single-story house. In several places along the pleats, it had worn away to threads. In others the fabric was as thin as a daydream. At last he sat with the bundle of cords in his lap, the cords that had been deliberately disconnected from the balloon. When it was stretched out before him, it was funny how much it all looked like a parachute.

They would've left me.

Aubrey was too tired to climb back onto the Junicorn, but it didn't matter. When he looked around, his ride had vanished.

He dragged himself between the dandy balloonist and the dead woman. He could've pulled a cozy blanket of cloud out of the smoke beneath him, but he was sick of mist and haze. Instead he drew the silk of the balloon over him, tucking it in around him, and holding the bundle of cord to his chest. The gun was digging into his leg, but not painfully enough for him to unzip his jumpsuit and pry it free.

How long did a bullet keep? he wondered.

19

"DYING LOOKS LIKE A LOT of hard work," Harriet said at the reception after the memorial, looking very smart in a white blouse and a trim gray
jacket. "When you're healthy, you think, no matter what, you'd want
to keep fighting. Squeeze every last drop out of your life. But cancer,
dude. That shit fucks you up. It must be such a relief to just let it take
you off. Like the best nap ever."

They were at the Morrises', drinking Pabst Blue Ribbon on the back
porch with June's brothers.

The bigger one, Brad, leaned against one of the screens, the glare
of the afternoon on his shoulders. Ronnie had plopped into one of the
deep lawn chairs, sending up a puff of dust and pollen to whirl and
glitter in a shaft of golden light. Harriet was perched on his armrest.

"There's no sense in it," Aubrey said, from one of the other chairs.
"Who gets to have a full life and who doesn't."

Ronnie was already drunk. Aubrey could smell beer on him from
three feet away, could smell it in his sweat.

"She did more in one day, without leaving her hospital bed, than
people who live three times as long." Ronnie tapped his temple mean-
ingfully. "She did stuff in here, where time is more elastic. The stuff
you think is all you ever know of the world. So if you can *imagine*
a thing, it's like you *lived* it. She told me once she'd been having an
affair with Sting since she was fifteen. In here." He gave his temple another profound tap. "She remembered hotel rooms. She remembered
sitting at an outdoor café in Nice with him when the rain began to

fall. That was her gift. She was predisposed to two things: imagination and cancer."

Aubrey thought this was a jarring association, the sort of wisdom you only ever heard from the mouths of drunks. Imagination was a cancer of the heart. All those lives you carried around in your head that you wouldn't ever get to live—they filled you up until you couldn't breathe. When he thought of Harriet slipping on to the rest of her life without him, he felt like he couldn't breathe.

"What about her list?" Harriet asked. "What about all this stuff she wants me to do for her? Jumping out of a plane, surfing the coast of Africa?" Harriet was beginning to cry again. She hardly seemed aware she was doing it. She cried easily and beautifully. "What about this list of regrets she left me with?"

Ronnie and Brad shook their heads. Harriet looked at them with wide-eyed wonder and hope, as if they were about to reveal some startling bequest that June had left behind for her beloved best friend.

"It's not stuff she wished she did," Ronnie said. "It's stuff she wants you to do, 'cause of how much fun she had doing it herself. In her head." Tapping his temple again. If he didn't give himself a headache with the beer, he would with all the tapping.

"What are we doing first?" Aubrey asked.

Harriet looked at him blankly. He had the uneasy idea she'd briefly forgotten he was there.

"We're jumping for her," Brad said. "Already made the booking."

"We're jumping *with* her," Harriet corrected him, fondling the little Junicorn she'd been carrying around all day.

"When do we go?" Aubrey asked.

"Oh, Aubrey," Harriet said. "You don't have to go. You're scared of heights."

"I haven't thought about heights once since I got on my antianxiety meds," he told her. "Thank God. I don't want to be too scared to share the most important things with the most important people in my life."

Harriet said, "You've already done a lot for June. You made our band worth listening to. She loved the shit out of you, you know." Leaning across the space between them to rap her knuckles on his thigh. "She told me that all the time in the last couple of months."

"She felt the same way about you. You were her favorite thing to talk about."

Harriet gave him a distracted smile and said, "What else did you and June discuss?"

Aubrey had the sense she was trying to steer the conversation somewhere, but he couldn't see where. He said, "We talked about how she wanted me to move on. That's what I want to do. I want to move right on to the first thing on her list."

"Good man," Ronnie said. "We're jumping in six weeks."

Aubrey lifted his chin in a mild nod of acceptance, although his stomach knotted with nervous tension. Six weeks was so soon. Maybe his unease showed on his face anyway. Harriet was watching him with quiet, damp-eyed concern and— What the fuck? How had she wound up sitting on Ronnie's knee?

The sight of her practically in Ronnie's drunk-ass lap bothered him, made him uncharacteristically resentful.

"Course, we could all just go skydiving in our imaginations," he said lightly. "And save money."

Ronnie furrowed his brow. "And be complete pussies."

"I thought you just said if you imagine something, it's the same as if you lived it."

"Jesus, man," Ronnie said, beginning to cry. "I just lost my sister, and you're going to make dick arguments?"

20

WHEN AUBREY AWOKE, ALMOST ELEVEN hours later, he knew something he should've understood months earlier. June had not told him he needed to move on from Harriet because she cared about *him.* June had told him to move on because she cared about *Harriet,* and Harriet was too sweet—or too lacking in assertiveness, take your pick—to tell Aubrey to get the fuck out of her life. That was what Harriet had been getting at on the day of the reception. *What else did you and June discuss?*

Harriet and June had maybe been only moments from breaking up their little goof of a folk act when he hijacked things that night in the Slithy Toves. He had made it all more serious than it had to be and than they had ever wanted it. The girls had made room for him in their lives, but only after he'd elbowed his way in and superimposed his own desires over their harmless fun.

There was, in fact, no one on the ground aside from his mother who would be unable to recover from his inexplicable disappearance. There was no life waiting for him down there, because he had never bothered to build one. He had left as little trace on the world below as the shadow of a cloud passing over a field—a notion that infuriated him and made him want to get back down there all the more.

He folded up the balloon silk just as he'd found it, following the timeworn creases. As he worked, he noted it had been reconfigured to open wider than a balloon normally would, although the ropes could still be drawn together to a single narrow point, about as wide as a man's waist.

Aubrey trod through the wispy billows of the cloud with the thick mass of silk under one arm and the bundle of ropes under the other. His breath smoked. He quivered, although whether from the cold or indignation, he did not know. He was ashamed of the way he'd yearned for Harriet when she had so obviously not wanted him, ashamed he'd tried to back out of leaping from the plane, ashamed to be twenty-four years old and not yet to have begun to live. He clung to his shame as if it were another kind of weapon, maybe one of greater worth than the gun.

His bed and bath and coatrack were where he'd left them. He hung the piles of silk on the rack, next to his skydiving harness. If there was a point to keeping it . . . well, it wasn't one he wanted to think about too closely. Not yet. Not when he had a gun. The gun had last been used for a suicide, but Aubrey thought it offered the possibility of a different, more satisfying form of escape. The silks and ropes, on the other hand, would do just fine later on, if all else failed and he truly had his heart set on killing himself.

He scooped up his helmet and buckled it onto his head (on the theory that you didn't march toward a fight without armor) and turned in the direction of the palace. The spires and soaring battlements reached high into the sky, with that central dome looming above all. He'd tried to climb the dome once before and had been driven back. It seemed to him it was time to find out what it might be driving him back *from*. It was protecting something up there, and if it had something to protect . . . it had something that could be threatened.

He set out for the castle gates. He wondered what he'd find if he could get all the way to the top of that creamy white globe. He had a wild, probably slightly hysterical notion that there was a *control panel* up there, a hatch into a hidden cockpit. He imagined a black leather seat in a tiny capsule filled with blinking lights, and a bright red lever with the words "UP" and "DOWN" stamped alongside it. The thought was so adorably goofy he had to laugh.

He was still laughing at himself when he got to the moat around the palace and discovered that the bridge had been withdrawn. Twelve feet of open sky separated him from the yawning gates opening into the courtyard.

That shut him up.

21

THE VERDANT FOLDED LAND BELOW shone with the buttery golden glow of first light. The hills threw vast lakes of shadow across the vales. He spied a red barn and a silver silo, a pale green field drawn into shaggy furrows, some yellow buttons that were probably haycocks.

His Harriet of the sky watched from the far side of the moat, twisting nervously in her gown. Her Greek-statue face was hopeless and frightened.

His pulse was a hand beating a barbaric drum.

"What are you going to do if I take a step forward? Let me fall? If you could drop me, wouldn't you have already?" he asked her. "It's against the rules—that's what I think."

He wasn't sure he really did think that. But the cloud had held on to the balloonists even after they died, had kept them for all the years since, when it could've drifted over Lake Erie anytime and dropped them unseen. What it caught, it kept. When he understood he was going to test this hypothesis, his abused insides seemed to overturn in a slow, heavy lurch.

"Not one thing you've shown me was real, and that includes your moat," he said.

He shut his eyes and lifted one foot. His lungs seized up in his chest. His balls drew so tight to his body his testicles ached.

Aubrey stepped forward.

And dropped. His eyes flew open as he fell headfirst.

Cloud foamed outward as he plunged, spilling before him. For an instant he was tipping into open sky. But as he collapsed to hands and knees, the living fog boiled in under him and caught him.

The billowing vapor continued to spread out across the moat until it formed a slender bridge across the gap. He looked around for Sky Harriet, but she had melted away.

Aubrey pushed himself to his feet, unsteady on his legs. A portcullis of fog had dropped down into the archway. He walked into it with his head down.

Bands of cloud stretched like bungee cord, pulled tight against the bowling-ball surface of his helmet. He strained against it, taking one small step forward, then another. The portcullis warped and deformed, as if it were made of yarn, and then all at once it tore and dumped him face-first into the courtyard.

He picked himself up and marched into the great hall.

A harem waited there: two dozen lithe girls of whitest white, slim marble perfections, some in wavering opalescent silks and some nude. Couches and beds had been brought into the open space, and the girls tangled upon them, writhed in one another's arms, between one another's legs.

Other girls glided to him with blind eyes and faces desperate with eagerness. A woman he didn't see grasped him from behind, pillowy breasts squeezed hard against his back, her lips on his neck. Sky Harriet was already on her knees in front of him, grasping for the zipper of his jumpsuit.

He dashed off her head with one backhand. Aubrey wrenched himself out of the arms of the woman clutching him from behind with so much force that her hands came apart in shreds of vapor. He waded through naked bodies. Every girl he'd ever jacked off to, from his first cello teacher to Jennifer Lawrence, tried to crowd in on him. He flailed right through them, tearing them into tattered banners of pearly mist.

He mounted the steps. Warriors waited in the dining hall: swollen marshmallow men, ten and twelve feet high, with cottony clubs, immense hammers of cloud. They were less fully formed than the girls in the hall below. They had Play-Doh hands and arms that bulged in lumps that had more to do with comic-book anatomy than with actual human bodies.

Aubrey Griffin, who had last been in a fistfight when he was nine, welcomed them. He was breathing hard, and his blood was up.

A warrior swung his cloud sledge—the hammer's head was as big as a Thanksgiving turkey—and caught him in the chest. Aubrey was surprised at how much it hurt, at the hard thud of pain that jolted through his torso. But he grabbed the business end of the sledge as it struck him and did not let go. Instead he pivoted, twisting and pulling the hammer along with him.

These things, these forms of hard cloud, were weak at the joints. They had to be, or they couldn't bend and move. He ripped the sledge free from his attacker and tore an arm off with it. He came all the way around, whirling 360 degrees, and let the hammer go. It whipsawed into the oncoming mass of giants. It tore one in half, slicing through his waist, the top half of his body tumbling to the floor. The sledge was on a rising arc and took off the head of the marauder behind.

The gladiators of cloud surrounded him with fists and clubs.

He wrenched off a nearby arm and used it as a scythe, mowing the first wave down before him, in much the way a boy might use a stick to hack at weeds. He struggled through them as if he were plunging along in a waist-deep flood of custard.

They shrank from Aubrey, recoiling less from his fists than from his cheerful fury, his upper lip pulled back to show bared teeth. The cloud lacked the courage of its own convictions, was no more willing to really abuse him than it would allow him to fall. He did not share its reserve. By the time he made it halfway across the hall, he was panting, sweating in the chill, and he was alone.

He went on into the castle, but there wasn't much to the place. After devising the entranceway and the feasting hall, the cloud seemed to have run out of ideas. He passed through the next soaring arch and found himself once again at the base of the dome.

The peak was a long way up, hundreds of feet above him. He felt a touch of light-headedness looking up there, and also something worse—the ghost of a glassy black pearl, hovering at the edge of his thoughts.

He pushed out a long, hard breath and began.

22

THE STOP COMMAND STRUCK WITH so much force it was almost a physical thing, snapping his head back. But when his thoughts returned to him, he had already climbed twenty feet. He blinked at tears, reached up, and drove his hand into the cliff face of cloud.

It nailed him again, a man stomping on a wounded wasp to make it stop crawling.

But he didn't stop crawling. He shoved back.

NO, he roared, although he didn't make a sound. It was a thought, reflexive and ugly.

His eyes watered over. The crest of the dazzling white globe blurred and doubled, then came back together. He was still climbing, seventy or eighty feet up.

Whatever was sending those psychic blows seemed to hesitate. Maybe it wasn't used to being yelled at. Aubrey went another forty feet, reached a place where he felt that the slope had rounded off enough so it was safe for him to try standing up. He was just rising on wobbly legs when the black pearl took a cheap shot, struck him again. He staggered, his balance wavering, one heel sliding out from under him. If he'd gone backward, he might've tumbled a hundred and twenty feet down to the base, but instead he belly-flopped onto his stomach, hard enough to drive all the air out of his lungs. He sprawled, arms and legs spread out in an X, pressed hard to the curving floor of the cloud.

"Oh, you bitch," he said, and forced himself up to his knees, then back to his feet.

He bore on. The frigid air tore at his lungs with each whooping breath. Gradually he became aware once more of a galvanic hum, felt as much as heard, right under his feet. It was like standing on a steel platform as a train approached. The thrumming sound increased as he climbed, until it was a deep, mechanical buzz that brought to mind the single note of feedback that opened "I Feel Fine" by the Beatles.

He stopped walking, fifty paces from the apex of the dome, and swayed on his heels. His head throbbed. His ears, too.

For the first time, he saw he was standing on something that *wasn't* cloud. It was cloud-*colored*, a dull pewter shade, but it was harder than anything he'd felt yet, and it was right *there*, hidden under a carpet of vapor not even an inch thick.

He fell to his knees and fanned away the smoke. It seemed to lack the will or the density to thicken here. Beneath was the curve of what might've been the world's largest pearl, a pearl the size of a ten-story building. It was not black but more closely resembled a polished sphere of ice. Except ice was cold, and this was warm and humming like a power transformer.

And something else. He could *see* something in it. Some dim form. It looked like an eel, frozen in the not-ice.

He crawled, sweeping cloud out of the way in puffs. The vapor did not resist him here. Aubrey uncovered what seemed to be a gold wire, as thin as a hair, running along the outside of the clouded glass. A dozen feet later, he discovered another gold filament. Soon he found a third, a fourth. All the gold wires were rising toward the very top of the globe to enwrap it in a fragile netting.

As his hand passed over one of the wires, he felt a cool breath against his palm. Aubrey paused and bent close and discovered that the lines were pricked with thousands of fine perforations, spilling wisps of white haze.

The whole impossible substance of the cloud began here, he thought. The pearl wore a coat of golden threads, which produced the cloud as a form of disguise, extruding a smoke that was lighter than air but as tough as human skin. It wasn't magic but machinery.

This idea was followed closely by another. He wasn't getting stepped on anymore. He had not felt the psychic impact of that black, glassy mace since finding the first golden thread.

I'm inside its defenses, he thought, certain without knowing how he could be sure. *It can't fight me here. And it can't hide either.*

He looked past the gold webbing and into the not-ice once more and spotted a second frozen eel, thick as a man's thigh. He followed it upward to see where it led, scooping aside the thin mist as he went.

At last he was at the very top. He pursed his lips and blew away a tissue of smoke, and finally he had a view of what he'd been hearing for the last fifteen minutes. The globe was crowned by what looked like an upside-down dish of beautiful gold foil. Hundreds of shining lines radiated out of it, spokes from the hub of a wheel. The dish produced a steady electrical drone that he could feel in the fine hairs on his arms, on the surface of his skin, in his fillings.

Aubrey stood, wiped an arm across his brow. His eyes shifted focus, peering beneath the golden cup and into that great ball of not-glass. It took him a moment to understand what he was looking at, and when it clicked into place, he was swept with an almost overpowering dizziness.

It was a *face*. The gray, smooth sphere contained a *head*, bigger than the head of a sperm whale. Aubrey saw a single closed eye, turned up toward him, an eye with the approximate diameter of a hot tub. Farther down was a beard of tentacles—those eels he'd seen—each ropy appendage thicker than a fire hose. It was hard to tell what color the creature might be. Everything within the sphere assumed a greenish-gray hue, like old, cold snot.

At some point he sank back to his knees. The gold platter set atop the pearl hummed steadily. He thought the thing inside the not-ice was either dead or in a state of coma very close to death, but the machinery that concealed it was alive and well.

He saw movement at the edge of his vision and turned his head. Sky Harriet waited a few yards away, nervously wringing her hands. The hem of her pale gown, ideal for a wedding, swept the steel-colored not-glass beneath her.

He gestured at the face in the sphere.

"What is that? Is that *you* in there?" he called out to her. "Is that the real you?"

He wasn't sure she understood, and he thought again of an illiterate thumbing through a magazine full of pictures. But then she shook her head, almost desperately, and hugged herself.

No. No, he didn't think so. He thought again (hoped was maybe more accurate) that whatever was down there was dead. She—the cloud—was more like . . . what? A security drone? A pet?

He was leaning forward a little, and he put one hand on that wrinkled, upside-down dish of gold foil.

It was like sticking a finger into a light socket, a charge so intense his whole body went rigid and his teeth clamped together, and for an instant his vision was wiped out by a flurry of silver lights, as if a dozen flashbulbs were going off in his face all at once. Only what galvanized him was not electricity but a five-hundred-thousand-volt shock of *loneliness*, a feeling of need so intense it could kill.

He yanked his hand free. When he blinked away the blurred afterglow of all those flashing lights, his Harriet of the heavens was regarding him with something like fear.

Aubrey held his left hand to his chest. It ached with pins and needles.

"I'm sorry," he said. "I'm so sorry for you. But you can't keep me here. You're killing me. I'm sorry you're alone, but you have to let me go. I—I don't want to be with you anymore."

She gazed at him with complete incomprehension.

He felt not surprise but only a kind of weary disappointment. A sentient and empathic life-form made of smoke had come to this world who knew how long ago, with a single purpose—to conceal and protect a head in a ball. A monstrous, silent thing that had maybe not even survived the voyage.

The cloud consciousness lived by one law: protect its freight from discovery. There was no going down. And there was no letting anyone free who might endanger that thing inside the sphere, a decapitated head the size of a house. The living smoke had kept the balloonists—and no doubt tried to please them—so it would not be alone. It was holding on to him for the same reason. It did not understand that this temporary easing of its agonizing, endless loneliness would inevitably come at the cost of the only life Aubrey had.

Perhaps it did not really understand death. Maybe it thought the balloonists were still there with it but only being very still and quiet, much like the creature inside the sphere. How much did the living cloud know, after all? How much *could* it know? That head inside the sphere no doubt had a brain the size of a two-car garage. But the thinking, feeling smoke . . . that was just some circuitry trapped inside a little gold dish.

"I have to get down," he said. "I want you to put me down somewhere. Leave me on a mountaintop, and I promise never to tell anyone about any of this. You can trust me. You can look into my thoughts and see that I mean it."

She shook her head, very sadly, very seriously.

"You don't understand. I'm not asking. This isn't a request. This is an *offer*," he said. "Please. Put me down, and I won't have to use this."

And he removed the gun from his pocket.

23

SHE COCKED HER HEAD, a bit like a dog who has heard an interesting far-away sound. If she knew what the gun did—and she *had* to know what it did, she'd certainly been present the last time it had been used—she gave no sign. Still he felt the need to explain.

"This is a pistol. It can do a lot of damage. I don't want to hurt you," he said. "Or your friend here. But I will if you don't set me down safely someplace."

She shook her head.

"I have. To. Get. Down." He punctuated his last three words by rapping the dish with the pistol, a little harder each time. *Bong, bong, bong.*

The third time he struck, her body of haze seemed to *ripple*, like tissue paper fluttering in a gentle breeze. She retreated a step. He wasn't sure she even *could* come any closer. The mist was at its thinnest here. There had barely been enough to cover the dome.

She was going to make him shoot. He hadn't thought it would come to that. He thought it would be enough to get up here and wave the gun in the direction of whatever she'd been hiding. He wasn't even sure a century-old bullet *would* fire, and if it did, he thought it was unlikely it could penetrate whatever he was sitting on. He had no doubts that the enormous pearl beneath him was from A Long Way Away and had been built to withstand worse than a slug from some nineteenth-century dandy's peashooter.

Did she know it could fire only once, at best? *No,* he thought, not with any certainty but with a kind of needy desperation. No, he had to play it out, had to push it as far as it could go. He was not yet sure if he'd just fire into the air to prove the gun worked or if he dared to fire into the ball, or at the gold dish. He just knew that if this was going to work, he had to keep going, had to be willing to pull the trigger.

"Don't make me do this," he pleaded. "If I have to shoot, I will. *Please.*"

She regarded him with an expression of wild, brainless anticipation.

The gun had four slender, elegant hammers, packed tight together, one for each barrel. In his mind he rolled them all back with his thumb in a single, awesome *CLACK*, like the Outlaw Josey Wales getting ready to deal some rough justice in the tumbleweeds. It surprised him when he pulled at them with his thumb and they wouldn't snap back into the ready position. Aubrey lowered the pistol and had a look at them. They were barnacled together with rusty lace, would have to be raised one at a time. He clenched his teeth and wrestled with the first. For close to a full ludicrous minute, nothing happened. He strained and strained, feeling the dramatic effect of his threat seep away by the second.

Then, all at once, it snapped back into place with a satisfying mechanical *crunch*, splinters of rust flying. His hand throbbed, was bruised from the effort, a deep blue indentation in the palm. He grabbed the next hammer and pulled back on it with both thumbs, wrestling at it with all the force he could muster. It was like trying to open a particularly frustrating jar of pickles. Then, as suddenly as the last time, it ratcheted back and locked into the ready-to-fire position. He exhaled, something like confidence returning, and grabbed at the third hammer with both thumbs, ready to pull against it with all his might.

Only the third hammer came free right away, flew back so unexpectedly that he let go and it fell, and the gun went off with a hot flash of light and a raggedy cough, like the backfire of a very old car.

Brimstone flared in his face, burned his nostrils. The barrels were no longer pointing at the gold cup but rather at an angle to the curved surface of that smooth gray orb. The slug cracked off the globe and clipped through one of those hair-thin gold wires. The severed gold line began to spray what looked like a billion glittery flecks of snow. A fine crack leapt through the sphere beneath, where the bullet had struck.

That continuous low thrumming sound seemed to shift, took on a reverberating note of strain.

Aubrey recoiled—from the change in sound, from the hissing spray of fine particles, from the crack in the curve of the not-glass ball. He looked at the gun, then flung it aside in horror. It was, he knew, the natural first impulse of any murderer: to get rid of the weapon. It banged off the glass, slid down the slope, and scudded out of sight in the suddenly agitated smoke.

He looked around for his Harriet of the sky. She was staggering away and melting as she went, not unlike the witch at the end of *The Wizard of Oz*. She sank into bubbling smoke, dissolving to her hips. Her arms were already gone, so that she looked more than ever like Greek statuary.

Aubrey turned in a circle. From here he could see the entirety of his cloud island. He looked out upon minarets and towers. They were caving in. As he watched, a tower quivered and sagged and fell into slop, a massive quaking pile of white whipped cream. Another folded at the middle, assuming the posture of a man bent over to look at his fly. Beyond the palace the rest of the cloud was in a wind-blasted torment. The surface was all chop, and the gusts caught the roiled waves and tossed smoke like sea spray.

His alarm stuck him in place. What got him moving was not the dissolving palace, the boiling cloud, or the shower of probably toxic particles hissing from the broken line. He could not find the will to move until he looked down between his feet.

Directly below, one eye opened to a slit in that grotesque, humongous face. The eyeball beneath was red, shot through with black specks, like a ball filled with blood and dead flies. It shifted dully, drowsily, this way and that, before seeming to settle: on him.

He ran. It was not a choice, not something he gave any thought. His legs were just going—*Feets don't fail me now*—taking him away from the top of the pearl, away from the hideous face, away from the increasingly wasplike buzz of the golden disk.

Aubrey fled down the curve of the sphere into the churning smoke until all at once the hard, smooth surface beneath his feet was a steep ramp and his heels shot out from under him. He struck on his ass and slid almost a hundred feet before he was able to roll over and catch himself. He went another hundred feet in a series of controlled drops, grabbing cloud, hanging, letting go, grabbing the next handhold, chimpanzeeing all the way to the bottom.

Aubrey leapt off the side and fell the final fifteen feet. He expected the springy jolt of impact when his feet found bottom. Instead he was, for one dreadful moment, plunging through a cloud like any other cloud.

When he stopped, it was because the cloud seemed to thicken and press in around him, a sensation like being buried up to the waist in wet sand. He had time, when he was half buried, to take in what had become of the banquet hall. It had collapsed in on itself, a ruin in the aftermath of a direct hit from a bomb. Craggy, shattered walls rose on either side of him. The floor was a tumbled mass of pillowy boulder shapes.

He wriggled up and free and began to climb across the debris. Even then there was a feeling as if the heaps and lumps of semi-solid smoke beneath him were bobbing in the fast current of a flood. It seemed at any instant that the unsteady blocks beneath him might roll and dump him right through the billowing paleness and toward the earth below. The cloud was losing its consistency, its ability to become solid— although he did not think of it as "consistency." The term that came to him, as he frantically clambered across the slurry, was "self-image."

He leapt down the grand staircase, three steps at a time. The last eight stairs bubbled and foamed away before he could get to them, and he hit and stumbled and was laid out, sliding through cloud like a kid dumped off his sled at high speed and eating snow.

Then he was up and moving again, leaping over deformities scattered across the floor of the entry hall. The slagged bodies of phantom lovers reached for him with grasping claws. Heads bobbed out of the milky soup of the floor, ruined faces set in expressions of panic. He stepped on at least one face as he ran for the gate.

It did occur to him that the bridge across the moat might be gone. He slapped through the limp threads of the dissolving portcullis. It was

like passing face-first into a cool, dew-damp cobweb. He was through it
and running full-out when he saw that the high arch of the bridge had
collapsed at the center. Not only that—it was shriveling at either end,
quickly shrinking back into the sides of the moat. His heart rose in his
chest like a hot-air balloon surging away from the world below. He did
not think or slow down. He sped up. One step, two, out onto the last
slender, decayed stub of the bridge, and he leapt.

He cleared the hole with a yard to spare, stumbled, and went down.
As he picked himself up, he threw a wild glance back, just in time to
see the palace drop, flattening like a magnificent pavilion caving in on
itself. He flickered back to a memory of lying in bed at the age of seven,
body clenched tight with pleasure, as his father snapped a sheet into the
air and let it float gently down over him, like a parachute.

The parachute—those folds of silk that had once been a hot-air
balloon—remained on the coatrack, although the rack itself was beginning to buckle under the weight. Beyond it the bed had lost all sense
of itself and now looked like the world's largest melted marshmallow.

Aubrey snatched up his jump harness and stepped into it, cinching it
tight over his balls, pulling it on over his jumpsuit. He was just shrugging the straps over his shoulders when he heard the cry. It was a blast
of noise, a cross between an air horn and a subway thundering through
a tunnel. The entire cloud seemed to shudder. He thought of that huge,
horrible, monstrous face and was gripped by a terrified, terrible idea:
Awake! The giant is awake! Down the beanstalk!

He grabbed the pile of silks just as the coatrack went noodle-soft and
collapsed. He began to run toward the edge of the cloud. As he went,
he discovered he was sinking. In a moment he was up to his knees.

Aubrey found the neat bundle of ropes, and as he struggled toward
the blue sky beyond the shores of the cloud, he began to clip old, rusted
D-rings to the carabiners on his harness. What he was about to do
amounted to little more than suicide, was a frantic act of lunacy, sure
to fail. So why, he wondered, was some part of him quivering with the
effort to restrain hysterical laughter?

The antique D-rings were a dozen in all. He clipped four to the front
of the harness and four to the back and let the rest dangle loose. He

still clutched the silk to his chest. When he looked up, he discovered his Harriet of the sky standing between him and the very edge of the cloud. She clutched the stuffed, dirty Junicorn in her arms as if it were their child, as if to block her faithless lover from leaving them both.

He lowered his head and plowed right through her. In two more steps, he was off the edge of the cloud.

Aubrey dropped like a brick.

24

HE FELL IN A STRAIGHT line, feetfirst. He hurtled eight hundred feet before he thought to let go of the bundle of silk in his arms. He had no idea how to release it and just threw it out from his body.

And he fell and fell and fell. Down he went in a wild corkscrew, dragging a long, tangled rope of silk behind.

The earth spun around and around below him: rectangles of pretty cultivated green, the humped mounds of forested hills, the flattened-squid shape of a small hamlet. He saw three white steeples, quite clearly, finely wrought spears of bone marking churches. In the distance he saw a wide horizon of filmy blue. It took him several moments to recognize it as either one of the Great Lakes or, maybe, the Atlantic Ocean.

The wind snatched his breath away from him. The very skin of his face rippled on his skull. He dropped faster and faster. Cords made loud popping sounds as they were pulled taut. The wind rattled and shook the knotted mess of silk trailing hilariously after him. How mad it had been to imagine it would catch his fall, that a balloonist of a hundred fifty years ago had left him a way off that lonely island in the sky.

Yet however worthless his half-assed antique quilt of old silk might be, he felt himself opening like a parachute—felt a steadily widening sense of joy. He let himself tip forward, spreading his arms and legs in the posture his jumpmaster had called aerobraking.

Cal. That was the guy's name. It popped into Aubrey's head all at once: cool Cal, the one and only. How had he forgotten?

He stopped spinning and fell toward the lush green earth below. If he weren't sure to die from the impact, he thought he might just about die from the glory of it all. Tears streamed from his eyes, and Aubrey Griffin began to smile.

25

HE WAS AT SIX THOUSAND feet when the long rope of silk trailing him came unwound and filled. The envelope erupted with a shocking bang—billowing wide, like a waiter tossing a tablecloth into the air. Aubrey was jerked upward, actually rose almost fifty feet, leaving his stomach behind, before his descent resumed—but slower now, with a sudden feeling of calm. He felt he was floating like a dandelion seed on a soft August breeze. He was warm again: sun on his face, gently roasting him in his jumpsuit.

He tipped his head back and saw a spreading dome of red and blue silk, scattered with enormous white stars. The sun shone through the thin places, wide patches where the fabric was just threads.

The ground rose up toward him. He saw a yellowing pasture almost directly below, pine trees at the back of it. To the east the field was bordered by a black strip of two-lane highway. Aubrey watched a red pickup glide along it, a black-and-white collie in the flatbed. The dog saw him and barked, his yaps flat and small and coming from a long way off. A farmhouse stood to the north, a dusty yard out back, a decrepit-looking barn nearby. Aubrey shut his eyes, smelling golden pollen, dry earth, hot tar.

When he opened his eyes, the meadow was rushing up at him. It occurred to him that landing might not be as peaceful as the slow fall to earth. Then he hit, heels first, a hard slam of impact that went up into his tailbone with a painful shock.

He found himself running through coarse yellow grass. Butterflies scattered before him in a bright panic. The raggedy parachute above wasn't done with him yet. It yanked him back up, dropped him, pulled him into the air again, yo-yoing him across the field. It made booming sounds each time it caught another scoop of ground wind and filled tight. Not only was Aubrey running—he couldn't stop. If he quit, the parachute would *drag* him. Aubrey began to unclip carabiners, wrestling with hard, cable-tight ropes.

He saw the road ahead, and a fence, rotten wood posts with three widely spaced lines of rusting barbed wire strung through them. The parachute inflated yet again, hauling him into the air. He lifted his knees almost to his chest and was carried right over the lines.

Aubrey put his feet down in a ditch on the other side, stumbled, and was remorselessly dragged out into the highway. He reached around behind him, grasping wildly for the carabiners on the back of his harness. He unclasped one, a second. The road burned his knees through his jumpsuit. He leapt up, did a hopping jig, found a third clip, snapped it free. He twisted from the waist, feeling for the last. It sprang loose all of a sudden, and Aubrey was thrown onto his chest, across the dotted yellow line.

He lifted his head and watched as the gay ruin of his parachute was sucked into the crown of an enormous oak across the street. Immediately it collapsed, draping itself upon the branches.

Aubrey turned over. He ached in the small of his back, in his knees. His throat was sandpaper dry. He gazed into the bright, hard blue, searching for his cloud. And there it was—a great white hubcap, barely indistinguishable from the other fat, puffy scraps of cloud up there. It still looked like a mother ship, just as Harriet had said. Harriet had said it was a UFO, and she'd been right.

He felt an inexplicable throb of affection for it—for the home his Sky Harriet had tried to make for him there. He felt in some ways that he was still gently floating to earth. He might be floating like this for days.

He was yet on his back in the road when a guy in a black Cadillac rolled down the highway from the north, slowing as he approached, then steering a wide berth around Aubrey. The Caddy stopped right next to him.

The driver—an old man with angry blue eyes under a thicket of storm-cloud-colored eyebrows—powered down his window. "Fuck you doin' in the road? Someone could go right over you, asshole!"

Aubrey, unoffended, sat up on his elbows. "Hey, mister. Where is this? Am I in Pennsylvania?"

The driver glared, his lean face darkening, as if Aubrey were the one who had called *him* an asshole. "What kinda drugs you on? I oughta call the cops!"

"So not Pennsylvania?"

"Try New Hampshire!"

"Huh. No kidding." Aubrey wasn't sure he could get out of the road just yet. It was awfully nice here, warm blacktop beneath his back, sun glowing on his face. He was in no rush to get to whatever was next.

"Jesus!" the old bird said, spittle flying from his lips. "Get your head out of the clouds!"

"Just did," Aubrey said.

The old guy powered his window back up and got out of there. Aubrey turned his head to watch him go.

When he had the highway to himself, he got to his feet, dusted off his rear, and began to walk. From above he had seen a farmhouse not too far away. If anyone was home, he thought he'd ask to use their phone. He figured his mother might like to know he was alive.

WHEN THE RAIN FELL, most everyone was caught outside in it.

You wonder, maybe, why so many people died in that initial down-pour. People who weren't there say, *Don't folks in Boulder know to come in out of the rain?* Well, let me tell you. This was the last Friday in August, you remember, and it was H-O-T, *hot*. At eleven in the morning? There wasn't a cloud to be seen. The sky was so blue it hurt to look at it for too long, and a body just couldn't stand to be inside. It was about as glorious as the first day in Eden.

Seemed like everyone found something to do out of doors. Mr. Wald-man, who was the first to die, was up on his roof, banging a hammer on new shingles. He had his shirt off, and his skinny old-man's back was baked as red as a boiled crab, but he didn't seem to mind. Martina, the Russian stripper who lived in the apartment below mine, was out in our dusty scrap of yard, sunning herself in a black bikini so tiny it felt like you ought to have to feed a machine quarters to keep looking at her. The windows were all open in the big, decaying Colonial next door, where the comet cult people lived: Elder Bent and his "family" of broken wackadoodles. Three of their women were outside in the silver gowns they all wore, ceremonial hubcaps on their heads. One of them, an obese gal with a sad, vacant grapefruit of a face, was turning sausages on the grill, and the blue smoke carried down the street, making folks hungry. The other two were at the wooden lawn table working on a fruit salad, one of them chopping pineapple and the other picking red seeds out of pomegranates.

Me, I was killing time with Little Dracula and waiting on the person I loved most in the world. Yolanda was driving up from Denver with her mother. Yolanda was moving in with me.

"Little Dracula" was a boy named Templeton Blake, who lived across the street from me, next door to Mr. Waldman. Yolanda and I both looked after the kid sometimes for his mother, Ursula, who was on her own after her husband had died the year before. Ursula tried to pay us sometimes, but usually we could convince her to settle up with some other form of compensation: a few slices of pizza or fresh vegetables from her garden. I felt sorry for them. Ursula was a slender, small, gracious dame who suffered from mild haphephobia. She couldn't bear to be touched, which made you wonder how she'd ever had a kid. Her nine-year-old had the vocabulary of a forty-year-old sociologist and almost never left the house; he was always sick with one thing or another, on a raft of antibiotics or antihistamines. The day the first rain fell, he was being treated for recurring strep and couldn't go outside because his medicine had made him hypersensitive to sunlight. A lot of healthy, vigorous children died in Boulder that day—parents all over town booted their kids outside to whoop it up on one of the last, most brilliant days of summer—whereas Templeton survived because he was too ill to have fun. Think about that.

Because he had been told he'd fry if the sun so much as touched him, he was going through a vampire phase, walking around in a black silk cape and a pair of plastic fangs. His mom was home, but I was keeping him occupied in the dark shadows of their garage out of sheer fidgety nerves—the good kind. Yolanda was on the way. She had called just as she and her mother had set out to make the one-hour drive from Denver.

We'd been together for eighteen months, and Yolanda had spent plenty of lazy afternoons in my apartment on Jackdaw Street, but she had only come out to her parents a year before and had wanted to give them some time to adjust to the idea before she officially moved in with me. She was right, they did need some time to adjust: about five minutes, maybe ten. I don't know how in life she ever imagined her parents could do anything but love her. The shock was how quickly they decided they were going to love me, too.

Dr. and Mrs. Rusted were from the British Virgin Islands; Dr. Rusted, Yolanda's father, was an Episcopal minister and a Ph.D. in psychology. Her mother owned an art gallery in Denver. All you had to see was the bumper sticker on their Prius—VOTING IS LIKE DRIVING: R GOES BACK-WARD, D GOES FORWARD—to know we were going to be all right. The day after his daughter came out to them, Dr. Rusted took down the

flag of the British Virgin Islands that hung from the pole on their porch
and replaced it with a rainbow-colored pennant. Mrs. Rusted got a new
bumper sticker for the hybrid, a pink triangle with the words LOVE IS
LOVE superimposed over it. I think they were secretly proud when someone egged their house, although they pretended to be steamed by the
bigotry of their neighbors.

"I cannot understand how they coo' be so intolerant," Dr. Rusted
announced in his big, booming voice. "Yolanda babysit halve the children on the street! Change their diapers, sing them to sleep. And then
they stick an anonymous note onder the windshield wiper to say our
child is a deviant and we should pay back oll the parents of children she
babysit." He shook his head as if disgusted, but his eyes glittered with
amusement. All good preachers have a little of the devil in them.

Yolanda and her parents had spent the summer in the BVI visiting the extended family and leaving me on my lonesome: Honeysuckle
Speck, the only twenty-three-year-old Joe Strummer lesbian look-alike
on my whole block, student of law at the University of Colorado Boulder, fiscal conservative, lover of horses, and reformed user of dipping
tobacco (the girlfriend made me quit). I hadn't had her in my arms in
six weeks, and I was so caffeinated waiting for her and her mother to
turn up this morning that I had the jitters.

It was lucky for me I had the little vampire to fool with. There was a
steel rack in the rear of the garage, a place to hang bicycles, and Templeton liked me to lift him up and turn him upside down so he could dangle from it by his knees like a bat. He said he went flying as a bat every
night, looking for fresh victims. He could get down—I had positioned a
mattress under the rack, and when he was ready, he would drop with an
uncharacteristically athletic flip, landing on his feet. But he couldn't get
back up without someone to lift him. By the time I heard the first crash
of thunder, my arms were rubber from scooping him up and hanging
him so many times.

That first bang of thunder caught me off guard. I thought a couple
cars had collided out in the road, and I hurried to the open garage door,
my nervous imagination already sketching a picture of Yolanda and her
mother in a head-on. It is odd how much we want to be in love when

you think about how much anxiety comes with it, like a tax on money you won in the lottery.

But there weren't any wrecks in the road, and the sky was just as brilliant and blue as ever, at least from my vantage point. The wind was gusting strong, though. Across the street, over where the comet-cult people lived, the breeze snatched at a stack of paper plates and scattered them across the grass and into the road. I could smell rain in that wind—or something like rain anyway. It was the fragrance of a quarry, the odor of pulverized rock. When I leaned my head out and looked at the peaks, I saw it, a great black thunderhead the size of an aircraft carrier, coming up fast over the Flatirons like they sometimes did. It was so black it startled me—black with bruised highlights of pink in it, a soft, dreamy pink like a color you'd see at sunset.

I didn't stare at it long, because at that very moment Yolanda and her mother turned onto Jackdaw Street in their bright yellow Prius, a velvet easy chair strapped to the top. They pulled up across the street in front of my house, and I started to walk over. Yolanda leapt from the passenger seat with a big scream: a gangly black girl with hips so round they were almost a parody of female sexuality, stacked on top of storklike, skinny legs. Yolanda was prone to screaming when things made her happy and also doing this funny stomping dance around and around a person when she was glad to see them. She did it around me a couple times before I grabbed her wrist and pulled her to me and . . . well, and patted her back in an awkward sort of hug. How I would regret that later: that I didn't snatch her around the waist and squeeze her against me and put my mouth on hers. But I was raised country. Anyone who so much as glanced at me would know me for what I was. One look at the strappy white muscle shirt and the trucker haircut and you'd spot me for a bull dyke. On a public stage, though, I lost all my don't-give-a-fuck spirit, was embarrassed to touch or to kiss, not wanting to draw stares or to offend. The sight of her made my heart swell so full my chest hurt, but I hugged her mother more firmly than I squeezed my beloved. No last embrace. No final kiss. I'll live with that shame the rest of my life.

We small-talked for a minute about the flight back from the British Virgin Islands, and I teased the girl about how much she'd packed for the big move. "You sure you remembered everything? I hope you didn't forget the trampoline. What about the canoe? You get that jammed in there somewhere?"

But we didn't talk long. There was another reverberating boom of thunder, and Yolanda jumped and screamed again. That girl did love a good thunderstorm.

"Yo-lan-da!" Martina called from her lawn chair. Martina was the Russian stripper who lived downstairs with Andropov. She had a teasing, flirty relationship with Yolanda that I didn't much appreciate, not because I was jealous but because I thought she liked to play friendly with the lesbians upstairs to rile her boyfriend. Andropov was sulky and overweight, a former chemist who'd been reduced to scrambling for driving gigs on Uber. "Yo-lan-da, your lovely thing is going to get wet."

"What'd you say, Martina?" Yolanda asked, just as blithe and innocent as a child listening to a teacher.

"Yeah, you want to try that one again?" I said.

Martina gave me a sly look and said, "Your chair, it get rained on. Big cloud make it all wet. Better hurry. You want to have nice place to put your fanny." And she winked at me and picked her cell phone out of the grass. A moment later she was chattering at someone in light, laughing Russian.

It nettled me, listening to her lewd talk and putting on an act like she didn't know what she was saying because English was her second language. But I didn't have time to stew over it. The next instant someone was tugging at my sleeve, and when I looked around, I saw that Little Dracula had joined us in the street. Templeton had his cape flapped up over his head to protect his face from the sun, and he peered out at me from beneath its sleek black folds. He liked Yolanda, too, and didn't want to be left out of our unpacking party.

"Hey, Temp," I said. "Your mom sees you outside, you won't have to *pretend* you sleep in a coffin."

Right on cue his mother shouted, "*TEMPLETON BLAKE!*" She had materialized on the front step of their pleasant, butter-colored ranch. "*INSIDE! NOW! HONEYSUCKLE!*" This last directed at me, like it was my fault he'd gone wandering. She was just about quivering—she did not take her son's health lightly—and as it was, her concern for his well-being saved my life, too.

"I got him," I said.

"We'll get the chair inside," Yolanda's mother told me.

"Leave it. I'll be right back," I told them—the last thing I ever said to either of them.

I walked Templeton across the street. You could see that no one knew whether to go in or not. The thundercloud was a lone Everest of darkness in the immensity of the sky. Anyone could tell that it was going to pour hard for six minutes and then be clear and hot and nice again. But the next time the thunder boomed, a blue flashbulb of lightning popped off inside the cloud, and that got folks moving, sort of. Mr. Waldman, who had been reshingling, hung his hammer on his belt and started making his way down the pitch of his roof, toward his ladder. Martina was off the phone and on the porch with her folded lawn chair, peering with a mix of curiosity and excitement at the darkening sky. That's where she was when Andropov slued in, driving his black Chrysler too fast, shrilling the brakes, and then jumping out and slamming the door behind him. She smirked at him while he came steaming across the little scrap of yard. He was so red in the face that it looked like someone had shown him a photograph of his mother having sex with a clown.

I nodded amiably to Ursula, who shook her head with a certain weary disapproval—it always distressed her whenever Templeton forgot to act like an invalid—and disappeared back inside. I led Templeton to the garage, scooped him up, and sat him on the stool at his father's workbench. The father was gone—had died when he got himself drunk and drove off the road and into Sunshine Canyon—but he'd left behind a manual typewriter missing the *h* and the *e,* and Templeton was writing his vampire story on it. He had six pages so far and had already drained the blood out of most every wench in Transylvania. I told him to write me something good and bloody, tousled his hair, and started back toward Yolanda and her mother. I never got to them.

Yolanda was up on the rear bumper of the Prius, wrestling with one bungee cord. Her mother stood in the road with her hands on her hips, offering her well-meant emotional support. One of the comet-cult biddies was in the street, picking up paper plates. The fat girl working the grill squinted up at the thunderhead with a sour look of resignation. Mr. Waldman perched on the top rung of his ladder. Andropov grabbed Martina by the wrist, gave it a twist, and dragged her into their apartment. That's what they were all up to when the storm hit.

I took one step into the driveway, and something stung my arm. It was like that shock of pain and then the achy numbness you get after the nurse sticks a syringe in you. My first thought was that I'd been bitten by a horsefly. Then I looked at my bare shoulder and saw a bright red drop of blood and something sticking out of the skin: a thorn of gold. I sucked in a sharp breath and wiggled it free and stood there staring at it. It was about two inches long and looked like a pin made out of needle-sharp amber glass. It was pretty, like jewelry, especially all bright and red with my blood. I couldn't think where it had come from. It was *hard*, too, hard as quartz. I turned it this way and that, and it caught the weird pink stormlight and flashed.

Mr. Waldman yelled, and I glanced around in time to see him slap at something on the back of his neck, as if the same horsefly that bit me had just bitten him.

By then I could hear the rain coming, a furious rattling, building in volume. It was *loud*, a roar like a thousand thumbtacks being poured into a steel bucket. A car alarm went off, the horn going *blat-blat-blat*, somewhere up the hill. It seemed to me that the very ground under my feet began to shudder.

It's one thing to be scared, but what came over me then was bigger than that. I had a sudden premonition of disaster, a sick flop in the stomach. I shouted Yolanda's name, but I'm not sure she heard me over the gathering *rackety-tackety* of the rain. She was still up on the rear bumper. She lifted her chin, looked into the sky.

Templeton called to me, and the anxiety in his voice made him sound like the very small boy he was. I turned and found he had approached as far as the entrance of the garage, drawn by the roar of the oncoming rain. I put my hand on his chest and pushed him back into the garage, which is why he lived, and why I lived, too.

I looked back just as the rain broke over the street. It crackled where it hit the blacktop and pinged when it hit cars, and some part of me thought it was hail and some part of me knew it wasn't.

The comet-cult gal who was picking paper plates out of the road arched her back, very suddenly, and went all wide-eyed, as if someone had pinched her rear end. I could see pins hitting the road and spraying this way and that by then: needles of silver and gold.

Up on his ladder, old Mr. Waldman went ramrod stiff. He already had one hand on the nape of his neck. The other flew to the small of his back. He began to do an unconscious jig on the top of the ladder as he was stung and stung again. His right foot dropped for the next rung, missed it, and he plunged, striking the ladder and flipping over on his way to the ground.

Then the rain was coming down hard. The chubby woman at the grill still had her face to the sky—she was the only one who didn't run—and I watched as she was torn apart in a downpour of steely nails. Her crinkly silver gown was jerked this way and that on her body, as if invisible dogs were fighting over it. She lifted her hands, a woman surrendering to an advancing army, and I saw that her palms and forearms were stuck with hundreds of needles, so she looked like a pale pink cactus.

Mrs. Rusted turned in a circle, keeping her head down, took two steps from the car, then changed her mind and went back. She fumbled blindly and found the latch. Her arms were prickled all over with needles. Her shoulders. Her neck. She struggled with the driver's-side door, got it open, and began to crawl in. But she had made it only halfway behind the wheel when the windshield exploded in on her. She collapsed and didn't move again, her legs still hanging out into the street. The backs of her round, full thighs were a dense thicket of needles.

Yolanda leapt off the rear bumper and turned toward me. She made a run for the garage. I heard her scream my name. I took two steps toward her, but Templeton had me by the wrist and wouldn't let go. I couldn't make him let go, and I couldn't go out there with him attached to me. When I looked back, my girl had been driven to her knees, and Yolanda . . . Yolanda . . .

Yolanda.

THE RAIN DIDN'T FALL FOR LONG. Maybe eight, nine minutes before it started to taper off. By then everything was covered in a blanket of glassy splinters, glittering and flashing as the sun came back out. Windows all along the street had been smashed in. Mrs. Rusted's Prius looked like it had been hit in a thousand places by little hammers. Yolanda was on her knees, forehead touching the road, arms over her head. Kneeling there in a hazy pink mist. My love looked like a pile of bloody laundry.

A final drizzle fell with a crackle and some pretty ringing sounds, like someone playing a glass harmonica. As the clattering faded away, other noises rose in its place. Someone was screaming. A police siren wailed. Car alarms throbbed.

At some point Templeton had let go of my wrist, and when I looked around, I saw that his mother was standing with us in the garage, an arm around him. Her slender, intelligent face was stiff with shock, her eyes wide behind her spectacles. I left them without a word, wandering out into the driveway. First thing I did was step on some needles and shout in pain. I lifted one foot and found pins sticking from the sole of my sneaker. I pulled them out and paused to inspect one. It wasn't steel but some kind of crystal; when I looked close, I could see that it had tiny facets, like a gem, although where it narrowed to points, it was as thin as a hair. I tried to snap it in two and couldn't.

I walked out into the road, sort of sliding my feet along to push needles ahead of me, so I wouldn't get stabbed by any more of them. Yolanda was at the base of the driveway. I sank to my knees, ignored the stick of pain as my weight settled onto all those slim, glittering nails. Nails. The sky had opened and rained nails. The idea was settling upon me at last.

Yolanda had wrapped her arms over her head to fend off the crystal downpour. It hadn't mattered. She'd been ripped apart, same as everyone else who hadn't made it to shelter. Her back bristled with needles, as dense as a porcupine's coat.

I wanted to hold her, but it wasn't easy, as now she was a lump of brilliant, glittering spikes. The best I could manage was to put my face close to hers, so we were almost cheek to cheek.

Crouched there with her was like being in a room she had just left. I could smell her sweet fragrance of jojoba and hemp, the products she used in the glossy whips of her dreads; could sense that her light, sunny energy had just passed through, but the girl herself was somewhere else. I took her hand. I didn't cry, but then I have never been much of a crier. Sometimes I think that part of me is broken.

Slowly, the rest of the world began to fill in around me. The whoop of car alarms. Screams and weeping. Tinkling glass. What had happened to Yolanda had happened from one end of the street to the other. Had happened to all of Boulder.

I found a place on Yolanda I could kiss—there were no quills in her left temple—and put my lips against her skin. Then I left her to check on her mother. Mrs. Rusted was facedown under an avalanche of blue safety glass, stuck through with a hedgehog pelt of shiny nails. Her face was turned to the side, and there were nails in her cheek, a nail through her lower lip. Her eyes were wide and staring, bulging in a grotesque parody of surprise. There were nails in her back, bristling from her hip.

The fob dangled from the ignition, and on impulse I turned the key to switch on the power. The radio sprang to life. A newsman spoke in a fast, breathless voice. He said that Denver was experiencing a freak weather event and that needles were falling from the sky and to stay indoors. He said he didn't know if it was an industrial accident or some kind of superhail or a volcanic event, but people caught outside were at high risk of death. He said reports were coming in from all over the city of fires and people killed in the street, and then he said, "Elaine, please call my cell and let me know you and the girls are inside and safe," and he started crying, right on the FM. I listened to him sob for most of a minute and switched the car off again.

I went to the rear of the Prius, opened the hatchback, and dug around until I found a quilt that Yolanda's grandmother had made for her. I took it back to Yolanda and rolled her into it, needles crunching and gritting underfoot. I meant to carry her up the stairs to my apartment, but no sooner had I finished folding her into her shroud than Ursula Blake appeared at one end of her.

"Let's take her to my house, dear," she said. "I'll help you."

Her quiet, forceful calm and the almost brisk way she settled into looking after Yolanda and myself brought me as close to tears as I would come that afternoon. My chest tightened with emotion, and for a moment it was hard to breathe.

I nodded, and we lifted her together. Ursula took her head, and I held her feet, and we walked her back to the Blake house, that little butter-colored ranch with its tidy yard. Or it had been tidy. The daylilies and carnations had been torn to rags.

We put Yolanda down in the dim front hall, Templeton watching us from a few paces away. His plastic fangs had come out of his mouth, and he was sucking his thumb, something he probably hadn't done in years. Ursula disappeared down the hall and returned with another bedspread, and we went back outside to collect Mrs. Rusted.

We put the two of them side by side in the foyer, and Ursula touched my elbow—just lightly—and steered me into the den and sat me on the couch. She went to make tea and left me staring at a television that didn't work. The power was out all over Boulder. When she came back, she had a mug of Irish Breakfast for me and her laptop, running off the battery. Her modem was down, but she was able to get Internet through her cell signal. She put the computer on the coffee table in front of me. I didn't move till after dark.

Well, you know what the rest of that day was like, whether you were in Colorado or not. I'm sure you saw all the same stuff on TV as I saw on Ursula's generic black laptop. Reporters went outside to kick through the needles and record the damage. The storm had cut a four-mile-wide swath down the mountain, through Boulder, and into Denver. There was a skyscraper with every window on its western face smashed in and people staring out from forty stories up. Abandoned cars littered the streets helter-skelter, all of them ready for the junkyard. Shell-shocked Coloradans wandered the lanes, carrying tablecloths and curtains and coats and whatever they could find to cover the corpses on the sidewalks. I remember one reporter yammering into the camera and a dazed man stuck full of pins walked through the shot behind him, carrying a dead Yorkie. It looked like a bloody mop with eyes. This guy's face was a blood-smeared blank. He had to have over a hundred nails sticking out of him.

The operating theory—lacking any other credible explanation—was terrorism. The president had disappeared to a secure location but had responded with the full force of his Twitter account. He posted: "OUR ENEMIES DON'T KNOW WHAT THEY STARTED! PAYBACK IS A BITCH!!! #Denver #Colorado #America!!" The vice president had promised to pray as hard as he could for the survivors and the dead; he pledged to stay on his knees all day and all night long. It was reassuring to know our national leaders were using all the resources at their disposal to help the desperate: social media and Jesus.

Late in the afternoon, this one reporter found a guy sitting on a curb cross-legged with a square of black velvet spread out in front of him and delicate nails of all colors scattered across it. At first glance he almost looked like one of these dudes you see selling watches on the street. He was studying his collection of pins with a jeweler's loupe, looking at one, then another. The reporter asked what he was doing, and he told her he was a geologist and he was analyzing the nails. He said he was pretty sure they were a form of fulgurite, and she asked what that was, and he said a kind of crystal. By that evening all the cable channels had experts saying much the same, talking about spectrographic analysis and crystal growth.

Fulgurite had formed in clouds before. It happened whenever volcanoes blew. Lightning would flash-cook flakes of ash into fangs of crystal. But there hadn't been any eruptions in the Rockies in more than four thousand years, and fulgurite had never formed into such perfect little needles before. The chemists and the geologists couldn't come up with any natural process that would account for what had happened—which meant it had to be the result of an *unnatural* process. Someone had figured out how to poison the sky.

So they knew what had hit us but not how it could've happened. Wolf Blitzer asked one chemist if it might've been an industrial accident, and the guy said sure, but you could see from the nervous-scared look on his face that he had no idea.

Then there were the plane crashes. Two hundred seventy people died in one plane alone, after it passed directly through the cloud. There were roasted bodies buckled into airplane seats bobbing in Barr Lake like corks. The whole tail section sat a few hundred yards away, in the north-bound lane of I-76, boiling with black smoke. Aircraft had come down all around Denver, crashes decorating an eighty-mile radius encircling the airport.

At some point I swam up out of my daze—the deep trance cast by scenes from the unfolding catastrophe, the same spell 9/11 cast upon us all—and it came to me that my parents might want to know I was alive. This was followed by another thought: that someone needed to tell Dr. Rusted what had happened to his wife and daughter, and that someone was going to have to be me. It was a Saturday morning, so he hadn't come to Boulder with them but had remained behind to write the sermon for that evening's services. It was inexplicable that he hadn't called me already. I thought that over and decided I didn't much like what it might imply.

I tried my mother first. It didn't matter we didn't get on. I don't care who you are. It's a human instinct to seek out your mother when you've skinned your knees, when your dog has been hit by a car, when the sky opens and rains nails. But I couldn't get through to her, didn't get anything but an annoying squawk. Of course it would've just been an annoying squawk if she answered, too!

I tried my father, who was in Utah with his third wife, and didn't get him either—just a long, staticky hiss. I wasn't surprised the cellular network was overloaded. Everyone was calling someone, and no doubt the relay towers had sustained a lot of damage. It was a surprise, really, that Ursula was able to keep us online.

By the time I tried Dr. Rusted, I wasn't expecting the call to go through. None of the others had. But after eight seconds of dead air, it began to ring, and then I found myself hoping he wouldn't answer. I still feel rotten about that. The idea, though, of telling him he'd lost his wife and daughter made my whole body throb with dread.

It rang and rang, and then there was his voice, sweet and happy and kind, saying to leave a message and he would be so glad to 'ear from me. "Hey, Dr. Rusted. You better call me, soon as you can. It's Honeysuckle. I need to tell you— Just call me." Because I couldn't let him find out what had happened from a recording.

I put the phone down on the coffee table and waited for him to call back, but he never did.

We watched streaming video into the late evening, Ursula and I. Sometimes the video fragmented and froze—once for almost twenty minutes—but it always came back. I might've watched until the laptop battery died, but then the CNN stream went to video of a school bus turned over on its side, full of six- and seven-year-olds, and that was when Ursula got up and closed her browser, shut her computer down. We had sat together on the couch most of the day, drinking tea and sharing a blanket tossed across our knees.

At some point I took Ursula's hand without knowing it, and for a while she let me, which couldn't have been easy for her. Maybe she'd been different before the husband died, but in the time I had known her, she could hardly bear physical contact with anyone except her son. She liked plants better, had a degree in agricultural science, and probably could've grown tomatoes on the moon. She wasn't much for conversation unless you wanted to shoot the shit about the best fertilizers or when to spray your fields, but in her own way she was comforting, even sweet.

She took the blanket that had been across our legs and flapped it over me, as if we had already agreed I was sleeping on her couch that night, and she tucked me in like a seed in a warm, fragrant bed of earth. I had not been tucked in by someone else in years. My father was a no-good drunk who stole the money I made on my paper route and spent it on women of negotiable affections; he was hardly ever home when I went to sleep. My mother was perpetually disgusted with me for dressing like a boy and said if I wanted to be a little man instead of a little girl, I could put myself to bed at night. But Ursula Blake enfolded me in that blanket just as if I were her own child, was so tender I half expected her to kiss me good night, though she didn't.

She did say, "I am so sorry about Yolanda, Honeysuckle. I know she was dear to you. She was dear to us, too." That was all. Nothing more. Not that night.

IT WAS GOOD OF HER to offer me the couch, but when she was gone, I took my quilt and carried it out into the foyer. I had myself a little pray, kneeling beside the two dead women bundled there. I don't mind telling you, I had some pretty warm comments for the Man Upstairs. I said whatever was wrong in the world, there were a lot of good people in it, like Yolanda and Mrs. Rusted, and if He thought slaying them in a hail of nails served some kind of just purpose, I had a revelation or two for Him! I said I was sure the world was full of awful sin, but riddling a pack of little kids headed to summer camp was going to eliminate absolutely none of it. I told Him I was disappointed in His performance over the last twenty-four hours, and if He wanted to make it up to me, He'd better hurry up and get to smiting whoever had set loose the nail-storm on us. I said Dr. Rusted had spent his whole adult life spreading the Good News, telling folks about how to find forgiveness and live the life Christ wanted for them, and the least God could do was let him still be alive and tend to him in his time of mourning. I informed Our Father that I thought He was a damn bad sport for taking away the doctor's loved ones. That was a fine way to show appreciation for all his service! One good thing about being a butch queer is you already figure you're going to hell, so there's no reason not to give God a piece of your mind when you feel like it.

After I was worn out cussing the Lord, my fatigue got the best of me, and I stretched out between Yolanda and Mrs. Rusted. I drew the quilt over me and threw an arm over Yolanda's waist. It's funny how tired I was, even though I hadn't done anything except stare at a computer all day. Grief is hard work. It'll run you down like you spent the day digging ditches. Or digging graves, I guess.

Anyway, I had a good sleepy talk with Yolanda, curled beside her on the floor. I told her I would owe her the rest of my life for sharing her family with me. I said I was sorry like heck we weren't going to have more silly times together. I said it always made me feel good to hear her laugh, so loud and free, and I hoped someday I'd learn to laugh that way. Then I shut up and held her as best I could. I couldn't quite spoon against her—even with her wrapped in a quilt, those hundreds of spines in her back made it impossible to cuddle. But I could drape an arm over her and put my thighs against the backs of her legs, and in that way I fell asleep at last.

Only an hour or two passed before I opened my eyes. Something had changed, but I didn't know what. I peered blearily around and discovered Templeton standing just above my head, Dracula cape tossed over his shoulders and his thumb in his mouth. He hadn't been outside in days, and his face was corpse pale in the dark. The lord of the vampires, visiting with his colony of the dead. At first I thought Templeton was what had stirred me, but it was something else, and a moment later he told me what.

"They're singing," he said.

"Who?" I asked, but then I shut up and listened, and I heard them myself.

A dozen sweet voices carried in the warm August night, all of them harmonizing to that Phil Collins song "Take Me Home." They'd been at it for a while. It was the sound of them, not Templeton standing over me, that had brought me awake.

I peeked out the thick square window in the center of the door. It looked like the whole Church of the Seventh Dimensional Christ were out in the night, dressed up in their shiny silver cowls and robes, carrying paper lanterns with candles in them. They had collected their dead, the three women who'd been out making lunch, and rolled them up in shrouds of metallic Bubble Wrap, so the bodies looked like monstrous burritos swaddled in tinfoil. The congregation had assembled in a pair of concentric rings, with the corpses in the center. The inner ring walked clockwise; the other ring marched in the opposite direction. It was almost lovely if you didn't think about how crazy all of them were.

I picked Templeton up, brought him down the hall to his bedroom, and tucked him back in. His window was open a crack, and the song of the comet cultists came through clear and rich and full. For a pack of deluded and pathetic wastrels, they sure could carry a tune.

I stretched out beside Templeton for a bit to see if I could settle him down. He asked me if I thought Yolanda's soul had gone up to the clouds. I said it had gone somewhere, because it wasn't in her body anymore. Templeton said his mother had told him his daddy was in the clouds looking down at him. Templeton said when he turned into a bat, he was always sure to go looking for his father in the sky. I asked him if he went flying often, and he said every night, but he hadn't spotted his father yet. I kissed his eyebrow on what Yolanda called his shiver spot, and he gratified me with a weak, happy shudder. I said no flying anywhere tonight, time for bed, and he nodded solemnly and said no more flying ever. He said the sky was full of nails now and it wasn't safe for an honest bat out there. Then he asked me if I thought it would rain like that again, and I said I didn't think so, because who imagined it would keep happening? If I'd known that night what we were all going to have to live through, I'm not sure I could've lived through it.

I told Templeton no more thinking and got up to shut his window and said good night to him. I could only keep my smile on my face until I got out into the hallway. I stepped around the bodies of my own loved ones and let myself out into the humid, perfumed summer night.

I meant to ask them to save their singing for some hour when people weren't trying to sleep, but as I approached, I saw something that irritated me even more than their harmonizing. Three hardy young men were at the edge of the lawn with Mr. Waldman, had dragged him across the street. They were busy winding him up in more of that shiny silver quilting. Elder Bent watched from a few paces away. His bald head was tattooed with a map of the solar system in black-light ink. Mercury and Venus, Earth and Mars, Saturn and Neptune shone with a spectral blue-gray glow on his skull, while phosphorescent dotted lines showed the path they would follow around a goblin-colored sun. I'd heard he'd been a trapeze artist in a former life, and he had the physique to back it up: lean muscle, ropy arms. He wore a silver gown, like all the rest. He also had a large gold astrolabe hung around his neck by a gold chain, a decoration allowed only to the men.

I call them a comet cult, but that's just a lazy tease and doesn't really sum up their beliefs at all. Most of them were middle-aged and visibly not right. There was one who had lost all three of her children in a house fire and who would tell you with a smile that they hadn't died at all—they had crossed into a new, seven-dimensional form of existence. There was a man who put a nine-volt battery in his mouth sometimes, to receive "transmissions" from various religious figures who he said were broadcasting from Neptune. He didn't hear their voices. He *tasted* their advice and ideas in the battery's coppery zing. One parishioner had a lazy eye and a tendency toward nervous spitting fits, as if she'd just gotten a bug in her mouth. Another of the devout had smiley-face scars up and down his arms, the result of deliberate cutting.

It made a person sad to even try to talk to them, the nonsense they believed and the embarrassing things they did. They were all of them waiting on the end of the world, and in the meantime Elder Bent was showing them how to prepare their souls for the seven-dimensional existence that waited beyond death. He kept them busy studying star charts and fixing radios (which they sold at street markets on Saturdays). All of them believed that the final Testament of the Lord would be written not in words but as a diagram for some kind of circuit. I can't pretend I understood all of it. Yolanda had more patience with Elder Bent's basket of crazies than I did, had always been sociable with them when she ran into them on the street. She was better than me that way. She felt sorriest for the same people who pissed me off the most.

I was pissed off then, and Yolanda wasn't on hand to calm me down. I crossed to the edge of their yard, where the three boys were getting ready to roll Mr. Waldman into their silver packing material, and I stamped on the edge of the fabric before they could flap it over him.

The fellows who'd been wrapping him into his sci-fi shroud looked up at me with surprised faces. They were the youngest of Elder Bent's crew. The first was trim and tall, with a golden beard and shoulder-length hair—he could've played Our Lord in a performance of *Jesus Christ Superstar*. The second was a soft, chubby boy, the kind of dude you just know is going to have damp, hot little hands. The third was a black fellow suffering from vitiligo, so the dark of his face was mottled with patches of bright, almost startling pink. They all had their mouths open, as if they were getting ready to speak, but none of them said anything. Elder Bent shot up one hand in a gesture to be silent.

"Honeysuckle Speck! What brings you out on this glorious night?"

"I don't know what's glorious about six or seven thousand people getting torn to shreds between here and Denver."

"Six or seven thousand people have stepped out of these sorry containers of the spirit"—gesturing at his dead—"and have transitioned to the next phase. They've been set free! They're everywhere now, in seven dimensions, their energy the background crackle of reality, the dark matter that holds the universe together. They prepare the way for the next great transmission."

"What I'd like to know is why Mr. Waldman is transitioning to your front lawn. What makes you think he'd want you to wrap him up in tinfoil like someone's leftovers?"

"He is one of the forerunners! He goes to mark the way, with so many others. It does no harm to honor his sacrifice."

"He didn't sacrifice himself for the likes of you. Mr. Waldman wasn't part of your cult. He belonged to a synagogue, not a crazy house, and if he's going to be honored, it ought to be by the precepts of *his* faith, not yours. Why don't you leave him alone? Go drink some poison Kool-Aid and ride a comet, you vulture! You don't know a damned thing."

He beamed at me, a tall, skinny geek with a glow-in-the-dark head. It didn't matter how you cussed him out, he always grinned at you like you were a charming scamp.

"But I do!" he said. "A damned thing is exactly what I know: The planet is damned, and I know it! I said the world would end on the twenty-third of November, this very year, at five A.M., and you see now . . . it begins!"

"What about when you said it was going to end in October, two years ago?"

"I said the apocalypse would come on October twenty-third, two

years ago, and indeed it did. But it has been developing slowly. Few
observers were attuned to the signs."

"You also said the world would end in 2008, didn't you?"

He finally looked disappointed in me. "The asteroid that was sure to
hit us was turned aside by the combined will of a thousand prayers, to
give us more time to perfect our minds for leaving the three-dimensional
world. But the day and the hour are almost upon us now! And this time
we will not turn the end aside. We'll welcome it with a happy song in our
throats. We'll sing the curtain down on this life. We have been singing
the finish for some time now."

"Maybe you could get back to singing it in the morning. Some of us
are trying to sleep. And while you're at it, can't you sing something that
isn't Phil Collins? Haven't we all suffered enough today?"

"The words don't matter! Only the joy the singing generates! We store
it like batteries. We are almost up to full charge and ready to go! Aren't
we?" he called to his people.

"Ready to go!" they shouted back, swaying a little, staring at the star-
scape on his bald, bony head.

"Ready to go," Elder Bent said placidly, lacing his fingers together
across his flat stomach. The tattoos on his head glowed in the dark, but
the stars on his knuckles had been printed there in plain black ink, while
he was in jail. He had served two years for what he'd done to his wife
and his stepchildren. He had kept them locked in an attic for most of
one summer, giving them a tablespoon of water to split in the morning
and one Nilla wafer to share in the evening, and making them map plan-
etary orbits all day. If one of them sassed or didn't participate in their
"studies," the others were commanded to kick her back into obedience.
One evening the wife escaped from him when he allowed the family
outside to make star observations. The police threw him in the clink, but
he wasn't there long. He got sprung on appeal, on account of his First
Amendment right to practice his religion, which apparently included
starving and abusing followers who didn't sing his hymns in the right
key. Worse yet, the stepdaughters rejoined him as soon as he was free.
They were devoted sisters of the faith now. They stood just behind him,

slim and pretty beneath their hubcap headgear, the both of them giving me the stink eye.

While Bent was blabbing, my attention had drifted from the three dopes crouched around Mr. Waldman. They had used the opportunity to begin wrapping him up again. I heard the crinkle of silver foil and stamped on the material once again, before they could finish cocooning him.

"You keep up with what you're doing, boys, and the apocalypse is going to fall on you a lot sooner than you think," I told them.

They gave Elder Bent a nervous look, and after a moment he gestured with one long-fingered hand. The three young men stood and retreated from the body.

"Do you think someone will sit shivah for him, Honeysuckle? Mr. Waldman's wife is dead. His son is a marine stationed in some foreign part of the world and who knows when he will learn of his father's passing, given the current crisis. And when he does hear the news —*if* he ever hears the news!—he may never make his way back to Boulder. The hard rains have only just begun to fall. More is coming, I assure you!"

"More is coming," repeated the boy who looked like the Christ. He fingered his own astrolabe necklace. "And we're the only ones ready for it. We're the only ones who know what's going to—"

But Elder Bent gave a brisk wave of one long-fingered hand and shut him up. Then he continued, "Shouldn't *someone* honor his life? Isn't *any* ceremony better than none? Does it do any harm? If his son appears back in Boulder, the discharged flesh will be here, to be mourned however he sees fit." He paused and then said, "Or *you* could take him. And how will you mark his passing, Honeysuckle? Will *you* sit shivah for him? Do you even know how?"

He had me there. I didn't like it, but I had my own dead to tend to.

"Well . . . at least keep it down," I said lamely. "There's a child trying to sleep across the street."

"You should sing with us! You shouldn't be alone tonight, Honeysuckle. Come sit. Don't be by yourself. Don't be afraid. Fear is worse than pain, you know. Let go of yours. Your fear of the rain. Your fear of us. Your fear of extinction. It isn't too late for us all to love each other and be happy—even here as the last chapter of mankind is written."

"No thank you. If we're all on the way out, I want to end my life sane, not wearing a sheet-metal skirt and singing my way through the greatest hits of Phil Collins. There's such a thing as death with dignity."

He gave me a sad, pitying smile and put his fingertips together in a gesture that made me think of Spock, and thinking of Spock made me sad again. Yolanda and I both had gay-girl crushes on Zachary Quinto.

Elder Bent bowed to me and turned with a rustle of his silver gown. It is hard to take a man seriously as a spiritual leader when he's swanning around in what looks like a prom dress made of Reynolds Wrap. The chubby kid and the boy with vitiligo bent back to Mr. Waldman's body, but the one who looked like Jesus ran his fingers through his yellow tresses and took a half step closer to me.

"If you knew what *we* knew," he whispered, "you'd *beg* to join us. We were the only ones ready for what happened today. A smart girl would *think* about that. A smart girl would ask herself what else we know—that she doesn't."

He sounded plenty ominous, but when he turned away with a dramatic swish, he stepped on a nail and yelped in a high-pitched voice that kinda ruined the effect. I watched him shuffle away—and then a movement, a flicker of light at the edge of my vision, caught my attention, and I glanced around.

It was Andropov, in his apartment on the first floor. He was standing behind the glass with an oil lamp, glaring out at us. Glaring at *me*. It made my stomach go funny, the way he was watching.

He lifted a sheet of plywood to the glass and disappeared behind it, and I heard him begin to wham away with a hammer. He was boarding up his windows, sealing Martina and himself off from the rest of the world.

WHEN I WOKE ON URSULA'S couch, the front room was flooded with strong, clear light, and I smelled coffee and warm maple syrup. Templeton stood over me, sipping espresso from a little mug, his Dracula cape flapped rakishly over one shoulder.

"It *was* terrorists," he said without any preamble. "And they're saying there's a sixty-percent chance of nails in Wichita. Do you want pecans in your waffle?"

Ursula was in flannel pajamas, tending to a waffle iron set on her gas range. She had news streaming on her laptop again. You know what was on the news that morning: I'm sure you watched it, too. Letters had come to the *Denver Times*, the *New York Times*, and the *Drudge Report*. They were displayed, discussed, and disdained all morning long:

> Sirs—
>
> Now is your day of ruin. A storm as big as Alla's fury is upon you. Blood will paint your roads. Bodys awaiting burial will cram your parks, vast farms for maggots. A million nails will rain upon you, for your wars to rob Muslim lands of oil, and your laws to bar Muslims from your racist nation. Soon you will fondly look back on 9/11 as a day of tranquility.

The names of schools and churches scrolled across the bottom of the screen, like when everything is canceled for a big snowstorm. That's what I thought it was at first: a list of cancellations. It wasn't until I was eating my first waffle that I realized it was a list of places to bring your dead.

They were saying at least seventy-five hundred killed in the metro Denver area, but law enforcement expected the number to go much higher by the end of the day. They showed a wedding, the bride in a red gown, all stuck full of needles. She was wailing and holding what was left of her husband. He had been torn apart, shielding her with his body.

They'd been married for less than an hour. They'd been dancing in an outdoor pavilion when the rain began. The bride had lost her husband, both sisters, her parents, her grandparents, her nieces.

On CNN they had a chemist in *The Situation Room*. He began by repeating what we already knew—that the hard rain was made up of crystal fulgurite, what was also sometimes called "petrified lightning." He said that while fulgurite could occur naturally, the crystals that dropped on Boulder and Denver were something new. They represented an artificial form of fulgurite that had to have been designed in a lab. Nothing else could account for the almost industrial perfection of the nails that fell on Colorado. He told Wolf Blitzer that it was possible—maybe even likely—that someone had seeded a cloud with it, perhaps using a simple crop dusting plane, which supported the terrorist hypothesis.

He added that the hard rain was doing things no fulgurite had ever done before. Instead of drizzling down *mixed* with rain, it *absorbed* water, using every bit of moisture it could get to power its growth. It didn't require lightning to turn to crystal; any old static electricity would do.

Wolf Blitzer said it was raining nails outside Wichita and asked his pet chemist if it was the same cloud that had rained nails on Boulder. The chemist shook his head. He said there might be a million grains of this stuff in the upper stratosphere and that it would collect in clouds like any kind of dust. Some would fall in needles and pins. Others would grow a bit, then fragment and break up, creating new grains of crystal to infect future cloud systems. Wolf asked him what that meant in simple terms. The chemist pushed his glasses up his nose and said that for all practical purposes this might become a permanent part of the global weather cycle. This new, synthetic crystal fulgurite was self-perpetuating, and it was in the atmosphere now. He said they'd need to do some modeling, but it was possible it might eventually make every rain cloud on earth into a farm for crystal. He called that the "Vonnegut scenario." That eventually ordinary rain might be a thing of the past.

That was when Wolf seemed to forget that the cameras were pointing at him. He just stood there, looking sick. After a moment he stammered that they were going to turn to the events unfolding in Wichita, and he cautioned parents against letting children watch.

Until then Ursula had been bent over the sink, briskly scrubbing out cups and pans and setting them to dry in the dish rack. But when she heard that bit, she told me, softly, it might be best to shut off the laptop and save the battery, and I knew she wanted to spare Templeton the sight of any more slaughter.

I joined her at the sink and began to towel off wet glasses. In a low voice, I told her, "Elder Bent says the world is going to end this fall. I think the scientist on CNN just agreed with him. I feel sick. Everything is terrible, and I don't know what to do."

Ursula was quiet for a while, sponging the waffle iron. Then she said, "In the days after Charlie died, I'd never felt so alone or scared or helpless. There is nothing that makes a person feel worse than helplessness. I was so angry I couldn't do anything about it. I couldn't have him back. I couldn't fix it. I couldn't rewind what had happened and change it. I understand how you feel, Honeysuckle. I've already visited the lost and lonely place at the end of the world, and all I know is, the only way to keep going is to do the things the people you loved would've wanted you to do. Try to imagine how Yolanda would've wanted you to use the time you've got left. That's the one way to keep her close. If you're scared and sick and can't think how to live for your own self, try to think how you can live for *her*. You won't feel helpless anymore. You'll know just what to do."

When she ran out of words, she gave the top of my head a twitchy pat, like a person who's nervous about being snapped at might pet a big, strange dog. It was lousy affection, but I knew it took a lot for her to even try, and I appreciated it. Besides, she had let me in far enough to show me a glimpse of her own pain, and an act such as that requires more courage than giving someone a hug.

She asked if I'd mind Templeton for a bit while she raked up the nails in her yard. I sat in the garage and watched the kid standing on a bucket of rock salt, banging the keys of the big iron manual typewriter, just about the only thing his father had left behind for him. I sat under his daddy's framed Ph.D. from Cornell; Templeton was the direct descendent of jumpy, pasty geniuses, people more comfortable with microbes on glass slides than with other human beings. I was unclear whether Charlie Blake had died by accident or on purpose, taking his car through a guardrail and down into a canyon after a couple of drinks. Yolanda had gone with Ursula to identify the body while I stayed behind to watch Templeton. Yolanda told me later that Charlie had only just been fired. His company was moving somewhere down south, and they were taking his research and all his best ideas with them but not him. All he got for a decade of work was a handshake and a gold iPad. The accident had smashed his skull down into his brain, but that iPad had been salvaged from the car crash with nary a scratch on it. Ursula gave it to Yolanda; Ursula couldn't bear to look at it.

I sat while Templeton banged at the keys, and I tried to think what Yolanda would've wanted me to do. I had about 30 percent charge left on my phone and used it to try her father again. This time I didn't even get voice mail. I walked to the open garage door. A mile of blue sky stretched above the Rockies, nothing in it but a few fat, scattered islands of cloud.

Ursula stood in the middle of her lawn, leaning on her rake, studying me. At her feet was a small mound of glittering crystal shards.

"What are you thinking about?" Ursula asked.

"Do you think it's going to rain?"

"Might be a sprinkle later," she told me cautiously.

"I was thinking I should go see Dr. Rusted. That's Yolanda's father. Someone needs to let him know what happened to his daughter. Easier for me to go to him than for him to come to me. He's sixty-four and not exactly a triathlete."

"Where's he live?"

"Denver."

"How were you planning to get there?"

"I guess I'd have to walk. No one is driving anywhere. The roads are full of nails."

"You know it's thirty miles?"

"Yes, ma'am. That's why I was thinking if I'm going to go, it better be soon. If I left in the next hour, I could be back by tomorrow night."

"You also could be dead by tomorrow night, if you get caught out in another downpour."

I scratched my neck. "Well. I'd keep a close watch on the sky and head for cover if it darkened up any."

Ursula clenched the handle of her rake and thought for a bit, frowning to herself.

"I'm not your mother," she said at last. "So I can't forbid you to go. But I want you to text me regularly to keep me up to date on your progress. And when you get back, you're going to come straight here and show Templeton you're all right, so he won't worry about you."

"Yes, ma'am."

"I wish I had a gun to give you."

"Why?" I said, genuinely surprised.

"Because law will be stretched thin, and there's a whole city of terrified people out there. Folks woke up today to a poisoned world, and some of them won't see any reason to hold back on doing the awful things they've always dreamed of." She thought some more and then lifted her eyebrows. "I have a big rusty machete you could take. I keep it around for hacking the brush."

"No, ma'am," I said. "If I got into a fight, I'd be just as likely to miss and whack it into my own knee as hit someone. You better hold on to it. I'll keep to the main roads. I don't think in the bright of day there'll be much to worry about."

I turned and went back into the garage. Templeton was all typed out and said he was ready to be a bat. I caught him around the waist and lifted him and hung him upside down from the bicycle rack. He dangled above the filthy stained mattress that was there to catch him if he slipped.

"Hey, kiddo," I began.

"I heard it all," he said. "I heard you talking."

"I don't want you to worry about me any. If it rains, I'll get under cover. I'll be fine. You stay in the house or the garage while I'm gone."

"Mom wouldn't let me out anyway."

"No, and good for her. Your days of flying around as a bat are over. Come to think of it, I might have to drop in on the FAA while I'm in

Denver and tell them what you've been up to. Let them know you've been flapping around at night without a license. See if they won't clip your wings once and for all."

"You better not," he said.

"Try and stop me."

He hissed like a snake and showed me his plastic fangs. I tousled his hair and told him I'd see him soon.

"Don't worry about Yolanda and her mother," he said to me solemnly. "If you don't come back, my mom will figure out what to do with them. She'll probably plant them in the garden."

"Good. I hope she grows something nice out of them. Yolanda would probably enjoy the idea of coming back as a batch of tomatoes."

"Mom doesn't like to hug people," Templeton said, still dangling upside down, his cape hanging almost to the floor. "Will you hug me?"

"You bet," I said, and I did.

ALL I HAD TO DO was stroll across the street to get a sense for just how hard hiking down to Denver might be. The road was covered in a carpet of steely needles, a half inch deep. One came through the soft rubber sole of my sneaker and jabbed me in the arch of my right foot. I sat down on the curb to tug it out and yelped and jumped back up with three more nails sticking out of my stupid butt.

I climbed the exterior staircase to my crib on the second floor. Below me Andropov's apartment was full of racket. He had a music player going, blaring operatic Russian music. Toward the rear of the building, there was a TV on, blasting just as loud. I could hear Hugh Grant saying witty things in a sly voice about as loud as God's. Remember, the electric was out all over Boulder; all his equipment had to be running off batteries.

I had swept and mopped the entire apartment in preparation for Yolanda's arrival. I had opened a bottle of sandalwood-and-sage oil, and the whole space had been kissed with the sweet fragrance of the high country.

We had only four rooms. The living room flowed into a small kitchen. There were a bedroom and a small office in the rear. The floor was old pine, the long-ago varnish yellowing to a shade of amber. We had hardly any furniture, aside from the bed and a cheap futon below a poster of Eric Church. It didn't look like much. But we had cuddled on that futon, had watched TV there, and sometimes kissed and held each other. Yolanda had kept her favorite pillow in my apartment, and when I looked in the bedroom, I could see it, long and flat in a faded purple pillowcase, neatly lined up at the top of the bed. At the sight of it, just about all the energy for expeditioning went right out of me, and I started feeling heartbroke all over again.

I lay down for a while and had a good snuggle with her pillow squeezed against me. I could smell her on it. When I closed my eyes, I could almost make myself believe she was there in bed with me, that we had only just taken a pause in one of the long, sleepy conversations we often had first thing in the morning. We could make a happy argument out of just about anything: which of us looked better in a cowboy hat, if it was too late for us to learn to be ninjas, if horses had souls.

But I couldn't make my lonesome feelbad last. It was too goddamn noisy downstairs. I didn't know how they could do it—listen to a Russian aria in one room and Hugh Grant in another, all of it turned up to a medium-size roar. They had to be fighting, I thought, trying to drive each other mad. It wouldn't be the first time the downstairs was full of furious clatter: crashing pans, slamming doors.

I leapt out of bed and stomped on the floor to tell them to shut up, and right away one of them replied by kicking the wall. He kicked so long and so hard it shook the whole house. I stomped even more furiously, to let him know I wasn't scared of him, and Andropov kicked back harder still, and suddenly I realized I was getting pulled into their childish game and quit.

I threw some water bottles into a backpack, some cheese and bread, my phone charger in case I found a place to use it, a multitool, and some other junk I thought I might want. I kicked off my Top-Siders and yanked on my cowboy boots, black with silver stitching and steel toes. When I went out, I left the place unlocked behind me. Didn't see the point. The rain had smashed in the windows on the exterior landing. The cops were no doubt too busy to worry about a little looting here and there. If someone came along and wanted my stuff, they could have it.

The noise from Andropov's shook my fillings and buzzed in my head and was more than any reasonable person ought to have to stand. On a last irritable impulse, I turned on my heel and clomped onto the porch and hammered on the door, meaning to ask him what was the big idea. But no one answered, even though I stood there pounding until my fist was sore. It was loud, but it wasn't *that* loud. I was sure they could hear me.

It nettled me, the both of them in there ignoring me. I went to one window, then the other, but both were boarded over on the inside. The glass wasn't even broken, not there in the shelter of the front porch.

I went back down the front steps and circled to the eastern face of the house. The nails had come in at a slant from the west, so the windows were intact on that side of the building as well. Andropov had nailed planks across the inside of the glass here, too. The first had been completely blocked up, but when I reached the second, there was an uneven space, about an inch wide, between two planks. When I stood on my tiptoes, I could just peer through the gap.

I saw a dark hallway and an open door looking into a dingy bathroom. Plastic tubing curled up out of the tub and into the sink. A glass beaker sat on the toilet, next to a gallon jug of some kind of fluid, what might've been water but which seemed more likely to be ammonia or some other clear chemical.

I rose a little higher on my toes, trying to see what was on the floor of the bathroom. My forehead bumped the glass. An instant later Andropov's eyes appeared in the crack, bulging and bloodshot and wild with fury or terror. The thickets of his eyebrows were black and overgrown. I could see the pores in his bulging nose. He belted something out in raging, sputtering Russian, and pulled a black curtain over the glass.

I WAS TRAMPING ACROSS THE campus of the University of Colorado Boulder when I saw a guy in a tree, forty feet off the ground: a man in a dark Windbreaker and a red tie, tilted almost upside down, with a branch going through his stomach. I walked right under him. He was reaching out with both arms, and his eyes were open wide, like he was about to ask for help getting down. I couldn't figure out for the life of me how he'd gotten up there.

It was a cool, shady morning under the big, leafy oaks on the Norlin Quad, but you couldn't fool yourself it was just any Sunday morning. A girl ran by me in a blood-soaked Josh Ritter T-shirt, sobbing her guts out. Who knew where she was coming from or where she was going? What might be the cause of her grief. What source of comfort she sought and if she ever found it.

There were shiny nails of finest crystal on the paths, broken windows in all the dorms, and dead pigeons littering the grass. The air should've been perfumed with the smells of late summer: roasted grass and blue spruce. Instead, though, there was a stink of jet fuel.

I didn't see the helicopter until I came down a gloomy alley between buildings and had a glimpse through a stone arch into the outdoor theater they have there for Shakespeare and the like. There was a TV news copter that had gone straight down into the flagstones. The cockpit was a bashed-in nest of steel and shattered glass and blood. The whole craft looked shot up, holes and dents and dings all over it. So that was where the guy in the tree had come from. He had tried to jump when he saw he was going down. Maybe he'd imagined that the oak would break his fall. It had.

I came out onto Broadway, which is four lanes wide and cuts a straight line through that part of Boulder. When I emerged streetside, I saw for the first time how bad everything really was. There were abandoned cars as far as you could see, windshields busted in, all of them beat up, pocked with hundreds of dents, shot through with holes. Cars had swerved off the road and up onto the curbs. I spotted a ragtop that was just rags and a pickup that had parked in the lobby of a real-estate office, driving right through the plate-glass window to escape the storm. Someone else had run their Lincoln Continental into a bus stop, plowed it right into the long Plexiglas booth where people had crowded together to take shelter from the rain. There was blood splashed up onto the Plexiglas, but the bodies at least had been cleared away.

Two blocks down the road, there was a stopped Greyhound riddled with holes. The door was cranked open, and a guy sat on the bottom step, feet in the road. Rangy Latin dude in a blue denim shirt buttoned at the throat but the rest flapped open to show his bare chest. He held a fist to his mouth as if to stifle a cough. I thought he was mewling to himself, but that was the cat.

A horrid, skinny hairless cat was in the street, one of those things that is all wrinkles and big, batlike ears. This thing was dragging itself around by its front legs, turning itself in a slow circle, trying to find a way to get more comfortable. It had a nail through its haunches and another in its throat.

The big guy, his face framed by long, greasy hanks of hair, was crying almost silently. Silently and bitterly. His nose had been broken more than once, and the corners of his eyes were wrinkled with scar tissue. He looked like he'd been in a hundred bar fights and lost ninety of them. From his dark hair and deep reddish hue—a color like polished teak—he had more than a little vaquero in him.

I slowed, crouched down by the cat in the road. It gave me a bewildered, helpless stare with very green eyes. I am no fan of the hairless breed of felines, but you couldn't help but feel dreadful for the sad thing.

"Poor little guy," I said.

"S'my cat," the big man told me.

"Oh, Lord. I am so sorry. What's his name?"

"Roswell," he choked out. "I was lookin' for him all mornin'. Callin' for him. He was under the bus. I half wish I hadn't found him at all."

"You don't mean that," I said. "You've been blessed with a chance to say good-bye. That's more than most got with those they love. He is glad to see you, no matter how much pain he might be in."

He glared. "You got a twisted fuckin' idea of what's a blessing."

"I'm not a fan of that kind of language," I said, "but I'll give you a pass since you're upset. What's your name?"

"Marc DeSpot."

"That isn't a real name."

"It's my fightin' name," he said, and opened his shirt slightly to show the Gothic black X inked across his pectorals and abdomen, the crux right over his breastbone. "I am a professional MMA fighter. Right now I'm five and seven, but I been undefeated in my last four scraps. Who are you?"

"I'm Honeysuckle Speck."

"Kind of name is that?"

"That'd be *my* fightin' name."

He stared at me in bewilderment for a moment over the fist he still held close to his mouth. Then misery overtook him, and his shoulders heaved with another sob, blowing snot and spit in the process. When movie stars grieve in the tragic third act of a love story, they always make mourning look a lot more beautiful than it really is.

Roswell peered from Marc to me and mewled in a weak, shivery voice. He was trembling. I stroked one hand along his smooth, downy flank. You never saw a creature asking for relief any more clearly.

"I don't know what to do for him," Marc said.

"There is only one thing left you *can* do for him."

"I can't!" he said, and another sob burst out of him. "Ain't no way. We have been friends for ten years."

"Ten years is a good life for a cat."

"He has been with me from Tucumcari to Spokane. I had him when I didn't have nothing else except the shirt on my back. I just can't do that."

"No. Of course you can't," I said. "Go on and pet him. He's looking for comfort."

He reached out one big, gnarly hand and rubbed at Roswell's head, as tenderly as a man stroking the face of a newborn. Roswell shut his eyes and pressed his skull up into Marc's palm and gave a soft, rattling purr.

He was stretched out in a sticky puddle of blood, but he had the bright sun on his flank and his companion's hand on his brow.

"Oh, Roswell," he said. "A man never had a better pal."

He drew his hand back to his mouth, heaving with fresh tears, and shut his eyes. I supposed that was as good a time as any, so I reached out and took Roswell's head in one hand and his neck in the other and gave a good, firm twist, same as I would've done with a chicken on my father's old farm.

Marc DeSpot's eyes flew open. He stiffened, went rigid with shock.

"What'd you do?" he asked, like he didn't know.

"It's over," I said. "He was suffering."

"No!" he shouted, but I didn't think he was shouting at me or shouting about what I'd done. He was shouting at God for taking away his cat. He was shouting at his own unhappy heart. "Aw, *shit*! Aw, shit, *Roswell*."

He slid off the bottom step of the bus and onto his knees. Roswell was curled up on his side in a red splash of blood. Marc DeSpot took his limp body in both hands, pulling him close, lifting him up, hugging him.

I touched DeSpot's arm, and he knocked my hand aside with his elbow.

"Get the fuck away from me!" he cried. "I didn't ask you to do that! You didn't have any right!"

"I'm sorry. But it was for the best. That cat was in agony."

"So who asked you? Did I ask you?"

"There was nothing that could've saved Roswell."

"You don't get moving, you filthy lez," he said, "there's nothing gonna be able to save *you*."

I didn't pay any mind to that. He was hurting. The whole world was.

I dug in my bag and offered Marc DeSpot a bottle of water. He didn't look at it and he didn't look at me, so I put it down in the road next to his hip. Close up I could see he was younger than I'd thought at first. He might've been no older than me. I felt sympathy for him, in spite of his nasty mouth and childish ways. I was all alone in the world, too.

I got up and went on, but when I'd covered another three blocks, I happened to glance back and discovered that Marc DeSpot was following me. He staggered like a drunk, about a hundred feet behind, and when I looked at him, he quickly turned away and pretended to be staring through a smashed plate-glass window into the darkened interior of a secondhand-electronics store. He had produced a white straw cowboy hat from somewhere, and with that on his head and a red bandanna around his throat he looked more like a youthful vaquero than ever.

The sight of him trailing along behind me made me ill at ease. In our brief encounter, he had struck me as the kind of person who is a victim of his own emotions, impulsive and immature. It occurred to me now that he might have made up his mind I was a sadistic breaker of hearts and slayer of felines and that he was cruising to express his displeasure with a closed fist. Or maybe he was looking to improve his fighting record to six wins by hauling off and belting a lonely lesbian with an unfortunate resemblance to Squiggy.

I went on, though, and in another block was able to take a deep breath. If he'd been hoping to jump me, he'd lost his chance. As Broadway descended south into Lower Chautauqua, it became steadily more crowded. I heard a noisy rumble, and an enormous dump truck with chains on its tires turned onto the street in front of me. Shiny nails of crystal imploded under its wheels. A big dude in a filthy yellow jumpsuit and elbow-length rubber gloves rode on the back end. Behind him the flatbed was stacked three deep with corpses.

The truck wove around abandoned cars, and when there wasn't room to go around, it went through, bashing wrecks out of its way. It joined a slow-moving caravan of other dump trucks. They were lined up to turn into a football field behind the high school.

It seemed like half of Boulder was there, wandering in a daze—packs of children with grimy faces, old ladies in housecoats. When I got closer, I could see dead people laid out in rows along the yard lines of the football field, from one set of goalposts to the other. The trucks were collecting the dead, and family members had followed in their wake to see that the remains of their loved ones were treated right.

You would expect them all to be sobbing, for the field to be a Greek chorus of wails and screams, but people were better behaved than that. We're people of the heartland, we don't make too much of a fuss. It seems impolite. I imagine that a lot of people were too sleepless and shocked to carry on. Maybe it would've felt rude to rend your clothes and tear your hair with so many other grief-stricken people around.

There were folding tables set up at one end of the field, manned by two crews: a team from Staples and a gang of kids from McDonald's. The McDonald's squad had a few charcoal braziers going. Under the diesel stink of the trucks, I could make out the cheery, greasy odor of McMuffins and burgers.

A line of about twenty people led up to the tables. I don't know why I got into the queue. Maybe it was that hungry-making smell, or maybe I was thinking I could see if there was a place here for Yolanda and her mother. Maybe I was just hoping Marc DeSpot would lose interest and decide to stop trailing me now that I was in a crowd. He was still there, pretending not to look at me but hovering at the outskirts of the action.

I waited my turn, and when I got up to the table, a tall, gawky gal wearing a pair of giant glasses and a red Staples shirt said, "Are you looking for someone or bringing someone in?" In front of her, she had a set of rotary files and a bag full of manila tags.

"Neither right yet. How does it all work?"

"Staples will tag your loved one and file their location on the field for future reference. If you have a Staples Rewards account, we'll even e-mail you all the burial information. It's all free to show our commitment to rebuilding the greater Boulder area through the combined forces of local volunteers and Staples' great products and services." She recited her lines in a dazed drone.

"I might want to bring my friend and her mom down. I don't know yet. It'd be a long way to haul them."

"We're arranging pickups, too, but it might be three to four days."

"Will there even be any room left on the field by then?" I asked.

She nodded. "Yes, absolutely. We're burying the first wave at one P.M. There'll be prayers from six different faiths, and Sizzler will provide catering." She pointed to some other trucks under the goalposts, filled with dirt and rocks. "After we cover them over, I'm afraid it'll be necessary to bury another group on top of them. We're hoping to manage three a plot."

"I'll think about it," I said, and she nodded, and then a teenager standing beside her asked if I wanted large fries or an Egg McMuffin and told me that McDonald's wanted to express their sorrow for my loss. It was the end of the world, but you could still hit the drive-thru on your way to oblivion.

Of course it was good of them all to be doing what they were doing, helping folks lay their loved ones to rest and making sure everyone got fed. When the sky starts raining nails, you find out pretty fast what parts of a culture are the sturdiest. One thing Americans do well is make an assembly line. Not twenty-four hours after a few thousand people were ripped to shreds by falling needles, and we were burying our dead with all the efficiency of packing a Happy Meal.

I got out of there, tucking into my fries. You might not think it's possible to have an appetite walking past a carpet of dead bodies a hundred yards long, but foreground becomes background pretty quick. Any pattern repeated over and over is bound to turn into wallpaper eventually, whether it's flowers or corpses.

After the fries were gone and I'd licked all the tasty grease off my fingers, I downed half a bottle of water in a hurry to rinse the salt taste out of my mouth. By then I was sometimes seeing faint little sparkles and flashes of light at the edges of my vision, which was maybe the sun glinting on all the scattered nails or was maybe just light-headedness. It didn't seem like I'd been walking long enough to get faint, but then the night before had been a restless one.

I hadn't gone far when I caught sight of Marc DeSpot again, hanging back about a block. He dropped his gaze straightaway and acted like he was interested in the football field, but I knew then he was still after me. I swerved toward a Starbucks on the corner, as if I wanted a latte to wash down my fries. The door was locked, of course—any fool could've guessed it wasn't going to be open—but I gave the handle a tug like I expected otherwise. I peered through the tinted glass as if there were someone in there to look at. Actually, the lights were off, and there was a paper sign taped up on the door: CLOSED FOR THE END OF THE HUMAN RACE. But I gave a thumbs-up and nodded as if someone had told me to use the side door.

I slipped around the corner of the building and then busted out the best run I could manage in my shitkickers. There was a wide swath of parking lot on the other side of Starbucks, filled with a thousand crystal nails, gleaming and throwing halos. It looked like all the treasures of Aladdin had been dumped off in front of Whole Foods.

I ran about halfway across the lot, then hunkered down behind someone's grape-colored Kia. I watched the Starbucks, looking through the space between the undercarriage and the asphalt. Sure enough, Marc DeSpot soon came wandering around the corner, peering this way and that, hunting for me. Then he looked over his shoulder, as if someone were following *him*. After a moment of indecision, he turned around and went back the way he'd come.

I sat and counted one-Mississippi, two-Mississippi, until I reached a hundred. I got up and went crunching on across the lot, down Baseline Road, and onto the ramp leading up to the turnpike.

I thought there might be sawhorses blocking the way, but the ramp was wide open, aside from a little hatchback that had somehow caught fire and burnt down to the frame. Once I reached the turnpike, I could see in a glance there was nothing to stop me from strolling all the way to Denver right along the dotted yellow line. When the rain had come down, it was going ten in the morning on a pretty Monday in August. On the turnpike, cars had been doing seventy when the storm broke. It must've been like driving into antiaircraft fire. I saw a black Corvette that had been peeled open, the whole roof twisted back, the red leather seats inside ground up into hamburger. Then I looked again and saw it wasn't red leather at all. They were *white* seats that had been painted red by what had happened to the people sitting on them.

There were other folks strolling along the pike, picking over the wrecks. One middle-aged lady had a shopping cart. I watched her stop alongside a Mercedes to mine the glove compartment. She was about forty, had a pink flowered kerchief over her graying hair, and the tidy, put-together look of a PTA mom. She dug through someone's bloodstained purse, found some bills, a gold bracelet, and a copy of *Fifty Shades Freed*, which she deposited into her cart before going on.

A mile away, on the other side of the road, I spied a crew dressed in orange jumpsuits, doing some kind of work. It was too far away to see what.

Well, it was a nice morning for walking, as long as you paid no mind to all the dead folks chewed up in their cars. I was down to about 25-percent battery on my phone, but I was longing to hear another human voice, so I stuck in my earbuds to catch some news.

That's why I didn't hear them coming up on me: the comet boys. That's why they got me.

WHAT I HEARD ON THE news was that preliminary evidence indicated the terrorists who'd made it rain nails might've been operating out of an area around the Black Sea. There was a company based in the region that had demonstrated a reagent that could rapidly produce synthetic fulgurite under laboratory conditions. The president had dashed to Twitter to promise a "BIBLICAL RESPONSE!" and a "HOLY WAR" and swore that the Islamists were about to learn that "WHEN IT RAINS IT PORES!!!" He said we'd be dropping a shower of our own soon enough, only it would be daisy cutters, not a bunch of namby-pamby crystal nails.

Then there was a story about a fierce downpour in Pueblo, all nails, that punctured natural-gas tanks and caused an explosion so tremendous it registered as an earthquake in Colorado Springs. They said the fire had swallowed half the town and the trucks couldn't get close enough to effectively battle it, because they couldn't traverse the nail-studded roads. A meteorologist said the crystal spikes in Pueblo were larger than the ones in Denver, with some darts as long as his thumb. A chemical engineer was just about to explain what it all meant, but I didn't hear what he had to say, because that was when someone clubbed me in the head.

I went down so hard and fast I don't remember hitting the ground. I wasn't knocked out. It was more like when the lights in your house flicker just a bit. There was a little mental flicker, and when my head cleared, I was on all fours, seeing stars. That's not a turn of phrase—I mean literally. I was looking down at a copper disk the size of a saucer, with constellations etched on it and my blood gilding one edge.

The comet kids were coming up through the waist-high blond grass at the side of the pike, moving fast in their tinfoil gowns. It was the three who'd been wrapping up Mr. Waldman. The boy who resembled Christ had thrown his astrolabe into my head. The other two had pulled their astrolabes off their necks and were whipping them around and around in big loops. The spinning gold medallions droned like a pair of didgeridoos.

My hands and knees were torn up from my fall. The road was carpeted in shiny tacks. I touched the crown of my head, and a pulse of blue light blinked in front of my eyes. I felt a deep throb of pain, like someone had whopped a railroad spike into my skull. When I could see again, my right hand had ten fingers instead of five, and all of them were wet with blood. I still had one earbud poked into my ear, and I heard a snatch of someone on the news, murmuring in a weird, deep, underwater voice:

"You juust dount beeelieeeve the skyyyy can really faaaalll on yoooou, but guesss whoooot? It's falllllling nowwwww. . . ."

I couldn't figure out why they wanted to pick a fight with me, and I didn't feel like hanging around to ask them. I scooped myself up and tried to run, but I was woozy and reeling from the thwack in the head. I staggered this way and that, and then another comet clown let go of his astrolabe, and it hit me in the small of the back. It was like getting stabbed. My knees folded, and I dropped again. I hit face-first and caught a chinful of fulgurite stickers. Fortunately, by then I had staggered to the edge of the road, and I fell into thick grass instead of against hard blacktop and rolled a few feet down the embankment.

I felt the way I imagine a caterpillar must when she's closed into the fuzzy shroud of her cocoon. I could hear, and I could see a little— although everything had gone cloudy and out of focus—but I couldn't feel my limbs, which were numb and boneless. All the thought had been knocked out of me. I wasn't even in what you might call pain. I didn't have enough sensation to feel pain.

They crowded in. I could see past them, too. The action had drawn the attention of the PTA mom pushing her shopping cart. She craned her head to see what was happening, her expression nervous but also excited.

The fat boy saw her looking and hissed, "Oh, man, oh, shit, we shouldn't have done this right here, Sean, where people can see—"

"Shut up, Pat," said the one who looked like Christ. Course the fat boy was named Pat. I've never seen anyone who was more Pat in his life.

Sean—Christ in a tinfoil gown—glanced up the embankment at the PTA mom.

"It's for her own good," he told her. "She's crazy. We're bringing her home to look after her. Right, Randy?"

The black kid who had vitiligo nodded with a frantic enthusiasm. "She gets like this when she's off her meds. She thinks everyone's after her!"

"Can't imagine what gave her that idea," the PTA mom said.

"You want her iPhone?" Randy gobbled. He had a querulous, jittery sort of voice. He picked my phone out of the dirt, dusted it off, and held it out to her. "It's the new one."

"The 7?"

"The 7 Plus! Take it. We just don't want any trouble."

"That's right," Sean said. "We're doing what's best for her—and for us. Same as you're doing what's best for *you* . . . even though the police might not see it that way. A cop might think you're looting, when really you're just surviving, aren't you?"

Her face assumed a faintly sulky cast. "The people I took from aren't going to complain."

"No, they won't. And this girl is mentally feeble and hysterical and needs looking after by her family. But some people might say we're committing abuse, dragging her back home this way. It's easiest to mind your own business, don't you think?"

She didn't reply for a moment but went on staring at the phone in Randy's hand. "I always wanted to try the bigger one. But I bet you can't unlock it."

"Bet we can. It's the one works off fingerprints," Sean said.

He nodded at Randy, who bent down and grabbed my hand and squeezed my thumb against the sensor. The phone unlocked with an audible click.

Randy tossed it to PTA Mom, who caught it in both hands. In his nervous, twitchy voice, Randy said, "You'll wanna reset the security right away, before it locks itself again."

"Enjoy it," Sean said. "Think different—we do!"

She laughed. "I can see that! Take care of the poor girl." And she turned and puttered off, playing with my phone.

My insides hurt at the thought of losing it. It had all my text messages from Yolanda on it. She would send me pictures of the sky, big blue western skies with little lumps of white cloud in them, and she'd write: The cloud in the middle is my pet unicorn. Or: That cloud over the mountains is you hiding under a sheet. Once she sent me a picture of a mountain pool, a cloud reflected in it as if it were a mile-wide mirror, and texted: I want to hold you like the water holds the sky.

Seeing that woman wander off with my phone was worse than getting my head smashed in with an astrolabe. It was like wrapping Yolanda in her shroud all over again.

Randy, Pat, and Sean watched her go, with hunted, rascally eyes. You never saw a more demented-looking pack of weasels. I tried to move—to rise onto all fours—and just the thought of the effort pushed a sound out of me, something between a sob and a groan. That got their attention back. They circled me again.

"You know what the best thing would be, guys? Guys?" Pat said. He was the kind of huffy, breathless boy who's always saying things that no one else listens to. "Guys? I think it would be easiest to kill this bitch. We could bang a nail into her temple. No one would ever know she didn't die in the rain."

"The Finders would know," said Sean. "The Finders would see homicide in your mind and leave your quantum energy to fall into dissolution with all of the others who are unprepared."

Or something like that. I've never had much of a grip on their cuckoo-bird theology. I think the Finders might be a higher breed of intelligence? And your soul, I guess, is your quantum energy? It's hard to believe anyone could choke down Elder Bent's fourth-rate Flash Gordon story. But humans are pack animals by nature and most will accept whatever they have to accept—wholly, enthusiastically—to keep an honored place in their tribe. Give a man a choice between reality and loneliness or fantasy and community, he'll pick having friends every time.

"It's not just the Finders we got to worry about," Randy said, wiping a hand under his nose and sniffing. "She dragged Yolanda and Yolanda's ma into the house across the street. You know, where the vampire kid lives."

"Yeah, the Blakes," said Sean. "Who cares about them?"

"Well, wouldn't the woman wonder when she never hears from Honeysuckle again? I bet she's expecting her to check in."

"If Ursula Blake and her creepy little kid turn out to be a problem, then we'll deal with them like we're going to deal with her," Sean said. "It's not like we have to worry about getting locked up. Humanity will be extinct before the year is out. There's not a prison in the world that can hold us, boys. We've got an escape tunnel that goes all the way to the seventh dimension!"

It's funny: The world always manages to ensnare you, even when you're most sure you're free and clear of its hooks. After I wrapped up Yolanda and said good-bye to her, it seemed to me that I'd come unplugged from the emotional charge that keeps most of us going, day in, day out. I was like a circuit board that had been popped out of the big, lively, whirring machine of human society. I didn't serve anyone; I didn't solve anything; I didn't have any useful functions to offer. Without Yolanda I was obsolete hardware.

Then Sean started talking about going after Ursula and Templeton—who had taken me into their house when I was in shock, fed me, and tended to me—and I felt a sick frisson of alarm that finally sent some strength to my limbs. Not enough to do me any good, mind you. I tried to get on my hands and knees, and Sean put his boot in my ass and slammed me back down onto my face. Lying there with my nostrils full of dust and needles sticking into my chest, it came to me that if anything happened to Ursula and her son on my account, I wouldn't be able to bear it.

"Yeah, that's right, Sean! The Big Flash is coming!" Randy said. "In ten weeks Ursula Blake, her kid, Honeysuckle—they're dead meat, along with all the rest of the disorganized, and we'll be with the Finders!"

"Learning how to make universes of our own," Pat whispered in a reverential hush.

"So . . . so what did we decide?" Randy said, and he licked dry lips with a sandpapery tongue. "Nail her?"

"No. Better. *Save* her," Sean said. "We'll bring her back to Elder Bent and force an awakening. Come on. Let's wrap her up."

He drew a big folded square of that crinkly, foil-like material out of a backpack and spread it on the ground next to me. The other two wrapped me in it just like they were rolling up carpet. I tried to kick my way loose. But I was too weak to work up a decent struggle, and in a minute they had me wound up with my arms pinned to my sides and that tough shiny fabric wrapped around me from ankle to throat. Sean was down on one knee, with a roll of black electrical tape, binding my silver cloak tight around me when I hawked a fat gob of spit into one of his eyes.

He flinched. Pat shrieked, "Gross!"

Sean wiped his eye and glared at me. "If I were you, I'd save my spit. Elder Bent takes the view that physical suffering prepares your spiritual energies to leave the body behind. You aren't likely to get much to drink in the next couple months."

"If physical suffering is good for building up spiritual energy," called someone from up in the road, "I am about to fully recharge your batteries. Get ready for a high-voltage ass-kicking, you sonsa bitches."

We all looked around, and there was Marc DeSpot, who I thought I'd ditched back at Starbucks. His stony visage stared out beneath the brim of his cowboy hat. His shirt flapped open to show the magnificent black X inked across his reddish-bronze chest. His right hand was clenched in a fist. Nails stuck out between his fingers.

The Three Stooges gathered around me had one moment to gawp before he fell upon them, dropping down the side of the embankment so fast his hat flapped off. Randy was the only one of them who still had an astrolabe to fight with. He was pulling it from around his neck when DeSpot got to him, throwing all his weight behind his right fist. He hit Randy so hard they both fell over. The side of Randy's face was raked off like he'd been struck with a gardening fork. DeSpot's nail-studded fist clawed deep red furrows in his cheek, puncturing straight through into his mouth.

The one named Pat screamed, then turned and ran. He tripped over me with both feet and hit the dirt. Well, that was his one and only chance to get away. By then Marc DeSpot was back up, growling like a dog sick from the heat. He caught up to Pat and kicked him in the ass and drove him back down onto his stomach. Pat flattened with a cough. Marc kept going, grabbed him by the collar, and yanked his head back. He grabbed Pat's nose and gave it a horrible twist. It made a sharp, brittle crack, a sound like someone stepping on a china plate. To this day I have never heard another sound so horrible. He dropped Pat, and the chubby boy went down squirming in a kind of palsy.

In all this time, Sean, the team's Christ look-alike, hadn't moved. He stood frozen, his eyes wide, his face rigid. When he heard Pat's nose crack, though, it broke his paralysis, and he turned to run. I guess it doesn't hurt your quantum energy none to be a lickspittle coward who leaves your buddies in the dirt.

DeSpot caught up to him in three lunging steps, snatched him by the back of the tinfoil gown, and yanked him right off his feet. As Sean fell backward, DeSpot snapped up his right knee and clubbed him in the base of the skull. If that was how he fought in the ring, I never wanted to meet any of the men who'd beaten him.

Sean stared up at him, his eyes rolling like those of a panicked horse. Marc was about to stomp on his face when I hollered, "Wait!"

Marc glanced at me with an irritable frown, like he thought I was going soft and womanly on him. I rocked to the left, then to the right, and finally I was able to roll across the slope until I thumped up along-side Sean.

We were stretched out side by side, me in my shroud of silver wrap, him in the weeds with Marc's boot resting on his chest.

I stared up into DeSpot's face and said, "They were following me?"

He peered down at me, his brow furrowed. "All morning long. I was sitting there with Roswell when I saw them the first time. Following you from two blocks back. Didn't look right, so I figured I'd trail along and see what they wanted with you. Thought it was the least I could do. When I had a minute to collect myself, I kinda got to feeling like I owed you."

We latched gazes, but only for a moment; he blushed and looked away.

I twisted my head to stare into Sean's dazed, frightened face. "Why the hell would you and your empty-headed pals follow me five miles just to bushwhack me, three against one? What'd I ever do to you besides make fun of the way you dress and the way you talk and all your stupid crackpot ideas?"

His voice, when he spoke, was rusty and thin. "You were going to tell! You were walking to Denver to meet with the FBI and tell them what we've been up to! You were going to tell them that Elder Bent, of all men, knew the rains would fall! He *knew*! He was foretold!"

"What do you mean, he was *foretold*?"

"*He* knew what was coming. He knew the hour and the day, when the ignorant would be cut down, leaving behind only the prepared. Only us!"

I considered that for a moment, then said, "And what gave Elder Bent the idea I was going to the FBI? Did he get that information from one of his contacts in the seventh dimension?"

Sean bit down on his lower lip as if he felt he had already said too much. Marc DeSpot put his weight on his left foot, pressing down against Sean's chest, and the air exploded out of the kid.

"The Russian!" he cried. "He left a message! It said you knew what we had been up to and if we didn't stop you, Elder Bent would be hauled away by the FBI! Because of what he knew about the rains!"

"Andropov left you a message?"

Sean let out a little laughing gasp. "Yeah." And in an atrocious Russian accent, he said, "'You must stop Miss 'Onysuck! Girl is going to talk to FBI.' I don't think he wants the law digging around the neighborhood any more than we do!"

"Who talked to him?" I asked. "Who took his message? Did he say anything else?" But it turned out we were all done talking.

This whole time the one named Randy had been surreptitiously crawling away through the high grass. When he reached the edge of the road, he got up and hotfooted it. DeSpot saw him making his break and snatched up one of the big astrolabes that had brought me down. He didn't bother with the gold chain but threw it like a Frisbee, and it hit the back of Randy's head with the kind of gong that would've been quite amusing in a slapstick cartoon. Randy collapsed.

While this was happening, Sean scrambled to his knees. A blade flashed in one hand. I recognized it right off—it was my own knife, part of the little multitool I had stuck in my backpack. Before he could poke it into Marc's kidneys, I twisted and threw my legs and swept his feet out from beneath him. Sean toppled backward down the embankment. His head struck the shallow, concrete-lined ditch at the bottom with a sickening crunch.

I shouted for Marc to have a look and make sure I hadn't just murdered him. Marc knelt beside him at the base of the slope, took his pulse, and looked into his eyes. He glanced up at me with a sorry, disappointed look on his battered face.

"Bad luck," he said. "I think he's fine. Just out cold."

He came back to me at a rangy lope and bent and started ripping tape free.

"You almost lost me back at Starbucks," he said.

"I didn't nearly lose *them*, I guess. I feel like a fool for not realizing they were after me. Dressed like they are, they should've stood out like flashing lights."

"It's easier for three people to tail a person than one. Besides"—he held up a set of connected brass cylinders—"they could stay farther back and still follow you. Your boyfriend down there had a telescope."

By then he was pulling that silver shroud free. It looked like tinfoil, but it was as resilient as canvas. It flashed the sun into my eyes, and in that instant it struck me that maybe I'd come close to spotting them after all. I remembered sometimes noticing a sparkle and glint at the very periphery of my vision and wondering if I was getting faint. That had been them, hanging back, hiding in doorways, shadowing me from a distance.

Marc was looking glum and avoiding my gaze, folding and unfolding that big sheet of silver packing material. I thought I knew what was troubling him.

"You can stop worrying about what you said to me when you were so upset," I told him. "We're even now. More than even. I'm awfully sorry about what I had to do to Roswell."

He nodded. "Yeah, well."

"What's your real name? Marc DeSpot is the kind of joke that would amuse a five-year-old."

He glared, then said, "DeSoto. No money in a name like that." He looked around him at the comet clowns. "Did you understand any of what he said to you?"

I sat up and stretched. Some of what Sean had babbled was the usual cosmic rubbish spouted by all of Elder Bent's people. But I thought there'd been fragments of something that mattered mixed in with all Sean's space-cadet nonsense. I needed time to try to untangle it in my head, see if I could make some sense of it.

When I didn't reply, Marc murmured, a little uneasily, "He said this Elder Bent . . . *knew* what was going to happen. That they were all preparing for it. You think there's any chance . . . ?" His voice trailed off.

I didn't know, and I didn't answer. Instead I said, "Some nasty old biddy gave me up to these white slavers here just to get my iPhone Plus. She walked off without a look back."

"The one with the shopping cart? I saw her." He picked his hat out of the dirt and set it on his head.

"I guess losing my phone isn't the worst thing. I could be on my way to a dank basement cell in a house full of end-of-the-world cultists, forced to do who knows what to satisfy their demented wishes." I had an urge to get up and walk around, kicking all of the comet kids in their heads. But it was hot and I had a long road still ahead of me. "Can you think of any way we can keep them from getting up and coming after me again? Or of going after you?"

He opened Sean's telescope and peered down the turnpike. "Those are convicts working on the highway, sweeping up nails under the eye of the state police. Why don't you wander down there and tell 'em you've got three more that belong in leg irons? I'll tape them up in their shiny dresses, the way they taped you up, so they don't wander off."

He offered me a hand, and I took it. He pulled me to my feet. We stood together in a tired, comradely silence for a moment. He squinted at the blue sky.

"You think these boys are right? You think these are the end times? I had an aunt who said it was a matter of fact that this was the last human century. That anyone who understood the book of Revelation could see a judgment was coming."

"I hate the idea these blockheads could be right about anything," I said. "Tell you what, though. If the apocalypse holds off another couple of days, why don't you stop by the white house on Jackdaw Street, with the staircase on the outside of the building? Or look for me across the street at the little butter-colored ranch, where my friend Ursula lives with her son. We can have a couple beers and try to brainstorm a better fighting name for you than Marc DeSpot."

He grinned, flapped his blue denim shirt open. "Too late. Once you got a big X on your chest, who else could you be?"

"The X-Terminator?"

"I thought about X-Rated, but a lot of kids come to the fights. You don't want to give their parents the wrong idea."

"Thanks for rescuing me, friend," I said. "Try to stay out of the rain."

"You, too," he said to me.

He squeezed my hand then, turned, and descended the hill to Sean. I hung out long enough to watch as he began to wrestle with Sean's gown, tucking his arms inside it, wrapping it tight around him. I didn't think I'd ever see Marc DeSpot again and wished there were more to say, but it seemed like we'd already said everything that mattered. Some people you can never thank enough, so you might as well quit after saying it once, because too much gratitude will just make them embarrassed.

I turned on my heel, crystal pins grinding under my boots, and went on into the noonday light. Behind me I heard the first loud ripping sound as Marc DeSpot tore off a strip of tape.

IT WAS A HOT, DUSTY half an hour walking up the turnpike to the chain gang. As I approached, a state trooper who'd been leaning against the hood of an abandoned red Audi stood up, and stared at me through a pair of mirrored sunglasses.

Strung out behind him there were maybe thirty convicts wearing orange jumpsuits that said SUPERMAX on the back. Most of the prisoners had push brooms and were sweeping the nails from the road. Maybe six others were working in teams of two to wrestle corpses out of cars and fling them onto a flatbed trailer, latched to a monstrous John Deere tractor down in the grass. The tractor had heavy chains on the tires, but I'm not sure it needed them. The tires themselves were as big as doors, so thick and massive that I doubt the sharpest of those crystal darts could've pierced them.

Another couple of staties were starting the cars that could be started and driving them to the center island between the east- and westbound lanes. They had cleared the turnpike all the way to Denver, the road open and empty and quiet. The skyscrapers of the city soared pale blue and distant below us.

"S'your business?" asked the cop who'd been sitting against the Audi. He adjusted the elephant rifle propped against his shoulder.

A lot of the convicts had paused to look up from their sweeping. They'd been at it all morning and smelled that way. It was a ripe man stink, mingled with the corrupted-meat smell of blood baking into the upholstery of all those ditched cars. A hundred thousand flies had been born overnight. The air seemed to vibrate from the beehive hum of them.

"There's three boys back that way you might want to talk to. They bushwhacked me as I was headed down from Boulder to Denver and tried to abduct me for their end-of-the-world cult. They would've got me, too, if I wasn't rescued by a Good Samaritan who beat the pants off them. He left them taped up in the silver gowns they were wearing. Also, there was a woman with a shopping cart who agreed to turn a blind eye to my kidnapping in trade for my iPhone Plus. But you don't need to bother with her. A cell phone seems a small thing to worry about in the midst of a national crisis."

"Got blood in your hair," said the state trooper in the aviator glasses.

"Yessir. One of 'em belted me with a chain." I didn't want to say they had attacked me with astronomical instruments, on account of I didn't feel that would make my story any more credible.

"Lemme see," he said.

I ducked my head and gestured to where I'd been struck. He pushed a few rough, callused fingers into my hair, then drew his hand back and wiped his red fingertips off on the hip of his uniform.

"This needs stitches." He had the clipped, disinterested inflections of Yul Brynner, but for all that, he'd inspected my injury with sensitivity and the blood on his hands didn't bother him. In the West you will find men like that, fellows with gentle hands and hard, flat voices. Horses and dogs are instinctively loyal to such fellows, while yellowbellies and equivocators instinctively fear them. They make mediocre husbands, good officers of the law, and top-notch bank robbers. He half turned and called out, "Dillett! You do a couple stitches for the lady?"

There was a skinny gink in a state-police uniform, a guy who was mostly knees and Adam's apple, standing in the flatbed behind the tractor, using a pitchfork to move bodies around. He paused and waved his gray felt campaign hat in acknowledgment.

The head guard looked down into my face and said, "You shouldn't be walking in this road anyway. We're in a state of emergency. Unless someone is dying, you shouldn't be in the open."

"It's not someone dying. It's someone dead. My girlfriend and her mother were struck down in the storm, and I set out for Denver to let her father know."

He looked away from me and shook his head, like his team just gave up a big lead in the late innings. He didn't express any condolences, but he did say, "And you were going to walk all the way there, from Boulder to Denver? What if it rains again?"

"I'd hide under a car, I guess."

"It can be hard to tell the difference between decency and stupidity sometimes. I'm not sure which side of the line this one falls on. But I'll take a couple of my guys up the pike, and if I come across this gang of girlnappers, I'll radio back. Officer Dillett will haul you down to Denver on his dad's John Deere. He's got a full load of dead folks to drag back to town anyway. You'll have to make a statement to authorities there."

"Yes, sir," I said. "What are *you* guys going to do if it rains? What are *all* of you going to do?"

"Take cover and start sweeping again when it's over. If the roads aren't clear, what good are they? If a government can't keep the roads open, what good is a government at all?" He cast an unhappy look at the sky and said, "Wouldn't that be a sad epitaph for the world? 'Democracy was canceled on account of rain. The human season will be suspended until further notice.'" If he knew he'd just said some poetry, his sunburned, hard-ass, Yul Brynner face didn't show it.

"Yes, sir. We'll hope for sun."

"And try not to worry about how we're going to raise crops when the clouds are spilling rocks instead of water."

"Yes, sir."

I crunched over the loose gravel of a thousand diamond-bright needles and said hello to Dillett, the skinny gink on the flatbed. He said to climb up on the bumper and he'd have a look at my scalp.

Strange to say, that was the best part of that whole long, menacing nightmare of a weekend. I took a shine to Dillett, who was as gangly and loose-jointed as the scarecrow in *The Wizard of Oz* and just as friendly. He pulled on latex gloves and threaded shut my scalp wound, working so light and careful that I didn't feel any pain at all and was surprised when he was done. Afterward he asked if I wanted an orange soda and a chicken-salad sandwich. I had them both, sitting on the bumper of the trailer with the daylight shining in my face. The sandwich was on sun-warmed slices of seeded rye, and the soda was in a can sweating drops of ice water, and for a while I felt almost human.

A convict—the sort of fat man who is described as morbidly obese— sat on the trailer with the dead folks. He had his right boot off and the foot mummied up in bandages. I caught his name—Teasdale—but didn't learn much more about him, not then. We didn't talk until later.

Just as I drained the last fizzy-sweet mouthful of soda, a voice, flat and staticky, burst from the walkie-talkie on Dillett's hip. It was Yul Brynner.

"Dillett, you there? Over?"

"Copy."

"I've got three males here in shiny silver dresses, claiming they were ambushed by the lady with you and her deranged boyfriend, Mr. X. I'm placing them all under arrest. If we can't make the kidnapping charge stick, we can still get 'em for crimes against fashion. Pack it up and haul that flatbed down to Denver. I want to remind you to get off at Uptown Avenue and take the cargo to the Ice Centre. If there's photos of what you're carrying on CNN tonight, you'll be lucky to wind up working as a crossing guard. That order is straight from the governor, y'hear, over?"

"Copy that," Dillett said. I noticed neither of them ever used the word "corpse" on the radio.

Dillett and Teasdale spent a few minutes arranging a crinkly orange tarp over their harvest of the dead and strapping the bodies down with bungee cords. Then all of us climbed up into the cab of Dillett's John Deere, the corpulent prisoner sitting in the middle. Dillett handcuffed one of Teasdale's wrists to a steel bar under the dash.

Dillett's John Deere was the size of a shed on wheels, and when I was up in the cab, I was a full nine feet off the road. This was no little family tractor. When he got it going, the engine roar was so loud I thought it might shake the teeth out of my gums.

"What'd you do?" I asked Teasdale.

"I cut my landlord's head off with a hacksaw," he said in a cheery voice. "It was self-defense, but you can't find a jury anywhere that isn't biased against people who struggle with their weight."

"No," I said. "I meant what happened to your foot?"

"Oh. I stepped on an eight-inch nail. Went right through the sole of my boot into my heel. Blame my extreme size. When there's been unhappiness in my life, my obesity has usually been the cause."

"Ouch! Eight inches? Are you messing with me?"

"No," Dillett answered for him. "I took it out myself. It was about the size of a walrus tooth."

"I didn't know the nails could get that big."

"She ain't heard about Enid," Teasdale said.

Dillett looked glum and nodded somberly.

"What about Enid?" I asked. "Enid, Oklahoma?"

Dillett said, "It's gone. It poured spikes as big as carrots there. Killed people in their houses! Storm only lasted twenty minutes, and they're saying over half the city's population was wiped out. The storms are tearing their way east and getting worse as they go. The sparkle dust—the stuff that grows into crystals—is following the westerlies right across the nation."

"We can't say we weren't warned," Teasdale told us in a contented tone.

"When were we warned it might rain nails?" Dillett asked him. "Was that on the Weather Channel and I missed it?"

"It's global climate change," Teasdale said. "They've been talking about it for years. Al Gore. Bill Nye. We just didn't want to listen to them."

Dillett couldn't have looked more stunned if Teasdale had opened his mouth and a dove flew out. "Climate change, my ass! This isn't climate change!"

"Well, I don't know what else you'd call it. It used to rain water. Now it's raining blades of silver and gold. That *is* a change of climate." Teasdale rubbed a thumb against his chin, then said, "Ghosts is next."

"You think it's going to rain ghosts?"

"I think we'll have ghosts instead of fog. The mist will wear the faces of the departed, all those we had and lost."

"You better hope for clear weather, then," Dillett said. "If a fog made out of ghosts rolls in, your landlord might turn up wanting his back rent."

"I count my blessings to live in a dry mountain climate," Teasdale told me complacently. "I'll face whatever blows in on the wind. It may come to blow gales of pure sadness instead of air and leave us all taking shelter from grief. Maybe time itself will begin to crest and drop instead of temperature. We might have the nineteenth century for winter. For all we know, we might've already slipped into the future without noticing it."

Dillett said, "Dream on, Teasdale. There aren't going to be ghosts, and there aren't going to be downpours of emotion either. We are dealing with chemical warfare, plain and simple. The Arabs who were behind 9/11 are behind this. Our president knew it was a mistake to ever even let 'em in here, because this is what happens. The NSA only just established that the company that invented hard-rain technology was financed with Arab money. They developed the science of it with American researchers, then brought the technology to their headquarters in old Persia. Congress is working on a declaration of war tonight. They think they unleashed a storm, they don't know the half of it. The president has already promised to go nuclear. There might be some more strange weather coming after all! I doubt they've had much snow in I-ran, so a faceful of atomic fallout should be quite the refreshing experience for them!"

By then we had reached a cloverleaf of on-ramps and off-ramps at the outskirts of Denver. Dillett steered us off the turnpike and onto US-287. Off the thruway things were in bad shape. Cars had been shoved to the sides of the road, but the blacktop was covered in broken glass and shards of crystal. A Tastee-Freez was boiling a greasy cloud of black smoke, but no one was fighting the fire.

We spent another fifteen minutes thundering down to the Ice Centre at the Promenade, a big indoor rink surrounded by a few acres of asphalt. A dozen official-looking black cars were parked in the area around the loading docks, along with several ambulances, a jumble of police cruisers, a pair of big armored prisoner-transport vehicles, and a fleet of hearses. Dillett pulled up to a stainless-steel garage-type door. He turned the tractor and carefully reversed, until the flatbed was right up against the closed roller door.

"You're sticking the dead here?" I asked, feeling queasy. Years before, when my parents were still together, they'd taken me to see *Disney on Ice* here.

"It's one place to keep 'em cold," Dillett said. He blatted his horn, and someone opened a regular-size door at the top of a loading dock.

It was another state trooper, a freckled redhead who looked like Archie from Riverdale. Dillett rolled down his window and yelled for him to open the garage door to the rink. The kid who looked like Archie shook his head and screamed something about a Zamboni, but it was hard to tell what he was yelling over the thresher roar of the tractor. They hollered back and forth like that, neither of them making any sense to the other, and finally Dillett opened the driver's-side door and stepped onto the running board.

No sooner had he straightened up than Teasdale stuck out his left foot—his bandaged bad foot!—and kicked Dillett in the ass. Dillett waved his arms and looked foolish for a few seconds before spilling down to the blacktop.

Teasdale pulled the driver's-side door shut and slid in behind the steering wheel. He put the tractor into gear. His handcuffed right hand couldn't reach the steering wheel, but it was in the perfect place to handle the stick. The tractor began to rumble across the lot.

"What do you think you're doing?" I asked him.

"I am making a bolt for freedom," he said. "They won't never come after me what with all that's going on, and I have family in Canada."

"Do you plan to drive there in this John Deere, hauling eighty dead bodies behind you?"

"Well," he said mildly, "one thing at a time."

Archie from Riverdale jumped up onto the running board. He had crossed the parking lot at a sprint to catch us before we got on the road. Teasdale opened the driver's-side door, hard and fast, and clouted him off.

We drove on, picking up speed. We were doing almost thirty when Teasdale swerved into the road, catching a piece of the curb. Bungee cables popped. Bodies sailed off the flatbed and into the air, rolled across the sidewalk like flung logs.

"Were you going to let me out, or were you planning to take me on your mad dash to the Yukon?"

"You can jump anytime you like, but I'm afraid it wouldn't be convenient to slow down just yet."

"I'll wait."

"I don't suppose if we passed a hardware store you'd run in and grab me a hacksaw so I can cut myself loose of the cuffs? I'd drive you on to see this fella you're looking for, even though it'd be going out of my way."

"Considering what you last used a hacksaw for, you'll have to find someone else to do your shopping."

He nodded in an understanding way. "Fair enough. I appreciate I don't have a great track record with household tools. I forgot to mention that I also took a hammer to my landlord's wife. I didn't kill her, though! She's fine! I understand she recently recovered full use of her legs."

I didn't recover full use of my legs for fifteen minutes. He tore along without stopping, taking corners hard, throwing corpses off the trailer at every turn. I didn't bother to tell him he was leaving a trail any fool could follow. A man who steals a ten-ton John Deere isn't thinking about being inconspicuous.

Finally we reached an intersection blocked by a jackknifed tractor-trailer, and the only way around was to drive up over the curb and across a small green park in front of a credit union. To navigate this new terrain, it was necessary to slow almost to a crawl. Teasdale shot me a friendly look.

"How's here?" he asked.

"Better than Canada," I said, and opened the door. "Well, take care of yourself, and don't murder anyone else."

"I'll try not to," he said. He peered speculatively into the rearview mirror, at the line of stony peaks behind us. "Keep an eye on the skies. I do believe it's clouding up."

He was right. A cold, icy-looking range of clouds stood above the mountains themselves. They weren't thunderheads but rather a great mass of vapor that promised a long, steady drizzle.

Teasdale chunked the tractor back into gear as soon as I was on the running board. I hopped down and watched him rumble away.

Once he was out of sight, I fumbled for my cell phone to call the police and report on what Teasdale was planning. I had to check the pockets of my jeans twice before I remembered I didn't have a phone anymore. I didn't have a clue where I might find the nearest cop, but I did know which way it was to Dr. Rusted's house, and I set out once more.

As I tramped into downtown, the wind rose behind me, funneled through the deep trenches between high-rises. It smelled like rain.

AS I ENTERED CENTRAL DENVER, I was struck most by the hush. No traffic. No shops open. On Glenarm Place I could hear a woman sobbing from an open third-floor window. The sound carried for blocks. The nails were scattered all over the streets, flashing silver and rose in the late-afternoon light.

The storm had lashed the high, vertical sign in front of the Paramount, so it just read R OU T. The other letters had come loose and dropped in the street.

A girl wandered along wearing a wedding gown that didn't fit and a homemade tiara fashioned from gold wire and crystal nails. She had on elbow-length silk gloves and carried a heavy-looking burlap sack. Close up it was possible to see that the gown was in tatters, and her cheeks were dribbled with smeared mascara. She walked beside me for a while. She told me she was the Queen of the Apocalypse and said if I'd kiss her and swear my fealty to her, she'd pay me ten thousand dollars. She opened the sack to prove she had the money. It was packed full with bundles of cash.

I told her I had to pass on the kiss—I informed her I was in love and didn't play around. I said she ought to use some of that money to get off the street and into a hotel room. Rain was going to fall. She said she wasn't afraid of bad weather. She said she could walk right between the raindrops. I said I couldn't, and at the next corner we went our separate ways.

The whole town wasn't a post-Rapture wasteland, and I don't want to give you the idea it was. The National Guard had cleared East Colfax for most of a mile and installed first-aid stations in storefronts. They had established a thriving HQ and information center at the Fillmore. The marquee promised BOTTLED WATER FIRST AID SHELTER INFORMATION. Generators roared noisily, and several places had lights on. The wrought-iron fence outside was plastered over with photocopies showing people's faces above their names and the words MISSING SINCE STORM PLEASE CONTACT.

But the soldiers I saw looked flushed and scared, barking at people to find shelter. A Humvee rolled up and down the avenue with PA loud-speakers on top, broadcasting information from the National Weather Service. A woman said an area of depression was building over the Boulder-Denver Metro Region and rain was expected within the hour. She didn't say what kind of rain and didn't need to.

I headed north to East Twenty-third Avenue and into City Park, the last stretch of my long hike. It was the quietest place I'd been yet, and the most mournful. I slowed as I neared the zoo.

An eighteen-wheeler had been parked in the road, and there was an adult giraffe spilled across the open flatbed trailer, legs sticking off the side and long neck curled up, so her head touched her breast. A guy in a hard hat motored a little crane over, crystal splinters snapping under its heavy tires. He pulled alongside the eighteen-wheeler. Hydraulics whined, and the crane operator lowered a net with a baby giraffe in it. He placed the calf daintily between its mother's legs. They were both stained with blood and filth, and the sight of them broke my heart like nothing else I'd seen all day.

The air was rank, and on my left, in a broad green meadow, arranged neatly in pairs, were dead lions and dead walruses and dead gazelles. It was like some horrible parade leading toward a cruel parody of Noah's ark, a ship for everything that was gone and never coming back, every-thing that would not be saved. There was a pile of penguins almost ten feet high. They stank like week-old fish.

I plodded the last dreary quarter mile under lowering skies, in a strange, pearly twilight. My sewed-up skull was banging, and the steady throb of it nauseated me. The closer I got to Dr. Rusted's house, the less I wanted to get there. It was impossible, after all I'd seen, to imagine I would find anything good. It seemed childish to hope for any small mercy now.

Dr. Rusted and his family had lived in a pretty brick Tudor east of the park, a place with tangles of ivy matting the walls between the mullioned windows. It looked like the sort of place where C. S. Lewis might meet J. R. R. Tolkien to share some scotch and discuss their favorite ancient Germanic poems. It even had a modest tower on one end. Yolanda slept in the round room at the top, and whenever I visited, I'd yell up, "Hey, Rapunzel, how they hangin'?"

I slowed as I stepped into the front yard. Leaves shivered in the aspens to either side of the house. I could not say why the dark and the stillness of the place so troubled my mind. Most of the houses on the street were dark and still.

Across the road a small, tidy, compact man was sweeping nails out of his concrete driveway. He quit what he was doing, though, to stare at me. I had seen him around: a fifty-something who sported square-framed glasses, a conservative haircut, and an air of chilly disapproval. He was packed into a shiny, violently green tracksuit that brought to mind radio-activity, the Jolly Green Giant, and Gumby.

I rapped twice on the door and, when there was no reply, turned the latch and stuck my head in.

"Dr. Rusted? What's up, Doc? It's me, Honeysuckle Speck!" I was going to call again, and then I saw a shadow I didn't like, near the bottom of the stairs, and let myself in.

Dr. Rusted was on his face, halfway to the kitchen. He wore a gray vest, a white oxford shirt, and charcoal slacks with a sharp crease in them. Black socks, no shoes. He lay with one cheek against the dark wooden floor. His face looked bare and bewildered without his gold spectacles. His hands were mittened in bandages, and the oxford shirt was torn and spotted with blood, but he hadn't died from those wounds. It looked as though a headfirst plunge down the stairs had killed him. His neck was swollen to the touch. I thought it might be broken.

I had walked a long way to carry a message I hadn't wanted to deliver, and now it turned out there was no one to receive it. I was tired and headachy and sick at heart. After I came out to my parents, my father wrote me a letter saying he'd rather his daughter was raped to death than be a lesbian. My mother simply refused to acknowledge I was gay and would not look at or talk to any of my girlfriends. When she was in a room with Yolanda, she pretended she couldn't see her.

But Dr. Rusted always liked to have me around, or if he didn't, he always made the effort to pretend. We drank beer and watched baseball together. Over dinner we'd rag on the same right-wing politicians, getting each other riled up, competing to see who could insult them the most creatively without actually being obscene, until Yolanda and Mrs. Rusted pleaded with us to talk about anything else. Is it odd to say I liked the way he smelled? It always made me feel cozy and content to catch a whiff of his bay-rum aftershave and the faint odor of the pipe he wasn't supposed to smoke. He smelled like civilization; like decency.

The phone was dead, no big shock there. I drifted from room to room, wandering the museum of the departed Rusted family. As I roamed, I was seized with the certainty that no one would ever live there again. No one would heave themselves down on that big striped couch to watch the latest UK imports, *The Great British Baking Show* and *Midsomer Murders*, the kind of programs Mrs. Rusted had liked best. No one would pick through the cans of tea in the kitchen cupboard, trying to decide between Lady Londonderry and Crème of Earl Grey. I climbed the tower stairs to Yolanda's room, my throat constricting with grief even before I pushed open the door to look in there for a last time.

Her round room was done in pinks and yellows like a hollowed-out birthday cake. She had left it in her usual state of manic disarray: a heap of unwashed clothes in one corner, a single sneaker in the center of her desk, half the drawers hanging out of her dresser, and a watch with a broken leather strap in the middle of the floor. Her jewelry was scattered across the top of her dresser instead of in the jewelry box, and tights had been hung over the foot of the bed to dry. I picked up a throw and pressed my face to it, inhaling the faint scent of her. When I left the room, I wore the blanket over my shoulders, like a robe. It was August outside, but in Yolanda's room it felt like late fall.

I descended the stairs and had a peek in the master bedroom. Dr. Rusted's gold spectacles were still on the end table, and the counterpane bore the rumpled imprint of a big man's body. His tasseled shoes stuck out slightly from under the bed. A framed photo of all of us—Dr. Rusted, Mrs. Rusted, Yolanda, and myself, on a trip we made to Estes Park—was faceup in the center of the bed. Maybe he'd had a sleepless night, worrying about his wife and daughter, and had dozed off with that picture of us all together cradled to his chest.

He could've been hugging any of the thousands of photographs he owned of Yolanda and Mrs. Rusted, but it made me almost feel like bawling that he'd picked one that included me. I never wanted to be liked by anyone so much as I wanted to be liked by Yolanda's parents. Understand: I wasn't just in love with her. I was in love with her family, too. It threw me at first, how often they held each other, and kissed, and laughed, and enjoyed one another, and never seemed to find fault. I'd never cared a damn about crosswords until I learned that Dr. Rusted liked them, and then I began doing them every day on my iPad. I helped Mrs. Rusted make ginger cookies just because it made me feel good to be near her and hear her muttering to herself in her lyrical island accent.

I left the throw blanket with the picture and made my way back outside. I stood just in front of the rainbow-colored banner extending from an angled flagpole bolted to one of the brick columns flanking the front steps. Gumby had retreated to the entrance of his garage, and a daughter had appeared. The daughter was maybe fourteen, willowy and bulimia thin, with sunken cheeks and circles under her eyes. She wore a tracksuit, too, black with purple piping, and the word JUICY across her butt. I wondered what kind of father let his fourteen-year-old wear that.

"You know there's a man dead over here?" I asked.

"There's dead folks everywhere," he said.

"This one was murdered," I said.

The fourteen-year-old girl twitched, tugged nervously at a silver bangle around her wrist.

"What do you mean, he was murdered? Course he was. Probably ten thousand people were murdered yesterday. Everyone who was caught outside, including a quarter of the people on this road." He spoke calmly, without distress or much apparent interest.

"He wasn't killed by the rain. Someone surprised him and shoved him down the stairs, and he got his neck broken. You hear anything?"

"Sure I have. People have been screaming and crying and carrying on all day. Jill and John Porter walked up the street this morning, each one of them carrying one of their shredded ten-year-old twins. The Porters were out looking for their girls all night. I prayed they'd find them, but maybe I should've prayed they didn't, considering the condition the children were in. The two little girls had hidden together under an overturned wheelbarrow, but it was too rusted out to stop the nails. Their mother, Jill, was sobbing and shouting that her babies were dead until John gave her the back of his hand and shut her up. After that I decided I'd heard all the awfulness I wanted to hear, and I haven't paid attention to any shouting or screaming ever since." He took a lazy, disinterested look at the back of his wrist, then shifted his gaze to me once again. "It was a judgment, of course. I'm lucky my own daughter was spared. Everyone on this street let your girlfriend look after our children."

I felt a clammy, cool feeling spread out from the nape of my neck, down my spine. "You want to elaborate on that?"

"What happened yesterday has happened before—to Sodom and Gomorrah," he informed me. "We let *your* sort mingle with *our* sort, as if we didn't know there would be a price to be paid. As if we hadn't been warned. He claimed to be a man of God, that one." Nodding to the house. "He should've known."

"Dad," said the teenage girl in a quavering, frightened voice. She'd seen the look on my face.

"Keep talking, buddy," I said. "And you won't have to worry about celestial retribution. You'll get some right here on earth."

He turned and took his daughter by the elbow and steered her away into the garage, past a gray Mercedes with a sticker saying that somewhere in Kenya a village was missing its idiot. He was walking his daughter up the step, toward the door into the house, when I called out to him again.

"Hey, sport, you got the time?"

He took another look at his naked wrist, then caught himself and shoved the hand into his pocket. He swatted his girl on the bum and urged her ahead of him into the house. Then he hesitated, glaring back at me, searching for one last insult to put me away. Nothing came to him. Quivering now, he took two last brisk steps up into his house and slammed the door behind him.

I WENT BACK INTO THE Rusteds' house. The stillness could be felt almost like a shift in barometric pressure, as if the interior of the brick Tudor existed at a different altitude, had a unique climate of its own. Maybe Teasdale was right and henceforth emotions would register as weather, as atmospheric change. The light was silver and gray, and so was the mood. The temperature hovered a little below lonesome.

I curled up on the big king in the master bedroom, under Yolanda's throw, holding the photo of us all together in Estes Park. I would've cried if I could've—but as I've said before, I've never been what you would call a crying woman. When my mother wept, it was a manipulation. When my father cried, it was because he was drunk and feeling sorry for himself. I never felt anything except contempt when confronted with someone in tears, until the first time I saw Yolanda weeping, and it twisted my heart. Maybe if we'd had more time, she would've taught me to cry. Maybe if we'd had more time together, I would've learned how to wash my infected parts clean in a good, healthy flow of tears.

As it was, I only curled up and dozed for a bit, and when I woke, it was raining again.

It was a soft *tick-tick* against the roof, not like drops of water but crisper, sharper, a kind of crackling. I left the bedroom and wandered to the open front door and peered out into it. The rain came down in a steady drizzle of shining needles, no bigger than what a tailor might use to pin up a sleeve. They bounced where they struck the flagstones and made a pretty tinkling. It was such a sweet sound that I stuck my hand out, palm up, as if to sample a warm summer shower. Youch! In an instant my palm was a flesh cactus. I admit the rain didn't sound so pretty after that.

I plucked the quills out one at a time, over a burrito of eggs, cheese, and black beans. The Rusteds had natural gas, and the stove could be lit. It was a comfort to have a belly full of hot food. I ate in the master bedroom, right out of the cast-iron pan.

After I was done, I got some packing blankets from the garage. I carried Dr. Rusted into the bedroom and stretched him out and covered him up. I set the picture of all of us together in his arms. I thanked him then for sharing his daughter and his home with me and kissed him good night and went to sleep myself.

THE RAIN STOPPED AT ABOUT two in the morning, and when Gumby from across the street slipped into the master bedroom, I was already awake and listening for him. I didn't move while he stepped around the body on the floor, under the packing blankets, and crept to the side of the bed. He reached for a pillow and put a knee on the edge of the mattress. He was wired, quivering with tension, legs shaking, when he drew down the blanket and pressed the pillow over the face of the sleeper.

His back was to me when I pushed aside the packing blankets and got up off the floor. But by the time I reached for the cast-iron frying pan, Gumby had realized that the person under the pillow wasn't struggling. He yanked the pillow back and gazed raptly and blankly into Dr. Rusted's calm, still face. Gumby had time to issue a little shriek and turn halfway around when I swung.

I was jittery and amped up myself and hit him harder than I meant to. The pan connected with a resounding *bong*. He went boneless, limbs flying in four different directions, head whopped to the side. It felt like I'd struck a tree trunk. I smashed his glasses, his nose, and several teeth. He went down as if he were standing on the gallows and the hangman had opened the trap.

I grabbed him by one foot and dragged him into the hall. I pulled him through the door at the end of the corridor, into the two-car garage. It was three steps down, and his head struck every one. I didn't even wince for him. Dr. Rusted's big black Crown Vic sat in the nearest bay. I popped the trunk, scooped Gumby up, and dumped him in. I slammed the trunk on him.

It took me about ten minutes, hunting around by candlelight, to find Dr. Rusted's battery-powered hand drill. I squeezed the trigger and punched a dozen breathing holes in the trunk. If it didn't get too hot tomorrow, Gumby'd be all right till at least noon.

You just can't sleep the same after belting an intruder with a frying pan, and by the time the sun came up, I was ready to go. I left through the garage, my backpack slung over one shoulder, loaded up with fresh bottles of water and a light picnic lunch. It would be dramatically satisfying to tell you I heard Gumby kicking and wailing to get out when I left, but there wasn't a sound coming from the trunk. He might've been dead. I can't swear he wasn't.

The evening rain had scrubbed the sky bright and blue, and the day twinkled. So did the fresh downpour of nails in the road.

Gumby's daughter was at the bottom of her driveway, staring at me with wide, frightened eyes. She was wearing the same black tracksuit with purple piping and the same silver bangle that had been around her wrist the day before. I wasn't going to speak to her—it seemed important to avoid acknowledging her, for her safety as much as mine—but then she took a nervous step toward me and called out.

"Have you seen my father?" she asked.

I stopped in the road, nails crunching under my feet. "I did," I told her. "But he didn't see me. Bad luck for him."

She withdrew a step, the fingers of one hand curling to her chest. I stalked a few more yards down the road, then couldn't help myself and went back. The girl stiffened. I could tell she wanted to run but was stuck in place with fright. An artery beat in her slender throat.

I grabbed the bangle around her wrist and yanked it off: a silver bracelet with crescent moons stamped on it. I hung it on my own arm.

"That's not yours," I said. "I don't know how you can wear it."

"He . . . he said . . ." she gasped. Her voice was small, and her breath was rapid and shallow. "He said he paid Yolanda a thousand dollars to b-babysit over the years, and her p-parents should've g-given it back. That they never should've let s-someone l-like Yolanda—like *you*—watch children!" Her face twisted in an ugly sort of way when she said that last bit. "He said they owed us."

"Your father was owed *something*. And I gave it to him," I said, and I left her there.

I WENT AROUND THE PARK this time. I didn't want to see a pile of dead penguins or smell them either.

Seventeenth Avenue borders the southern edge of City Park, and a squad from the National Guard had been deployed there to do some cleanup. A couple guys used a Humvee to drag wrecks out of the road. A few others plied push brooms across the blacktop to sweep aside the latest shimmering carpet of nails. But all of them worked in a despondent, desultory way, the way folks will when they know they've been assigned a pointless chore. It was like trying to bail out the *Titanic* with a teacup. Denver was sunk, and they knew it.

The road crew were the lucky ones, though. Some of the other soldiers had been assigned the job of bagging corpses and lining them along the curb, same as Parks & Rec used to leave bagged trash for garbage collection.

Just past where Seventeenth crosses Fillmore, there's a handsome entrance to the park: a wall of glossy pink stone in a welcoming crescent that opens on an expanse of green as smooth as the surface of a billiard table. A couple of park benches, fashioned from steel wire, had been placed artfully to either side of the park entrance. An elderly couple had tried to squeeze in underneath one of those benches together for shelter from last night's drizzle, but it hadn't done them any good. The nails had gone right through the wire.

A crow had found them and was in under the bench plucking at the old lady's face. A soldier in camo approached and bent down and yelled at the bird and clapped his hands. The crow jumped in fright and hopped out from under the bench with something in his mouth. From a few yards away, it looked like a quivering, soft-boiled egg, but as I approached, I could see it was an eyeball. The bird walked up the sidewalk with its fat, pearly prize, leaving bloody footprints behind. The soldier took three brisk steps to the curb and vomited in front of

me, a hard cough followed by a wet spatter, a mess that smelled of bile
and eggs.

I came up short to keep from getting any of the spray on me. The
soldier, a black guy, average height, downy little mustache, heaved again,
and coughed and spit. I offered him a bottle of water. He took it and
swigged and spit once more. Drank again, long, slow swallows.

"Thanks," he said. "Did you see where that bird went?"

"Why?"

"Because I think I'm going to shoot him for being a pig instead of a
crow. His eyes are bigger than his stomach."

"You mean *her* eyes are bigger than his stomach."

"Ha," he said, and shivered weakly. "I'd like to shoot *something*. You
can't imagine how badly I want to put a bullet somewhere it would do
some good. I wish I was in with the *real* soldiers. There's a fifty-fifty
chance we'll have boots on the ground in Georgia by sunup tomorrow.
Shit about to go down."

"Georgia?" I asked. "They think Charlie Daniels might've had something to do with all this?"

He gave me a sad smile and said, "I thought something similar when I
heard. Not *that* Georgia. This one is in that puddle of crap between Iraq
and Russia, where everything is Al-frig-i-stan and El-douche-i-stan."

"Next to Russia, you said?"

He nodded. "I think Georgia used to be part of it. The chemists who
dreamed this shit up—clouds raining nails—work for a company out
there. A former U.S. company, if you can believe it. The Joint Chiefs
want to strike with a dozen battalions. Biggest ground operation since
D-Day."

"You said it's only a fifty-fifty chance?"

"The president has been on the phone with Russia to see if they'd be
okay with him dropping a couple tactical warheads on the Caucasus. His
stubby little fingers are itching to stab the button."

After all I'd seen in the last forty-eight hours, the idea of thumping
our enemies with a few hundred megatons of hurt should've given me
a rush of satisfaction—but it only made me antsy. I had the nervous,
fidgety sensation that there was somewhere I needed to be, something I

needed to be doing; it was the way a person feels when she's away from home and suddenly begins to worry she left a burner running on the stove. But I couldn't for the life of me identify what it was I needed to do to ease my anxiety.

"You want a bad guy to whup, you don't have to fly halfway around the world. I can point you to one right here in Denver."

He gave me a weary look and said, "I can't help you with looters. Maybe the Denver PD can take a complaint."

"How about a murderer?" I asked. "You got time to deal with one of them?"

Some of the exhaustion left his face, and his posture improved just slightly. "What murderer?"

"I walked down from Boulder yesterday to check in on my girlfriend's father, Dr. James Rusted. I found him dead in his front hallway. He took a tumble down the stairs and broke his neck."

My soldier softened up a bit then, shoulders slumping. "And you know it was murder . . . how?"

"Dr. Rusted was caught out in the rain, like so many others, but he was able to get inside before he suffered anything worse than light injuries. He bandaged himself up and stretched out to rest and recover in his bedroom. I believe he was awakened by the sound of someone moving around in his daughter's bedroom upstairs. He was so surprised he didn't even bother to put on his glasses but went straight up to see who was there. Perhaps he thought his daughter had returned home. But when he got up there, he found a looter. There was a confrontation. Only God and Dr. Rusted's assailant could tell you what happened next, but I believe that in the course of the struggle Dr. Rusted toppled down the stairs and suffered the fatal injury."

The soldier scratched the back of his head. "You don't want to bring the National Guard into a crime scene. You want someone who knows about the art of detection."

"There's nothing to detect. The man who killed him is locked in the trunk of Dr. Rusted's Crown Victoria. He visited the house last night to kill me as well, but I was ready for him and slugged him with a frying pan. He won't suffocate—I drilled some holes in the lid of the trunk—but he might get awfully hot, so I recommend going right over there."

When I said that, the soldier's eyes about came out of his head. "Why'd he try to kill you, too?"

"He knew I had identified him as Dr. Rusted's murderer. The guy in the trunk has a grudge against the entire Rusted family. Yolanda Rusted, the doctor's daughter and my girlfriend, used to babysit this guy's daughter. After he found out Yolanda is gay, he was horrified and demanded that the doctor refund every cent of the babysitting money he'd paid over the year. The doctor rightly refused. Well, after the rain fell, this neighbor noticed that a car was missing from the garage, assumed the house was empty, and decided it would be a good time to do some stealing and settle the bill. I'm sure he thought he was justified in looting Yolanda's jewelry box, but the doctor had a different point of view. While they were grappling, the intruder lost his watch. Later, when I asked this neighbor if he'd heard any ruckus in the doctor's house, I saw him looking at his bare wrist, as if to check the time."

"You figured out he killed your girlfriend's daddy just because he glanced at his wrist?"

"Well, it didn't help that his daughter was wearing one of Yolanda's bracelets. I recognized it straightaway," I lifted my wrist to show him the silver bangle. "I asked for it back this morning. Besides, if there was any doubt about what the neighbor did, it was cleared up when he entered the house at two in the morning to suffocate me with a pillow."

He studied me for a moment longer, then turned his head and called to a couple of his compadres pushing brooms in the street. "You guys want a break from cleanup?"

"To do what?" one of them asked.

"To grab a murdering bigot and drag his ass to the lockup."

The two soldiers looked at each other. The one leaning on his broom said, "Shit, why not? It'll give us something to do while we're waiting on the world to end."

My soldier said, "Come on. Let's go. Jump in the Humvee."

"No, sir, I can't. I'm afraid you'll have to go back to Dr. Rusted's house without me."

"What do you mean, you *can't*? We haul this guy in to Denver PD, they're going to want you to give a statement."

"And I will, but they'll have to contact me at my house on Jackdaw Street. I left Dr. Rusted's daughter up in Boulder. I need to get back to her."

"Oh," he said, and looked away from me. "Yeah. All right. I suppose she'll want to know about her old man."

I didn't tell him the girl I wanted to get back to wasn't waiting on news of her father, on account of being just as dead as he was. I was glad to let my soldier think what he wanted, as long as I could keep moving. As restless and antsy as I was, I couldn't bear the thought of returning to Dr. Rusted's and maybe losing another day in Denver.

I told him where the police could find the doctor and his assailant and where they could locate me in Boulder when they wanted my statement.

"*If* they want a statement. If this even goes to a judge." My soldier took an uneasy look at the sky. "If the rains keep falling, I think trial by jury might be a fond memory in a few months. We'll be back to frontier justice soon enough. Hanging people on the spot. Saves time and trouble."

"Eye for an eye?" I asked.

"You know it," he told me, and turned to glare at the crow. "I hope you're paying attention, you filthy beast."

The crow, half a block away, squawked at us, then lifted its prize, opened its wings, and flapped laboriously away—getting while the getting was good.

I WAS ALMOST BACK TO the pike when I came across Dillett's John Deere, crashed through a fence of slender wooden posts and dumped in a dusty lot, just shy of a bridge over the brown, noisy rush of the South Platte River. The windshield had been shattered into a dozen spiderweb fractures from the evening's rain. The driver's-side door hung open on darkness.

I climbed up on the running board for a peek inside. The interior was empty but scattered with bloody hundred-dollar bills. The handcuffs hung from the steel bar under the dash. Someone had left what at first looked like a filthy, uncooked sausage on the driver's seat. I leaned close, squinting at it, trying to figure out what it was, then realized it was a thumb and recoiled so fast I almost fell out onto the dirt. My stomach turned. Someone had clipped Teasdale's thumb off so he could slip the cuffs, and then his mystery accomplice had attempted to stanch the bleeding with money. There were some torn strips of bloody white silk on the floor and something glittering in the footwell of the passenger seat. I reached in and picked it out. A fake golden tiara.

I don't know for sure that Teasdale met the Queen of the Apocalypse. I can't swear that she cut off part of his hand to enable his escape or that she bandaged him with ribbons torn from her wedding dress, padded with money out of her carpetbag. I could not tell you if the two of them went to Canada together. Maybe they did, though.

Maybe she taught him how to walk between raindrops.

I LEFT THE JOHN DEERE behind and went on. I was no tractor thief and didn't have the confidence to try to drive a vehicle the size of a *Tyrannosaurus rex* anyhow. But I did miss having a ride. I was seven hours hoofing it through the hot, dry grass along the side of the Denver-Boulder Turnpike. I walked until I was footsore and weary and then walked some more.

The state troopers and the prisoners from the supermax weren't to be found on the eight lanes of pike that day. Maybe, after yesterday's escape, it was decided there was too much risk in trying to use them as a road crew. Or—and this struck me as more likely—maybe they didn't see the point. After last night's rainfall, the road was a trough filled with brassy spokes of sharpest crystal. All of yesterday's sweeping hadn't accomplished anything.

I wasn't alone on the road. I saw lots of folks picking over abandoned cars, looking for loot. But this time no one bothered me. It was a quiet walk, no cars going by, no planes droning in the sky, no one to talk to, almost no sound at all except the buzzing of flies. To this day there are probably more flies feasting in the wrecks along those eighteen miles of the pike than there are human beings in all of Colorado.

As I was coming down the off-ramp in Boulder, I heard a boom that gave my heart a leap. People sometimes compare thunder to cannon fire. This was less like hearing a cannon go off and more like what you'd hear if you were *shot* from one. The sky was an expanse of filmy blue haze. At first it seemed there wasn't a cloud in it. Then I spied what was almost like the ghost of a cloud, a towering blue mound so big it would've made an aircraft carrier look like a kayak. Only it hardly seemed to be there at all. It was like a halfhearted sketch of a cloud, lightly penciled in over the peaks. The afternoon heat was mounting, though, and I thought we would get pounded again at the end of the day, harder than ever. It wasn't just that single blaring crash of thunder that made me think another storm was building. It was the almost airless quality to the late afternoon, a feeling like no matter how deeply I inhaled, my heart and lungs were never getting a full supply of oxygen.

The crews from Staples and McDonald's were gone, and the football field was abandoned. A few earthmovers had been scattered about, and the field itself had been blanketed with a layer of dry yellow sod, concealing the recent dead. Numbered white posts stood in ranks, all they had for grave markers. I'm sure there were enough dead in Boulder to plant the field thrice over, but the project seemed to have been discontinued. The whole town was hushed and still, almost no one out on the sidewalks. There was a terrible sense of the place steeling itself for the next and worst blow.

That clamped-down air of silence went on for block after block, but there was nothing quiet about Jackdaw Street. Andropov had the radio and the TV going, top volume, just like when I left. You could hear it from the end of the street. That was interesting enough on its own. Power was out all over town, but he had his own source of juice: a genny or just a lot of batteries.

That wasn't the only sound on the street. Elder Bent's house throbbed with carefree song. They were singing what at first sounded like a religious hymn but after a more careful listen turned out to be Peter Cetera's "Glory of Love." What a strange thing, to hear voices lifted in joy after a long hot day of walking with nothing to listen to except the idiot harmonic of the flies.

As I closed in on my house, I saw Templeton watching from the open bay door of his garage. He had come right up to the edge of the shadows but, as always, had held up there, knowing how sick the sunlight would make him. He had his cape over his shoulders, and when he saw me coming, he spread his arms out to either side and showed me his fangs. I made a cross with my fingers, and he obediently retreated into the gloom.

I stood in the street looking at Ursula's house, thinking how nice it would be to go in there and sit on the couch and rest my feet. Maybe she would bring me some sun tea. Later, when the evening was cool, I could stretch out with Yolanda and slip the silver bracelet off my wrist and on to hers.

Then I considered the boarded-up windows of Andropov's apartment, shaking from the noise behind them. I thought about the fat, surly Russian calling next door to tell Elder Bent that old 'Onysuck was going to make trouble for him with the FBI. I thought about the way the former chemist had come in burning rubber right before the first thunderstorm hit, the way he'd grabbed Martina by the arm and manhandled her into the house while she protested. Then there was what I'd seen in his bathroom when I peered through the window around the side of the house: plastic tubing, glass beakers, a gallon jug of some clear chemical solution. I wondered what part of Russia he was from, if he had emigrated from anywhere near Georgia.

There was another boom of thunder, loud enough to make the air quiver. If I thought it over long enough, I could probably devise a sly way to lure him out of his first-floor apartment so I could slip in while he wasn't around and have another look in his bathroom. Then again, if I waited another night and he knew I was around, he might come for me himself.

I decided subterfuge was overrated and that it was better, as Admiral Lord Nelson supposedly said, to "go right at 'em!" I sank to one knee, took the water bottles out of my knapsack and lined them up on the curb. Then I began to collect fistfuls of crystal spikes. I piled them in until the bag was two-thirds full and as heavy as a sack of marbles. I zipped it shut, hefted it once to get the feel of it, and went up the steps to Andropov's porch.

I booted the door once, twice, a third time, hard enough to jolt it in the frame. I roared, "Immigration, Ivan, open up! Donald Trump says we got to drag your ass back to Siberia! Either you let us in or we'll kick the door off its hinges!"

I stepped to the side and pressed myself against the wall.

The door flew open, and Andropov stuck his fat, sagging face out. "I immigrate my cock to your hole, you lesbeen beetch—" he started, but he didn't get any further than that.

I brought the sack down on the top of his head with both hands, and he collapsed to one knee, which was where I wanted him. I brought my own knee up into the center of his face and connected with the bony crunch of a snapping nose. He groaned and dropped to all fours. He had a big, rusty wrench in one hand that I didn't intend to give him a chance to use. I brought the heel of one cowboy boot down on his knuckles and heard bones split. He screamed and let go.

I scooped up the wrench and stepped over him, into the front hall. It was dark and bare and had a sour smell of mildew and body odor. The green flower-print wallpaper was peeling away to show the water-stained plaster beneath.

A left turn took me to a squalid living room. The couch and end tables were the kind of stuff most folks put out on the sidewalk, next to a cardboard sign that says FREE. There was a bong made out of a two-liter Coke Zero bottle, five inches of brown slop that looked like diarrhea water in it.

He had an iPod jacked into a Mophie Powerstation, next to a big Bluetooth speaker. Twitchy synth loops played over a steady *whop-whop* beat. I jerked the power cable out of his sound deck, and that killed his St. Petersburg electronica. But the apartment was still filled with bellowing noise. Somewhere in the rear of the apartment, Hugh Grant was shouting over a background soundtrack of swelling violins. Beneath that came a stream of angry, muffled cries.

I stumbled in the short, dim hall between the living room and the bedroom. An enormous hot-pink vibrator in the shape of a horse's phallus rolled under my foot. I lurched and put a hand out against a door to my right, and it swung open to show the dingy little bathroom I'd glimpsed before.

He had arranged a lab for himself in there. I wasn't any chemist, but it for sure looked like he had a sinkful of crystal, glassy yellowish-white shards. Several big brown jugs labeled as brake fluid—brake fluid?—sat in the bathtub. Rubber tubing ran between flasks of amber liquid. The whole place had the sharp stink of nail polish.

The muffled cries were closer now. I backed out of the bathroom and went on to the bedroom.

Martina was on the big brass bed, handcuffs on her wrists, hands behind her back. A black leather bracelet had been buckled around her right ankle. One end of an extension cable was clipped to it. The other end had been elaborately knotted around one of the shiny brass bedposts.

The bedsheets were a tangle under her bony, light frame. She peered out from beneath the twisted Debbie Harry coils of her golden hair, like a bright-eyed fox peering out from a heap of briars. Andropov had strapped a piece of duct tape across her mouth. A laptop was open on a nearby dresser, playing what looked like *Notting Hill* at top volume.

She glared at me and kicked the wall with her free foot, same as she'd been doing the day before—the only way she could let anyone know she needed help. She struggled to rise to her knees, writhing from side to side and lifting the sharp edges of her hip bones into the air. It just about looked like porno: a twenty-two-year-old alabaster-skinned stripper in cheap white underwear and a tight little Ramones T-shirt that was so threadbare and thin it barely looked fit for use as a dishrag. What made me hold up, though, wasn't my surprise to find her a prisoner in Andropov's bedroom. It was the sight of a glass pipe, on the end table, with more yellowish chunks of crystal in it—crystal that was looking less and less like lethal rain and more and more like you-know-what.

I was taking it all in, waiting for my brain to catch up to my eyes, when the mad Russian crashed in. He stumbled past me—it was dark, and the floor was carpeted in sour-smelling unwashed laundry—then turned and stood between me and her. The lower half of his face was sticky with blood, and his broken left hand twitched against his chest. Tears crawled down his bristly cheeks.

"You stay away from her, lesbeen! She not go away with you!"

The way he called me a lesbian, like it was the dirtiest word he knew, got the better of me. I slapped him with an open hand. I didn't have any words, just an overwhelming desire to smack his fat, foolish, tragic face. The instant I did it, he erupted into sobs that shook his whole body.

I moved around him and snatched the duct tape off Martina's mouth. If I wrote down all the four-letter words that came pouring out of her, this page would catch fire in your hands.

When she finally started to make sense, what she said was "I try to leave, and crazy asshole lock me here, two days now! Crazy fucking piece of turd!" And she stretched toward him, getting as close as she could, and spit on his head. "Two days he run *Notting Hill* over and over, only unlock me to piss! He smoke too much his own shitty drugs!"

Andropov turned to face her, holding his head in his hands and sobbing wretchedly. "You said you run away with thees lesbeen! You said you have me arrest and live with girls who have the pussy to eat, leave me for women at end of world!"

"I said it, and I meant it! You go to jail a meelion years!"

He looked at me with pleading, miserable, lunatic eyes. "Every day, all the time, she parade herself almost naked to you lesbeens. Always she is calling to tell me she plan to sleep with you both! She say only women make her cum, and she laugh at me—"

"Yes, I laugh at you, I laugh at your penis, always soft—"

And then they were screaming at each other in Russian and she was spitting at him again and my head was about to split from the way the both of them were carrying on. He drew back one arm like he was going to backhand her, and I thumped him in the stomach with the wrench—not hard but hard enough to drive the air out of him and bend him double. He swayed, sank to his knees, and curled up on his side, crying his guts out. You never saw a more pitiful sight.

I stepped around Andropov and paused *Notting Hill*. I spotted a chrome key by the laptop and figured I'd try it on the handcuffs. I sat on the edge of the bed with Martina, and her bracelets popped off with a *snick!* She rubbed her bruised wrists.

"Filthy, horrible, soft-dick man," she said, but her voice was lower now, and she was shaking.

I picked up the glass pipe with the crystals in it. "What's this?"

"Drug he make me take to shut me up," she said. "I try to leave him before, and he hit me, choke me. He use what he sell, is like mad killer. He punch me because he can't *fuck me anymore*!" Throwing this last at him.

"What kind of drug?"

"Crystal meth." She bit her lower lip and began to wrestle with the buckle around her ankle.

"Okay," I said. "Tell me something else. He isn't from the area around Georgia, is he?"

Her brow furrowed. "What? No. Moscow."

"And I guess he doesn't know how to make the kind of crystals that are falling from the sky?"

"What you mean? No. No." She barked—a harsh, ugly laugh. "He is washed-up pharmacist, not geeenius."

"I love you," he said to her from where he was curled up on the floor. "If you leave, I shoot myself."

By now she had freed her ankle from the strap around it. She leapt up and began to kick him.

"Good! I hope so! I buy you the bullets myself!"

He did not attempt to escape from his place on the floor. Her foot found his ass again and again.

I'd heard about all I could stand. I dropped the wrench on the bed and left the two of them to the pleasure of each other's company.

I STOOD ON THE PORCH, leaning against the railing, inhaling the clean, clear air with its taste of the mountains and summer. A few members of the comet cult had heard the commotion and come out onto the porch, Elder Bent among them, his stepdaughters flanking him. The girls were pretty brunettes in their early twenties, and each of them wore matching ceremonial hubcaps on their heads. It was only the best for Elder Bent's pretties: golden '59 Lancer hubcaps that looked like UFOs from a black-and-white movie.

Martina emerged in a pair of jeans so tight I'm surprised she could get into them without lubricant. She stood beside me, pushed her crazed hair back from her face.

"You do me favor?" she asked.

"I think I just did."

"Don't call police man for a while," she said. She gave me a haunted, harried look. "I haff my own legal problem."

"Yeah. All right," I said, but I found I couldn't look at her, and my voice curdled with distaste.

I was sorry for her and glad she was safe, but it didn't mean I had to like her. She'd had her fun, teasing Andropov about how she was going to jump into bed with the dykes upstairs, using us as a cudgel to batter his masculinity. She'd been doing it the day the hard rain fell. That was why Andropov had come home in such a hurry—not to beat the storm but to beat his girlfriend. In her own way, she wasn't much better than Gumby, who loathed Yolanda for being a queer. We had never been people to Martina. We were just a blot on the local environment, something she could rub her ignorant boyfriend's face in when she needed a cheap thrill.

Maybe she registered some of the contempt in my tone. She softened, took a step toward me on her delicate feet. "I am sorry for Yo-lin-dah. She was very special. I see her die from the window." Her cornflower-blue eyes took on a guilty, shamed aspect, and she added, "I am sorry about things I say to Rudy. About how you both make me lesbeen. I am shit, you know?" She shrugged, then smiled and blinked at tears in her long lashes. "You a real badass beetch, you know? You safe my worthless ass today. You are like if Miss Maple haff baby with Rambo Balboa."

She turned and put her hands in the pockets of a tight leather coat she'd found somewhere and went down the steps, crystal nails crunching under her heels.

"Where are you going?"

The air was heavy, so heavy it required an act of will to draw a full breath. In the ten minutes I'd been inside, that ghostly impression of a distant thunderhead had darkened and filled in to become a looming mass, pretty as a facial tumor.

Martina turned back, answered with a shrug. "Maybe down to university. I haff friends there." She laughed bitterly. "No. This is lie. I haff people I can sell drugs to there."

"So they'll think of you fondly then. Go on. Just don't take any detours. The weather is about to turn ugly."

She looked up from under her carefully tweezed eyebrows, then nodded and turned away. I sat on the top step and watched her go, walking at first—then breaking into a half jog.

Martina had only just disappeared around the corner when the door crashed open behind me and Andropov stumbled out. Blood and snot had dried over his upper lip, and his eyes were bloodshot as if he'd been up for twenty-four hours with only a bottle of vodka for company.

"Martina!" he screamed. "Martina, come back! Come back, I am sorry!"

"Forget it, brother," I said. "That plane flew already."

He staggered to the edge of the porch and dropped down to sit beside me, clutching his head and crying helplessly.

"Now I haff no one! Everything fuck me in the ass! Everyone is dying, and I haff no friend and no woman." He opened his mouth so wide I could see his back teeth, and he sobbed in a great, booming voice. "I haff no place to go where I am not alone!"

"There's a place with us," Elder Bent said softly. "There's work for you to do and secrets to learn—a bed to sleep in and dreams to dream. Your voice belongs with ours, Rudolf Andropov. Singing the curtain down on the world."

While I was lost in my thoughts and Andropov was lost in his sorrows, Bent had come to the bottom of the porch steps. He stood there with his hands folded at his waist, smiling placidly. In the weird gathering stormlight of the afternoon, the planets on his skull seemed alight with a sickly glow.

His daughters and a small delegation of worshippers were behind him in their gowns. The girls began to hum softly, a melody I recognized but couldn't place, something sickly sweet and almost sad.

Andropov stared at them with wide, straining eyes and a dazed wonder on his face.

I kind of wished I'd held on to the wrench. I stood and backed off a few steps, putting the railing between me and the crazies.

"All that harmonizing together is going to be good practice for singing on a chain gang," I said. "If you haven't heard from the state police yet, count yourselves lucky. They've got the three who jumped me on the interstate, and they'll be coming for you next."

"The police have come and gone," Elder Bent said, and he smiled apologetically. "Randy, Pat, and Sean acted without my knowledge. They were the ones who first saw Andropov's note slipped under the door, and they decided to spring upon you without ever discussing their plan with me. I think they believed they were protecting me—as if I have any reason to fear the law! Yes, I knew that the storms were coming, but prophecy is not culpability. When I saw the note myself and my daughters told me what Sean and his friends were off to do, I immediately contacted local authorities to warn them what was afoot. I am so, so terribly sorry the police weren't able to prevent them from attacking you, but of course law enforcement is badly stretched thin right now. You weren't hurt, were you?"

Andropov and I spoke at almost the same time. The Russian said, "What note?"

I said, "Wait, Andropov left a *note*? Sean said they got a *message* from him, but I thought they meant a voice mail or something. How do you know this note was from Andropov? Did he sign it?"

One corner of Elder Bent's mouth turned up in a wry smile. "He has a rather interesting phonetic spelling of your name. 'Onysuck! It's quite unmistakable."

"I leave note?" Andropov said, sounding genuinely baffled. "I must haff been so high! I don't remember thees note."

"Good," Elder Bent said. "Let it all go. The note. Martina. Your sadness. The whole life you had until this moment. A new life begins right now, today, if you want it. You're looking for community, for a place where you don't need to be alone. And we've been looking for you, Rudy! If you're ready to do work that means something and to be among people who will love you and ask you only to love them, then we're here for you. We're ready to say hello."

And on cue the girls behind him broke into Lionel Richie's "Hello," asking Andropov if it was them he'd been looking for. If I hadn't been so confused and stunned, I would've gagged.

Andropov, though, stared at them like one inspired, his tears drying on his cheeks. Elder Bent held out one hand, and Andropov took it. The bald, gangly monk of madness pulled the Russian to his feet and led him down the steps. One of the comet cultists zoomed in and hung an astrolabe around his neck and kissed his cheek. Andropov stared down at it in wonder, fingered it in fascination.

"A map to the stars," Elder Bent said. "Keep it with you. We'll be going there soon. We wouldn't want you to get lost."

They moved away across the lawn, gathered around Andropov and singing in their sweet, harmless, senseless voices. As they slipped one by one into the house next door, their music faded and another sound took its place—a loud, steely clack, like someone cocking a gun. Only it wasn't a gun. It came again and again. It was a manual typewriter.

I turned and looked at the open bay door to Ursula's garage. From where I stood, I could see only darkness within.

I crossed the street, worn down from the heat and the walk and fighting evil. Except that wasn't it. What had tired me out the most was thinking about all the hours I'd spent in that garage, seeing everything and observing nothing.

Templeton stood at his daddy's workbench, feet planted on a big white plastic tub of rock salt so he could reach the keys of the antique typewriter.

"Hey there, Templeton," I said.

"Hello, Honeysuckle," he said without looking up.

"Where's your mom, kiddo?"

"Inside. Lying down. Or maybe on her computer. She spends a lot of time on her computer watching the weather."

I settled in behind him, ruffled his hair. "Hey, Temp? Remember when you told me you go flying every night to look for your daddy in the clouds? Is that something you do in your dreams?"

"No," he said. "I go with Mommy. In the crop duster. I pretend I'm a bat."

"Uh-huh," I said. My gaze drifted to the framed Ph.D. hung above the workbench. I'd never wondered what Templeton's father had a Ph.D. in but wasn't surprised to see that his field of study had been applied chemical engineering. I wondered if the company that had fired him still had offices somewhere in the United States or if they'd completely relocated to Georgia. Yolanda had told me that Mr. Blake's company had moved down south—a natural mix-up. When you heard that someone was moving to Georgia, you didn't think they meant Russia.

"Can I see something, Templeton?" I said. "Jump down for a moment, will you?"

He obediently hopped down off the white plastic tub of rock salt. I pried off the lid and looked in at glittering silver dust. At a glance a person might've imagined it was salt, but when I stuck a finger in, it pricked my finger like a pile of broken glass. I wiped my hand on my hip and stood up.

Templeton had backed a few steps away, ceding his place at the typewriter. I cranked the silver carriage-release lever to start a new line and began to type. Little steel hammers fell, *bang, bang, bang* . . . all except for the *h* and *e,* which wouldn't fire. I wrote "onysuck" and quit. I thought about the letter in the paper, "Alla" with no *h*, the word "bodies" spelled "bodys" to avoid the *e*.

"What'chu writing, Hemingway?" someone said from behind me, a male voice.

I spun, my heart banging like the keys of Templeton's typewriter.

Marc DeSpot had crept to the entrance of the garage and stood peering in at me, tall, rangy, muscular son of a bitch in a white straw cowboy hat, blue denim shirt buttoned only at the collar so it flapped open to show the ornate X on his chest.

"Marc!" I cried. "Why are you here?" Not that I cared. I'd never been so happy to see a friendly face.

He wandered into the dim garage. It was increasingly looking like twilight outside. "Why you think I'm here? I'm looking for you."

"Here? How'd you know to find me here?"

"You told me, Sherlock. 'Member? You said if you weren't in the big white house across the street to look in the butter-colored ranch. You got anything to drink? I've walked half the day to bring this back to you, and I've worked up a considerable thirst in the process." He pulled a rectangle of slick black glass out of his back pocket.

"My phone! How is it you have my phone?"

He thumbed his hat back on his brow. "Well, I caught up to the lady that took it from you and asked nice. The trick is to use the magic word, which is 'please.' It works 'specially well if you're holdin' 'em upside down by the ankles at the time."

"Let me have it."

"Catch," he said.

He gave it a soft underhanded lob, and it rapped me in the chest and fell into my hands, and I had it for an instant and it slipped through my butter fingers and struck the concrete with a crack. As a finishing touch, I kicked it and heard it skid under the worktable.

"Oh, crickets!" I shouted. "Give me your phone."

"It died six hours ago. Where's the fire?"

I got down on all fours and scrambled into the dark beneath the worktable, a space that stank of mice, dust, and rust.

"I've got to talk to people. FBI maybe," I said. "See that typewriter? There's no *e* on it. And no *h* either!"

"And you want the FBI to investigate? I don't think crimes against the alphabet fall under their jurisdiction."

I put my face through a cobweb and snatched it off my nose. I set my palm down on the blade of a rusty screwdriver and hissed. "I can't see a damn thing."

"I can help you look," Templeton said, getting down on all fours and scrambling in under the worktable with me.

"Here," Ursula said. "I've got a flashlight. Maybe this will help."

"Thanks, Ursula," I said automatically, for a half an instant forgetting who I was calling the FBI about.

Then my insides throbbed with a kind of cold ache, and I went still. She'd heard us talking and slipped into the garage just as I was scrambling under the table. I turned in a circle and peered out at her and Marc.

"Thank you, ma'am," said Marc DeSpot, taking the flashlight from her, pointing it under the worktable, and switching it on. I opened my mouth to scream but couldn't get any air. My lungs wouldn't fill. Marc hadn't seen what was in her other hand. He bent over and looked under the table at me. "But listen, girl, if you've got someone to call, you aren't going to be able to do it with that phone either. That's out of charge, too. It's like a law of nature. The more you need something, the more likely it is the damn thing is just going to drop dead on you."

"Isn't that the truth," Ursula said, and hit him in the back with the machete.

It sounded like someone swatting a carpet with a broom. His legs wobbled, and his knees knocked. She yanked back with both hands and all her strength to free the blade. Marc dropped the flashlight, and it rolled a little to the right, pointing its beam out the garage door and leaving Temp and me in shadows. As the machete came out from between his shoulder blades, he toppled backward, pulled off his feet. He fell to the floor with a weak cry.

I scuttled all the way back under the table.

"Templeton," Ursula said, leaning forward, her face as serene and calm as if she hadn't just nearly cut someone in half. "Come on out,

Templeton. Come to Mama." She held out her left hand for him, gripping the machete in her right.

Templeton didn't move, paralyzed with shock. I put my arm around his neck and stuck the blade of that rusty screwdriver under his eye.

"Back away, Ursula."

Until that instant her voice and expression had been perfectly placid. Now, though, her face darkened to a shade of tomato and a tendon stood out in her neck.

"Don't you TOUCH HIM!" she shouted. "HE'S A CHILD!"

"Streets are full of 'em," I said. "All stuck through with nails. One more dead kid won't matter to anyone. Except you."

Templeton shivered in my arms. My scalp burned, and my own legs trembled, squatting there under the worktable. My voice had so much nasty in it that I almost believed myself.

"You wouldn't," she said.

"Wouldn't I? I don't doubt you love him more than anything in the world. I understand how that feels. I felt just exactly the same about Yolanda."

Ursula took a step back. Her breath echoed in the concrete-and-aluminum cavern of the garage. Thunder detonated outside, shook the floor.

I began to crab-walk forward, edging Templeton along with me.

"He's innocent in this, Honeysuckle," she said, trying to regain her calm but unable to keep the tremor out of her speech. "Please. He's all I have. His father was already stolen from me. You can't take him, too."

"Don't talk to me about what you've lost," I said. "Colorado is full of folks who've lost loved ones, all because you couldn't mourn in a reasonable fashion. Couldn't you just plant a tree in his memory like a normal person?"

"This state, this *nation*, took my husband's *life* away from him. My good man. A bunch of Georgian oligarchs stole Charlie's life's work—all his ideas, all his research—and this state said he wasn't entitled to a dime. They stole his future from him, and he couldn't bear it. So now I'm taking away *their* future. The president authorized a tactical nuclear strike. The entire nation of Georgia has been radioactive ash for three hours.

And as for Colorado—and the rest of this hideous, money-worshipping country—they didn't recognize my husband's rights. They didn't appreciate the power of his ideas. Well. They're learning to appreciate their power now, aren't they?"

I clubbed my head on the edge of the worktable as I came out from under it, and my eyes just about crossed. Temp could've lunged away, but I think he was too terrified in that moment to bolt for it. I kept the tip of the screwdriver a quarter inch beneath his right eyeball.

"I don't understand why you sent Elder Bent's people after me," I said.

"Templeton told me you knew we went flying every night. He said you were going to tell the FAA about our trips in the crop duster. I wasn't even sure I believed him, but then isn't that how people always get caught? Someone robs a bank, then gets pulled over 'cause of a broken taillight. I didn't think I could afford to take any chances. I hope you know I don't have anything against you personally, Honeysuckle."

I kept the boy between Ursula and myself, turning, putting my back to the driveway. I saw Marc lift one hand weakly, fingers curled, and heard him groan faintly. I thought if we got help soon enough, he might live. I began to retreat toward the road.

"No!" Ursula shouted. "You can't! He can't go outside!"

"My fanny. That's just another lie. He isn't taking any medicine that makes him allergic to sunlight. That was just a story you told to be sure he'd never get caught out in the rain if you weren't around to watch him. Keep moving, Temp."

"NO! *It's about to pour!*" Ursula screamed.

"Come on," I said. "Come on, Templeton. We'll make a dash for it."

We turned, and I shoved him ahead of me, down the driveway, and at that moment the world turned into a negative image of itself in a stroke of lightning followed by a shattering blast of thunder. We ran. I clutched one of his shoulders with my left hand, held the screwdriver with the other. As we crossed the road, I felt something stab me in the arm. I looked and saw a diamond-bright nail sticking out of my biceps.

I heard a mounting, rattling roar, less like a downpour, more like an avalanche, building in strength as it approached. I saw the far end of the street disappear in an advancing wall of whiteness, a flashing, brilliant curtain of falling crystals. The Flatirons danced, disappeared, and reemerged, like an image glimpsed through a kaleidoscope.

We weren't going to make it to Elder Bent's house. A nail struck my hand and went all the way through it, like a bullet. I yelped and let go of the screwdriver.

I still had Templeton around the neck, and I pushed him four more steps, to the rear end of Mrs. Rusted's car. I put a hand on top of his head and shoved, driving him to his knees. I dropped beside him. A nail struck me in the small of my back, four inches of icy crystal. Another hit my upper left shoulder. I ducked under the bumper and wriggled beneath the car, hauling Templeton with me by his cape. Over the deafening, obliterating roar, I heard Ursula screaming his name.

I don't think Templeton realized I'd lost the screwdriver until we were under the car. I was flat on my belly, squeezed so tightly between the undercarriage and the road that I had almost no mobility at all. He began to squirm. I grabbed a fistful of his cape, and it came right off him.

I lunged to grab a hold of him again and banged my head on the undercarriage. It was the second time in the last minute I'd managed to catch my skull, and this time I struck myself right along the stitches. A galaxy of black suns exploded and faded before my eyes, a map of the stars and Elder Bent's seventh dimension visible on the far side. By the time my vision cleared, Templeton was out from under Mrs. Rusted's Prius.

"Mom!" he screamed. I could barely hear him over the bellow of the crashing rain. The road shook like I was sprawled on the rails with a freight train thundering straight toward me.

I turned myself around to watch him sprint back for his house. Nails struck him in the back of the thigh, in one heel, in the upper back, and he was flung to his face at the foot of the drive. That's where he was when his mother reached him.

He was trying to stand again, up on one knee. Ursula covered him with her body, curving herself over him and enclosing him in her arms. She held him down and beneath her as the full force of the rain struck at last—the obliterating August rain.

AND THAT'S ABOUT ALL I have to tell.

Templeton was transferred to a unit at Boulder Community Health. A six-inch spike pierced his right lung before his mother could get to him, but Ursula shielded him from the worst of it, and he was released to state foster care two weeks ago.

Ursula herself had, I heard, 897 nails in her by the end. She was a red carpet stuck full of blades. I hope she died knowing her boy was going to live, that she had saved him. What she did to us—to the world, to the sky—is unforgivable, but I wouldn't want any mother to die feeling she'd failed to protect her child. Justice and cruelty are not the same, and knowing that is the difference between being right in your head and being someone like Ursula Blake.

This was all five weeks ago, and as you know, in the time since, the sparkle dust has coated the entire troposphere. The last rain that was water, not nails, fell on the coast of Chile in mid-September. The only other precipitation since then has been radioactive ash. Our armed forces nuked Georgia, wiping out the firm that had developed Charlie Blake's vision of crystal rain and annihilating most of the scientists who might've been able to reverse the process. ISIS fell for fake news claiming that the crystal rain was the work of Jewish scientists and launched rockets at Israel. In response Israel obliterated Syria with half a dozen warheads; they leveled Tehran while they were at it. Russia took advantage of the international chaos to storm the Ukraine. In Jakarta it rained nails the size of broadswords and killed nearly 3 million people in an hour, which was almost as bad as a nuke. The president's latest move has been to offer tin umbrellas on his web store, $9.99 a pop, made in China. Admit it, the guy knows how to turn a buck.

It isn't all a nightmare, although some days it seems close. A single colleague of Charlie Blake's, a researcher named Ali-Rubiyat, was in London when Georgia was baked at 5 million degrees Fahrenheit. Although crystal generation was not his area of study, he had some crucial files on his laptop, and the scientists in Cambridge have cooked up a neutralizing agent that stops crystal growth and might make it rain normal again. It works half the time in the lab, but no one is sure what it will do in the wild.

I remember how Yolanda used to send me photographs of clouds and tell me what she saw when she looked at them. This one was an island paradise for the two of us, where we would live the rest of our days in hula skirts, feeding each other pineapple. That one was a big smoky gun that we would use to shoot the moon. Another was God's own camera, taking a picture of us as we kissed. All I'll ever see when I look at the clouds from here forward is weapons of mass destruction.

That's how we got to now—all of us watching the Internet (what's left of the Internet) to bear witness when the drones take off from Heathrow to disperse the neutralizing powder. *If* they can take off. There's a 60-percent chance of nails in that part of the United Kingdom this evening.

I'll be watching myself, on the couch with Marc DeSpot, who has taken up digs in Andropov's old apartment and who often limps upstairs to see how I'm doing. We'll be surrounded by half a dozen purring felines. Marc and I have kept ourselves busy rescuing neighborhood cats. Or, really, I rescue them and he pets them and gives them silly names, like Bill Due and Tom Morrow. His mobility isn't what it used to be, although Marc has assured me he'll be back to chasing tail soon enough.

Less than a quarter of the world has power or web access, but everyone who does will be tuned in tonight for the most watched public science experiment since the moon landing. I'm sure the comet cult will be watching next door, Elder Bent and his stepdaughters and Andropov, hoping the powder doesn't work. They've got the end of the world penciled in for just a couple weeks from now. They'd hate to be wrong again.

Me, I've got my fingers crossed and a heart full of H-O-P-E, *hope*. The meteorologists predict that a big storm front will pass across the Rockies at the end of the week. If the Ali-Rubiyat formula works, it'll be coming down cats and dogs. If it fails, it'll be pins and needles instead.

If we do get real rain, I'll run right out to dance in it. I'll stomp in puddles like a little kid, all the rest of my days.

They say into every life a little rain must fall.

God, let it be so.

AFTERWORD

THESE STORIES WERE WRITTEN IN LONGHAND over the course of four years. I began the first of them, *Snapshot*— then titled *Snapshot, 1988*— in Portland, Oregon, in 2013, while I was on tour for *NOS4R2*. It came to fill two notebooks and the back of a placemat from one of those 1950s-t hemed diners. After the story was done, I put a rubber band around the notebooks and placemat, stuck the whole mess on a shelf, and more or less forgot it existed.

I completed my fourth novel, a very long book titled *The Fireman*, in the fall of 2014. I wrote *The Fireman* in longhand as well; it wound up occupying four and a half giant Leuchtturm1917 notebooks. That left half of a very large notebook untouched. I hate to see so much paper go to waste, so I used the remaining pages to write *Aloft*. At that point it occurred to me that I was working on a collection of short novels.

Most of my favorite stories as a reader come in at this length. Short novels are all killer, no filler. They offer the economy of the short story but the depth of characterization we associate with longer works. Little novels aren't leisurely, meandering journeys. They're drag races. You put the pedal to the floor and run your narrative right off the edge of the cliff. Live fast and leave a pretty corpse is a shitty objective for a human being but a pretty good plan for a story.

My favorite novel, *True Grit,* is just over two hundred pages long. Maybe the best novel published in this century, David Mitchell's *Cloud Atlas,* is six tightly constructed novellas, thematically laced together in an elegant cat's cradle of story. Neil Gaiman's most perfect novel, *The Ocean at the End of the Lane,* is not one sentence longer than it needs to be and came in at less than two hundred pages. Tales of horror and fantasy especially thrive at a length of about twenty-five thousand to seventy-five thousand words. Think of *The Time Machine, War of the Worlds, Jekyll and Hyde,* most of Richard Matheson's brief, sinewy novels, and Susan Hill's (no relation) brilliant *Woman in Black.* You want to be able to read such stories in just one or two sittings. You want them to feel like a hand on your throat.

And for me, after writing a couple seven-hundred-page novels back-to-back, it felt particularly important to get lean and mean, if possible. Nothing against long novels. I love discovering a big, fantastic world to explore, to get lost in. But if epic-length works are all you ever write, you risk becoming the bore at the dinner party. As the deejay Chris Carter says, don't overstay your welcome or you'll never be welcome to stay over.

I think *Rain* arose from a desire to spoof myself and my own sprawling end-of-the-world novel, *The Fireman.* I'm a big believer in making fun of yourself before anyone else can. I wrote it in the early part of 2016, as the presidential race was heating up, and initially the president in my story was a fatigued, besieged, but basically competent woman. Also the tale had a much happier ending. After the election . . . things changed.

Loaded is the oldest story in the book, although I only got around to writing it in the fall of 2016. I've had that one in my head ever since the massacre of twenty children in Newtown, Connecticut. *Loaded* was my attempt to make sense out of our national hard-on for The Gun.

That said, my politics are my own. Lieutenant Myke Cole (U.S. Coast Guard, Ret.) read over *Loaded* and helped me get my facts right on the subjects of guns and military service. He isn't on the hook for my fuckups, and you shouldn't assume he in any way shares my agenda or point of view. Myke is more than capable of speaking for himself and does, in his novels, on his TV show *Hunted,* and on Twitter. That goes, too, for Russ Dorr, who also vetted *Loaded* for accuracy and provided me with first-rate research on the subject of law and disorder in Florida.

Each story in this collection was enriched with illustrations by a different artist. *Snapshot* features the art of Gabriel Rodriguez; Zach Howard armed *Loaded* with a pair of fine images; Charles Paul Wilson III graced *Aloft* with a couple of visuals; and the team of Renae De Liz and Ray Dillon delivered some crystalline eye candy for *Rain*. The book is a far more beautiful thing because of their craftsmanship and care.

HarperCollins produced a lovely audiobook of *Strange Weather*, employing the vocal gifts of four remarkable performers: Dennis Boutsikaris, Wil Wheaton, Stephen Lang, and Kate Mulgrew. My gratitude to them all—thank you for being my voice.

An earlier version of *Snapshot* appeared in a double issue of *Cemetery Dance* magazine. My thanks to Brian Freeman and Richard Chizmar for giving the story its first home and for treating it so well.

Quite a few people lent their talents and hard work to make *Strange Weather* look good. In the United States, they include my superstar of an editor Jennifer Brehl, Owen Corrigan, Andrea Molitor, Kelly Rudolph, Tavia Kowalchuk, Priyanka Krishnan, and Liate Stehlik. Maureen Sugden has done the copyediting in every single one of my books and has always made my prose much more direct and clear. Over in the UK, this book was loved and nurtured by editor Marcus Gipps, Craig Leyenaar, Jennifer McMenemy, Jennifer Breslin, Lauren Woosey, Jo Carpenter, Mark Stay, Hannah Methuen, Paul Stark, Paul Hussey, Jon Wood, and Kate Espiner.

My mother and father looked at each of these stories as they were written and offered their usual encouragement and editorial suggestions. My brother, the novelist Owen King, gave *Strange Weather* a read and offered several astute observations. Jill Bosa is a sweetheart for reading a late draft and correcting the sorts of goofs that slip in when you've lived with a thing for too long and can no longer see the glitches staring you right in the face. I'm grateful to my agent, Laurel Choate, for looking after this book from its earliest stages to final delivery, and to Sean Daily for representing *Strange Weather* on the film and television fronts. My gratitude to Dr. Derek Stern for his support, thoughts, and advice.

Finally: Thanks to my three sons for sharing the sunny days and the stormy ones alike. And my love to Gillian, who is the best of company and the best of friends, no matter what the weather.

Joe Hill
March 2017
Exeter, New Hampshire

ABOUT THE AUTHOR

JOE HILL is the author of the *New York Times* bestsellers *The Fireman,* *NOS4A2, Horns,* and *Heart-Shaped Box* and the prizewinning story collection *20th Century Ghosts.* He is also the Eisner Award–winning writer of a six-volume comic-book series, *Locke & Key.* He lives in New Hampshire.